DARK SHORES

ALSO BY DANIELLE L. JENSEN

THE MALEDICTION TRILOGY

Stolen Songbird

Hidden Huntress

Warrior Witch

The Broken Ones (prequel)

The Bridge Kingdom

DARK SHORES

DANIELLE L. JENSEN

A TOM DOHERTY ASSOCIATES BOOK
NEW YORK

DARK SHORES

Copyright © 2019 by Danielle L. Jensen

A Tor Teen Book
Published by Tom Doherty Associates
175 Fifth Avenue
New York, NY 10010

www.tor-forge.com

Tor® is a registered trademark of Macmillan Publishing Group, LLC.

The Library of Congress Cataloging-in-Publication Data is available upon request.

ISBN 978-1-250-31772-8 (hardcover)
ISBN 978-1-250-31771-1 (ebook)

Our books may be purchased in bulk for promotional, educational, or business use. Please contact your local bookseller or the Macmillan Corporate and Premium Sales Department at 1-800-221-7945, extension 5442, or by email at MacmillanSpecialMarkets@macmillan.com.

First Edition: May 2019

Printed in the United States of America

0 9 8 7 6 5 4 3 2 1

Dad, this one is for you

DARK SHORES

1

TERIANA

The *Quincense* launched off the peak of a swell like she dreamed of taking flight. Her blue sails were full of the southerly wind that had been propelling them up the coast with an eagerness mirroring Teriana's own. It had been months since they'd last been in Celendrial—and since she'd last seen Lydia. Her feet itched with excitement at the prospect of being reunited with her closest, albeit most unlikely, of friends.

The ship failed in her dream to remain airborne, crashing down against the turquoise sea and sending a salty spray into Teriana's face, forcing her to finish tying the knot blind before wiping a damp sleeve across her face. Rising to her feet, she instinctively shifted her weight to keep her balance as the *Quincense* reared up on another swell. Her eyes she kept on the horizon as the ship slid around a rocky peninsula and Celendrial, the crown jewel of the Celendor Empire, came into view.

"Hello, lovely," she shouted at the gleaming white sprawl stretching out beyond the enormous harbor, flanked on one side by a villa-encrusted hill and on the other by a towering statue of a legionnaire holding a standard bearing a gleaming gold dragon. A dozen enormous stone wharves reached out like fingers, countless ships originating from every province of the Empire busy unloading freight for sale in the markets beyond. Through the middle of it ran the river Savio, spilling its filthy contents into the harbor and turning the azure waters a murky greenish brown.

Grinning, Teriana gave the city a one-fingered salute before weaving her way back through her sea-soaked crew to where her mum stood at the helm. All Teriana's anticipation would earn her were hours of cutting deals in the harbor market unless she negotiated some free time from the captain now.

Captain Tesya stood with one hand resting on the railing, the other holding a pipe that had gone cold from neglect, her ebony skin gleaming in the sun. Her hair was wrapped tight against her head with blue silk, but a few black curls had escaped to frame an older, grimmer version of Teriana's own face, both of them possessing full lips, arched eyebrows, and rounded cheeks. On her mother's neck, three small blue sapphires were pierced into the skin to form a triangle, marking her as a Triumvir of the Maarin Trade Consortium. At her elbow stood Teriana's aunt Yedda, who peered intently through her spyglass at the coastline. Teriana caught the last of her words: ". . . Chersome's sigh of relief will mean another nation is catching its breath."

"No nation on this half of Reath *left* to catch its breath," Teriana's mother muttered. "Yet still, no good can come from *them* being here. Not with elections just round the corner. Might be time to take our leave. Time for *all* Maarin ships to take their leave."

"Who you talking about?" Teriana asked, squinting at the coast beyond the glowering statue and outside the city proper. She could make out rows and rows of white tents rising up from the sandy beaches, marking the camp of one of the Empire's legions. All across Celendor, along with most of its provinces, families were bound to deliver their second-born sons to the grounds of Campus Lescendor for legion training. Groomed for combat from early childhood, the legion's soldiers were deadly and not to be crossed under any circumstance. Yet given their ever-presence across the East, she did not see how they were cause for comment.

It was her mother's words, not the soldiers, that caused a tightening in her chest. *Taking leave* didn't just mean going west—it meant staying there. And that meant never seeing Lydia.

"Don't recall inviting you to join the conversation," Teriana's mother replied, turning her back to the wind to relight her pipe.

Teriana crossed her arms. "It's my business where we sail." Which was technically true. On her seventeenth birthday she'd been promoted to second mate, and the ship herself was Teriana's birthright. If her mother intended to take the *Quincense* back through the paths, then—

"Methinks it's self-interest and not ship's business that's brought you up here," Aunt Yedda said, interrupting Teriana's thoughts. "Am I wrong?"

The veracity of her comment warred with Teriana's desire to know what the two had been talking about, but in the end, the former won out. "Can I leave once we're docked?"

"You a passenger?" Tesya asked, lighting her pipe and blowing a smoke ring into Teriana's face, which was no small feat given the gale-force wind.

"We don't take passengers," Teriana replied, because no Maarin ship did, but instantly regretted rising to the bait when both her mum's eyebrows cocked.

"That's because passengers are useless. Much like you, at present. Now hop to."

There was no sense arguing. Her mother wasn't fond of Teriana's friendship with Lydia, whom she referred to as the child of a godless Cel landlubber, and picking a fight now would only see Tesya inventing excuses to keep Teriana in the harbor until it was too late to climb the Hill. Then fashioning a reason why the *Quincense* needed to sail at dawn. And then more reasons still why they shouldn't come back, despite Celendrial providing them more income than nearly any other harbor on Reath. So instead Teriana said, "Aye, Captain," and went off in search of busywork.

"No luck?"

Bait's voice caught Teriana's attention as she trudged down from the quarterdeck. Her friend sat on a pile of ropes sharpening one of his diving knives, exempt from general labor for the fact that he was god marked. Didn't hurt that he had a wide smile that could charm anyone with eyeballs.

Kicking the ropes, Teriana scowled at the approaching city. "They want to go back west."

Bait's dark hands stilled; then he said, "Good."

Teriana aimed her next kick at his shins, but her heart wasn't in it. Anytime they were in a Cel-controlled port, which was every port in the eastern half of the world, Bait had to remain on the ship. The last thing anyone needed was Bait's, or any other Maarin diver's, god mark being discovered. The Cel were godless and bent on wiping what they referred to as paganism from the world, which meant they wouldn't understand his differences. And she didn't relish the notion of having to visit her friend in a specimen exhibit for the rest of their days.

Bait's expression softened, and he shoved the knife back into the sheath strapped to his calf. "If she won't let you go, Magnius and I will sneak you to shore tonight."

An echo of affirmation from the *Quincense*'s guardian filled Teriana's head, and she thumped her boot heel against the deck, knowing he'd hear it from where he swam beneath the ship.

"Drop sails!"

Her mother's voice cut through the noise, and the crew devolved into a flurry of organized chaos as the massive stone wharves loomed closer, one of the trade magister's boats already moving in their direction, crimson and gold banner snapping above the oarsmen's heads.

"Teriana!"

Teriana turned in time to see her mum clap her hands together, golden bangles gleaming in the sun, and she gave her mother a resigned nod. *Hop to.*

The sun hung low in the sky by the time they'd secured a berth, unloaded their freight, paid the taxes, and satisfied the dour-faced magister that while they might indeed be carrying contraband, they had no intention of off-loading it in his precious harbor.

"Blasted godless Cel pigs and their rules!" Tesya pounded her fist against the rail with every curse, then spit on the pristine dock.

The magister turned and inclined his head. "Always pleasure doing business with the Maarin," he said in passable Mudamorian, which the Cel knew as Trader's Tongue, earning a reluctant smile from Tesya.

"That one isn't so bad," she said, then turned on Teriana. "Well? You going to stand there dancing from foot to foot like a child about to piss her pants, or are you going to get going?"

"I'm gone," Teriana replied, stepping onto the gangplank even as her mother jerked her back onto the deck, pressing a dusty bottle into her hand.

"One does not show up at a senator's door empty-handed, girl." Then she exhaled softly. "Give Senator Valerius my regards. And Lydia, too. Then be back by dawn. There's trouble brewing, and I'm not fixing to be part of it."

Teriana sprinted down the plank before her mother had the chance to change her mind.

2

TERIANA

The Cel believed Celendrial to be the heart of the world. While they were incorrect in that presumption, the city had fair claim to being the heart of the Empire, and by virtue of the Empire controlling all of the eastern landmasses of Reath, the heart of their *half* of the world. Celendrial was an enormous sprawling place, home to over a million souls hailing from the far northern reaches of Sibern, to the fertile lands of Atlia, to the towering mountains of the Sibalines, and everywhere in between, including Celendor itself.

The quality of the streets improved exponentially as Teriana climbed uphill and away from the harbor and the always-ripe river Savio. The cramped insulae and narrow alleys of the city's underbelly gave way to wide boulevards with elaborate stone aqueducts running down their centers. Towering public buildings that were all columns and arches lined the streets, and every corner featured a statue of some famous legionnaire or politician, the latter usually bearing profane, and often amusing, graffiti. Farther still had Teriana surrounded by the domus of the wealthier citizens, set back and often gated from the street, their entrances flanked by columns, the walkways leading to them bordered by gardens.

Yet it wasn't until the streets ended, replaced by narrow, meandering pathways and staircases of carefully maintained stone, that she was faced with the true wealth and power of the Empire. The Hill was covered with palatial senatorial homes barely visible past the shading of ancient trees and cultivated gardens, the air full of the scent of flowers and citrus trees, all of it contained by high walls and elaborately wrought gates.

Teriana was both panting and sweating by the time she

reached the top, where the grandest of all the villas overlooked not the city, but the ocean beyond. There she stopped to allow the breeze to dry her skin before marching up to a set of gates. There was no bell, and she waited only half a heartbeat before hooking a toe into the bars and climbing over, the contents of the bottle her mother had sent along sloshing as she landed with a thud.

Columns linked with elaborately carved arches flanked a pathway made of square marble tiles, at the center of which ran a narrow pool filled with water lilies and golden koi. At the far end, a statue of a nude woman holding out a slender hand in greeting sprayed water gently upon the pool, and Teriana paused to rinse her hands before climbing the marble steps to the heavy door inlaid with small squares depicting Celendor's conquests. Not bothering to knock, she pushed it open and stepped inside.

The atrium was open roofed, revealing the first stars of the night sky. Beneath the opening sat an enormous bronze basin to collect the rare rainfall. Small benches framed the perimeter, behind which were alcoves containing busts of stern-faced men. To the left and right were curved staircases leading up to the second level, but Teriana continued through the door at the back of the atrium. The air was slightly damp and filled with the scent of flowers from the soaked linens stretched taut across the sea-facing windows. During the day, the corridors of the home were filled with the soft sounds of servants going about their duties, but it was now past sunset and the only noise was the jarring notes of male laughter coming from the rear of the villa.

Teriana strolled down the corridor in their direction, stepping into a brightly lit room filled with a miasma of food, booze, and scented oil, none of which did anything to cover up the smell of sweat.

"Of course, I'll fund the entire event," said one of the men sprawled across a divan, his back to Teriana. "It seems only fair given that I'm coming out ahead in our transaction."

"You are kind to say so," replied a young patrician lounging across from him, his toga gaping enough that his companions deserved accolades for keeping straight faces. "Really, truly, you are doing us the most *tremendous* of favors. We are in *your* debt for you doing us this service."

Teriana was in the midst of wondering how the young man could breathe with his head shoved so far up the other man's ass when the obsequious buffoon caught sight of her. "What is this? What is this?" He nearly fell stumbling to his feet, obviously drunk, and leveled a finger at Teriana. "What is this?"

"Good evening to you, too," she drawled, then nodded to Lydia's father, who had also climbed to his feet. "Evening, Senator."

The man whose back had been turned was now facing her, the expression on his gold-skinned face both amused and . . . cold. "Fine night, isn't it?" she said to him.

"That it is." He smiled, and Teriana fought the urge to take a step back, sensing something *off* about him. Something dangerous.

"How did you get in here?" the young patrician demanded, dragging Teriana's attention back to him.

"Front door."

"How is that possible?"

"I opened it."

"You opened it?" The man was spluttering with indignation and alcohol, and Teriana leaned back on her heels, trying to keep her grin in check. The Empire was rigidly hierarchical, with patricians, who were all Celendorian, at the top, followed by the plebeians, who were common Celendorian citizens. Then came the peregrini, who were those from the conquered nations—now provinces—that made up the bulk of the Empire. Plebeians and peregrini did *not* wander uninvited into the homes of patricians, but given that the Maarin were neither, being the only people in the East *not* under the control of the Empire, Teriana did not consider herself bound to that particular protocol. She was a peer to these men, even if they didn't know it.

"I'm afraid there's little to add to my account of the opening of the door," she said. "Though I could demonstrate, if that would assist your comprehension of such a grand tale."

The young man's golden skin began to take on a distinctly purple hue, but the cold-eyed man laughed and lifted his glass to toast her.

"Now, now," Senator Valerius finally spoke, hurrying between her and the young man, who was straightening his toga as though preparing for some great defense of the villa's unlocked doors. "This young woman is known to me." His eyes latched on to the bottle in Teriana's hand. "You needn't have brought it here yourself, my dear. I would've arranged for its retrieval had I known your mother's ship was in port."

The warning look in his eye chased away any confusion she might've had, and Teriana shrugged. "Best of service for the best of customers, Senator. Now if you'd be kind enough to settle . . ."

"Of course, of course." He placed a hand on her shoulder and shuffled her out of the room. "What was the price we agreed upon?"

She named an obscene number, but it wasn't until they were down the hallway that Senator Valerius dropped his arm and shook his head at her. "I appreciate your cheek, Teriana, but you really do push your luck. Perhaps next time a note to warn us of your arrival."

"Seems like a waste of time and paper," she said, handing him the bottle.

"Why am I not surprised that you think so." He sighed, the hand gripping the bottle trembling. "She's in the library. Do keep your voices down until my company has departed."

"Will do." Teriana gave him one backward glance, noting that Lydia's foster father's gold skin was sallower than it had been the last time she'd seen him, then trotted down the corridor and up the stairs to the library.

Soft lamplight filtered out of the large room, and Teriana paused in the doorway, casting an appreciative eye over the bookshelves stretching up to the ceiling, all filled with rare and precious volumes written in every language of the East. While she wouldn't trade her life on the *Quincense* for anything, living on a ship did mean certain space constraints.

Lydia sat at a desk on the far side of the library, shoulders hunched over whatever it was she was working on. The fact that she was adopted aside, Teriana's friend was an anomaly on the Hill. A head (and often shoulders) taller than most of the Cel, she had dark hair where theirs was fair, and her ivory skin was distinctly *not* native to scorching-hot Celendor. What she looked like were the people from northern Mudamora in the West, especially with those angular green eyes with their quartz-like luster. She was the spitting image of High Lady Dareena Falorn, which was comical in that Dareena was a god-marked warrior and Lydia had never wielded anything sharper than a pen. Striking as the resemblance was, though, it was impossible that Lydia had been born in the West. Only Maarin vessels were capable of traversing the Endless Seas, and her people did *not* take passengers. Ever.

Teriana and Lydia had met five years ago while the Maarin were negotiating a new trade agreement with the Senate. As Triumvir, Teriana's mother had been one of the captains doing the negotiating and had been invited to Senator Valerius's home for dinner, Tesya dragging Teriana along to do "some learning." Lydia had been in attendance, looking like a raven among a flock of yellow ducklings, nearly as out of place as Teriana. Which was saying something, given Teriana's skin was black as night, her multitude of waist-length braids decorated with gold and priceless gemstones, and her arms corded with muscle from laboring on the *Quincense*. Still, Teriana had assumed Lydia was just another Cel girl who'd only speak when spoken to. Pretty as one of the flower arrangements, but just about as interesting.

How wrong she'd been.

One of Valerius's fellow senators—a man notable only because he was even more of a condescending bigot than the typical patrician—had insisted on speaking in Trader's Tongue, which might have been commendable had he not clearly stated that it was "so as not to listen to the Maarin abuse the Cel language." It had been everything Teriana could do not to laugh as he butchered the conversation, Tesya grinding her boot heel into her daughter's toe after a particularly egregious mistake regarding the size of the man's property holdings. Then Lydia had stood.

"Senator," she said. "With respect, you just told the captain that you are possessed of a very large"—she coughed delicately—"member." Then she gave him an innocent smile. "I correct you only because I've been told time and again that accuracy is of the utmost importance in these negotiations."

It was then, despite the two of them having *nothing* in common, that Teriana had known that this girl was a twin to her soul, their friendship ordained by the gods themselves. And so it had been ever since.

Coming up behind Lydia, Teriana leaned over her friend's shoulder, amused that she was so lost in the piece she was translating that she didn't even notice she was being watched.

"You spelled *chicken* wrong," Teriana said loudly. "And your Bardeen grammar is shit."

"It's not—" Lydia sat up straight and then twisted in her chair, a grin blossoming on her face even as her spectacles slid down her nose. "Teriana!"

They went down in a heap of arms and legs, hugging and shrieking in complete disregard of Senator Valerius's request. "I wasn't expecting you," Lydia said, bracing a skinny arm on the floor and adjusting the silk of her dress.

"There's a lot of that going around." Teriana pulled off her boots, tossing them aside before crossing her legs. "Your father keeps poor company tonight."

"Oh?"

Teriana described the two men, and Lydia made a face. "The younger is my father's nephew, Vibius."

Her father's nephew—not her cousin. Another reminder that

despite having been adopted by the senator when she was a babe, Lydia was not a true Valerius and never would be. Pulling off one of Lydia's rings to examine the gemstone, Teriana considered asking her friend once again whether she remembered anything about her life before being taken in by the senator. Except Teriana knew the answer: Lydia's mother had been found dead from a knife wound in front of the Valerius manor, a squalling child clutched in her cold arms. Too young to do more than babble. Too young to remember where she'd come from. "Who was the other man?"

Lydia took her ring back, twisting it round her finger a few times before saying, "Lucius Cassius."

Teriana lifted both eyebrows. It was well known that Lucius Cassius had been born to a minor branch of his patrician family, but due to a series of accidents and illnesses, had managed to inherit the family's wealth and seat in the Senate when his cousin, or whoever it had been, had died. Now he was considered a powerful member of the Senate, but his politics were quite at odds to those of Lydia's foster father, which made his presence here strange. And not in a good way. He was the sort of man who everyone agreed had a rotten reputation, though no one could give specifics as to why. Like a bad stench from an unknown source.

"Elections," Lydia said, by way of explanation, then hauled Teriana to her feet. "Let's go out into the gardens. It's cold in here."

It wasn't, but Teriana didn't argue, following Lydia back downstairs.

Where they came face-to-face with Lydia's father. And his nephew.

The young man looked Teriana up and down, swaying on his feet, then cast a disparaging glare at Lydia, who shrank.

Her reaction had Teriana reaching for a knife. Only Lydia's hand closing on her wrist kept Teriana from poking a few holes in the bastard and his unearned sense of superiority.

"As if you aren't embarrassment enough, you have to fraternize with a sailor," the nephew said to Lydia, and then to Senator Valerius, "You indulge her."

The senator's normally warm expression was icy. "And I'll continue to indulge her while it is within my power to do so." He nodded once at Lydia, who dragged Teriana around the corner and out into the gardens.

"That pompous prick," Teriana snarled. "He better watch his back, because I'm of a mind to cut off his—"

Lydia held up a hand, silencing Teriana's diatribe. "While that's a delightful visual, I really need you to curb your tongue in his presence."

Teriana stared at her. "Not like you to be a shrinking violet."

"Yes, well." Lydia passed a weary hand over her face, then said, "He's my father's heir."

Understanding smacked Teriana in the face as she recalled Senator Valerius's shaking hand and sallow skin. *I'll continue to indulge her while it is in my power to do so.* He was sick. Maybe even dying. And Celendor's laws were not favorable to women at the best of times. At the worst of times, they were downright ugly. The worst she'd encountered across all of Reath. "You'll be his property when he inherits."

Her friend's face scrunched up in the way it did when she was trying not to cry.

Teriana's throat felt thick, her words sticking. "Any way around that?"

"If I were to be married."

Which wasn't getting around it at all—it only meant she'd become another man's property. Still, there were better men than Vibius. Teriana said, "Surely there would be men falling over themselves to gain a connection with your family?"

"Perhaps they would be if everyone didn't know my father was ill. It would be a short-lived union."

"What about someone who isn't a patrician?" Teriana persisted. There were only a few hundred patrician families, but there were countless wealthy plebeians dying to gain a connection to the influential houses. "A financial incentive might—"

"Enough, Teriana. This conversation makes me feel like a broodmare. Let's discuss something else." Lydia made a small gesture, and a servant appeared out of nowhere carrying a tray with wine and fresh fruit. "Tell me of your travels. Where have you been? What have you seen? How is your family? How is Bait?"

It was easier to let her change the subject. To regale Lydia with tales of the high seas, of her crew's hijinks in various ports and the pranks she and Bait played during idle moments. Happy stories. Funny stories. Anything but the hopelessness of her best friend's situation. And Teriana's helplessness to do anything about it.

Retreating to Lydia's rooms, they guzzled more wine and Teriana tried on half of Lydia's silken dresses. They were all a good six inches too long and not cut for Teriana's muscular frame, both of the girls laughing hysterically when Teriana tried to make up the height difference in a pair of high-heeled shoes. Moving to the balcony, they sat on a divan, Lydia weaving Teriana's bejeweled braids into a coronet on her head, switching from language to language as they spoke, because Lydia liked the practice. Eventually, they curled up nose to nose in Lydia's massive bed. Surrounded by too many cushions and just the right amount of darkness, Teriana finally asked, "Are you afraid?"

The only sound was the hum of insects outside the window and the faint crash of waves from the ocean below. Then Lydia whispered, "Yes. I think the day after my father passes, Vibius will sell me to the highest bidder. And if no one will pay, he'll have me killed."

Teriana's heart beat staccato in her chest, fear for her friend's life turning the wine in her stomach sour. Senator Valerius might last a year, but unless he secured Lydia a husband, her fate was certain. There had to be another way out. A place Lydia could escape to outside the Empire's reach. A place only a Maarin ship could take her.

East must not meet West.

The only thing curtailing the spread of the Empire's dominion was the Endless Seas and the Senate's ignorance of anything on the other side worth conquering. Madoria was the most benevolent of the Six, but keeping the two halves of Reath unaware of each other was one of her most stringent commandments. Breaking it might see Teriana's soul forsaken to the underworld.

And yet . . .

In her mind's eye, she imagined her friend, everything about her screaming that she'd been born in the West, from a nation that held to the gods as firmly as the Maarin did themselves. That Lydia belonged to the Six as much as Teriana did.

Which meant . . .

Before she could lose her nerve, Teriana said, "What if you left? What if you ran away?"

A choking laugh. "To where? There is nowhere the Senate doesn't control. Nowhere that its legions couldn't find me."

"There is."

Silence.

"Where?"

Teriana's heart was racing, sweat pooling beneath her breasts. Because this was forbidden. *Forbidden, forbidden, forbidden.* "Across the Endless Seas."

"What do you mean?" her friend asked. "There's nothing but water."

"There's a whole other world."

Teriana heard Lydia's breath catch. To the Empire, what lay beyond the Endless Seas was nothing more than speculation and myth, the seas too expansive and treacherous for their ships to test the theory that there might be more. Not that they hadn't tried.

Lydia whispered, "Do you mean the Dark Shores? They exist?"

To say yes was more than Teriana could stomach, so she nodded. And then, praying she wouldn't have cause to regret it,
she said, "If you decide you want to leave or if you're ever in
desperate need to reach me, this is how it's done."

3

MARCUS

Marcus stretched one leg in front of him and eyed the cards in his hand. He did not remember Celendrial being this hot. The Thirty-Seventh Legion had been back for little more than a week after seven years abroad, and he was ready to be gone again. Judging from the look of his friends, he wasn't alone. It was only just past dawn and Servius and Felix were both stripped to the waist and sweating profusely.

Felix threw his cards on the table. "I'm out."

"Me too." Servius leaned back, staring up at the sun. "I never thought I'd miss the snow, but damned if I don't."

"Go for a swim," Marcus told him, pulling the coins off the table into an already-bulging purse.

"Not a chance." Servius grimaced. "Celendrial's waters are full of beasties."

"Just take a slower swimmer with you," Marcus said, shifting again on his stool. This idleness was enough to drive him mad.

"No, I'll have none of that. Would rather sweat."

"Shame." Felix waved a hand in front of his nose. "You stink. I'm surprised the combined stench of your sweat and farts hasn't seared off my nose hairs."

"You'd look better if they had, you golden-skinned shit," Servius retorted, but Marcus had already tuned them out. His mind was for other things—namely, why the Senate had called them back. It was true that Chersome had been subdued, yet their departure felt premature. The island contained more violence and unrest than all the other provinces combined. There was no better place for the Thirty-Seventh. And given that it was about as far away from Celendrial as one could get, there was no better place for him.

A small voice from behind him broke his reverie. "I'm looking for the Thirty-Seventh Legion."

Marcus turned to find a young servant standing a few paces away. He held a rolled sheaf of parchment, his sandaled feet shifting nervously in the dirt.

"The Thirty-Seventh?" asked Servius. "What reason do you think to find them here?"

The boy's gaze flicked anxiously between them, not hearing the sarcasm in Servius's voice. The number was everywhere. Wrought in gold on the dragon standard wedged in the ground a few paces away. Emblazoned on countless banners flapping in the wind. Tattooed large and black on the chests of all the 4,118 young men lounging around the camp. The boy opened his mouth, then closed it again, the parchment shaking in his hands.

Servius laughed, the sound making the child cringe.

"Shut your mouth, Servius," Marcus said. The boy wasn't stupid; he was terrified. And rightly so. Judging from the curved blue tattoos across his forehead, he was from Chersome. The Thirty-Seventh had decimated his country and forced his countrymen into indentured servitude. Whoever had chosen him to deliver this message either was exceedingly ignorant or had a malicious sense of humor. "We are the Thirty-Seventh," Marcus said, rising to his feet.

The boy took a step back.

"Who is your message for?"

The parchment crumpled under the servant's grip. "Legatus Marcus. Legionnaire number one five one nine."

"You've found him." Marcus held out a hand for the message, but the boy clutched it to his chest.

"I'm supposed to ask for proof." His chin trembled.

"You disrespectful little—" Servius was on his feet in an instant, reaching for the boy.

Marcus swung an arm, catching his friend in the face and knocking him back. "Sit. Down."

Servius sat.

Taking hold of the neck of his tunic, Marcus tugged it down. Turning around to reveal the number tattooed across his back, he asked, "Is this satisfactory proof?"

The only response he got was stifled sobs. Sighing, he pulled the tunic back into place. Moving slowly toward the kneeling boy, he extracted the sweaty parchment from his grip. "Go tell your master that you've done your duty."

The boy scrambled to his feet and bolted through the camp.

"Rude little shit," Servius mumbled through the rag he held to his face. "Marcus, I think you broke my nose."

Marcus ignored him. Walking a few paces from his friends, he unrolled the parchment, taking in the few, precisely written lines.

"They going to let us into the city?" Felix asked.

"No." Marcus reread the message, then tucked the parchment away. "They'll not give this legion leave to enter Celendrial at will."

"'S not fair," Servius said through his rag. "They let the Forty-First in."

"The Forty-First's different," Felix answered. "It's like letting a legion of kittens loose in the streets."

"I can purr."

Marcus sidestepped the spray of blood and spit from Servius's demonstration and made his way toward his tent. Inside, he stripped off his sweaty clothes and motioned for his man to bring him a clean tunic. Pulling the fabric over his head, he again cursed the heat of Celendrial as the wool glued to his back. Amarin, his Sibalese manservant, was strapping on Marcus's armor when his friends decided to follow him in.

"Social call?" Felix asked, one eyebrow rising.

Marcus grunted a negative at his second-in-command. "Been summoned."

"Senate?"

"No." Picking up his gladius, he belted it on while his red cloak was fastened to his shoulders, the thread of the golden dragon emblazoned on it gleaming. "But by a senator."

A slow smile worked its way onto Felix's face. "Answers, then? A mission."

"Maybe."

"You got the itch?"

"I've always got the itch." Servius laughed, scratching his ass. They both ignored him.

Marcus did have the itch, as Felix called it. The feeling he got before a battle or a mission assignment. Or when something meaningful was about to happen. Except something didn't feel right. Why had they been recalled? Why, given their reputation, had the Senate left them to languish outside their precious capital? Why had he been called, not to stand before the Senate, but to meet with one man? And what did it say about this man that he would send a Chersomian to deliver his message? This was more than an itch; it was like trying to sleep in a hair shirt.

"You going to tell us who?"

"The man whose name is on everyone's lips this morning." Marcus picked up his red and gold crested helmet and shoved it on his head. "Lucius Cassius."

4

TERIANA

Dawn was in the distant past by the time Teriana made it back to the harbor.

Sweat soaked into the back of her blouse as she dodged between the Cel sailors working on the wharves, then scuttled up the gangplank, eyes searching the deck for her mother, who, thank the Six, was nowhere in sight.

"Couldn't pry yourself out of the feather bed?" Aunt Yedda asked from where she sat drinking from a steaming cup, her light brown skin, courtesy of a Mudamorian father, striking against the yellow of her blouse. Other than the grey in her braids, time didn't seem to touch her. Ripples like gentle waves crossed the serene blue of Yedda's gaze, reflecting her mood in shades of the sea, as did the eyes of every individual with any amount of Maarin blood. The Cel scholars at their fancy colleges believed Maarin eyes similar to a chameleon's skin, but her people knew it was Madoria marking them as her own.

"Sorry. We stayed up late talking."

"How is Lydia?"

Teriana made a face. The truth was a conversation she didn't want anyone to overhear, and most of the crew were moving around on the deck, eyes sleepy but hands deftly performing the tasks required before they could set sail. Her head hurt from all the wine she'd guzzled the night prior, and her mind waffled back and forth between being convinced that it was the booze that had made her tell Lydia about the West and knowing it was a real, desperate need on her friend's part that had made Teriana tell. Because once she had started talking, it had been like the floodgates had opened, secret after secret passing from her lips to Lydia's ears until they'd both fallen asleep in the wee hours.

And it was hard not to feel a touch panicked about what she'd done. *East must not meet West* was a mantra that had been chanted in her ears since childhood, and she'd never even *heard* about one of her people violating Madoria's command that they keep the two halfs of Reath ignorant about each other's existence. If anyone found out about what she'd done, Teriana wasn't even sure *what* the consequences would be—

Loud voices and banging drums coming from the city tore Teriana from her thoughts, everyone turning to scan the market for signs of the commotion. Minutes later, a group of men marched into sight, waving their arms and shouting something indistinguishable. Then another group arrived, behaving in much the same manner, the two stopping a dozen paces from each other and squaring off. More and more people joined their ranks, the cacophony growing.

As it was through all of Celendrial.

The city was coming alive with protest, plebeians taking to their balconies and to the streets to add their voices to the mix. And there was only one thing that incited the Cel this way: politics.

Two of the *Quincense*'s crew who'd been out all night loped toward the ship.

"What's going on?" Aunt Yedda demanded.

"Lucius Cassius has announced he's running for consul," one of them replied.

The sweat on Teriana's back turned cold with the sense that she was much too close to a bad situation. "Cassius was at Lydia's home last night," she said to no one in particular. "He was meeting with her father."

Yedda's brow furrowed, her multitude of braids swaying as she turned back to the city. But it was Tesya who spoke, having coming up silently behind the group of them. "We need to set sail. Is everyone aboard?"

Yedda shook her head. "Might be a few hours yet."

"Shit." Tesya slammed her fist against the rail. "We'll miss the tide." Her dark skin strained as her jaw muscles worked back and forth; then she said, "No one leaves the ship. There's destined to be riots today, and I don't want any of our crew caught in the mix." Then she turned and strode toward her cabin.

Teriana followed her.

Her mother was washing in a basin, and Teriana watched her finish, then tie a scarf to keep her thick black hair out of her face. It did little to hide the droop in her eyelids and, seeing the stacks of ledgers sitting on her mother's desk, Teriana assumed she'd been up all night working.

"Enjoy yourself last night?"

The question made Teriana jump. "I did. It was good to see her. But . . ."

"But?" Her mum turned away from the mirror.

"I'm worried about her." Hoping the darkening shade of her mother's eyes was on Lydia's behalf, Teriana explained the situation.

"What did you expect?" her mother asked when she was finished. "The Cel are block-brained fools, and though Valerius is better than most of them, he's only better by comparison. The thought of marrying Lydia to a plebeian won't even have crossed his mind—the patricians chart their ancestry the same way the Gamdeshians do for their hunting dogs, though at least the latter serves a purpose. Which is why it's going to cost Senator Valerius a gods-damned fortune to get anyone to overlook that girl's lily-white skin. Not a drop of Cel blood in that one."

Not a drop of *eastern* blood in her, in Teriana's opinion, but she didn't voice it. Instead, despite knowing what the answer would be, she asked, "Can we take her with us?"

"No."

"But—"

"I said no. Do you think her father wouldn't suspect it was us who'd taken her? And just how well do you think that would go for this ship and her crew? For all the Maarin, if it was learned we'd spirited away a senator's daughter. We'd have the navy on our heels and legionnaires waiting for us at every port."

"We'd go west," Teriana argued. "She'd be safe there."

Her mother made a rude noise. "We'd be damaging the relationship with the Empire and all Maarin ships. Many whose livelihoods are based around ports on this side on Reath. Would you ruin countless lives for the sake of one girl?"

"You're being—"

"The answer is no, Teriana. I pity Lydia's lot, but there is nothing we can do for her."

And just like that, the conversation was over.

Kicking open the door so that it slammed against the wall, Teriana stormed back on deck, hurrying over to the rail to look at the ships anchored farther out, because that way no one would see her cry.

The sun was fully risen. It was hot and she was hungover, and she'd given her best friend hope where there was none. Scrubbing tears from her cheeks, Teriana caught sight of movement beneath the surface of the water, and she had a heartbeat to wonder why Magnius was braving the filth of the harbor when his voice echoed in her thoughts. *Lydia needs your help.*

It took a second for the words to register, then another second for her to come to grips with Lydia having risked performing the ritual to summon Magnius, then another second still for the question of *what* could've motivated her to do so to begin its march through Teriana's head. "This better not be an experiment, Lydia," she muttered under her breath; then she turned.

The entire crew was staring at her, and her stomach plummeted as she realized it hadn't been just in *her* mind that Magnius had spoken. It had been in *everyone's.*

The captain's cabin door swung open with enough force that the glass pane shattered, and Teriana's mum stormed out. "You idiot!" she shrieked. "What have you done? What were you thinking?"

Teriana's mouth opened and shut, but she'd spent her argument already and her mother hadn't cared. Tesya stormed toward her, pulling her belt free, the tirade coming from her mouth white noise in Teriana's ears. Aunt Yedda tried to step in Tesya's way, but she only pushed her aside.

"Turn around," Tesya ordered, and it wasn't the anger in her voice that made Teriana comply but the fear in her mother's eyes. Ignoring the laughter and catcalls from neighboring vessels, Teriana rested her forehead against the rail, bracing for the snap of her mother's belt, when Magnius's voice cut through the fray. *Let her go see the girl.*

The jeering on the neighboring ships continued, but no one on the *Quincense* spoke, everyone waiting to see how their captain would react.

"Go. Go then." Her voice was shaking, and Teriana avoided looking her mum in the eye as she straightened.

"She's not going through the city by herself," Aunt Yedda said, her calm voice doing little to slow Teriana's thundering heart. "It's not safe."

Tesya's eyes went to Celendrial. "Bait, take one of the boats and row her around to the base of the Hill."

"We're being watched," Aunt Yedda said. "Magister will think we're moving contraband."

"Then make a distraction," Tesya shouted. She turned away from the crew, rubbing at her temples, but Teriana saw the gleam of tears in her eyes. "Deal with it, Magnius."

The *Quincense*'s guardian didn't respond—at least, nothing Teriana could hear. But Bait moved to lower one of the longboats, expression uncharacteristically blank. Instead of helping him, she said, "Mum, I—"

"Just go, Teriana."

Uncertainty kept Teriana fixed in place. She'd pissed her mother off countless times before and suffered any number of punishments for it. But not like this. Never like this.

"I'll talk to her," Aunt Yedda murmured. "You see to Lydia."

It didn't feel right to leave, but it felt even worse to stay.

Unease was biting at her guts like overgrown ship rats. What had happened to Lydia? Had she been harmed? But even worse was the question of what Teriana would be able to do to help her.

Bring the book. Magnius's voice filled her thoughts, along with the vision of a tome that was deeply familiar to her—deeply familiar, in one form or another, to anyone who hailed from the West.

Have you lost your mind? she thought back at him. *What possible good could come from giving her that book?*

There are as many paths as there are travelers.

A typically cryptic response, but Teriana knew from experience that he'd give her no more. "Fine," she muttered, hurrying into her cabin to retrieve the item. "Might as while jump out of the frying pan and into the fire."

Bait had the boat in the water, and Teriana slid down the ladder to join him. "You rowing?" she asked.

He nodded, but his eyes were distant, seeing yet unseeing, and she knew he was in conversation with Magnius. "We just need to wait—"

Whatever he said was drowned out by shouts of alarm as the whole harbor turned to chaos.

5

MARCUS

The Via Metelli was dry as old bone, and by the time Marcus walked through the sprawling gates of Celendrial his skin was coated with a fine layer of dust. From the direction of the harbor, he could make out the drums and shouts of political protestors, and he avoided going anywhere near the Forum, knowing that there'd be oratores on every corner shouting out the promises of the consular candidates. Not that you'd be able to hear them over the hecklers.

Marcus strode through the streets, marking the changes in the city as he went. It seemed smaller than it had seven years ago, but perhaps, he thought, that was because he was larger. Or perhaps it was because now that he had seen so much of the world, Celendrial no longer seemed like the center of it.

Breathing shallowly, he crossed the river Savio, the ripe stench of sewers thick on the nose, all the filth of a million people draining into its murky waters. It was another thing he had forgotten about the city of his birth—how much it stank like shit and piss. It was the same in all cities, he knew, but Celendrial always seemed worse for the fact that it looked so clean from a distance. Gleaming white buildings rising out of a blue sea disguised a core coated with physical and moral filth. He hated it here, and being back had put a permanent scowl on his face that had people leaping out of his path as he cut through one of the city's many marketplaces.

Anything that could be found in the Empire was for sale in Celendrial, from spices to narcotics to fabrics to things he couldn't even name. This market catered to jewels and metal-work, stall after stall of precious wares glittering in the sunlight. Marcus passed a pair of Maarin sailors examining the work of a silversmith, their skin like polished ebony, bright silk shirts tucked into leather trousers, voices rhythmic as they negotiated. There was little doubt in his mind that they'd come out ahead in the transaction.

He wove around a group from Sibern who, despite the heat, wore robes trimmed with fur dyed in vibrant hues, both men and women wearing their hair cut chin length so that it danced around their cheekbones as they moved. They spoke Cel, but their voices carried the lisping accent of their homeland, most of them carrying silken sunshades to protect skin so fair, it was nearly translucent.

Beyond them, his eyes were drawn to a trio of Bardenese women, their dark fingers playing elongated stringed instruments that created a rippling music, their narrow forms swaying to the rhythm as they sang. The youngest of them was fairer than the other two, her skin a golden brown that suggested one of her parents was Cel, a not uncommon occurrence in Celendrial. A not uncommon occurrence across the *Empire,* which had been thoroughly colonized by retired legions.

Exiting the market, Marcus climbed higher, his sandals clacking loudly against the stone walkways as he strode up side paths half-remembered from his childhood to the top of the hill overlooking the sea. All the wealth and power of Celendor resided on this villa-crusted slope, each plot of land fenced off from the next as though those men didn't spend half their lives closeted together plotting the next steps of the Empire. As much as he disliked the city, his hatred for those toga-clad men eclipsed all else.

The most powerful families had homes overlooking the sea, but Cassius's villa faced the city, easy to find with the description Marcus had been given. Stopping at the gated entrance of a villa so large it dwarfed those on either side, he paused to give it a once-over. Most of the senatorial homes were ancient structures steeped in history, gardens lush from centuries of cultivation. Not this villa. Whatever had stood here before had been razed to the ground, and a monolithic monstrosity had been erected in its place. The grounds were nothing but stone and statuary, not so much as a blade of grass in sight.

A servant with a pinched expression appeared from behind the locked gate. He was tall and thin to the point of emaciation, as if he might disappear if turned sideways. The man waited for him to speak, but Marcus did not. His regalia was introduction enough.

"The senator expected you some time ago, *Legatus*."

The man stared at Marcus. Marcus stared back.

"He is not *accustomed* to waiting." The man's face became even more pinched, an expression most would reserve for over-sour lemonade.

The silence stretched as the man waited for an apology. Cracking his neck, Marcus squinted up at the sun to mark the time. He was overheated and wouldn't have turned down a glass of water, but he was used to discomfort. The pinched-faced man, it seemed, was not. He sighed the sigh of one who had suffered a grave injustice, unlocked the gate, and motioned for Marcus to follow, leading him to a room filled with cushioned divans.

"Legatus Marcus of the famous Thirty-Seventh Legion, it is an honor." Lucius Cassius stood as Marcus entered, then motioned for his servant to leave. There was no one else present. The senator was a man of middling height and age, his golden skin oily, as if he had just come from a masseur. He wore his light brown hair clipped short and combed forward, and his blue eyes were too small for his narrow face.

"The undefeated Thirty-Seventh!" Cassius pumped his fist in the air. "We do not fall back. We do not fall back," he repeated the legion's motto. "Is it true that you've never retreated? Remarkable," he continued, not waiting for an answer.

Grasping Marcus's hand, he shook it hard. Marcus withdrew his arm as soon as he could, wishing he could wipe the dampness from his palm. The senator smelled cloyingly of flowers, and his beady eyes were filled with a cunning at odds with his demeanor.

"Who would've thought that the legion of twelve-year-olds we sent off to cut their teeth on the Sibalines would have come so far?" Cassius shook his head, eyes stretched wide with feigned awe.

All legions went active when their youngest member turned twelve, departing Campus Lescendor for their first campaign. Given that every family living under the Empire's control was required to give their second-born son to the military, there wasn't a soul who didn't know it.

"From the Sibalines to Phera to Bardeen, and finally, to Chersome." The senator shook his head. "Never has a nation been quelled quite so thoroughly, and so violently, as Chersome. The market for indentured servants is still down from the glut in supply." He paused, looking Marcus up and down. "Your reputation precedes you, Legatus. I must confess, I felt something of a chill when you walked in, knowing all the atrocities you ordered your men to commit. Ohh." Cassius shivered, his jowls swaying. "There it is again. Like having someone walk across your grave, pardon the pagan expression."

Marcus's jaw clenched, but he said nothing. Some of the stories out of Chersome were just that: stories. However, much of it was true, and he didn't care to be reminded of that fact. His dreams were troubled enough.

Cassius gestured for him to come deeper into the room, and Marcus reluctantly complied. There was something about the situation that wasn't right. Why wasn't he standing before the entire Senate?

"I expected you to arrive somewhat earlier in the day," Cassius said, settling gingerly on a silk-covered divan.

"I walked."

"And he speaks." The senator raised one amused eyebrow. "A horse would've been faster."

The truth was, horses made Marcus sneeze. That, combined with the dusty air of Celendrial, would be enough to set off one of his attacks, and he'd rather walk a thousand miles over hot coals than have a man like this see him so reduced. He raised one shoulder, then let it drop. "True."

Cassius's brow creased ever so slightly. "And here I thought legionnaires were good at following orders." His voice was hard, the polished veneer gone.

"They are." The corner of Marcus's mouth turned up. "And I'm good at giving them."

"You aren't what I expected," said Cassius. "And perhaps that's a good thing."

"Why is that?"

"Because I need a man with vision, not a follower." Leaning forward, Cassius filled two glasses from the decanter sitting on the table, passing one to Marcus. "You'll have heard that I'm running for consul in the next election."

"Yes."

"I want your assistance, Legatus, in ensuring that I'm successful in my bid."

Marcus hadn't expected him to say that. He could vote in the elections—all legionnaires were granted citizenship, the status of their birth and their original nationality wiped away when they left their families to begin training—but what was one vote? "What sort of assistance?"

"All your men are nineteen, or will turn nineteen in the coming months. They are old enough to vote. I want you to ensure they vote for me."

Which entirely undermines the purpose of voting in the first place, thought Marcus. The consul led the Senate—he controlled the entire Empire, and he was chosen by the citizens of Celendor. Forcing individuals to vote one way or another happened, but it was illegal. Forcing an entire legion? They'd hang him for it. "No."

Cassius's face turned sour, but only for an instant. "Don't be so hasty, Legatus. There are those campaigning for consul who do not have the legions' best interest in mind. Those who no longer see your necessity and would see your wages cut, your ranks dismantled and dispatched to the provinces to make babies who'll amount to nothing. Who'd turn the blades of the Empire into farmers and tradesmen, leaving you to toil and struggle like common men."

Over half of Marcus's men had been born in the Empire's provinces, and many—regardless of where they'd been born—would leap at the chance to be *common,* but that wasn't something he necessarily wanted a senator knowing. "Even if every one of them voted for you, it wouldn't be enough. You need the Optimates."

Cassius was not popular among the moderates who'd held power for the last decade—he was too power hungry for their tastes. They called him a warmonger. His chances of winning the consulship were not strong.

Yet if Marcus's words angered him, Cassius didn't show it. "You know of Senator Valerius?"

"Of course." Valerius had been consul when Marcus was a child—he was an Optimate, a scholar, and known as the voice of peace. He also lived at the very top of the Hill.

"He has an adopted daughter of questionable heritage who he is most fond of and keen to see well placed. I've agreed to marry her—for a price."

Marcus set down his glass. "Then you do not need us," he said, turning to the door. "Good day to you, Senator. We await instructions from the Senate on our next mission."

"You will do what I say!"

Marcus turned to face him. "I will not order them to vote for you—they have little enough freedom as it is. I won't take this."

"That's surprisingly moralistic, coming from you."

"Do not presume to know me."

"I know you well enough," Cassius said. "Unless you show your solidarity, I'll make sure to send you and yours to the worst hole in the Empire and leave you there for the next twenty years to rot."

"You're threatening the wrong man." Marcus's hand went reflexively to his gladius, and the senator's eyes went with it. He took a step back, glancing at the walls. Of course they were being watched. Men like Cassius didn't put their lives in danger. Spinning on his heel, Marcus reached for the door, but the senator's next words stopped him in his tracks.

"I think I'm threatening precisely the right man, Domitius."

Marcus hadn't been called by his family name since he was eight years old. Since he had lived on the top of this very hill. Family names were struck when boys were sent to Campus Lescendor to begin their training. The Empire was their father and their mother. Their fellow legionnaires their brothers.

"I'm well acquainted with your family," Cassius said, coming up behind him. "Of course, you would know that."

"The Thirty-Seventh is my family," Marcus replied, but he had to force the words out of his tight throat. "I know no other."

"Please, Legatus. If you were from some obscure plebeian family, I might believe that."

Marcus could feel the man's presence behind him, smell the sweet stink of flowers and oil. "Believe what you will. It is the truth."

Cassius chuckled. "As you like. Though you might find it interesting to learn that your elder brother stopped suffering from his fits after you left for the legions. As I understand it, he hasn't had one since. Don't you find that fascinating?"

Ice ran through Marcus's veins. The compulsion to pull his blade and silence the man standing behind him was overwhelming. An almost unbearable need to stem the tide of words coming from Cassius's mouth that threatened everything he cared for.

"I see your brother often, and I find it fascinating how you, the younger, seem so much more mature. Perhaps it's your reputation. Perhaps it's the gravitas of your rank and its accoutrements. Then again," he continued, "perhaps it's not."

"My legion is my family." Clenching his teeth, Marcus reached for the door, forcing his legs to take him out of the room and down the hall.

"Succeed in convincing your men to vote for me, Legatus, and I'll ensure you're rewarded," Cassius called, his voice bouncing off the empty corridor. "Fail, and your . . . *family* pays the ultimate price."

The words sounded hollow and distant, drowned out by the scream inside Marcus's head. *He knows.*

He knows.

6

TERIANA

The alarm bells reverberated through the air, making Teriana's ears ache. And around them, all the ships began to rock violently, one by one, as though being disturbed by something beneath the murky harbor waters. Which was precisely what was happening.

Go.

Bait rowed hard. Teriana sat with her head resting on her hands, elbows balancing on her knees, eyes on the water pooling around her boots. To look anywhere else would invite questions she didn't want to answer.

Not that it saved her.

"By the Six," Bait said once they'd made it around the rocky outcropping and out of sight of the trade magister. "What were you thinking, Teriana?"

"She's in danger."

"I don't care if she's in open water with sharks circling," he snapped. "East must not meet West. What you told her is forbidden for a *reason*. If the Cel were to learn about the West . . . you know what they'd do. Conquest is in their blood!"

"First they'd have to find their way across the Endless Seas," she said. "And that seems unlikely." Twisting around, Teriana pulled the brim of her hat down to shade her eyes. High on top of the Hill were the senatorial villas, but pathways zigzagged their way down the steep slope toward the series of small coves at its base. They were distant yet, but she could make out the lone figure of a girl sitting on the beach in one of the coves, her gaze fixed on the sand.

"Lydia! Lydia!" she shouted, and when it became clear that her friend was not mortally wounded her fear slid aside to make room for her anger. Anger that melted away the second the other girl lifted her face to reveal an expression as grim as Teriana had ever seen it. "I need to talk to her alone," she said to Bait.

Jumping out of the boat once they reached the shallows, she held the wrapped book high above her head until she was on dry sand, then trotted up the beach to where her friend sat. "The only thing it appears you need help with is escaping the sun. You look like a boiled lobster." Pulling off her battered hat, she plunked it down on Lydia's head. "There."

Lydia's only response was a slight tremor in her jaw. Her friend finally said, "You might have mentioned Magnius was a sea monster."

"He isn't." Teriana grinned, determined to diffuse the situation with levity. "He just looks like one. What did you think he was? Some sort of handsome merman who'd swim up to the beach and give you a kiss?"

The corners of Lydia's mouth crept up. "I thought he was going to eat me."

"Why would he do that?" Teriana punched Lydia gently on the shoulder. "You've got less meat on you than the half-eaten wing of a scrawny chicken. Besides . . ." She hesitated, knowing this subject was dangerous territory.

The power of the gods was dependent upon belief. In an age past, they'd held sway in the East, but the rulers of the then-young Empire had railed against the idea of a power higher than their privileged seats. They condemned those who placed their faith in the Six, slowly eradicating the practice through punishment and the erasure of knowledge until the gods lost their hold. And as the Empire's control spread north and south, faith in the Six dwindled until the gods could no longer touch these lands. Could no longer even see them.

If Teriana was caught admitting her belief, she could be arrested for paganism, which risked all her people being persecuted. But Lydia was different. Lydia, she could trust. "Magnius is a demigod. A scion of Madoria, Goddess of the Seas. He isn't ruled by hunger."

"There is no such thing as gods," Lydia muttered. "All can be explained by logic and reason."

Or maybe she isn't so different. Teriana made a face. "Well, aren't we just a good little parrot today. Though if I do say so myself, you'd be a lot more convincing if you hadn't just confessed to speaking with an overgrown sea snake."

"True," Lydia said, staring at the sea.

"What's wrong?" Teriana gave her arm a shake. "Tell me what's happened to keep you from walking down to the harbor yourself."

Lydia's straight white teeth sank into her bottom lip. Then she said, "My father has forbidden me to go to the harbor."

"That so?" Teriana frowned, feeling her pulse racing beneath her skin as trepidation filled her. "Hate agreeing with a senator, but you were well to stay away today. Whole city's in an uproar since Lucius Cassius announced he's running for consul." Her brow furrowed. "If he wins, all Maarin ships will be giving wide berth to harbors under the Empire's control."

"Did you hear as well that Lucius Cassius has decided to take a new wife?"

"Hadn't," Teriana said, wondering when Lydia would explain herself. "Though I pity the poor girl he's chosen."

Then she saw Lydia clench her fingers around handfuls of sand, and realization stabbed like a knife into her core. "No . . ."

Lydia nodded slowly. "My father signed the contract. A week after the elections, I will be the property of Lucius Cassius." Lydia lifted her face, eyes full of desperation. "I need you to take me with you."

Which had been exactly what Teriana had said she would do.

And it was exactly the one thing she *couldn't* do.

Resting her chin on her knees, Teriana said, "If it were my ship, I would, but my mum refuses to even consider the idea. It's forbidden for us to take passengers, and she's . . . rigid."

"I know she is." Lydia pressed her fingers to her forehead, jerking them away when they touched burnt skin. "And I know it's not your decision."

"I'm sorry—" Teriana started to say, but Lydia held up a hand to stop her, giving her head a weary shake.

Then she poked the package sitting on the sand. "Did you bring me a gift to soften the blow?"

There was no good answer to that, so Teriana pulled the wax covering off the thick tome, passed it to Lydia, then spun a pair of gold bangles around her wrist, casting her mind out to Magnius. *You sure this is a good idea, old man?*

The only response she got was the mental version of a shrug, which was little comfort.

"*Treatise of the Seven.*" Lydia traced a finger over the embossed cover. "The seven what?"

"The Seven Harem Girls." Nerves made the joke sound jarring and not even a little bit funny. She swallowed hard. "The Seven Gods of the West—the Dark Shores." The tome told the stories of the rare occasions the gods had stepped onto the mortal plane, as well as detailing the acts of the individuals they marked with their gifts.

Her friend blinked. "I'll be in all sorts of trouble if I'm caught with this, Teriana."

"So you don't want it?" Teriana reached for the book, but Lydia hugged it to her chest, sun reflecting off her spectacles. "I didn't say *that*. Almost no one reads Trader's Tongue, anyway. I could tell them it was a cookbook and they wouldn't know the difference."

Teriana flopped back on the sand, shading her eyes, wondering if she should inform her friend that what the Cel called Trader's Tongue was the language spoken in Mudamora, the largest kingdom of the West, then decided against it. "The Six preserve me from crazy Cel girls and scholars. Do you even know how to cook?"

"Of course I don't." Lydia flipped through the pages. "What about the seventh god?"

"The Corrupter." Teriana licked her lips in a failed attempt to moisten them. "Only a select few invoke his name, and they aren't the sort you'd care to cross paths with."

"And why are you giving me this?"

Teriana swallowed, her throat dry and scratchy. "You said you needed help."

"And your suggestion is that I ask your gods for it?" Lydia's lips pinched together, turning almost colorless.

"There are as many paths as there are travelers," Teriana said, repeating what Magnius had told her. "You must find the right one."

"What does that mean?"

Before Teriana could answer, Bait approached. "Captain wants to sail with the next tide."

Which wasn't for hours, but what good would she do by lingering? "I need to go."

Lydia nodded, and then Bait came a few steps closer, holding out a glittering object. "I think this is yours, Lydia."

The three of them stared at the bracelet. It was engraved with Celendorian marriage vows of obedience, and to Teriana it had all the appeal of wearing a poisonous snake around her wrist. Lydia's scowl suggested she thought the same as she slid the bracelet onto her wrist.

Teriana rose, pulling Lydia to her feet, then embracing her tightly, her chest constricting as Lydia pulled away first. "I'm sorry. I wish—"

"It's fine," Lydia said. "Vibius is apparently thrilled about the union, so even after my father passes, I'll be of value to Cassius. I'm sure he'll treat me well enough."

"Right." Teriana stood frozen in place, knowing she should say something but for once at a loss for words. And when Bait took her hand, tugging her insistently away from Lydia, she didn't resist.

"She'll be all right," he said when they reached the boat, squeezing her fingers. "Lydia's clever."

Instead of answering, Teriana took hold of the boat and

shoved it into the surf, feeling Magnius's presence as the water splashed against her skin. *That was a waste of time,* she thought. *Might as well have given her a washtub and soup spoon and told her to start paddling.*

She waited for the guardian to answer, and when he did not she snatched the oars from Bait's hands and set to rowing, hoping the tears burning on her cheeks would be confused for sweat. It was only when the beach was far from sight that Magnius's voice echoed in her mind.

She found her way here, Teriana. With faith, she will find her way back.

7

TERIANA

Three months later . . .

Teriana perched on the railing of the *Quincense,* idly watching a body rise from the depths as she toyed with a gold and diamond bead decorating one of her dark braids. The corpse bobbed to the surface, features bloated beyond recognition. Another floated to join him, the two bobbing side by side in the surf like two comrades deep in conversation. Out of habit, Teriana searched for the gleam of jewels or gold on their fingers, but found none.

It had only been chance that they'd come across the wreck of another Maarin ship, Magnius catching sight of it as they sailed down the coast of Celendor, selling silks they'd picked up in Bardeen in some of the smaller port cities. They'd get a better price in Celendrial, but even though it had been three months since Teriana had left Lydia on that beach, her mother still refused to consider returning to the Empire's capital.

Frowning, Teriana turned to the hourglass mounted on the rail. Bait had been down there a long time—he'd better have found something more interesting than dead sailors.

Watching the corpses float away, Teriana lifted her chin to regard the island of Atlia. From where she stood on the ship, it seemed grey and inhospitable, but that was only a trick of light and mist. The lush smells of foliage and fertile earth betrayed the island's true colors. She half-imagined the aroma of the dark drink the islanders brewed. The scent grew stronger, and she turned at the sound of footsteps coming up behind her.

"Quit fretting," her mum said. "Bait knows what he's about. Or at least he better, given what I pay him."

"I'm not fretting." Teriana took the porcelain cup her mum was holding and blew on the steaming liquid before taking a sip and handing it back. Despite her words, her attention drifted back to the turned hourglass, the last grains of sand raining down to form a perfectly peaked mountain. "Just enjoying a moment of free time."

"Free time was not part of the terms of your punishment."

Teriana was not quite forgiven for what she'd told Lydia. She fought the urge to tell her mum to let it go. That what was done was done. But doing so would probably earn her another month of swabbing the decks.

"Those were not your secrets," Tesya said under her breath, as though reading her daughter's thoughts. "They're the secrets of our people. Secrets that Madoria forbids us to reveal to anyone, under any circumstances. The East and the West must be kept apart. They must be protected from each other." Her mouth thinned into a tight line. "Your immortal soul may be lost to the underworld for this."

Teriana thought her mum was overreacting. After all, Magnius hadn't been angry with her for telling Lydia about him—and he was the goddess's scion, which meant his opinion mattered more. Not that she'd ever say that. Magnius's opinion might hold more weight, but that didn't mean her mother wouldn't give her another hiding for arguing.

"And telling a Cel girl of all people," her mum muttered, setting her cup on the railing.

"She's not Cel, and you know it. I'd bet my last copper that she was born in the West." The words were out before she could think.

"That may be true," her mum replied. "But she's been raised as a Cel lady. And in a few days, she'll be wed to the worst of them."

"Not by choice." Teriana dug her fingernails into the wood railing, easily calling to mind the misery on Lydia's face when she'd told her about the contract. "Don't know what her father was thinking."

"Bah!" Tesya spit into the ocean. "Stupid Cel—always thinking women need men to survive." She shook her head. "Lydia's father might be motivated by emotion, but Cassius is motivated by politics. He's using the girl to get to her father." She gave Teriana a sharp jab in the shoulder. "And thanks to your loose lips, he might use her to get to us as well."

A serpentine shadow rose up from the depths, ending their conversation. "There they are," her mum said. "Let's see what Bait has found for us."

"Took your time, boy!" Tesya shouted once they broke the surface.

Bait grinned from where he sat on the guardian's back, gloved hands gripping Magnius's rear dorsal spike. "Sorry, Captain, she was deeper than I thought."

"Broken up?"

"Not too badly, though it looks like they went down quickly. Hold's intact."

"And?"

Bait shrugged. "Plenty of silks and fabrics; we can bring them up, but I doubt they can be salvaged."

Tesya swore and slammed her fist down on the rail.

"And a chest full of these." Bait stood up on the guardian's broad back, and as they passed by the ship he revealed a handful of glittering green emeralds.

Tesya hooted with delight, the watching crew echoing her. Teriana added her voice to the racket, but her relief at seeing Bait back above water far eclipsed her enthusiasm for the gemstones. As Magnius lazily circled the ship, Bait met her gaze and shot her a smile. Before she could smile back, a hand shoved her shoulders, sending her toppling off the railing. Teriana managed one shocked shriek of laughter before plunging under the surface of the water.

Rising on a swell, she heard her mum shout, "Ready the equipment, my friends; we've got a cargo to bring up!"; then Bait's hand was reaching toward her, pulling her onto Magnius's back. The guardian's skin was cold and rough against hers, but Bait's hand was warm.

"What took you so long?" she asked once she was settled. "Was starting to worry."

Bait frowned. "I can take care of myself, Teriana."

"Aye. Only . . . you were down there an awfully long time."

"Didn't seem long." He scratched his head. "Something about the ship didn't seem right."

"How so?"

"Something about the way she sank . . ." He trailed off with a shrug. "Doesn't matter."

"Bait!" They both looked up to see Tesya leaning over the railing. "Did you see any sign of the captain? Big man, black beard?"

"Aye, Captain. I saw him."

"Well, then be a good lad and retrieve the rings on his fingers. Likely you'll need to cut them off."

The *Quincense's* diver grimaced.

"If you bring him up, I'll do it," Teriana whispered, keeping her face lowered so her mum wouldn't hear.

"I can do it myself."

"He's dead," Tesya shouted. "He's beyond caring if his fingers are attached or not."

Refusing to meet Teriana's gaze, Bait said, "It's not that, Captain. I was a mind to take them while I was down there, but before I could get to it, Magnius ate him."

Tesya swore. "We'd be as rich as kings if we could find a way to attach a sack to the old man's rear end." Leaning over the railing even farther, she pointed a finger at the guardian. "It's a wonder you still keep up to the ship with the way your eyes are always searching for your next meal, you gluttonous overgrown sea snake."

Bait and Teriana howled with laughter right up to the point when Magnius rolled, spilling them both into the water. Magnius's black eyes rarely showed much in the way of emotion, but Teriana swore the guardian gave her a look of indignation before diving into the depths.

Bait looked ready to follow him when the lookout bells

clanged a warning. "White sails two points off the starboard bow!"

And then a heartbeat later, the lookout added, "She flies the Celendorian dragon."

8

MARCUS

Marcus brushed an invisible fleck of dust off his armor, half-listening to the thousands of men readying themselves throughout the camp. After three months of languishing outside of Celendrial, today they would vote in the elections. And if all went according to plan, Lucius Cassius would become consul.

"Ready?" Servius came into the tent, helmet in one hand.

Marcus cracked his neck, then nodded. "Let's get this over with."

"I've got your horse outside," Servius said. "Made sure he was given a good brushing, then I took him down to the ocean and scrubbed him within an inch of his life. Bugger is as clean as a whistle. Still a bit damp, but he'll be dry by the time we get to the gates."

"I thought you were avoiding the ocean?" Marcus asked, fighting to keep a smile off his face. Servius's phobia of sea creatures had only increased since the rumor had passed through the camp that there was a monster living in the Celendrial harbor.

"Oh, well." Servius rolled his wide shoulders so that his armor settled more comfortably. "I figured any sea monster worth its salt would prefer your horse to me. And besides, you're the first of us that the people will see—can't have you riding a grubby steed. Would make us look bad."

"Thank you for safeguarding my image." Marcus clapped a hand against his friend's shoulder and stepped out of the tent. He doubted anyone would notice the cleanliness of his horse, but they would certainly notice a legatus who sneezed every two strides. He idly wondered how many times over the years

Servius and Felix had helped hide his illnesses. Without them, he wouldn't have made it through the first year of basic.

Taking the reins, he swung into the saddle and started through camp. In the distance, Felix was on horseback, shouting instructions to the men. They were already in march formation, but at the sight of Marcus shoulders squared and lines straightened. He scanned the ranks, noting with pride that they showed no sign of having lost their edge in their months of leisure. They looked as sharp and ready as ever. He trotted his horse to the front of their line, each century saluting him in unison as he passed, the sounds of fists striking armored chests echoing across the hills.

The line of men stretched down the Via Metelli, but it wasn't long before he could see the Thirty-Seventh's gleaming dragon standard marking the front. "All is in order?" he asked Servius, who, despite sitting a horse about as well as a sack of potatoes, had managed to make it there ahead of him.

"Yes, sir. Ready to show that blasted piss hole of a city what a real legion looks like."

Marcus lifted a hand to get the attention of the line. "Let's have some music, shall we?" he shouted. "Something triumphant." Wheeling his horse around, he started at a fast walk down the road. Drums and horns blared to life behind him, but they seemed loud only until the rhythmic beat of the marching legion drowned them out.

Though he'd never admit it aloud, Celendrial did need a taste of what it felt like to be marched on. The city deserved to feel the force of what it had created.

It seemed to take an eternity to reach the Forum, even once they entered the city. Marcus refused to look to either side, fixating on the never-ending streets rather than the never-ending sets of unwelcoming eyes. He could feel their judgment thick upon his skin, and he wanted to scream, "These are your sons! Sons you served up to the Senate." Only there was no point. They had all washed themselves clean of the children they had given up—thanks to Chersome, there was no pride in claiming a son belonging to the Thirty-Seventh.

When Marcus reached the great Forum square, he and his officers trotted to the far side to stand before the rostrum, stairs arching up both sides toward the marble poll. Golden tubes exited the small structure, leading to massive cisterns labeled with the candidates' names. The structure was designed so that it was impossible to see where an individual vote went but allowed anyone to see who was in the lead. Marcus glanced surreptitiously at the cisterns: it appeared Cassius was in second place behind an Optimate named Basilius, though the votes were close. If the Thirty-Seventh all voted for Cassius, he would win. Whether that was a good thing or a bad Marcus wasn't sure.

The legion syphoned into the Forum, arranging themselves into neat rows until the square was full of young men. Seeing they were all settled, Marcus held up one hand, silencing the music. Then he dismounted and strode toward the stairs, his footsteps echoing through the silent Forum. An official standing at the base handed him a token, and he walked swiftly up the steps and into the little building. It had an open roof, the sunlight bright on the list of six names cast in stone across the raised table. Beneath each name was a hole where the voter was to drop his token.

Marcus stared at the names. Were these other men better or worse than Cassius? Better for the Empire, maybe, but not for him. Not for his legion. His stomach felt in ropes and the token grew slick with sweat from his palm. He tried to imagine a circumstance where he was voting without the pressure of blackmail to guide his choice. Would he vote for Cassius then? Or a circumstance where he wasn't a soldier—just a common citizen. Who would he vote for?

Tapping the token against the table, Marcus took a deep breath. What-ifs didn't matter; what mattered was what *was*. Holding up the sweaty token, he dropped it into the hole. It clattered down the tube and into the cistern below.

When he came out, his attention went immediately to the steps of the Curia, its towering columns running the length of the Forum. They'd been empty before, but now they held a dozen toga-clad patricians, Cassius among them.

"Well, that wasn't nearly as exciting as I thought it would be," Servius said, coming up behind him. His friend had already voted, clearly not lingering on the decision as Marcus had. "This is going to take forever."

"Keep it orderly," Marcus replied absently, starting across the Forum toward the senators.

The senators were broken into two groups, one surrounding Cassius and one surrounding Basilius. Only one woman was present, a willowy girl with porcelain skin and black hair that was braided into a coronet around her head. Judging from the way Senator Valerius hovered next to her, this was the foster daughter Cassius was marrying in exchange for Valerius's support.

"Legatus," Cassius said as he approached. Marcus nodded in greeting. Basilius's shoulders jerked as he realized that Marcus and Cassius were acquainted, the implications dawning on him.

"Lydia, darling," Cassius said. "This is Legatus Marcus of the Thirty-Seventh Legion. Legatus, Lydia is my intended, and I'm sure you know her father, Senator Valerius."

"Senator," Marcus said, inclining his head. "Domina." He didn't bother congratulating her on the forthcoming nuptials. The way she recoiled from Cassius's greasy grip on her skinny arm was telling. Her father appeared deeply unwell, his skin sallow and dripping sweat despite the servants vigorously fanning the party.

The girl, whose slanted eyes had a peculiar luster—like shards of quartz—turned her head to regard him. "It appears your legion favors Lucius, Legatus. Though I suppose that's unsurprising given that he favors the legions."

Out of the corner of his eye, Marcus saw Cassius's face darken but he answered anyway. "In my experience, men vote for the individual they perceive will act in their best interest. Only a few vote for the good of society, altruism being a rare quality."

"Which sort of man are you, Legatus?" she asked. "The sort who desires to save the world? Or to save himself?"

"That's enough, Lydia," Senator Valerius said, taking his foster daughter by the arm. "Perhaps we might go inside out of the heat. Excuse us."

"Apologies," Cassius said, taking a glass beaded with condensation from a servant. "She's yet to realize that her company would be more desirable if she kept silent." His eyes never left the cistern or the legionnaires efficiently filing up and down the steps.

Marcus said nothing, the girl the least of his concerns. Even from here, he could see Cassius's cistern slowly filling, with no change in those of the other candidates. Within a half hour, Cassius was in the lead, and half the legion had yet to vote. The polls closed at sunset, and by then Cassius would unofficially be consul.

Basilius and his friends knew it, too. Marcus watched them whisper angrily to one another; then Basilius was walking toward him. "Fool of a boy," the senator barked. "Do you have any idea what you've done?"

Marcus stared back at him, silent.

"You're barely more than a child, and you come home thinking you can do this . . . this . . ." Basilius waved a hand at the cisterns. "You know nothing of anything but killing, you ignorant—" He broke off, pressing a hand to his chest, head shaking rapidly. "There will be a reckoning for this, mark my words." Basilius and his friends stormed back into the building.

"Some people handle defeat poorly," Cassius remarked, a faint smile crawling across his face. "But you don't know much about defeat, do you?"

"Or about much of anything, apparently," Marcus replied, keeping his voice light. The senator's words troubled him—it was as if the man had heard every doubt that had run through his mind while holding that blasted token.

"Ignore him," Cassius snapped. "He's an old doddering fool."

Marcus watched the procession until the last of his men had trooped through to vote, the horns blasting to indicate the polls had closed. He wanted to be away from this conversation, from this place. "It's finished," he said a little too quickly. "We'll excuse ourselves from the city and return to camp. Consul," he added, with a slight incline of his head. For better or worse, Cassius was in power now.

Cassius licked his lips. "Indeed. Send them back, but I want you to stay. We've business to discuss."

Marcus kept his face still, but his stomach twisted. "With the Senate?"

"No," Cassius replied. "You and I. Attend me at my villa within the hour." Not waiting for a response, he strolled into the Senate, leaving Marcus alone on the steps.

Marcus found Cassius in his home, once again sprawled across a divan. "I see your promptness is improving, Legatus." The soon-to-be consul chuckled. "I'll have you trained yet."

A statement that implied that Cassius had further use of him. Marcus's jaw tightened. "Why am I here? I gave you what you wanted."

"Unfortunately, your manners still need work." Cassius shook his head. "I suppose blood isn't everything."

"Or anything at all."

"I'm not so sure about that." Heaving himself to his feet, Cassius gestured to the far door. "If you'd come with me, I think now is an appropriate time to discuss how I might reward you and your men for your solidarity."

"Keep your money. Just have the Senate send us back to the field. Preferably somewhere far from here."

"I thought you might say something like that, Legatus. And as your reward, I'm going to give you exactly what you want."

Curiosity piqued despite himself, Marcus followed Cassius into the next room. In its center was a large table covered with maps and parchment. The senator poured two glasses of yellow wine, handing one to Marcus. "What would you say if I offered you the opportunity to lead an army on the most ambitious mission undertaken in the history of the Celendor Empire?"

Marcus's fingers twitched, and though he rarely drank, he took a large mouthful of wine. "I'm listening."

Cassius gestured to a large map dominating the table. Heedlessly setting his cup on a pile of parchment, Marcus took in the totality of the Empire, which was wrought in exquisite detail. The writing was in the Trader's Tongue spoken by the Maarin—a language of which he only knew a few phrases, not having had much contact with the Maarin, despite his travels. "How did you come by this?" Marcus asked. "Any Maarin captain would rather lose a hand than give up a map."

"Let's just say the captain in question lost more than his hand."

Marcus felt his eyes drawn away from the map until they came to rest on Cassius's face. The senator wore a cruel smile as he said, "Legatus, it is long past time the Maarin were brought to heel."

War with the Maarin? The seafaring race was the only nation of people *not* under the dominion of the Empire, and the Senate had never shown any inclination to change that relationship. For one, the Maarin had no known lands for the Empire to claim, and two, the Senate made a tidy profit off of a tax the Maarin paid as the price for their uncontested liberty. For the Senate, above all else, was ruled by profit, and the Maarin were consummate business people. Starting a war with them would cost everyone money, and trying to make them sail under Cel command would, in Marcus's opinion, be far more headache than it was worth. And given the general goodwill the plebs held toward the Maarin, causing them trouble for no reason other than to put a leash on them smacked of political suicide. "To what end would the Senate consider such a move?"

"To the end of the world." Reaching out with one hand, Cassius unfolded the map, smoothing it flat against the table. "Behold, the Dark Shores of Reath."

Marcus sucked in a deep breath.

The world had suddenly become a lot larger.

Two continents, one in the north and one in the south, plus several large islands, dominated the unfolded half of the map. He scanned the unfamiliar names, his mind racing. "Are they inhabited?"

"Indeed. The crew we captured were reticent about providing details, but the maps and ledgers pulled from the hidden compartments on their ship provided a wealth of information. It will be no easy conquest, but well worth it in the end."

Marcus's heart skipped, the chance to go to a place he'd never seen—never *heard of*—before more alluring than all the riches or girls in the Empire. Except there were two large and wet problems that his mind couldn't get past. "These are to scale?"

"They are."

Marcus shook his head. "What you suggest is impossible, then. Even if the Maarin can show us a way across the Endless Seas, it would take months over open water. Half my army would be dead from starvation or disease by the time we got there. The rest would be in no condition to fight."

"I'm not suggesting you sail directly across."

Marcus's brows rose. "Xenthier?"

Xenthier could transport both man and beast from one place to the next in a matter of moments, and it had been integral to the success of Celendor's conquests since the dawn of the Empire. Marcus could move his whole legion a thousand miles in a matter of hours, men and supplies transported between provinces as easily as game pieces on a board. There were dozens of mapped veins of xenthier crystal crisscrossing the Empire, all heavily fortified, the Senate using them for its own purposes, traders and travelers paying heavy tolls for the privilege. But the paths only flowed in one direction, like arteries, so consuls regularly sent men through unmapped stems with the promise of riches if they returned with answers as to where the xenthier had landed them. It was entirely possible one of them had made it to the Dark Shores. But none had ever found a route back.

Cassius hesitated, then shook his head. "I'm not certain how, but the Maarin have a way."

"Do you have proof?"

"Of a sort." Cassius pulled several ledgers in front of him. "These are from Maarin ships we detained."

"What motivated you to detain them?" Celendor's ironclad treaty with the Maarin included terms that prevented their ships from being boarded unless they broke the Empire's laws.

A slow smile worked its way onto the consul's lips. "An unexpected piece of information fell into my lap that allowed me to charge them with paganism."

That was unexpected and yet . . . not. The Maarin kept apart and always had. That they had practices and beliefs that didn't fall in line with the Empire's wasn't surprising, but that Cassius—and the Senate—had been willing to endure the disruption to trade that would come from this *was*. A far better thing to just purchase the information from the Maarin rather than to force it from them.

"One set of ledgers," Cassius continued, "shows the ship's activities throughout the Empire. But this set, which we found in the secret compartment with the maps, shows activities in the places whose names correspond with the western half of the map."

It was an incredible revelation. The existence of a whole new world. The ripples of the news would extend up and down the Empire, especially the news that the Maarin were moving back and forth between them. But the problem of the Endless Seas and their many hazards remained. "Even if the Maarin could be compelled to share their route through the doldrums, there is a huge difference between one merchant vessel and her crew sailing for months and a fleet carrying a legion or two."

"Not months. Days." Cassius smiled. "Look at the dates."

Marcus paired the ledgers, eyeing the circled dates. "Could be an error."

"An error made dozens of times?" Taking the ledgers back,

Cassius flipped through the pages, showing example after example of instances where the Maarin appeared to have leapt from one side of the world to another. And there was only one way that could be done.

"It has to be somewhere at sea for them to be taking their ships through it," Marcus murmured, trying to conceive of the amount of nerve it would require to sail a vessel through one of the crystal pathways. He'd used the established land-based paths with their well-guarded terminuses, but each time it was almost more than he could do to reach out and take hold of the crystal, never knowing for certain what would greet him on the other side. Fire. Flood. An enemy waiting to pick his men off one by one.

"I'm inclined to agree," Cassius replied. "But nothing is marked on any of the maps. And we were unable to excise the information from any of the crew. Not with any amount of force."

Which likely meant the crew in question were now dead. Or wished they were. Marcus asked, "They denied its existence?"

"Not precisely." Cassius's lip curled with distaste. "Though it's of no matter. Even as we speak, our navy is moving to intercept several influential Maarin ships. They have the information we need; it's merely a matter of extracting it."

"And when you do?"

"Then we send an . . . *exploration* party across the Endless Seas." Cassius's smile was feral. "A party *you* could lead, Legatus. An endeavor which, if you were successful, would make you the most famous commander in Celendor's history."

Fame was the least of Marcus's concerns, just as *exploration* was the least of the Senate's desires. But to walk on the far side of Reath, to see lands that until now had been nothing more than myth . . . that *was* worth something to him. As was the opportunity to be out from underneath the Senate's thumb. To do things *his* way.

But one question remained to be asked. "Why me?"

"You are said to be the sharpest mind to ever graduate from

Campus Lescendor, Legatus. Undefeatable. I'd be a fool to choose anyone else."

And Marcus would be a fool to believe such flattery. Crossing his arms, he waited for the man who'd soon control the entire Empire to name his price.

Cassius was quiet for a long minute before he spoke again. "I suppose there is no point circling the issue. In exchange for the command, I want you to kill someone for me. Kill her, and make sure the body is never found."

Marcus's chin jerked up. "I'm no murderer."

"On the contrary, Legatus, that is exactly what you are. A professional killer. Which is precisely what I need. I don't want some hack to botch the job or lose his nerve at the last moment. Or to hesitate because she's a girl. I can't see you hesitating. Man, woman, babe—it makes no difference to you, does it?"

Marcus laughed, the sound harsh. It always came back to Chersome. He wondered what people would think if they knew what really happened on that forsaken isle. "You're dreaming. If I were caught, they'd hang me for it."

The soon-to-be consul's expression was cold. "If you don't do it, you'll hang. And you won't hang alone."

Blood roared in Marcus's ears. Blackmail. That was why Cassius wanted him—because he could control Marcus. Even on the far side of the world, he could control him.

The consul gestured for him to sit, but Marcus ignored him.

"I was hoping it wouldn't come to this," Cassius said, sighing deeply.

Denying it was futile, but Marcus still asked, "Come to what?"

Cassius snorted and shook his head. "I know that you are the eldest son of the Domitius family. I know that your parents sent you instead of your brother to Campus Lescendor. And everyone knows *that* is a capital offense. No one, not even a senator, gets to cherry-pick which of their children to send to the legions, else the blade of the Empire would be made up of . . . well, it would be made up of young men like *you*."

There was no sense pretending it wasn't the truth. "If you harm them," Marcus said quietly, "I will gut you from stem to stern and stake you out in the sun for the crows to feast on."

"Now, now, Legatus. No need for threats. The last thing I want is for your family to come to harm. I've known them for a good many years, after all." He leaned back on the divan. "My memories of you as a child are as vivid as if they were yesterday. You were such a wheezy, runty little thing—always chasing after the other children only to collapse in a faint, their dust settling on your pale little face."

Marcus glared at him, wanting to cut him off but knowing it was the prudent course to hear him out.

"It is, even now, easy to see why your father chose to do what he did." Cassius smiled. "They sent you two boys off to the healing mineral springs. One last brotherly adventure before young Marcus was sent to join the legions and Gaius returned to resume his position as heir to the Domitius fortune." Cassius flung up his hands. "And lo and behold, six months later young Gaius returned as hale and healthy as a young man could want to be and his brother, Marcus, disappeared into the great machine of our legions, never to be heard from again."

"Get to it, Cassius."

"Of course, of course. As it so happens, I partook of the healing waters myself some years after." Cassius peered into his cup and made a face at seeing it was empty. "A moment. I find myself parched." He poured himself more wine, obviously enjoying his performance. Settling back on the divan, he took a long mouthful. "By chance, I met the physician who treated young Gaius, and though he was reluctant to divulge information about his patients, he eventually confessed that the young boy had not improved at all with the treatments."

And there was the proof. All the rest was speculation, but the word of a university-trained physician in the courts would be damning, because any physician worth his salt would be able to examine Marcus and his brother to determine which one of them possessed the affliction.

"I can only imagine what it must have been like for you," Cassius said. "Not only were you disinherited of one of the greatest fortunes in the Empire, but you were abandoned by your family. Because they wanted you less than your brother."

Marcus forced himself to appear calm. Having this man drag the worst moment of his life out into the open and rub it in his face was bad enough, but allowing Cassius to know he was getting to Marcus was worse. "You've a flair for the dramatic. And it seems you've spent far more time thinking about my past than I have."

"Perhaps. Though there was always one aspect of the story that troubled me."

"And what was that?"

"Why you went along with it." Cassius leaned forward. "It's easy to understand why your brother did. In one fell swoop, he was spared the grueling life of a legionnaire and became heir to the Domitius fortune. But why did you? What possible reason could a young boy have to protect the family who abandoned him?"

"None."

Cassius smiled. "One. And I think you'll do whatever it takes to keep her safe. Including murdering my future wife."

9

TERIANA

"Everyone out of the water," Tesya ordered.

By the time Teriana and Bait climbed up ropes and onto the ship, the white sails were visible to the naked eye.

"She flies the golden dragon, Captain," the lookout shouted from above, lowering her spyglass. "Doesn't look to be a merchantman."

A Celendorian naval vessel, Teriana thought. She'd be easy enough for them to outrun, but to do so would arouse suspicions. They'd no reason to cause the *Quincense* trouble, but that didn't mean her mum was of a mind for them to know they'd been salvaging a wreck. Maarin seas, Maarin secrets. "What do you want to do?"

"We'll see what they want." Tesya took her pipe out of the pocket of her trousers and filled it with some fine Gamdeshian leaf, lighting it with a flame one of the sailors passed her. The smoke trailed behind them as the ship drifted and they waited for the top-heavy frigate to pull alongside. The Celendorian sailors tossed up hooks and pulled the ships together, leaving deep gouges in the wooden rails.

Teriana's mum leaned over the side. "Admiral."

The short, bald man looked up at her. "Captain . . . ?"

"Tesya," she replied, taking a long pull on her pipe and then blowing smoke rings.

"And your ship?"

"Has that blasted paint worn off already?" She bent farther to look at the prow. "No, it appears to still be there." She pointed at the flowing golden script and blew another smoke ring. "The *Quincense.*"

"Hmm." The admiral poked his scribe, who made a note in a book. "And your business in Atlian waters?"

"None. We are merely passing through."

"To where? And what is the nature of your cargo?"

"Silk cargo destined for Celendrial."

Tesya pulled Teriana to her side and muttered, "Make certain anything we shouldn't have is well hidden and bring some wine back with you."

Teriana gave the admiral a wide smile and trotted toward her mother's cabin. Bait was already inside, stowing the maps into their secret compartments. "What do they want?" he asked, not looking up from his task.

"Don't know." Teriana extracted a bottle of wine from a crate, along with two pewter glasses. The Maarin had a treaty with the Senate ensuring their ships would never be boarded or searched without just cause; *just cause* being the violation of one of the Empire's innumerable laws. But the *Quincense* hadn't been caught doing anything it shouldn't, so this was uncalled for. Her mum's words resounded in her ears: *He might use her to get to us as well.*

Please don't have said anything, Lydia, Teriana thought. To Bait, she said, "Make sure everything is stowed away."

Teriana came back on deck in time to hear the admiral say, "Something to hide, Captain?"

Tesya took a long pull on her pipe and shook her head. "Just thought you might enjoy a glass of wine. We've Atlian vintage aboard."

"Perhaps we'll share a glass or two after we inspect your cargo."

From the rigging, one of the lookouts whistled a short tune. The title of the song was "Mutiny and Murder," a black song of betrayal, but more importantly, it signaled another ship was approaching from the windward side. The sailor continued with the second verse and then the third: three ships approaching. Something was happening.

"Pour the wine, girl," her mum said. It was an effort to keep her hands steady as she uncorked the bottle and poured a glass, handing it to the man. The other ships were in sight now, and they were coming in fast.

"What are your intentions, Admiral?"

"The Senate is of the belief that the Maarin are in possession of certain pieces of information that are of value to the Empire. We are here to escort you to Celendrial so that you might share what you know."

Teriana's stomach hollowed, all the blood draining from her face. *No, please no,* she silently prayed.

Her mother said, "The Maarin have a long-standing treaty with Celendor. I hope the Senate isn't of a mind to violate it."

The admiral smiled, but his shaved head was slick with sweat. "They wouldn't dream of it."

He was lying, Teriana was sure of it. But why? The Senate wouldn't jeopardize trade with the Maarin on a whim . . . unless they believed the cost worth the information they'd gain.

Something is amiss. Magnius's voice echoed through her thoughts. Her vision dimmed, the admiral's face disappearing only to be replaced by the faintly illuminated depths of the ocean. Through the guardian's eyes, she saw the wreck of Castrick's ship on the seafloor, tattered sails drifting in the current. Magnius circled the wreck, his distorted vision making her dizzy. He swam closer, and through the damage enacted by the sea she saw something that made her blood run cold: an iron ball stamped with the Celendorian dragon.

Her vision cleared, and she blinked back tears at the sudden brightness of the sun. Her mother was blinking, too. She'd seen as well.

"Captain?" The admiral's voice was tinged with impatience. "Do we have your cooperation?"

Tesya took a final pull on her pipe and then tapped it out, the smoldering tobacco floating down to land on the deck of the other ship. "Tell me, Admiral, did you sink Castrick's ship before or after he cooperated with you?"

The man's face paled and he took a step backward.

"You're floating over the bones of your victims, you Celendorian liar," Tesya hissed. "Angry spirits, who'd be more than happy to have you join them in Madoria's depths!" The words had scarce left her lips when the Cel ship jerked and shuddered, wood cracking as Magnius slammed his bulk into the hull. Pulling a coin from her pocket, Tesya tossed it through the air, the gold glittering in the sunlight. "To pay your passage to the underworld, you godless dog!"

The admiral reached for his blade, but Tesya punched him in the face, sending him staggering.

"Full sail!" Teriana screamed. Drawing her cutlass, she ran to the railing and brought the blade down hard, cutting the rope binding the two vessels as her crew did the same to the other lines. The admiral had extracted his sword, but the dozen armed Maarin had him climbing onto the rail.

The ships slammed together, then broke apart as Magnius rose out of the water. Teeth flashed and the admiral screamed once before he was dragged beneath the waves.

The sails billowed, catching the wind and snapping taut. The *Quincense* rotated, the stern slamming into the smaller ship and sending the terrified Cel sailors sprawling. Teriana clung to the rail as the ship leapt forward, smashing through the waves as she gathered speed.

Faster, Teriana thought, watching the encroaching ships. One dropped sail to pick up the survivors from the sinking ship, but the others didn't hesitate. She watched in grim silence as they armed their catapults. A thousand curses on Celendorian planning and ingenuity.

"We're still in range!" Tesya snarled.

The beams of the catapults crashed against their stops with each launch, the iron balls splashing into the sea to either side of her ship. Then the crunch of wood and screams from those below.

Her mum's hands remained fixed on the helm, lips moving in silent prayer to Madoria.

Another twang and the shattering of glass as the ball flew through the captain's cabins below them, bursting through the door and across the deck, sending sailors diving out of the way.

Only a few moments more and the *Quincense* would be out of reach.

Leaning over the side, Teriana watched as the Cel ships fell farther behind. Then a catapult on the front runner snapped forward, a black speck flying toward them. "Incoming!"

It was too late. Wood splintered and sails ripped as the ball tore through the rigging, smashing into a mast. The ship lost momentum, listing to the leeward side as mast and rigging splashed into the water. Teriana watched helplessly as her mother was thrown off her feet, head smacking the deck. "Mum!"

Crawling toward her, Teriana felt for a pulse. It was strong, but she barely had a chance for relief. With her mum unconscious, she was in command.

"Cut it loose." The words came out as barely a croak, forcing Teriana to repeat herself. The crew hopped to, cutting away the fallen rigging and seeing to the injured, but their faces were grim.

Bait hobbled up the steps, eyes widening at the sight of Teriana's mother cradled in her arms. "How bad is she hurt?"

"Don't know." Tears were streaming down Teriana's face. "If I don't surrender they'll see us at the bottom of the ocean. You must bring word to our brethren that no port in the Empire is safe."

He shook his head. "I'm not leaving you. Not like this."

An iron ball landed off the port side, spraying them with water.

Laying her mum down, she clambered to her feet. "No one else can swim so far. It must be you. Now go! Find Magnius and warn the other ships." He hesitated and she shoved him toward the stern. "That's an order."

With one final look at Teriana, Bait leapt over the rail to disappear into the foam of their wake.

"Drop sail and run up the white flag," she ordered the crew. It was time to find out the depths of Lydia's betrayal. And how much it would cost her.

10

TERIANA

Teriana spent three days locked in the brig. Alone. She didn't know whether the rest of her crew were alive or dead. Whether her mother was alive or dead. She'd never been more terrified in her life.

Or felt more guilty.

"This is all your fault," she told herself every time she sensed a bout of self-pity coming. "You brought this upon yourself. You deserve everything you get." And her verbal flagellation might have been some comfort except for the fact that her mother and her crew hadn't deserved this. None of them had opened their big mouths and told all the secrets of their nation to a bloody weakling of a Cel girl.

Because that was what she told herself: not that Lydia had maliciously betrayed her, but that she'd been too weak to stand up to the inquisition of her future husband. That Teriana had placed her secrets in a wicker basket rather than the steel box they deserved. Her mother had been right. It was straight to the underworld for Teriana's soul for what she'd done. There was no argument for it being otherwise.

Not that she didn't try. Day and night she knelt with her head pressed against the floor, praying to Madoria for forgiveness. Even when her Cel captors gave her foul water and food, which made her sick from both ends and almost glad she was imprisoned alone, she prayed. Curled up in a ball on the damp deck, she prayed, promising she would do whatever her goddess asked in order to earn forgiveness. In order to make up for what she had done.

But Madoria was silent. As was Magnius. She hoped fervently that he was far, far away with Bait, warning their people of the danger. But part of her feared that the *Quincense*'s guardian had turned his back on her, too.

As sickness caught hold of her mind, sending her into wild fits of delusions, fear fled in the face of her anger. "You trusted her, too!" she screamed at the serpentine shape swimming before her. "You should've warned me against her. You were supposed to protect me!" She pounded her fists bloody against the boards, tears running in torrents to join the murky seawater slowly flooding the leaky ship.

But there was only silence.

"Wake up, you little twit."

Teriana coughed and choked as a bucket of water splashed against her face. With one shaky arm, she pushed up onto an elbow, blinking against the unaccustomed brightness of the sun. She was lying on the deck of the Cel ship, though she had no memory of getting there. One of the sailors must have carried her. She cringed at the thought of their fingers on her unconscious body.

"Where?" she croaked. They were docked, but her bleary vision and dizzy head couldn't place the port.

"Celendrial." The sailor kicked her in the ribs. "Now get up."

Clutching her side, Teriana dragged herself upward, holding the railing for balance. A wave of blackness threatened to send her back down to the deck, and it took several measured breaths until the feeling passed. Once it had, she noticed about a dozen of her crew with their wrists bound on the far side of the deck. Some were injured. All of them were afraid.

"Where's the rest of my crew?"

The sailor shrugged. "Some's on the other ships." Then he grinned. "Some's dead."

A sob tried to tear out of her throat, but she forced it down. The crew members were her friends, her family. Most of them she'd known her entire life, and now who knew how many were dead because of her? "And my mum? The captain?"

The sailor didn't answer and dread filled her. "Please, no," she whispered. "Don't let her be gone."

"Speak Cel," the sailor said, then backhanded her.

"That's enough!" someone shouted, and she saw a flash of red and a gleam of metal. Legionnaires. Teriana clutched the rail of the ship, trying not to cower.

"I don't take orders from land grunts," the sailor snapped.

The legionnaire leading the group shrugged. "Have it your way." He jerked his chin at two of the other soldiers, who rushed the sailor and tossed him overboard.

The legionnaire glanced around at the rest of the navy crew. "Anyone else have opinions they'd like to voice?" The crew all shook their heads. "Good. Get the rest of them cleaned up. Give them food and clean water. We need them alive and functional, not half-dead from dehydration and gut rot. We're taking the girl."

He started in Teriana's direction, and she recoiled. Not because he was as broad as a rain barrel or because of the gleaming gladius at his waist. It was because of the number embossed on his breastplate. 37. The legionnaire reached for her and she screamed and tried to run, but he caught hold of her arm.

"Easy, girl," he said. "We don't mean you any harm."

"I don't believe you." Tears and snot ran down her face, but she was too weak to pull away.

"I don't blame you." A waterskin was pressed against her lips. "Drink."

Cold, clean water filled her mouth, dribbling down her chin as she guzzled it. Nothing had tasted as good in all her life.

"That's enough." He pulled it away from her lips. "Any more and you'll be sick."

"Where's my mum?" she asked, clutching at his arm. "She's the captain. Is she alive?"

"Was the last I saw her. She's talking with the consul and the rest of them now."

"Consul?"

"Cassius." The legionnaire pulled her upright. "We're taking you there now. Can you walk?"

"Yes." With him half holding her up, she staggered toward the gangplank. "What does he want? Why is he doing this?"

The legionnaire's shrug almost lifted her off the deck. "Information. You tell them what they want to know, maybe you live another day. You don't, I suspect they'll kill you."

Teriana swayed on her feet.

"You're scaring her, Servius," one of the other legionnaires said.

"Am not. She's a pirate, not some silly patrician girl. Bet she ain't scared of nothing."

Teriana was terrified, but she appreciated the sentiment.

"She just needs a few sips. Here." He extracted a flask from a pouch at his waist and pushed it against her lips.

She took a long swallow. The rum burned down her throat, making her cough. "That's not water."

Servius grinned, his teeth bright white against his deep brown skin. Not Cel. Probably Atlian, one of the many provinces that supplied children to the Empire's legions. "Sometimes you need something a bit stronger, wouldn't you say?"

"Aye." Teriana took the flask and downed another mouthful. "I reckon that's exactly something I'd say."

Teriana had thought they'd bring her to the hill that loomed over Celendrial, its slopes filled with senators' villas, of which Cassius's was certainly one. A home like Lydia's, cool and scented with perfumed oils, tinkling fountains filling the air with music. Instead, the legionnaires took her to the slums. The insulae were four, sometimes five, stories tall and filled with tiny apartments into which entire families were crammed. Unlike the rest of Celendrial, these buildings weren't plumbed, and the people living within them threw their waste out their glassless windows. The gutters were full of piss and shit. It was into one of these buildings they took her. The inside was oppressively hot, the dust in the air threatening to choke her if she breathed too deeply. But that wasn't what made sweat break out on her forehead. Above the smell of the streets, she could make out the iron tang of blood on the air. A soft whimper escaped her lips. Servius didn't say anything.

"Down here." The door to the basement swung open, and with it came the stench of blood and bowel. She gagged, and Servius swore. "Blasted useless bastards. I told them to deal with this before I got back."

Teriana wasn't listening. A dull roar filled her ears as her eyes fixed on the pile of forms lying in a heap at the bottom of the stairs. With a shriek, she tore out of the legionnaire's grip and stumbled down the steps. "Mum!" She wildly pulled apart the still bodies, searching their faces for the most important one.

"None of them are your mother."

He was right. But she still knew them. All of them. All captains and first mates of ships without guardians, which explained why no warning had come when they'd been captured. All of them bore signs of torture, and she tugged one of them, Illria, into her arms, the old woman's grey braids stained brown from drying blood. "I am so sorry, so sorry," she whispered into the woman's ear. "May Madoria accept you into the realm of the Endless Seas."

"I told you to get rid of the bodies." Servius's words reached her ears.

"Consul's man told us to leave them here."

"He ain't consul yet. You take your orders from the legatus or from me, no one else. Is that clear?"

A hand shook her shoulder, and she looked up through blurry vision.

"What do you do with your dead?"

She stared uncomprehending at Servius for a moment before mumbling, "We return them to the sea."

"Not going to happen. Second choice?"

Teriana swallowed the lump in her throat. "Burn them then. Or leave them out for the carrion. Just don't put them under the ground."

"Right." He let go of her shoulder. "Take them out back and burn them. Get ahold of some oil and do it right."

Nothing about this was right. Nothing at all.

"Come on, then." Servius hauled her to her feet. Once inside, he dropped her arm and slammed his fist against his chest in salute, but Teriana didn't note where it was directed. Her eyes were on the woman shackled and on her knees in the dirt. "Mum!"

Flying across the room, she flung her arms around her mother's strong shoulders. Blood ran down the side of Tesya's swollen face, the fingers of her right hand broken. "The Six preserve us, what have they done to you?"

"Tell them nothing," Tesya responded. "For the sake of your immortal soul, for the sake of all of Reath, tell them nothing."

"What do they want to know?" Teriana asked, but her mother stayed silent. Reluctantly, Teriana pulled back and assessed the situation. A man with oily golden skin wearing the white toga of a Cel patrician sat watching her—the same man she'd seen the last night she'd spent with Lydia. Lucius Cassius. She scowled at him before turning to look at the legionnaire leaning against the wall. He wore officer's regalia, but she could not make out much more in the shadows.

Teriana could've sworn there'd been another figure in the room when she came in. She rotated her head in the other direction, then froze when her gaze settled on a pair of legs standing only an arm's reach from where she crouched. Her eyes drifted up, taking in the black trousers and tunic. Up and up until they reached a face shrouded by a black mask. Terror filled her veins and she clutched her mum tightly.

She was about to face the questioner.

11

TERIANA

Before Teriana could think to move, the questioner clapped iron manacles around her wrists and dragged her toward a ring embedded in the floor. He attached the chain to the ring and then strolled to a table full of tools on the far side of the room.

"Why are you doing this?" she demanded of Cassius, knowing that he was the instigator. "What do you want to know?"

He shifted on the well-stuffed chair, entirely out of place in the damp cellar. "How nice to see you again, Teriana. You're here because it has come to my attention that you are in possession of valuable information about the lands across the Endless Seas."

His words were a punch to the gut, confirming the fear that had been lurking in her heart ever since the *Quincense* had been boarded. "I don't know what you're talking about."

"I'm afraid we're past the point where denials will do you any good." He sighed dramatically. "You ought to have taken more care with your secrets if you wished to keep them that way." Reaching out with one hand, he lifted a heavy book, revealing a title deeply familiar to Teriana: *Treatise of the Seven*.

Lydia, how could you?

Teriana's eyes slid to her mother, certain she'd see disappointment in her mother's gaze, but Tesya's lids were closed, her lips moving. Praying. She was devout, but Teriana had never seen her like this. Had never seen *any* of her people like this. It was almost as though she weren't there—like her mind was somewhere else entirely.

But Teriana didn't need her mother's disappointment to feel it herself. Lydia was the *only* person to whom she'd told Maarin secrets. The only person she'd told any of her secrets, and her friend had done the same. Dreams. Hopes. Desires. All whispered in each other's ears while they lounged on silken pillows in Lydia's home, or wandered the enormous Celendrial markets, or perched in the top of the *Quincense*'s rigging the one time she'd convinced her friend to climb to the lofty heights. Precious moments, which now seemed more like regrets. But she'd be damned if she confirmed the secrets Lydia had spilled, would be damned if she'd confirm having told anything to Lydia at all.

Teriana spit at Cassius, and he grimaced before continuing. "We know you and your people travel regularly to what we call the Dark Shores. We know from your maps and your records that these lands are diverse and populated, and that you trade with them. Speak their languages."

"Let me guess," Teriana interrupted. "You want me to tell you how to get there so that you can conquer and enslave them like you've done to this half of Reath."

Cassius clapped his hands together like a small child. "Marvelous! Finally, someone who understands. And speaks! If only we'd started with you in the first place."

"Save your breath, you old sloth. I'm not telling you anything." She closed her eyes and began praying, hoping her imitation of her mother would put them off, make them think she was no more likely to spill her people's secrets than anyone who had come before.

Except you are, a voice inside her head whispered. *That's why all of this is happening.*

The questioner took hold of Teriana's left wrist. Cold metal touched the tip of her finger, and her eyes snapped open as he tore off her fingernail. Pain lanced up her hand and into her arm and she screamed.

One by one, he tore the nails off her hand. Teriana cried, "Mum, Mum, help me," but Tesya didn't even twitch, much less acknowledge her pleas. When the questioner finally lowered his tool, she curled up on her side, clutching her hand to her stomach. "You cannot tell, you cannot tell," she repeated to herself through the agony. "Better to die than to tell."

"Reveal the Maarin route to the Dark Shores, Teriana," Cassius said. "Reveal it now, and this will all be over."

Slowly, she pushed upright, and with her bloody left hand made a gesture that was universally insulting.

"Break her fingers."

Teriana recoiled, but it was the legionnaire's voice that saved her. "Enough! This is getting us nowhere." He shoved himself away from the wall, stalking toward them.

"You've no business interfering," the questioner hissed.

"Interfering in what, precisely?" the legionnaire demanded. "All afternoon I've watched you ply your trade on half a dozen people and for what? Nothing. The only thing we've learned is that the Maarin care more for keeping this secret than they do for their own lives."

Teriana tried to stifle her sobs, but her shoulders continued to tremble and jerk. Her mum, it seemed, was unaware of what was going on. Her eyes were still closed, her lips moving in silent prayer.

"You aren't going to break the captain," the legionnaire continued, bending over to examine her mother's face as though she were some strange creature he'd never seen before.

"You don't know that."

"Yes, I do." The legionnaire peeled back one of her eyelids, but her eyes were black and unseeing. "There is something she fears more than pain, more than death. More than the torture of her own daughter."

"We'll see about that." The questioner reached for her mum with his pinchers.

"Leave her be!" Teriana tried to intercept the steel clamps, but the shackles on her wrists kept her latched to the floor. She wouldn't have been fast enough anyway. With shocking speed, the legionnaire's fist struck, catching the questioner in the gut. As the man staggered, the legionnaire snatched off his mask and threw it on the floor. A glob of spit followed suit.

"You twisted bastards make me sick," he said, shoving the questioner up against the wall. "Covering your faces so the world doesn't see the pleasure you take from your work."

"You know nothing," the questioner hissed.

"I know a real man owns his actions. He doesn't hide behind a mask." The legionnaire jerked the keys off the questioner's belt. "Your methods are ineffective. Get out."

"Legatus . . ." Lucius Cassius's voice had a note of irritation in it.

"Shut up, Cassius."

Teriana sat back on her haunches, hugging her throbbing hand to her stomach as she watched. Who was this man who dared to speak so to a consul?

"I don't like repeating myself," the legionnaire said, his tone frigid.

The questioner's face darkened, but he nodded. Snatching up his mask, he scuttled from the cellar. The legionnaire turned around, and Teriana averted her gaze. But not before she got a good look at him.

He was far younger than his actions had suggested, but otherwise he could've been the model for one of the many statues of famous legionnaires scattered throughout Celendrial. Even in the dim light, she could tell he was fair of eyes and hair, his skin a golden tan. His chiseled features were strong and not at all marred by the faded scar across one cheek. There were four deep scratches on his neck, and unlike the scar, they were fresh. She hoped they were courtesy of her fallen people.

"While that was an impressive display of temper, Legatus, I'm not sure it was entirely productive," Cassius said, not moving from the chair in which he seemed permanently ensconced.

The legionnaire ignored him, and Teriana's heart beat faster, tears running down her face as he knelt before her. "What does she fear so much?" he asked, one hand gesturing to her mother.

Despite what Cassius had called a display of temper, there was no anger on the young man's face. There was nothing: no empathy, no curiosity, no distaste. Nothing.

"Why do you think she fears anything?"

"Because bravery and willpower have their limits," he said. "Fear does not. And there are worse things than pain."

"A godless dog like you wouldn't understand," she choked out between sobs, realizing her error the second the words passed her lips.

One of his eyebrows rose. "I suppose this is when I should slap you and call you a pagan fool?"

Teriana cringed away from him, waiting for the impact.

Instead, a calloused hand grasped her wrist, and she heard the click of a lock turning, felt the shackles fall away from her skin.

"It's only recently come to light that the Maarin worship gods," he said. "Makes one wonder how many other secrets you harbor."

He pulled Teriana to her feet, then pushed her into one of the chairs. Turning, he poured a glass of water, then dragged another chair over to face her, sitting before he handed her the glass.

"If you think being kind will get me to talk, you're sorely mistaken." She drained the glass, hoping the gesture looked suitably defiant.

"Do you know who I am?"

She jerked her chin at the 37 on his armor. "Everyone knows you," she replied in Chersomian.

"Then do you really expect kindness from me?"

"I expect to burn alive," she said, hoping to get a reaction out of him.

She was disappointed.

"It's hard to get answers from ashes." Turning his attention to her mother, he asked, "She fears punishment from your god should she reveal Maarin secrets?"

After a lifetime of keeping the Cel from learning about the gods, it was hard to speak of them. But given what Lydia knew, Teriana supposed that ship had sailed.

"Goddess." A hot tear rolled down her cheek. "And no. She

fears the goddess will not claim her immortal soul when she dies, and that she will be taken by the Seventh god into the underworld to burn for all eternity."

"I see," the legatus said. "I don't believe the questioner realized he was competing with eternity."

Teriana scowled and looked away.

"And all for telling a secret," he mused, rubbing his chin. "Tell me, do you fear the same?"

"Course I do. You'll not meet any Maarin who doesn't."

"Since you are clear on the consequences of helping us, I'll clarify the stakes of hindering us," he said. "If you don't tell us how the Maarin move so quickly between here and the Dark Shores, your mother and your crew will be executed and buried in the deepest hole my men can dig."

She stared at him, horror tying her tongue into knots.

"However," he said, straightening in his chair, "if you tell us your way to the Dark Shores, I will personally guarantee the lives of you, your mother, and all of your crew. I will also guarantee that none of them are ever in a room with the questioner again." He frowned, as though thinking. "I'll even have it ratified by the Senate."

"Blast you, Marcus!" Cassius hauled himself out of his chair. "What are you thinking?"

"Sit down, Consul. I don't want you to strain yourself."

She was damned if she told him, that much was certain. But was her eternal damnation worth the lives of her mother and crew? More than just their lives, their souls? If he buried them in the earth, their souls would be stuck in limbo until the sands of time reshaped the earth and revealed their bones.

"Why should I believe you?" she asked.

"Because I always keep my word."

Teriana looked to her mum, hoping she'd snapped out of her trance and would give her some sort of guidance, but her eyes were still closed, lips still repeating the same prayer. She stretched out her mind, hoping to feel the touch of Magnius upon it, but they were too distant from the water. If he was even listening. She was on her own.

"Choose carefully, Teriana," Cassius crooned. "You know who the man sitting before you is. You know what he's capable of. And I promise, if you don't agree to these terms, it will be him whom I deliver your people to for their execution. Have you ever seen someone burned alive?"

The legatus was right. There were far worse things than pain.

Teriana's willpower fractured like glass, and she choked out one word: "Xenthier."

Legatus Marcus leaned toward her. Cassius did the same. The Senate controlled countless shorter xenthier pathways. The crystal was what had allowed them to conquer the East, as it could transport anything—and anyone—it touched from genesis to terminus in a matter of a heartbeat. But the ocean veins crossed the world, and that made them a far greater prize. A prize her people were sworn to protect . . .

"Where is the stem located?" Legatus Marcus asked.

"You got a map?"

"Yes." He rose swiftly from his chair. Picking up a lamp, he revealed one of her mum's maps of Reath.

"The genesis of one of the great ocean veins lies here." She pointed to the spot on the map where the stem was hidden, leaving a bloody fingerprint. "And it takes you here." She pointed to the terminus at the midpoint of the southern continent.

"That's in the middle of the Sea of the Dead," Cassius snapped.

"Aye," she replied. "Under it, in fact."

"She's lying." Cassius's face reddened with anger. "The Sea of the Dead's doldrums make it impassable for sailing ships."

"That's true," she said. "But I'm not lying." It was a struggle to keep a smile off her face. They had the knowledge, but it would do them no good. "Me and mine will be leaving now," she said, taking the keys that sat on the table and starting toward her mother. "That is, if you are actually a man of your word, Legatus."

"I am," he said, "but I don't recall agreeing to you leaving."

Teriana froze.

"I said you would live, unmolested by the questioners. I don't believe your freedom was part of the bargain."

"I called you godless, but I must be wrong," she hissed, fury rising instead of fear. "Because of a surety, you are a minion of the Seventh."

"I'm just a man, much like any other."

"No," she said. "You are far, far worse than any other." But nothing she could say would make an impact on the heartless creature before her.

"I'll offer you a new bargain," he said. "You agree to take the Thirty-Seventh and Forty-First Legions safely through the Sea of the Dead to this xenthier stem and land us on the Dark Shores. Your mother and the crews of the other Maarin vessels we captured will remain here and kept in comfort as hostages. You will travel with me as my advisor until we discover land-based xenthier paths to and from the Empire. Once we have done so, I will allow you to return and retrieve your mother. Then both of you can go free to do as you will, as can the crews of the other ships."

"And if we never find routes?" Teriana demanded. "What then?"

"Then your mother will be kept a comfortable prisoner to the end of her days, at which point she will be buried at sea."

Teriana looked down at her mum. The damned bastard knew exactly what to say. The only life on the line would be hers. The only soul in jeopardy was hers.

"We know the Dark Shores exist," he said. "It is only a matter of time until we find our way there. And I can tell you with certainty that Cassius will not hesitate to destroy your entire people in the pursuit of his goal. You can save them by agreeing to help us now."

And damn the other half of the world in doing so, she thought.

The Celendor Empire had conquered the entire Eastern Hemisphere—did she dare open the West to them? How many would die if this man and his armies were unleashed across the sea?

But how many of her people would be saved?

"If I bring you there and help you, you'll swear the Maarin will be left alone?"

"Yes."

She looked at Cassius. "Do you?"

A sweat had broken out on the man's already-greasy brow. He hesitated a long while, beady eyes shifting between her and Marcus. "Fine."

"I want the Senate to agree to it as well. All our terms, in writing. And I want a signed copy."

Cassius's face darkened, but he nodded.

"And I'll only do it once," she said, not even sure if once was going to be possible. She needed Magnius to open the path, which he might very well refuse to do. "It's a very difficult thing to do, especially given the number of ships you'll need to bring through. So don't think you can run a supply line from here to there."

Marcus's brow creased.

"Once there, and if you still have the ships you need, I'll open the other ocean path to get you back," she amended. "I suppose it's only fair to give you an avenue of escape."

Marcus tilted his head. "It makes me nervous how easily you're agreeing to this."

"You should be afraid of what you're getting yourself into. These aren't helpless people you'll be fighting, but kingdoms with trained warriors and armies." *And powers you've never even dreamed of.* "And I haven't agreed yet."

"What else do you want?" he asked quickly. Too quickly, in her opinion. She'd expected her words to bring a touch of fear to his expression, but what she saw was excitement. He *wanted* the Dark Shores to be a challenge, and she was certain he'd agree to just about anything to get there.

"I entirely expect that you will be defeated," she said. "And I don't want to pay the price for your over-ambition. I want your guarantee that you won't withhold our freedom out of spite. That if I get whatever remains of your army back to Celendor, you'll consider our bargain fulfilled."

"I don't have any intention of coming back," Marcus said, and even in the dim light Teriana could see his cheeks were flushed.

"Then you won't mind agreeing to it."

"All right. As long as I don't deem my retreat the result of some act of sabotage on your part, I'll deem our contract fulfilled."

This was the moment of reckoning. The moment she needed to make a decision. She meant what she had said: the Cel legions weren't setting sail to fight powerless nations. They would be fighting lands under the dominion of the Six, and defeating them would be no easy task. She was gambling everything, but it was the only way she could save the people who mattered to her most. And if everything went according to the plan growing in her mind, Legatus Marcus's overconfidence would see him defeated and her mum freed in one fell swoop.

Teriana spit on her bloody hand and held it out. "I think we have an accord, Legatus."

His smile grew and he replicated her gesture, grasping her hand. "We have an accord."

12

MARCUS

"When do you suppose we'll leave?" Servius asked, kicking a rock and sending it tumbling down the road ahead of them.

"When we're ready," Marcus replied. "This campaign will be different. Once we're across the seas, we'll be entirely on our own. We need to make sure we're prepared. And the Maarin must finish repairing their ship."

"So . . ." Servius picked up a pebble and threw it into the trees.

"A week. Maybe less." Marcus hoped it was less—the sooner they were away from Celendrial, the sooner he could forget about everything that had happened today. Unconsciously, he reached up to touch the scratches scored across his neck.

"Looks like one of the Maarin got a piece of you," Servius said, picking up another rock. "The girl? Teriana?"

"Not her."

"Ah. I thought it would've been. She's a fierce one—looks more likely to stick a knife in your gut than kiss you."

"She *is* likely to stick a knife in your gut if you try to kiss her," Marcus replied, giving his friend a dark look. "So don't even think of trying."

"Wouldn't dream of it." Servius held up his hands in mock defense, his laugh echoing through the hills. "Though it would be nice. She's good to look at, but those Maarin eyes . . . Looking at them too long made me seasick."

"You're an idiot," Marcus muttered, though he didn't entirely disagree. The girl *had* been good to look at. More than *good*. And that had been despite the fact that she'd been filthy, battered, and bloody. He'd been to nearly every corner of the Empire, met individuals of every single nation and race, but the Maarin were distinct with their eyes that rippled like the waves of the seas they lived upon, shifting color with their moods. Beautiful as the girl was with those rounded cheekbones, full lips, and that flawless dark skin, Marcus thought her eyes were the best part of her. They were honest. After the way she'd been treated, he was certain he'd never see them another color than that of inky pools of hate and fear. But after all the politics, lies, and deception he'd waded through of late, he liked the idea of being around someone whose feelings were clear, even if they were negative.

"Will be strange taking a girl along, don't you think?" Servius chucked the rock at a tree. "She'll have a lot of eyes on her."

Too many. A good portion of his men preferred the companionship of each other, but the rest of them had to content themselves with paid company. Relationships outside the legion were forbidden for a myriad of reasons, and he had no doubt his men would be falling over themselves to make the Maarin girl's acquaintance. "She'll be along to advise me and to translate, not to entertain soldiers."

"I heard you the first time, Marcus, but as you said, we're going to be on our own out there."

Marcus skidded to a stop, dust flying in clouds around his knees. "Hear me the first time on this, Servius: if anyone touches her, I will personally strip the skin off the perpetrator's back."

Servius didn't respond straightaway, which was a sure sign Marcus had offended him. "Do you really think I'd do *that* to her?"

He didn't. Servius had left behind six sisters in Atlia when he was sent to the legions, and he had a soft spot in his heart for girls, personally doling out the punishment for transgressions against those the legion came in contact with. Even if Servius's life was on the line, Marcus didn't think his friend was capable of harming a woman—if they ever came against an army of them, the Thirty-Seventh might be forced into their first retreat based on Servius's principles alone.

But Marcus wasn't in the mood to placate anyone today.

Servius picked up yet another rock and threw it with impressive force, sending it sailing far out of sight. "I'll make sure to spread the word. Sir."

"Do." They were at the edge of the camp, and though Marcus could smell food cooking, the thought of eating turned his stomach. "Cassius will be sworn in as consul tomorrow morning. Afterwards, the Senate will deal with the Maarin and with us. Be ready to leave for the city at dawn." He started walking. "I'm going for a swim."

Marcus discarded his armor in his tent and walked down to the beach in only a tunic and sandals. The sun had long since set, but the moon had risen and he could see as well as he needed to. Dumping his clothes on a rock with his belt knife sitting on top, he waded into the surf, letting the cold water strip the day's grime from his body.

If only it could wash away the invisible filth coating his soul.

He'd stood silently while the Maarin sailors were tortured and killed in front of him, but though their eyes had joined the ranks of those who haunted him, it wasn't their screams that echoed in his head. Wasn't scratches from their fingers that stung the skin of his neck. Wasn't strands of their long black hair that he still felt tangled around his fingers, the sensation lingering no matter how often he checked to ensure his hands were clean.

Murderer.

He ducked his head under the waves, trying to drown out the sound of Lydia Valerius's voice as she'd begged for her life, but it grew louder with every wave.

Murderer.

He could have saved her. Could've smuggled her out of the city and arranged to have her taken somewhere no one would ever find her. The idea had been heavy on his mind while Cassius had subjected her to that dreadful speech. If Marcus hadn't had such a recent reminder that secrets never stay buried, he probably would have done it. Except Cassius would not be kind if he discovered he'd been betrayed. Marcus had had no choice.

The only way to keep his family safe from the Empire's executioners had been to kill the girl.

Murderer.

"What else could I have done?" he asked the ocean, but the waves only splashed him in the face and repeated their accusation.

Something else. Anything else. Which was why at the last moment he'd hesitated. But the fierce current they'd been standing in had finished the job for him, ripping the girl out of his grip and pulling her underground, drowning her, leaving little chance of her body ever being discovered.

Marcus's nausea rose and fell with every swell. Stumbling back onto the beach, he sat naked in the damp sand with his eyes squeezed shut, but visions of all the Maarin who'd fallen to the inquisition marched across his mind. Everything that could be done to inflict pain had been done to them, but not one screamed.

Except for the girl.

Her screams had been too much. Five fingernails had been all he could take.

Then you threatened the lives of everyone she knew. Everyone she loved.

"But she's bloody well still alive!" he shouted at the waves. "And so is everyone she was so desperate to protect!"

"Umm, Legatus? Sir?"

Marcus twisted around. One of his men was standing where the sand met the scrub grass, studying the ground with more interest than it deserved. Marcus cringed internally at how it must look, him sitting naked on the sand, shouting curses at the waves. "What is it?"

"There's a patrician in the camp to see you, sir. We told him you were busy, but he won't leave."

"Cassius?" Marcus picked up his tunic and pulled it over his head.

"No, sir. A Gaius Domitius."

Marcus's hands fumbled on the buckle of his sandal. His day was not improving. "Tell him I'll be along shortly."

It had been a lifetime ago when Marcus had last seen his little brother, who, at nineteen years old, could no longer be described as little. Not when Marcus was only twenty himself, the small gap in their ages being what had allowed them to switch identities. And there was no mistaking them for anything other than siblings. Servius was in the process of handing a cup to Gaius when Marcus came in, and it was clear he'd noticed the resemblance as his gaze flicked between the two of them.

"I'll ensure you have no interruptions, sir." Saluting, he exited the tent.

"What are you doing here, *Gaius*?" Marcus asked, walking to the table and setting his knife on top of a pile of maps.

"I should ask you the same thing." His brother's face was flushed and he reeked of wine.

"By orders of the Senate." Marcus gestured at Gaius's white toga. "As you should know."

"By the Senate or by Cassius?" Gaius crossed his arms. They were thin and soft. The arms of a politician. "How much did he have to bribe you with to coerce your entire legion to vote for him? Or was being put in command of this fool's errand of a mission enough for you? Yet another piece of land for you to burn and pillage your way across?"

Staring at his brother for a long moment, Marcus considered his response, then settled with, "Cassius knows we switched identities."

The color slowly drained from Gaius's face. "How?"

"The physician at the healing springs. Cassius is adept at digging up dirt, but I suspect you know that."

Gaius took a mouthful of wine, the cup in his hand trembling as the ramifications of what Marcus had told him settled. "This is all happening because of you," he finally said.

"And you." His brother's hair was long, as was fashionable,

and sandy brown. Marcus wondered if his would be the same if allowed to grow. They had the same color eyes.

"No." Gaius shook his head rapidly. "This wouldn't be happening if you hadn't come back."

Marcus pressed the heel of his palm to his forehead; the room was faintly spinning. "No. I rather think that I am back because Cassius decided it was time for things to start happening."

"Liar!" Gaius tossed the cup across the tent, splattering the pale canvas with red wine. "He's going to ruin me because of you!"

Marcus shook his head, studying the red stain. It looked like blood. "Not if we keep him happy." He coughed, the action making his muscles ache. *Blast this dusty country.*

"You mean if *you* keep him happy." Gaius's words sounded distant. "You're the one who put him in power."

"Be glad of that," Marcus said, pouring a glass of water and downing it. "He'd have taken it out on you otherwise."

"Don't pretend you did it for me. You did it to protect yourself and to ensure he sent you on this insane mission to conquer the Dark Shores. Who knows what other sordid tasks he has you doing."

"I'll dirty my hands so you don't have to." The ground was moving, and Marcus felt a familiar tightness in his chest. *Not now, not now!* his mind screamed. "I'll do what it takes to keep our family safe."

"They aren't your family."

The air in the tent was tinged with red. After all he had done, everything he had given up, how dare Gaius come here and try to disown him?

"You were supposed to die. They said you would—that there was no chance you'd survive." Gaius shook his head from side to side. "I wish you had. I wish you would."

The comment carved out a hollow in Marcus's stomach. It was one thing to know his parents had made a pragmatic choice between him and his brother. Quite another to realize that his brother actually wanted him dead. "I'm sorry my continued existence has inconvenienced you." He heard the faint wheeze in his voice. So did Gaius.

His brother laughed. And laughed. "After all this time," he finally managed to get out, "you're still sickly. You've come so far and yet not far at all." He shook his head. "I can't believe your men follow you. Or. Do. They. Know?" he asked, pantomiming one of Marcus's attacks, just as he had done when they were children. "Maybe your illness will do me a great favor and finally carry you off tonight."

Marcus's self-control snapped. He tackled Gaius and they fell through the side of the tent. Marcus could barely breathe, barely think, but that didn't stop his fists. All that mattered was making Gaius hurt as badly as he'd been hurt. Making him suffer the way he had suffered. Through the haze of his attack, he could see his brother holding his hands up in pathetic defense, hear him squealing. Then arms had Marcus around the waist and were dragging him off. Dimly, he heard Servius's voice in his ear and Felix's farther off shouting orders. Then he was back in his tent, Servius laying him down on the pallet.

"Can't. Breathe."

"I know," Servius said. "But no one else needs to. You tough it out, my friend, and we'll take care of the rest 'til morning."

Marcus dug his fingers into the bedroll, desperately trying to suck enough air into his lungs. Maybe Gaius was right. Maybe his illness would take him tonight.

And if it did, maybe he deserved it.

13

TERIANA

"Rise and shine, pirate girl!"

Teriana jerked, her eyes struggling to focus on the legionnaire standing on the far side of the room. "Oh, it's you," she said, recognizing Servius.

"At your service," he said with a grin. "Unless you were hoping for someone else?"

"I was hoping to be left alone," she snapped, sitting upright. The motion jarred her injured hand.

"Nah. That would be boring," he said. "Nothing to do in here but watch the rosy-cheeked ladies of the Forty-First marching about and making a racket." He crossed the room and peered out the window. "And not even a very good view of it."

Now that her senses were clearing, Teriana could hear the sound of marching feet accompanied by horns and drums. She couldn't believe she'd slept through it. Pressing her uninjured hand to her face, she pieced together the bits she could remember of the prior evening. After that demon of a legatus had finished with his endless questions, his men had brought her to a building near the Forum. A Cel physician accompanied by two older servant women had treated her hand, but not before giving her something to dull the pain. That something had dulled her senses, because she had no memory of anything after.

Teriana blinked away tears. She'd had every intention of finding a way to escape in the middle of the night. To rescue her mum and her crew, steal back the *Quincense,* and bugger up all the plans of *Legatus Marcus.* She made a face as she thought of him and his self-assured expression.

Instead of doing any of that, she'd slept, her dreams plagued by visions of Lydia laughing as she revealed every secret Teriana had ever told her. Now it was morning, and in a few hours Cassius would officially be consul and she'd have to stand in front of the entire Senate and promise to take *Legatus Marcus* and his pig legion across the Endless Seas.

"What about him?"

"What?" She turned to look at Servius.

"You've just said the legatus's name twice. *Legatus Marcus*," he said, parroting the sarcastic tone she hadn't realized she'd used aloud.

"I'm cursing his name," she snapped, feeling her cheeks warm.

"Right." He grinned. "You're not the first." Coming across the room, he emptied the sack he was carrying. "Brought you some choice of clothes. The ones you have on aren't fit for wearing."

"You went through my things?" she demanded, recognizing the garments.

"No!" He frowned at her. "I did no such thing. I had one of your lady crew members retrieve them. She wanted me to take only black shirts for you—kept saying some sort of nonsense about it being fitting—but I liked this one better." He nudged the bright blue silk blouse with his foot.

Teriana barely heard him. Black was for days of mourning, but it was also what traitors and blasphemers were forced to wear. Her crew knew what she had agreed to. And they hated her for it. She could only hope they'd forgive her once she had a chance to explain that she'd been trying to save their lives.

Teriana coughed to clear her throat. "How is my mum?"

"Recovering. She's down the hall from you."

She'd been so close! If only she hadn't let them drug her, she might have been able to get them both away. Teriana shoved her fingertips against the bedroll, punishing herself with the pain that she should have suffered through last night. "Can I see her?"

Servius shook his head. "We don't have time for that now.

I'll speak to the legatus and ask if you might see her before they take her away to the safe house."

"What?" Teriana demanded, tugging off the blouse she'd been wearing for days, along with the snug undershirt beneath, both reeking of sweat and worse. The blue silk Servius had chosen felt glorious in comparison, the fabric holding the faint scent she associated with the *Quincense*. Wood polish and the brine of the sea, along with the faint hint of cedar and orange blossoms from the sachets her aunt Yedda always tucked in her clothing chest. "What do you mean, they're taking her away?"

He made a distressed sound and covered his eyes with one hand until she was finished dressing. "It's for her own safety," he said. "Not everyone is pleased about the Empire taking on another expensive campaign. They'd rather spend the gold on other things, like, er-r . . . schools and . . . whatnot. And without you, the mission would at the very least be delayed."

"And if my mum were to die, they think I'd have no reason to help you." Teriana's mind raced. How soon would they take her mother away? How much time did she have?

"True. But even if she were to die, it isn't as though Cassius doesn't have other methods of making you do what he wants, and his opposition knows that." He grimaced. "That's why you'll both be under guard by my men day and night until we leave. And the sooner that happens, the better."

That is all a matter of perspective, Teriana thought as she laced up her vest, then pulled on one boot. "I heard some of the schools were to be built in Atlia. I'd have thought you'd prefer to see that than to travel to the far side of the world in search of war."

"Why would I care about schools in Atlia?"

"Given you're brown as a nut and as big as an ox, I assumed that was where you were born. Where your family lives. Am I wrong?"

He looked away. "I was born the day I walked through the gates of Campus Lescendor. The Empire is my father and my mother. The men of the Thirty-Seventh are my brothers. I am a legionnaire."

The words slipped off his tongue like he'd been made to repeat them many times. Which perhaps he had. "Nice speech," she said. "Make it up yourself or did you have help?"

Huffing out an amused breath, Servius shook his head. "We are made to forget everything that came before Lescendor, Teriana. And there are consequences to not doing as Mother Empire demands."

"Right." Teriana reached for her other boot, pulling the soft leather up to her knee and then accepting the apple Servius handed to her.

"You can eat while we walk. Cassius wants you there for the ceremony."

Men waited for them on the street, all saluting when they saw Servius. One handed him a helmet, which he jammed on his head. "To the Forum," he said. "If we don't all perish from the heat on the way."

For all she hated the Cel, their capital city was a work of art: all columns and archways, statues, and fountains. This close to the Forum, the roadways were wide and clean, the pristine white of the structures unmarred by the mud and splattered waste found in the district nearest to the harbor, where the narrow and cluttered alleys welcomed such behavior. Golden dragons flapped on the faint breeze, and panels of Bardeen silk hung from balconies, turning the route they traveled into a rainbow of color. The men arrayed themselves around her and Servius, walking swiftly and silently, their eyes always moving as they scanned the shadows between buildings and the faces of the civilians milling about the streets. Servius kept unnervingly close to her, continually switching from her left to her right side as they walked. She had the uncomfortable sensation of being herded. Sunlight glinted off their armor, off their shields, off the tips of their spears, making her feel like she was being cooked alive in a giant metal oven. The scent of the sweat dripping down their necks mixed with the inevitable stench of a large city and filled her nose.

The shouts and cheers from the Forum grew, thousands blending together into one deafening voice. As they rounded the bend, the entrance reared high, crimson and gold flags dancing above. A great line of legionnaires marched through, eight abreast. As the tail end of the line snaked out of sight, the sound of trotting hooves became audible. Servius called for his company to halt, and they all slammed the butts of their spears against the ground in unison, standing stock still but for their searching gazes.

A trio of red-plumed horses appeared, their white heads tossing as they swiftly pulled the chariot up the street. Teriana recognized Lucius Cassius as one of the passengers. The other she thought for a moment was Legatus Marcus, but when he turned his helmeted head the weak chin revealed otherwise. "Who's that?"

"Legatus Titus of the Forty-First."

"Why's he riding with Cassius? Thought he and *Legatus Marcus*"—she injected as much sarcasm as she could—"were as tight as ticks."

"You tell me," was all the answer she got. Squinting, she took another look at the approaching chariot. There was something familiar about the young officer. Cassius caught sight of her just before turning into the Forum and he lifted his hand to waggle his fingers. Titus turned to see who the consul was waving at, and his beady eyes bored into her own. "They're related," she muttered. "His son?"

"If you believe the gossip."

"Didn't realize legionnaires gossiped," Teriana said, her curiosity about Legatus Titus chasing away her fear of having a passerby stick a knife in her back.

"Oh, we're worse than a sewing circle of meddling matriarchs," said a soldier standing next to her. It was the first time one of them had spoken, and she turned to look at him with a start. Beneath his helmet, grey eyes and a boyish smile accosted her. He had a nick in his chin where he had likely cut himself shaving that morning.

"Especially this chatterbox." Servius gave the other legionnaire's spear a shove, knocking it against the man's helmet. "Mind on the job, Quintus."

"Yes, sir." The legionnaire turned his head away, but a faint smile remained on his face.

"Thought you were supposed to forget where you came from and who you were?" she asked.

"Some people have less incentive to forget."

They stood in silence while Cassius ascended the rostrum, the crowds shrieking in delight. Then Servius gave her a gentle push on the shoulder.

"Look sharp, lads," he said. "Forward!" Surrounded by her marching bodyguard, Teriana stepped into the Forum.

The Forum was a rectangular open space surrounded by buildings on all sides, and it was currently full to the brim with civilians, the ranks of soldiers the only thing keeping the path to the rostrum open. The crowd's noise diminished as they caught sight of her, and Teriana heard whispers questioning why a Maarin girl was part of the consul's ceremony. She realized at about the same time the crowd did why she was here. Like the legions of old who used to parade in triumph after a great victory over a foreign people, Cassius had added her to his march to show he had triumphed over the Maarin. She might not be in chains, but the symbolism was the same, and as soon as the crowd realized it their volume grew. Only now there were jeers on their tongues, their faces malicious and taunting.

It scared her. But more than that, the crowd's reaction *hurt*. The Maarin were well regarded across all of Reath, by people of every nation, and the Cel were no different. Or so she'd thought. But these men and women were screaming for her blood. For worse things than her blood, and Teriana didn't understand why. Didn't understand how they could swing so far in the opposite direction in the space of an instant. Didn't understand how they could feel so much hate for her when neither she nor her people had done anything to deserve it. The Maa-rin brought knowledge and trade, but the Cel were treating her like she was their enemy.

"Chin up," Servius said. "This is Cassius grandstanding for his supporters—it's naught to do with you."

But the crossbow bolt that bit into the ground in front of her said otherwise.

14

MARCUS

A trio of horses appeared at the entrance of the Forum, and Marcus squinted into the sun, watching them tow Cassius and Titus down the lane created by ranks of the Forty-First. He'd fought hard against the choice of the younger legion. They were untested, and there were commanders of other legions with whom he had a better rapport. With whom he had fought alongside. Frankly, he'd rather have taken the newly minted Forty-Fifth with him than this lot. Five thousand twelve-year-olds would have been better than Cassius's son. Yet therein lay the reason the Forty-First had been selected. While Cassius could never officially claim Titus as his son, everyone knew it, and any victories Titus won would, unofficially, bolster Cassius's reputation. There was a great deal of honor to be had from a son achieving officer status in the legions, all gained from carefully made comments at luncheons and dinner parties. Under other circumstances, Marcus's own father might have benefited from his success, but he doubted the patriarch of the Domitius family would risk drawing attention to his crime. Better to behave as though his son had never existed.

Titus reined in the chariot in front of the rostrum, and Cassius strode up the steps to the center of the platform, holding up his hand in greeting, to the roaring delight of the crowd.

With the ceremony about to begin in earnest, the patricians poured out of the cool interior of the Curia, the senators' red sashes like splashes of blood against the gleaming white of their togas. None of them paid him any mind except for one: Both eyes bruised black and nose so swollen it must be broken, Gaius glared malevolently at him. Then, with an almost imperceptible motion, he nudged their father with his elbow.

Marcus held his breath, unable to move and barely able to think as he waited for his father to turn his head. To see him. To know him. But the senator did not so much as twitch, and in an instant Marcus was transported back in time to the cool winter morning when he'd last seen his father's face. *There is honor in this, my son,* his father had said, eyes on the dirt between them. *I will not forget the sacrifice you've made for the sake of our family.*

Even as a child, Marcus hadn't believed him.

Marcus snapped back to attention as his own men started marching down the lane toward the rostrum, Servius and Teriana in their midst. This was yet another concession Marcus had been forced to make. He'd wanted the Maarin girl holed up and protected by his men until they left, but Cassius had insisted on parading her about and risking her life every minute that he did so. He was spinning circumstances to make the whole city believe that he had done the impossible and conquered the Maarin. That he had been the consul to bring the last holdout of civilization in the East under the Empire's control.

The crowd was jeering now, pressing against the line of legionnaires and shouting vulgarities. It was made up of Cassius's supporters, and there was a marked difference between these people and the enormous crowds he'd seen protesting the imprisonment and planned execution of the Maarin crews earlier that morning. A certain righteousness in the eyes of the men and women before him that made Marcus's breakfast sit poorly in his guts, because just like them, he had voted for Cassius. But unlike them, he took no pleasure in Cassius's posturing. In truth, most of the city didn't. The peregrini, in particular, were incensed, demanding the release of the Maarin, promising violence if they weren't, and given the people from the provinces made up half of Celendrial's population, it was no small threat. The consul had fractured the city with this move against the Maarin, and it remained uncertain whether the Dark Shores campaign would make things better or worse.

Teriana sauntered with her head high, waist-length braids swaying back and forth, face not showing any signs that the crowd's insults mattered or that she heard them at all. If she didn't look conquered, it was because she wasn't. Teriana still had some tricks up her sleeve, and Marcus was keen to discover what they were.

A flash of metal caught his eye just before Teriana leapt backward.

"Shit," he swore, then leapt off the rostrum, shouting at Titus, "Control the crowd," as he sprinted past the other legatus. Servius had Teriana on the ground, and the men had pulled their shields together to form a protective dome. It took a bolt bouncing off those shields, then another puncturing the armor of a boy in the Forty-First, before the crowd reacted. Screams filled the air as the crowd turned into a mob, pushing and shoving, everyone trying to flee the confines of the Forum. Marcus ignored them, searching the surrounding buildings for sign of the crossbowman.

There. He spotted the man crouched behind a cornice on the Great Library. The would-be assassin scampered across the roof in the direction of the public offices. There was no way Marcus could make it through the crowd to cut him off, and once the assassin had mixed in with the mob there would be no tracking him down.

Snatching a spear out of the hands of one of the Forty-First, Marcus hefted it to throw, then thought better of it. He didn't have the arm for this great a distance. "Servius!"

His big friend clambered out from under the interlocked shields, and Marcus tossed him the spear. "There." He pointed.

Servius needed barely a heartbeat to mark the path of his target. He took a few running strides and heaved the spear through the air with a grunt. Marcus watched as the spear sliced through the air and into the assassin's back, knocking him facedown. The body lay still for a moment, then slid down the roof, gaining speed as it went, dropping like a lead weight onto the steps of the library below.

Ignoring the pressing mob, Marcus stepped closer to the dome of shields protecting Teriana. "Stand down." With the ease of much practice, the men disentangled themselves, revealing the Maarin girl sitting cross-legged in the dirt. Only the midnight waves of her eyes revealed her as anything other than as cool as a cup of water.

"I hope you are providing better protection for my mother than you are for me, Legatus."

"You complain a great deal for someone who is still alive," he said. "And your would-be assassin is dead." He gestured toward the corpse bleeding all over the library steps.

She glanced at the body, and only the slight tightening of her jaw indicated that she thought anything of it at all. "You killed him?"

He blinked. "No. But—"

"Then don't take credit for it," she interrupted. Without another word, she walked toward the rostrum.

"Lunatic of a woman," he muttered under his breath. He realized his men were all staring at him. "Well? Go after her!"

Feeling oddly unnerved, Marcus scanned the Forum. It had cleared, but not without cost. Dozens of plebeians lay on the ground, some moaning and crying, some still. And Titus's legion was doing nothing to help them.

"You!" he shouted. "And you." The two centurions hurried in his direction. "Get your medics working on the injured and send someone to the physician's college for assistance. Put the dead in the corner out of the sun before they start to stink." He watched long enough to ensure the centurions complied before he made his way over to the corpse of the assassin.

Crouching, he examined the assassin's face, but it was no one he recognized. Habit made him pull down the corner of the man's tunic to check for a legion number, but as he had expected, there was none. If there had been, Teriana would have been dead and this man would have disappeared into the city.

Catching sight of the fallen crossbow, Marcus picked it up, the weapon familiar the second he had it in his grip. He hardly needed to examine it to know it would have the Cel dragon stamped on it. This crossbow was made for the legions, and it wasn't old enough to belong to a retiree. Straightening, he cast his gaze upon the men standing on and around the rostrum. Most of the senators were hurrying in the direction of the Curia, their eyes searching the building tops. His attention shifted to Cassius.

The consul was shouting and waving his hands about, demanding answers for the disruption of *his* ceremony and the attack on *his* asset. Except Marcus knew Cassius was a coward. That if he believed there was a chance a crossbow bolt was coming in his direction, he'd be the first in that pack of sweating senators scuttling for cover. No doubt he'd play this off as an Optimate assassin intent on disrupting a military campaign, but Marcus was not so easily fooled.

Yet the question remained, why would the consul want Teriana dead? She'd been the only one of her people they'd been able to crack, the only one willing to unlock the door to the West. Killing her seemed counter to everything Cassius wanted.

Had it been a ruse? A subversive attack on the opposition?

Or was it motivated by the contract between the Empire and Teriana that was about to be signed?

Marcus himself had given the terms to the lawyers drafting the document, not wanting to leave anything to chance. He'd already read it to ensure it was to his liking, and he would read it again before he'd sign it, just in case. The crux of it was simple: Teriana guided the legion fleet through the xenthier stem to the Dark Shores, then remained on as his advisor until Marcus was able to discover and secure land-based xenthier stems between the Dark Shores and the Empire. At that point she, her mother, and the captive crews would be allowed to go free. She'd also insisted that the agreement include a clause pardoning all Maarin ships and crews from the charge of paganism, which carried a death sentence. Once the agreement was signed, and once Teriana had delivered, the Maarin would be free to go about their business unmolested, much as they always had.

And given that Cassius had just grandstanded in front of his peers and his supporters that he'd been the consul to bring the entire East under the dominion of the Empire, Marcus could see how the man might consider that aspect of the agreement a problem. The contract was with Teriana, specifically, not with her people, which meant if she died and was therefore unable to fulfill her obligations, the contract would be void. Cassius would be free to dedicate his term to conquering the Maarin, ensuring his place in Celendor's history books even if his actions netted the Empire nothing but blood.

Killing Teriana was a gambit, risking their ability to reach the Dark Shores, but given the number of ships they had captured across the Empire, Cassius had close to six hundred Maarin sailors he could work through to find a replacement who wouldn't be so demanding in his or her terms.

"Shit," Marcus muttered under his breath, his eyes shifting back to where Teriana stood speaking with Cassius on the rostrum with Servius hovering nearby. Cassius had one hand resting on Teriana's shoulder, either not noticing or not caring that she was cringing away from him in disgust. Handing off the crossbow to one of Titus's men and giving the order to have the dead man sketched to see if he could be identified, Marcus strode toward them.

"Perhaps we might go inside where our backs are somewhat less exposed to errant crossbow bolts," he said, shouldering his way between Cassius and Teriana, then nudging her in the direction of the Curia.

"Worried about your own back, Legatus?" Cassius quipped, following them at a leisurely pace.

Marcus rapped his knuckles against the thick steel protecting his torso. "Not mine, Consul. Not mine. But it seems not everyone is pleased about your plans for your consulship, so you should be worried about yours." Best to let Cassius believe him fooled by the ruse.

They entered the Curia, the cavernous building infinitely cooler than the Forum, and as Servius moved in closer, Marcus said, "Triple the guards on her, Tesya, and the *Quincense's* crew. Anytime we take her anywhere, I want the route cleared of civilians and ours on the roofs."

Teriana looked up at him, her eyes turbid seas of grey. "Worried?"

Yes.

"Let's get your paperwork signed," he said. "I want to be underway tomorrow."

Her eyes widened. "Tomorrow?"

If they could be at sea today, he'd do it. If he could be at sea in the next hour, it would be even better. Because with every step he took, Marcus grew more convinced that there was a target painted on Teriana's back and Cassius was the one pointing the weapon. And not just at her, but at her entire people. But Marcus had no intention of allowing Cassius to slaughter hundreds of Maarin for no reason beyond the pursuit of glory and fame, just as he had no intention of allowing Cassius to jeopardize the only chance he had to get his legion out from beneath the Senate's thumb. And himself beyond Cassius's reach to blackmail.

The consul could come at Teriana all he wanted, but he'd have to go through Marcus and the Thirty-Seventh to get her.

15

TERIANA

She was almost out of time.

Teriana waited until long after dark, when her guards would think she was fast asleep, before making her move. She'd greased the hinges on the window with butter from her dinner, carefully easing it open and closed a few times until she was certain no creaks would betray her.

Not that anyone was likely to notice a squeaky hinge over the noise of the celebrations in the city. Cassius had put his considerable wealth to work, and all of Celendrial seemed to be out in the streets. Firecrackers banged over the harbor, and she prayed her crew had truly finished the *Quincense*'s repairs. This would all be for naught if her ship wasn't at least close to seaworthy. Never mind that they'd need to fight their way free of the legionnaires standing guard over them. Three times the number of guards who had been on the ship this morning, thanks to Legatus Marcus's *caution*.

Tying her bootlaces together, she draped them over her neck and climbed onto the sill, scanning the darkness for guards. She suspected they were there, but it was a moonless night and with her dark skin and black clothes no one would be able to make her out in the shadows as long as she was quiet. The street below was obscured by darkness, but her earlier assessment had shown that it was flat and free of anything she had to worry about landing on. Teriana had no fear of heights, having grown up in the rigging of her ship, but she still felt a wave of vertigo as she flipped around, toes clinging to the narrow ledge and hands reaching for the even narrower ledge above. Her injured fingers screamed where they rubbed against the stone as she slid along, but the pain was nothing in comparison to her fear of losing this opportunity.

A hot wind caught at her hair and clothes, blowing bits of dust into her eyes. Teriana squeezed them shut, burning tears running down her face as she inched sideways. She made it to the first window without incident, clinging to the frame while she struggled to catch her breath. Every moment she lingered was one they could be using to get away, so before her nerves had settled she eased back onto the ledge.

The wind picked up again, swirling around and pulling at her from all angles. Teriana pressed herself tight against the wall, her heart racing. Even if the fall wouldn't kill her, she'd probably break enough bones to wish it had. Her arms trembled from the effort of staying balanced and her toes were cramping. She reached the next window with no small amount of relief.

It was short-lived. There was faint light coming from the room, and to her horror, she could hear voices.

"What are you doing here? Have you lost your mind?"

Teriana recognized Legatus Marcus's voice.

"You're leaving tomorrow." A young woman's voice. "This was the only opportunity I had to see you, and for obvious reasons, I couldn't do it through more legitimate channels."

If she hadn't been in such a precarious position, Teriana would've rolled her eyes. Lydia had told her about patrician women taking legionnaires into their beds, so it was no surprise to her that that a young man as attractive as Marcus would have caught their attention. Tuning out their conversation, Teriana debated what steps to take next. Obviously she couldn't go across the window—Marcus might see her. That left climbing over or going under.

It was concern over going any higher that made her decision. Holding on to the edge of the window, she bent her knees and, reaching one hand down, she placed it on the ledge. Taking a deep breath, Teriana let herself drop.

Her arms shuddered with the effort of holding her entire

weight, the tips of the fingers of her left hand growing slick with blood. Moving as quickly as she could, she slid one hand sideways. Then the other. She prayed neither of them would see the movement of her fingers in the darkness.

Once she was across the window, the ledge grew narrow again, barely wide enough to span the first two joints of her fingers. Icy sweat trickled down her arms, and the wind buffeted her legs from side to side. She tried to dig her toes into the tiny cracks in the mortar, but she couldn't get a grip. Her only chance of making it to the next window was to move quickly.

Her breath rasping in and out, Teriana moved painstakingly across the gap between the windows. She was almost there. Almost to her mum.

But her fingers were slipping.

Little whimpers sneaked past her lips as she fumbled to keep her grip. Her injured fingers slipped, and abruptly she was hanging from one hand, her fingernails scratching against the stone as she desperately reached with her bloody hand to grasp the ledge.

And missed.

16

MARCUS

The table in the center of the room was littered with reports on supplies, ships, and sea conditions, men constantly coming and going with updates on the progress of preparing to load two legions' worth of men into a fleet of vessels only now making port. Marcus would've preferred to have run things from the Thirty-Seventh's camp, where things were organized to his liking, but this building was where they were keeping Teriana, so in this building he would remain.

"Feels bloody amazing to be going on campaign again," Servius said, practically vibrating with energy as he signed off on costs for provisions. Ensuring the legion was supplied and fed was Servius's domain, the big man always seeming to have a sixth sense about what the Thirty-Seventh might need, particularly when it came to libations.

"Stand still," Felix muttered. "I'm trying to write and you're shaking the rutting table." Then to Marcus, he said, "Do we really need this many men—"

"Yes," Marcus interrupted. "And all of them on point until she's on the ship and we're sailing out of the harbor."

"You really believe Cassius would take her out now? On the eve of a campaign that hinges upon assistance from the Maarin?"

"Yes, Felix. For the hundredth time, I do believe that." Marcus was tired, his patience for Felix's questions about Teriana's importance shot.

"But we need her," said Servius. "He needs her! How else does that sheep lover think we're going to get to the Dark Shores?"

"He thinks she can be replaced with someone less difficult. He doesn't like the deal I made with her. And he especially doesn't like that Senator Valerius will be the one holding on to our most important hostage, but Valerius wouldn't take no for an answer."

"*Can* she be replaced?" There was worry in Servius's voice. He'd grown fond of the girl. Most of the men who'd had contact with her had, Teriana's ire seeming to be reserved for Marcus, and Marcus alone. Which was probably fair.

"I'm not so certain," he replied. "Teriana was the only one we could get to talk. The rest of them all went into a sort of trance the moment they were brought in. I've never seen anything like it."

"Rutting paganism." Felix made a noise as if to spit, then eyed their fancy accommodations and seemed to think better of it. "Maybe it's well that Cassius intends to hold them to account for breaking the Empire's laws. There's no reason they should be exempt when all the rest of the peregrini have to abide."

"They *aren't* peregrini," Marcus reminded him. "They aren't part of the Empire—they're a free nation only subject to the Empire's laws when they are in port."

"And why is that?" Felix snapped. "Why should they be free when no one else is? What makes them so special that they don't have to pay the taxes, and follow the rules, and tithe their second-born sons?"

Frowning, Marcus eyed his second, disliking hearing political propaganda like that coming from Felix's mouth. "Talk like that makes you sound like one of Cassius's sycophants."

Felix blinked in surprise, but before he could say anything further on the matter there was a knock at the door and Quintus stepped inside. "There's, uh, a young woman here to see you, sir," he said. "Fancy-like. Patrician."

Exhaling a breath of annoyance, Marcus nodded, and a moment later a slender silk-clad woman stepped through the door, all but her grey-blue eyes concealed by a gauzy veil. "Legatus," she said, inclining her head even as the familiarity of her voice hit Marcus like a punch to the gut. To his friends, she said, "Please excuse the interruption, sirs, but I need a moment in private with your commander."

Two sets of eyes turned on him, and Marcus nodded. Servius chuckled and slapped him on the shoulder hard enough to make him stagger. Felix only strode out the door, his face a thundercloud over the interruption.

The door shut, and Marcus's older sister, Cordelia, dropped the veil covering her face.

"What are you doing here?" he demanded, hoping she didn't notice the faint shake to his voice. "Have you lost your mind?"

"You're leaving tomorrow," she replied. "This was the only opportunity I had to see you, and for obvious reasons, I couldn't do it through more legitimate channels."

"They think you're here to—" He broke off, not even able to say it, heat rising to his face.

"I'm well aware of why they think I'm here," she said, "because it was part of my plan for them to think it." Shaking her head, she added, "You weren't the only one in the family born with brains in your head, but it appears you were given an extra helping of prudishness, dearest brother."

"Enough." He'd stood in front of thousands of men and given orders, but right then his voice had all the authority of the twelve-year-old he'd been when last they'd talked.

"Always so easy to tease," she said; then her face abruptly crumpled and she flew across the room, flinging her arms around his neck. "I didn't think I'd ever see you again."

"Neither did I," he admitted, tightening his arms around her for a moment. She seemed so small, so fragile, so unlike the indomitable young girl who'd sneaked out of the city dressed as a servant to visit him at Campus Lescendor. Then she pushed him back, a line appearing between her brows as she took hold of his chin and turned his face from side to side.

"I'm pleased to see you decided not to stay scrawny," she said.

"I'm not sure it was a choice." Last time he'd seen her, she'd been taller than him, but now the top of her head was beneath his chin. He was still caught up with considering how much she'd changed—twenty-one and, if what he'd heard was true, married to one of the rising stars of the Senate and mother to two children—when she ran her thumb over the scar marring his right cheek. "Your face . . ."

"It's nothing. It's old—from when we were in Bardeen."

The furrow between her brows deepened. "You're in command. You aren't supposed to be fighting."

A laugh tore from his mouth even as he considered how sheltered his sister was. She'd never bled in the mud and never would, if he kept Cassius happy. "I'll inform the enemy of that the next time they come at me."

"That might be sooner rather than later," she said, stepping back and resting one hand against the table, eyes skipping over the stacks of documents.

"Is that why you risked coming here, Cordelia? To say goodbye before I crossed the world?"

"No, Ga—" She bit her lip and frowned at her almost slip on his name. She'd always struggled with that particular lie. "No, Marcus. I'm here to try to convince you *not* to cross the world."

One of his eyebrows rose. "Bit late for that. And even if it wasn't, I'm sure you know that I don't have much choice in the matter."

Her eyes went to the door. "They aren't eavesdropping, are they?"

"No."

"Are you sure?"

"Yes."

Exhaling, Cordelia walked to the window and looked out, though there was nothing to see but darkness. "Gaius, of course, told us what you told him about Cassius." Looking over her shoulder, she smirked. "Two black eyes and a broken nose, and not even Mother felt an ounce of sympathy for him when she heard what happened. Only handed him a bottle of wine and told him to go out into the garden and whine to the flowers."

"I shouldn't have done it."

"He deserved it. Gaius took your name and you took his place at Campus Lescendor, and never once has he expressed any gratitude for that sacrifice. He's an entitled, spineless little shit who never would've survived legion training. He doesn't just owe you his privilege; he owes you his life."

Marcus exhaled a long breath. This was well-trodden ground, Cordelia's anger over their parents' choice far greater than his own. She'd never forgiven them, or her and Marcus's brother, judging from her words. "There are more pressing concerns than our brother's self-involvement."

"True." She rotated a gold bracelet around her wrist. "I knew what was going on with Cassius the moment you and yours marched into Celendrial and handed that maggot the consulship."

He opened his mouth to speak, but Cordelia cut him off. "I know that he blackmailed you. That he threatened to reveal that our parents had broken the law. That you, and Father, and Gaius would be executed. That Mother and our little sisters would be stripped of the Domitius fortune and sent into exile."

"And with the Domitius name in ruin, you would cease to be an asset to your politician husband," he reminded her. "Don't think that you'd make it through unscathed, Cord."

Her expression hardened. "My mind is what makes me an asset to my husband, Marcus, not my name."

The corner of his mouth turned up in a smile. "Father made a good match for you, then."

"I made the choice of whom I'd marry, not Father."

His smile grew, her ferocity welcome after Gaius's whimpering. "Even better."

Turning from the window, she strode back toward him, her skirts whispering against the mosaic tile of the floor, her jeweled sandals sparkling in the lamplight. She suited these ornate rooms with their gold-painted walls and frescoed ceilings, the furniture all heavy wood with padded velvet seats and tasseled cushions. The comfort made him uncomfortable. Made him long for the familiarity of his command tent with its flimsy folding table and chairs, the floor nothing more than naked earth.

"Cassius is the worst possible man to hold the position of consul, Marcus. Celendor was already struggling beneath the burden of endless conquest. Of supporting an army over two hundred thousand strong. We thought after Chersome that it was over, that we could focus inward rather than eyeing new lands like slavering dogs. But now?" She threw up her hands. "A whole other half of the world has presented itself and we have a warmonger in power who has no compunctions against taxing the people to within an inch of their lives in order to fund this monstrous venture. Bad enough the practice of taking second sons; do you know what he's talking about doing? Cassius plans to take the fourth sons of families who can't afford to pay."

The fingers of Marcus's hand twitched, and he balled it into a fist. "What do you expect me to do about that, Cordelia? Only the Senate has the power to temper Cassius, and I don't sit in it. So perhaps your concerns are better directed to our father. Or to your husband."

Her face darkened. "Don't stand there and act powerless. You're in command of a legion, and that means that you *can* march into the Senate and tell them you think this campaign is a mistake. You're bloody well the most famous living legatus, the Prodigy of Lescendor. They'll listen."

"It wouldn't make a difference," he said, feeling his temper rise. "You think I have power, but let me assure you, it only exists within the framework of the Empire's making. I have power over my men. Over how I conduct a campaign. And that. Is. It." Reaching for a cup of water, he drained it, slamming it back down against the table, swearing silently when the crystal cracked.

"The Senate tells me where I must go. What I must accomplish. And if I don't do as they say, my life will be forfeit and precisely nothing will change, because I'm nothing more than a number to Mother Empire and I can be replaced."

Her jaw clenched. "That's not true."

"It is." Resting his hands on the table, Marcus stared at the map on which Teriana had marked the route to the xenthier stem, the location itself stained with a bloody fingerprint. "I don't have the power to change our world, Cordelia. All I can do is protect those I care for as best I can."

"No matter the cost?" She came around the table, staring him down in a way no one had in a very long time. "Was what happened in Chersome worth our family's lives? Was what happened to Lydia Valerius?"

He flinched, and she gave a weary shake of her head. "They say she's missing—that she fled her marriage to Cassius on a ship. But that's all lies, isn't it?"

Blood roared in his ears, and he didn't answer, only stared at a painting on the opposite wall of a woman holding an infant to her breast.

"Did you kill her?"

Silence hung between them, and finally he said, "Does it matter?"

"I think it is better if you answer that question yourself, Legatus," she said, stepping back. "It is *your* conscience that must bear the burden of your choices."

Hurt and anger rose within him like a tide. For twelve years he'd answered to a name not his own, and now she took even that from him. He was just a title. Just the number tattooed in black across his back.

"For your sake, be glad my conscience bears its burden well," he said, feeling a terrible mix of misery and pleasure when she recoiled.

Then a shriek echoed through the thick stone of the walls, and a second later a fist hammered against the door. "Legatus? Sir? We've got a problem."

Crossing the room in three strides, he flung it open to find Quintus standing outside. "What is it?"

"It's the girl, sir," Quintus responded. "She escaped."

17

TERIANA

Her fingers slipped from their hold, and Teriana bit down on a shriek as she dropped.

Then a hand closed around her wrist.

She gasped in shock and relief, especially when she saw that her savior was her mum. With a grunt of effort, Tesya heaved, pulling Teriana up far enough that she could grasp the windowsill with her other hand.

"Have you lost your bloody mind?" Tesya hissed, helping her clamber into the room.

Teriana was relieved to see her mum sounded right in the head again, though her flesh still bore testament to the questioner's torture. "I'm rescuing you," she said once she had caught her breath.

"That what you call this?" Tesya snatched up Teriana's bloody hand, holding it in the lamplight. "What've you done to yourself?"

"What do you mean, what did I do to myself?" Teriana asked, her mouth dropping open. "You were there! You saw what they did to me."

Tesya pressed her unbroken hand to her eyes, and Teriana's chest tightened when she saw tears seeping out from underneath it. "I don't remember anything—only the soldiers taking me to a building, and then waking up here with . . ." She trailed off. "The Cel did this to you? Why? What did they want?"

"Cassius," Teriana whispered. "They know about the West. I think . . . I think Lydia told them." She swallowed hard. A cowardly part of her had been hoping her mum already knew what she'd done and had had time to come to terms with it.

"They knew that we had a way of getting there quickly, and they wanted to know how."

"You didn't tell them, did you?"

Teriana looked away, unable to meet her mum's piercing stare. "They threatened to kill you—to kill all of our crew and then go after other ships. I had no choice."

Her mum sucked in a ragged breath of disbelief. "You should've let us die!"

Teriana jerked her head up. Her mother was one of the Triumvir—the closest thing the Maarin had to royalty. Her duty was to protect their people and their interests. And as heir, Teriana's duty was the same. "How can you say that? How can one secret be worth the lives of everyone we love?"

"Because it's the only thing protecting the West from these dogs!"

Teriana shivered, her skin feeling like ice. She should've known that this was how it would go. Should've known her mother wouldn't side with her decision. "It's easy for you to say," she choked out. "Your body might've been there, but your mind wasn't. You didn't have to make the choice."

"Madoria protected me."

"And everyone else." The words were strangled, but Teriana forced them out. "But not me. There was no one there to help me. Not Madoria, not Magnius, not even you. You left me alone with them"—the tears were flooding down her cheeks now—"and I had to make a decision. And I chose to save those I love."

"And you've been forsaken for it. She did not protect you because she's turned her back on your soul."

"You don't know that. Let's leave here—they can't use the paths without us. We'll steal back the *Quincense* and flee."

"There is no escape. And there is no undoing the damage you've done. They know the West exists now, and they'll stop at nothing to conquer it. Your soul is forsaken."

"Mum, we need to at least try!"

"You are forsaken."

Then her mother did the worst thing that she could possibly have done and turned her back on Teriana.

"Mum," she pleaded, tugging on Tesya's shirt. "Mum, please, don't do this."

Tesya kept her back turned and said nothing.

"Please," Teriana repeated. "Please!" It came out as a shriek, and seconds later the door to the room slammed against the wall.

A surprised legionnaire stared at her. "How did you get in here?" His gaze jumped to the window. "Shit. Get the legatus," he said to the men peering over his shoulder.

There was a commotion in the hallway, and Marcus strode into the room. He looked from her to Tesya and then went to the window and leaned out. "Impressive," he muttered. "I wouldn't have thought it possible."

Teriana didn't resist when he took her arm. "One of you stay in here with Tesya," he said to his men. "I don't want her left alone for so much as the length of time it takes for you to piss."

Teriana barely heard him. She was forsaken, not only by her goddess but also by her mum. Her own mother, who had never left her alone for more than a day in all her life.

Marcus steered her into her room, returning a moment later and shutting the door behind him.

"Sit."

She sat on her pallet, watching dully while he poured water from a jug into a basin and carried it over to her. Setting it on the ground, the legatus of the infamous Thirty-Seventh Legion sat cross-legged in front of her, took her wrist, and dunked her injured hand in the water.

Teriana bit back a hiss of pain. "What're you doing?"

"Tending to your injury." He turned up the lamp's flame.

"I can see that. Why are *you* doing it?"

"Because I can," he said, removing her hand from the basin and examining it in the light. "We're all given basic medical training. No one with more is here at present."

He hadn't answered her question. He knew it, and she knew it.

Frowning at her fingers, he pulled out a pair of tweezers and started plucking out the bits of rock jammed into her skin. It hurt like the fires of the underworld, but she embraced the pain. It distracted her from what had happened. First Lydia had turned on her. Now her mum.

"I take it you didn't go through all that effort just to visit your mother," he said, not looking up from his task. "Particularly given that you knew you would see her in the morning before she left."

Teriana refused to meet his gaze, glaring instead at her bloody fingers.

"I *am* curious as to what your plan was," he said. "Her hand is broken. There's no way she could've climbed down."

"Blankets," she muttered. "I was going to lower her."

"Tried, but true. And you were going to climb?"

She nodded reluctantly. It didn't really matter now.

"You might've done it," he said, his face turning to the window. "I didn't think it was possible, especially by two prisoners with injured hands, but you proved me wrong."

"Just because *you* can't do something doesn't make it impossible."

"You could try taking the compliment." He dunked her hand in the water again to wash away the blood.

"Doesn't matter anyway. She wouldn't go with me."

"Why not?" He carefully dried her hand, then smeared her fingers with a numbing salve.

"Because I am forsaken."

"By your god? For helping us?"

"Goddess."

"Sorry." With surprising gentleness, he wrapped the bandage one finger at a time, cutting and pinning it so she could use her hand rather than having it reduced to a paw. "You didn't get much choice in the matter."

"She believes I made the wrong one."

His hands hesitated in their motions. "How old are you, Teriana?"

"Seventeen." She answered honestly, surprised by the question.

"I was sixteen when I made my first decision that cost men their lives."

"What did you do for your first four years of being in charge of your own legion?" she asked. "Delegate the hard decisions?"

He grinned, his teeth white in the dim light. It was, she thought, the first time she'd seen him properly smile. It made him seem like a real person rather than a soulless bastard.

"No," he said. "During those years, we were under the guidance of older, more experienced legions, who were responsible for finishing our training. Their commanders made the tactical decisions, the hard decisions. It wasn't until we were stationed in Bardeen that I had moved up enough in the Senate's eyes to take command." He moved on to her ring finger. "It was an easier campaign than any we've had since—quite clear what had to be done from a tactical standpoint, but I knew going in that we would have casualties. Everything went as planned, but we lost thirteen men. Men whom I'd known since we were children together. It was . . . difficult."

"Why are you telling me this?"

"Because if anyone deserves to have their soul burn for eternity, it's someone like me. Not a girl trying to save the lives of the people she cares about." He'd finished her little finger while he spoke, but she didn't notice until he withdrew his hands from hers.

"There's something you should know, too," he said. "The *Quincense* and the other vessels you likely saw in the harbor weren't the only Maarin ships captured. The navy took several of them, and they're being kept in various harbors throughout the Empire."

Her stomach plummeted. "How many?"

"Over six hundred Maarin sailors are being kept captive."

Six hundred? Her eyes burned, and it was a struggle to keep her tears in check.

"The deal you signed today protects them. If you follow

through, they'll be released. Even if Cassius isn't happy about it, the Senate will hold him to his word. As will I. But you have to hold to your word in order for that to happen. It's the only way."

Despite her best efforts, a tear dribbled down Teriana's face.

"I won't go so far as to say that our goals are the same, Teriana, but when it comes to protecting your people, our interests are aligned." Digging into the medical kit, he extracted something, then grew still. "The Maarin have done nothing to deserve persecution by the Empire, and the Empire has nothing to gain in the genocide of your people beyond putting a very bloody feather in Cassius's cap. I'll use the means at my disposal to ensure he doesn't get the opportunity, but everything I do will be for naught if you don't cooperate."

"Pretty words, Legatus," she said, still reeling from the revelation of how *many* of her people had been taken. "But you are *not* my ally. You are my enemy."

He nodded slowly. "I am. But so is Cassius, and I assure you, he is a far greater threat to you and yours than I ever could be."

There was no right path. No good choice. No solution that would protect everyone.

"If the Empire has nothing to gain from killing my people, then why do they support Cassius in doing so?" Teriana's voice was thick, every word sticking in the intensity of her grief. "Why do your people hate mine?"

"What you saw today were Cassius's supporters. They do not represent all of the Empire." He hesitated, as though uncertain of whether to continue, then added, "There are a good many who are protesting what Cassius has done to the Maarin, but he's recalled two more legions to assist with policing the city, so there is only so much they can do without fear of consequence."

"A good many?" She laughed, but it felt like a sob. "There were thousands in that Forum screaming their support for Cassius. And for him to have won, it means thousands more feel the same. Why? Why do they take pleasure in seeing our downfall?"

"Some resent your . . . *freedom* from the laws and taxes and obligations that come with being part of the Empire."

"They weren't screaming that we should pay more *taxes*," she choked out. "They were screaming for me to be beaten and slaughtered and—" She broke off, unable to repeat the words the crowd had thrown at her. "They were acting like I was their enemy."

Tension filled the space between them, cloaking the room in silence despite the noise filling the city streets.

"When I was in the final years of my training, I once asked why the Empire glorifies conquest," Marcus finally said. "One of my teachers reminded me of the history of Celendor. Reminded me that once we were a race of mighty warriors who all bled and fought in a world where conquest—and the defeat of our enemies—was a necessary part of survival. Reminded me that the blood of those men and women still flows in the veins of those born today." His brow furrowed. "Except now my people toil in different ways to survive, and some—like those you saw today—find little satisfaction in their labors. They suffer a feeling of . . . *impotence*. Cassius knows this. He knows that when the Empire is victorious that these people see *themselves* as victorious. That it makes them, in the moment of the triumph, feel mighty again. And for some, that feeling is an addiction that can never be sated. But for there to be conquest, there must be something—or someone—to be conquered. There must be an enemy."

"Did your victories make you feel *mighty*?" She spat the word, furious because his answer was no relief to her pain. "Do you enjoy bringing your enemies low?"

"No." He exhaled a long breath. "When I win, I feel relief that I've survived. Grief over the fallen. But mostly I feel fear, because for me and my legion, the fight is never over."

Teriana closed her eyes, a tremor running through her. There was no way out of this, not for anyone.

"Drink this." Marcus pushed a small vial into her hand. "It will make you sleep."

She tried to give it back, remembering how heavily she'd slept the last time she had taken it, but he shook his head. "Your ship has been repaired, and the rest of the fleet will arrive through the night. We leave tomorrow with the tide, and I need you sharp and ready to sail the *Quincense*."

Reluctantly, she swallowed the contents of the vial. It might be the last time she ever slept easy. The drug took hold of her quickly, and she rested her head on the pillow. "If Cassius thinks he can torture more information out of my people, he's wrong. Madoria will protect their minds. They won't feel it."

"Why didn't she do the same for you?"

Through the fog of the narcotic, it struck her that he didn't deny the existence of the gods like every other Cel person she'd met. So she answered him. "Because I'm forsaken. I'd already broken the mandate and spoken about the West to an easterner, and Madoria has turned her back on me as punishment."

Marcus paused in the process of packing the rest of the bandages. "The question you should ask yourself is this: If your goddess is so desperate to keep the ocean paths a secret, why did she silence her loyal followers and leave loose the lips of the girl she had most cause to doubt?"

A good question, Teriana thought, her eyelids drifting lower. Marcus crossed the room and leaned against the window, looking out. "What are you doing?" she asked.

"Someone needs to watch over you," he said, not turning around. "And no one will do it better than me."

18

TERIANA

Marcus was gone when Teriana awoke, replaced by another, unfamiliar legionnaire. He had the markings of an officer and his Cel heritage was as apparent as his commander's. He was not much taller than her and, courtesy of his shorn hair, his ears were unfortunately prominent. He was eating an apple that she suspected had come from the tray sitting next to her pallet.

"You eating my breakfast?" she asked, slowly sitting up. Every muscle in her body ached with an ungodly fierceness, and her mouth tasted like a midden heap.

He grinned, but his expression wasn't friendly. "First to the fire gets the best pickings."

"I'll keep that in mind." Picking up the tin cup of water sitting on the tray, she guzzled it down and then went to work on the food. "What's your name?" The question came out around a mouthful of meaty stew.

"I'm the tribunus of the Thirty-Seventh."

She rubbed her chin, eyeing him thoughtfully while she chewed. "Tribunus . . . Is that what they call the soldier who blows the horns?"

He huffed out an annoyed breath. "It means I'm second-in-command. Which means you can call me sir."

Teriana raised one eyebrow. "I'm your prisoner, not your underling. Give me your name or I'll come up with something worse." She swallowed her mouthful of food. "With ears like that, it won't be hard."

His face darkened. "You wouldn't dare."

She scraped her spoon along the bottom of the bowl and shoved the last bit of food into her mouth. "Try me, Sir Elephant Ears."

His fists clenched.

"I did give you the choice," she said, rising to her feet. "And since I'm under the protection of *Legatus Marcus*, who I believe *you* refer to as sir, there isn't much you can do about it. Unless you give me your real name, that is."

He crossed his arms, his face almost the shade of plums.

The door swung open and Marcus strode in. "Felix, is she ready to go?"

"Sir Elephant Ears and I were just finishing breakfast."

"Pardon?" Marcus shook his head and sighed. "Never mind, I don't want to know."

They followed him into the hallway, where the waiting legionnaires fell in, front and behind. The room where they'd kept her mum was unguarded. *Maybe she's already waiting downstairs?* Teriana's shoulders were tense—would her mum even say good-bye to her?

There was no one outside the building except more soldiers.

"Where's my mum?" she demanded, looking up and down the streets for any sign of Tesya. "You said I could see her before she left."

Marcus turned away from the man he'd been speaking to. "You *did* see her," he said, his fingers tugging at a buckle on his armor.

Teriana's stomach sank. "I didn't even get to say good-bye."

He shrugged one shoulder, looking away. "Valerius and his people took her at dawn. Even if I knew where he was planning to keep her, I don't have the time to take you there before the tide turns. I loaded over nine thousand men onto ships this morning, and I don't relish the thought of unloading them for the sake of missed good-byes."

The tiny bit of goodwill he'd built up the prior night vanished in an instant. Teriana's skin flushed, and she felt an almost uncontrollable urge to lash out. She should've known he'd find a way to punish her for trying to escape. Marcus turned his back on her and started walking down the street, but Elephant Ears shot her a smirk before following his commander.

As they walked down the wharf, Teriana's skin chilled despite the heat of the sun. Sweat slicked her palms, and she wiped them on her trousers, barely noticing the sting of her fingers. She could see her crew now—their bright-colored clothes standing out among the soldiers on the deck. What if they all turned their backs on her the way her mum had? What if every single person she'd tried to save abjured her for her actions? What if they would all rather be dead than take the Cel across the ocean paths? She'd be completely and utterly alone.

Several of them caught sight of her at the same time, and she watched as word passed across the ship and they all came to the port side to watch her arrival. Their faces were expressionless, but that didn't necessarily mean anything. Regardless of what they thought of her, they wouldn't want the Cel involved.

"I don't have to worry about *them* trying to kill you, do I?" Marcus asked, frowning at her crew.

"No. It's not our way. If they're done with me, they'll turn their backs. Pretend I don't exist. But they won't kill me."

"That's the stupidest thing I've ever heard," Elephant Ears said.

"Then you clearly haven't been listening to anything that comes out of your own mouth," Teriana retorted. "Believe me, there's some things that are worse than death. Like having to spend the rest of your life as a pariah to your people, and knowing at the end of it, your soul is destined to burn for eternity."

"You aren't going to put up with her spouting this pagan drivel, are you, sir?"

Annoyed, Teriana said, "It's this pagan drivel that's going to get you across the Endless Seas, Elephant Ears, so maybe you should shut your big mouth before any more stupidity comes gushing forth."

"That remains to be seen," he snapped. "How do we know you aren't planning to sail us around the ocean on a wild-goose chase?"

"Maybe I am." She winked at him, getting to enjoy the rising flush on his face for about a second before she collided with something hard. Stumbling back, she determined that the something hard was a very unamused Marcus.

"Felix," he said.

"Sir?"

"This is your ship."

Surprise drove the anger out of the legionnaire's face. "What?"

"This is the ship you'll be sailing on," Marcus said, pointing at the monstrous Cel creation bobbing next to the dock, onto which dockworkers were loading casks marked as *Dangerous* and *Explosive*. "It's the biggest—has four hundred of our men on it. I want you with them."

"I thought I would be sailing with you."

Teriana blinked. The young man looked almost hurt.

"It makes no sense for my second-in-command to be on the same ship as me," Marcus said. "If something happens, I need someone I can trust to lead."

Elephant Ears' face paled, and it occurred to Teriana that perhaps the sentiment between the two ran deeper than comradeship. Deeper, even, than friendship. "Maybe he's tired of your conversation," she said, knowing it was stupid to bait him but unable to resist.

Felix's hands balled into fists, and she readied herself to leap out of the way if he attacked. But he only said, "If anything happens to him, I'll gut you like a pig. Is that clear?"

Teriana held up her hands and smiled. Not that she doubted he was telling the truth. Or that he was capable of following through.

Giving her one final scowl, he saluted Marcus and started toward the gangplank. When he was halfway up, Teriana shouted, "Good-bye, Elephant Ears! Maybe if the crew attaches you to the mainsail you might have a chance of keeping up." Chuckling to herself, she started walking down the dock. She didn't make it far before she found herself flying through the air and into the filthy harbor water.

Kicking to the surface, she treaded water, trying to ignore the debris floating around her. "What was that for?"

"For insulting one of my men." The legatus stared down at her. "I will ensure they respect you, and in turn, you will respect them. Am I clear?"

Teriana wanted to argue with him, but nothing she said would carry much weight given there were turds bobbing next to her. "Clear."

He was already on her ship by the time she climbed a ladder back onto the docks and dumped the filthy water out of her boots. Not bothering to put them back on, she trudged up the gangplank and tossed them on a pile of ropes to dry. Then she started grimly in the direction of where her crew was assembled. None of their faces were readable, and the speech she'd rehearsed had disappeared from her head. "Lydia . . . She . . ." Swallowing hard, Teriana said, "The Cel know about the West."

Then there were arms around her. "Girl, we thought you were dead." It was Yedda's voice whispering in her ear. "You and your mother both. Wasn't until this morning that we learned otherwise."

Teriana's shoulders trembled and she buried her face against the old woman's shoulder, feeling the hands of her crew patting her back and hearing their welcoming words. The ship's cook, Polin, immediately began unraveling the soaked bandages on her hand, his enormous fingers gentle and familiar, having tending Teriana's injuries since she was a child. "Thought you'd abjure me for what I've agreed to," she said into Yedda's shirt.

"As if I could ever do such a thing to the girl I held as a wee babe."

"Mum has."

Yedda pushed her back, her wrinkled gaze searching Teriana's face. "She may come to regret that. In her own way, your mother is as impetuous as you." She pointed her finger to a distant dock. It was set up with gallows, and Teriana's stomach lurched when she saw the decomposing corpses hanging from them.

"That one—" She jerked her chin in Marcus's direction. "He came and talked to us this morning. Said the only reason we hadn't joined those poor souls was because of a bargain you made." She frowned. "He took pains to make sure we understood the bargain was with you and not your mother."

"True tale," Teriana admitted. "You know who he is?"

"Aye. The one who supposedly set Chersome on fire." The old woman smiled. "I didn't expect him to be so pretty."

"Yedda!" Teriana's cheeks warmed. "He's a blackhearted devil. What he looks like doesn't matter. And what do you mean *supposedly*?"

Yedda shrugged. "I think there's more to that tale than has been told. And if we're going to take these Cel bastards across the world, I might as well have something nice to look at. Or a few somethings." She whistled at a pair of legionnaires who'd wandered too close. They both jumped like they'd been stung by bees.

Teriana groaned and shook her head. The rest of the crew hid grins behind their hands. "So you know the plan?"

"Oh, aye. There was only ever one reason they'd do this. Though perhaps you might fill us in on the details."

While Polin cleaned and bandaged the raw spots where her fingernails had been, Teriana explained what had happened since she'd been taken. Her crew stood in a circle around her, expressions tightening as they listened. When she'd finished, Yedda rubbed her chin. "So you spy on them and we use Magnius to smuggle out their plans to the greater powers of the West?"

"Isn't much of a plan," Teriana admitted. "But I didn't have any other options that didn't involve all of us ending up dead."

More than a handful of the crew glanced uneasily at the dangling corpses.

"They don't know I'm heir to the Triumvirate," Teriana said.

"They think I'm just the daughter of a merchant captain. They don't realize that my word carries weight with kings."

"Or that where we're going has gods who might have something to say about the Cel scourge invading their shores," her aunt added.

Teriana only nodded, because those same gods might have something in store for her for the choice she'd made.

"Teriana! The tide." It was Marcus's voice. She scowled over her shoulder. Servius stood next to him, and he waved cheerfully.

"Make ready," she told the crew, then motioned for Yedda to follow her to where Marcus stood by the helm.

"You heard from Magnius or Bait?" Teriana asked quietly as they walked.

"They'll turn up once we're at sea. You worried?"

Teriana knew she didn't mean about their well-being. "Very."

Climbing to the quarterdeck, they stopped in front of the two legionnaires. "This is Legatus Marcus and Praefectus Servius of the Thirty-Seventh," she said. "This is Yedda, my second mate."

"First mate now, Captain," Yedda said, nudging her in the ribs.

Teriana's chest hollowed. "Just until we get my mum back."

Yedda only shrugged.

"Anyway. Taking into account the speed your tubs with sails will manage, it'll be a day until we reach the doldrums of the Sea of the Dead, then another two to reach the mouth of the greater ocean path. Once there, I'll have specific instructions that the crews of your ships will need to follow in order to safely make it through. It's . . ." She hesitated. "It's far more dangerous than a land path, you understand?"

Marcus nodded.

"All right. Good." She surveyed the deck. "You have everything we need, then?"

"Not quite." Marcus nodded at a group of his soldiers who were lingering next to a longboat. "Cut them down."

The men dropped the longboat, rowing it swiftly across the harbor to the dock with the gallows, where they climbed up and began cutting down the bodies of her people, carefully depositing them in the boat before rowing back to the *Quincense*. With her aunt at her elbow, Teriana watched it all in silence, but when they reached the ship she asked, "What are you doing?"

"You bury your dead at sea, yes? The ground is unacceptable?"

She nodded, unable to speak.

"I heard you tell Servius as much," he said. "And if I heard, so did Cassius. He's petty when given the opportunity."

Yedda glanced at Teriana, both grey eyebrows rising nearly to her hairline; then her aunt said, "That's good of you, Legatus."

Snorting, Teriana shook her head as she watched the legionnaires lift the bodies on deck and stow them below out of the sun. "Good would've been keeping them from the noose in the first place."

No reaction showed on Marcus's face. "When we're in open water, I'll bring my men belowdecks to give you the time to do what you do. Now shall we?"

Teriana placed a hand on the smooth wood of the helm. It should've felt familiar and comforting, but it didn't. "Let's get out of this gods-forsaken city."

Yedda immediately shouted orders at the crew, and moments later the *Quincense* drifted away from the docks.

They had to pass the scaffold that had held the corpses of Teriana's countrymen, but it wasn't the cut ropes her eyes went to. It was to the living person standing next to them. He was dressed in the white toga and crimson sash of a senator, but she would have recognized him even if he weren't. Cassius lifted one hand, not in farewell but to an unused noose, its loop waiting for a neck to fill it.

"He's warning you," Marcus said under his breath, but an instant later Cassius moved his arm, finger pointing not at Teriana but at the legatus. Teriana looked up at Marcus right as he looked down at her, and their gazes met. In that instant she realized that not only did he hate Cassius like she did but also that just as she did, the legatus of the Thirty-Seventh had something to lose.

19

TERIANA

After not a half day of sailing, the *Quincense* started to take on the odor of sick landlubber.

"Did you have to put all the seasick ones on my ship?" Teriana asked, wrinkling her nose at the stench rising from the hatch.

"It isn't all of them," Marcus replied from where he leaned against the railing, steady as though he stood on dry land. "Only forty-three are sick, and of those, only thirty-six are bad."

"*Only* thirty-six," Teriana muttered. "Well, what are you doing for them?"

"They have fresh water. They'll survive."

"*I* might not survive," Teriana replied, shaking her head. "Bring the pukers on deck."

He frowned. "You said you wanted the deck clear so your crew could work."

"That was before I realized your men were going to fill the hold with puke," she replied. "Send all those ones"—she gestured at the men loitering on deck—"below, and bring up the sick ones."

"I need able bodies on deck."

"Why? We're at sea and the only ships I can see are full of Cel legionnaires. And I'm quite sure your second-in-command would sense if you were in any danger and fly over here on those wings he calls ears to protect you."

"I don't need anyone to protect me," he snapped. "And frankly, I'm starting to tire of your foul mood." He started down the steps, shouting orders as he went.

Teriana *was* in a foul mood, but she had a good reason for it. Once they had gotten out of the harbor, she'd gone on a tour about her ship to see how well the damage had been repaired. But it wasn't the repair work that had set her eyes thundercloud grey—it was what else the Cel had done to her ship.

The *Quincense* was their home, where they kept everything they owned. And everything she owned was gone to make space for soldiers, including the small fortune in gold they'd kept aboard.

"Where's my money?" she'd shouted at Marcus upon discovering the chests were gone.

He'd had the decency to look embarrassed. "It's in trust back in Celendrial. It will be returned to you once you've fulfilled your end of our bargain."

"Gods-damned thieves," she'd muttered at him, though in truth, the gold was the least of her concerns. With the exception of her clothing, all her books, art, and bits of memory had vanished, and no one was able to give her a straight answer about where it had gone. And not only *her* possessions—all the crew had suffered the same. The ship seemed barely theirs anymore—her home had been invaded and taken over by the enemy. She hadn't even gotten to keep her tiny room. All her clothes were piled on the small bed in her mother's cabin. Which would have been fine, if she'd been in there alone. It would have been fine if she'd been squished in there with every last member of her crew. But no, she had to share the room with *Legatus Marcus,* so that he could keep an eye on her.

She'd argued against it, of course, but she would have had more luck moving a mountain than changing his mind. She'd offered to bunk with her crew or even in the midst of the legionnaires squished into the hold. She'd even gone so far as to offer to sleep right next to Servius and have him watch over her, which Marcus had taken entirely the wrong way, threatening to tie her to a mast if she so much as thought of sleeping with one of his men. As if she'd ever even consider such a thing.

The legionnaires on deck disappeared below, replaced a few minutes later with a pale-faced lot, who looked relieved, if a little confused, to be out in the fresh air.

"Take the helm, and make sure you keep the Cel ships in sight," she said to one of her sailors, Jax, then started toward the seasick soldiers. As she watched, one of them ran to the side and heaved his guts into the ocean.

"Well, aren't you a sorry-looking lot," she said to them.

Marcus's face darkened, but she held up a calming hand. "First things first: keep your eyes on the horizon." She pointed to where the sea met the sky. "It doesn't move. Watching it will settle your gut. Secondly, stay on your feet. Doing so will force you to keep your balance, and you'll get used to the motion of the ship. Thirdly"—Yedda had read her mind and arrived at her elbow carrying a bowl of hazelnuts and a few strips of old cloth—"you all need to do this." Taking the elbow of one of the young men, who was Sibernese judging from his red hair, she removed his armguard and tied a strip of fabric around his pale wrist so that the nut pressed against the two tendons.

"What's this for?" he asked suspiciously, the impact of his glare reduced by the splatter of freckles on his nose.

"For growing a tree out of your arm." She rolled her eyes. "What do you think? It will make you feel better."

"I think I don't like your pagan witchery," he said, plucking at the fabric, clearly of a mind to pull it off.

"You'll do what she says," Marcus ordered.

"Yes, sir!" they all shouted, saluting sharply despite how they wobbled each time the ship crested a wave. Teriana tied a nut to each of their wrists, and by the time she was finished most of them were starting to look less green around the gills. Leaving them to wander the deck, she made her way back to the helm. She hadn't noticed that Marcus had followed until he caught her arm.

"Thank you," he said. "For helping them. You didn't have to do that."

"I did it for the sake of my nose, not for them," she said, even though it was a lie. She didn't want to admit that she'd felt bad for them—that she, the daughter of a Triumvir and the closest thing her people had to a princess, knew what the ceaseless nausea felt like.

"Right." He fussed with a buckle on his armor, looking as though he wanted to say more, but instead turned and walked away.

"Legatus," she called after him, keeping her eyes on the horizon. "Unless you got rid of it, too, there should be gingerroot in the galley. Get Polin to make you some tea out of it—he'll know how. Give it to those who are still sick."

He didn't thank her a second time.

She stayed at the helm for the rest of the day, leaving only to eat a quick meal, which she shared with Yedda, half-listening as the woman pointed out the legionnaires she found most attractive. It wasn't that Teriana wasn't watching them, but rather that she was more interested in how they functioned as a whole. Everyone knew the Cel were efficient in all things: organized, methodical, and persistent. It showed in how they built: every building, bridge, and road designed to last. In the way they governed themselves: with laws, rules, and regulations that left nothing unaccounted for. In how they had conquered the eastern half of Reath, slowly, but resolutely. And the legions were the ultimate testament to what it really meant to be Cel.

Despite being crammed into her ship with barely room to move, they functioned with absolute order. With the exception of the sick ones who remained topside, the rest of them rotated about with the precision of clockwork. When they were on deck, they marched around in groups of ten, doing various stretches intended to keep themselves limber. They ate in shifts, forming neat lines and eating with mechanical efficiency. No one argued or stepped out of line, every one of them seeming to know exactly where he was supposed to be and what he was supposed to be doing at every moment.

She knew there were 170 men aboard, excluding her crew, and that 8 of them were servants who served the legion in some capacity. From the variations in their armor, she could tell that

Marcus and Servius were the only two senior officers, but there were another two who seemed to be the ones giving the most orders. About half of them appeared to be Cel, with their ubiquitous golden skin, the rest hailing from the provinces, their skin ranging from the nearly translucent white of those born in Sibern to the deep brown of Atlia, along with dozens who looked to be the product of interracial relationships, which were common given that the Empire colonized the provinces with retired legions. Yet despite so many of them having been born to places that spoke a language other than Cel, none of them bore even a trace of an accent, their training having made them uniform even in that.

Their efficiency made her nervous.

Her plan depended on the West being able to defeat them—on her belief that if she could provide its rulers and armies with details about Marcus's plans and strategies, it would be enough for them to prevail. That a warrior backed by the power of the Six would be able to defeat any one of these godless Cel vermin. Except she was beginning to realize that it wouldn't be *just* one legionnaire. They didn't function as individuals, and they wouldn't fight as individuals. The legion was an enormous cohesive entity, and her uncertainty was growing over how well thousands of individuals would fare against them. Her doubt felt like a sickness inside of her, working its way through every vein and growing in strength as it progressed.

Would it be better to refuse to open the path and suffer the consequences? Was her mother right? Was it better to martyr herself and her captured people for the sake of the countless thousands of lives she was putting at risk by bringing the Cel across?

"You heard from Magnius?" Yedda asked as they walked back to the helm.

"No." If Magnius didn't come back to the ship before they reached the mouth of the ocean path, Teriana wouldn't have to make a decision—it would be made for her. If her guardian refused to help, she would know for certain the state of her soul in Madoria's eyes. A cowardly part of her wanted to turn this into Magnius's decision. If he agreed to open the path, then it wouldn't be her who'd put the West at risk. And if he refused, then it wouldn't be her fault when the Cel slaughtered her crew. Sighing, she took hold of the wheel.

"There is still time," Yedda said, patting her shoulder before heading off in the direction of legionnaires doing their stretches.

When the sun set, Magnius had still not shown himself.

Leaving specific instructions with her night crew to keep the storm lanterns lit and the Cel ships well in sight, Teriana retreated to her mother's cabin. Marcus was inside with Servius and a scarred man with dusky skin named Gibzen, who she'd learned was a centurion, which was an officer of sorts. They had one of her maps out on the table, but their discussion of supplies and such didn't interest her, so she climbed into bed, clothes and all. Someone had kindly hung a sheet that concealed the bed from the rest of the room, but it did nothing to block their shadows.

Moments later, she heard Servius and Gibzen leave and she listened to Marcus talking to the man who attended him.

They were speaking in Sibal, which surprised her a little. She didn't think a Cel legatus would condescend to speak in the language of his servant—especially when the man spoke Cel fluently. Leather creaked and metal clicked as Marcus's armor was removed and put aside; then the door shut and the lock fell into place.

They were alone.

Teriana held her breath, wondering if he would say anything to her. But the only sound was the faint tread of bare feet against the floor. The lamp dimmed to a barely perceptible glow, and blankets rustled as he lay down. Nothing was said, but Teriana remained frozen on her side until she heard the measured breaths of sleep. Only then was she able to roll on her back and relax.

Teriana woke to a cool breeze brushing across her face, goose bumps rising on her arms. She frowned, trying to remember if the window had been open when she'd come in. Maybe Marcus had opened it during the night? She had risen, intent on closing the window whether he liked it or not, when a large hand clamped down over her mouth.

20

TERIANA

Teriana shrieked and slammed her elbow against her assailant's ribs. He grunted and let her go, stumbling into the sheet hanging from the ceiling. She heard the rapid *thud thud* of Marcus coming across the room and then a collision as he tackled the man to the floor.

"Teriana, it's me!"

The voice was familiar.

"It's Bait!"

It took her a second to react; then she flung herself on top of the two men. "Marcus, stop!" she shouted, trying to figure out who was who in the tangle of sheets. "He's one of my crew."

The hard shoulders beneath her hands froze. "Teriana, get the light." His voice was angry and she jerked her hands away, running to fetch the faintly glowing lamp. Turning up the flame, she swung it round so that the light illuminated the two.

Bait had gotten the worst end of the struggle. Marcus had one of her friend's arms twisted behind his back and his face pressed into the floorboards. Blood dripped from his nose, making tiny splattering sounds against the wood.

"He's mine," she said. "See, look. Maarin as they come."

Marcus's only reaction was an irritated grunt, and he didn't let go of Bait. If anything, his grip tightened. "Let him go," she demanded.

He ignored her, and Bait started thrashing and cursing.

"Bait, shut up. Marcus, let him go. He's one of my crew. How many times do I have to tell you?"

"Considering I've met all of your crew and this is the first time I've ever seen this boy, you'll excuse me for not believing you." In one swift action, Marcus flipped Bait onto his back and then pinned him down. "How did you get aboard?"

"Get off me, you filthy Cel scum!" Bait snarled. "I'm going to slit your throat and string you up for the seagulls!"

"Really?" Marcus lifted him up and thumped his head against the floor. "How did you get aboard?"

Someone pounded on the door, and the locked handle jiggled. "Legatus, sir? Is everything all right?"

Marcus stared at the locked door, then glanced at the window and swore. "Let them in," he snapped at Teriana. She scuttled across to the door and unlatched it. Two legionnaires were inside in an instant, pushing her out of the way.

"Who's he?" one of them demanded.

"Good question." Bait struggled furiously under Marcus's grip, but he was all gangly limbs compared to the solid muscle of the Cel legatus. "How did you get aboard?"

"I stowed away," Bait spit. "It was easy. You Cel are all blind dogs." He then let loose a string of curses that included no fewer than six languages, three of which he had no business using in front of the Cel. Not that it mattered anymore.

The two legionnaires grumbled angrily and Teriana winced. Only Marcus seemed immune to Bait's insults. All he did was glance in her direction and say, "I wouldn't have thought it possible, but he's even worse than you." He then surprised her and Bait both by letting her friend go and sitting back on his heels. Bait sat upright, and for a moment Teriana worried he was going to take a swing at Marcus, but he clearly thought better of it.

"Magnius with you?" she asked quickly in Mudamorian. She knew he had to have been at one point; there was no other way Bait could have caught up with the ship.

"Aye," Bait replied. "And he's got plenty of questions for you. And so do I, the first of which is: Why in all the depths of the underworld are you sharing a room with him?" He scowled in Marcus's direction.

The legatus frowned. "Enough. You don't have to speak in Cel, but you bloody well use a language I speak fluently."

Bait smiled; then he started barking.

In an instant, both legionnaires had their gladii out. Teriana's heart leapt into her throat, and she readied herself to push between them and her friend. She was *fairly* certain neither of them would stab her. Fortunately, she was saved from having to test that theory when Marcus waved a calming hand in their direction. "Either you're a fool or you've got a death wish, boy. You do realize there is nothing stopping me from gutting you and tossing you overboard to feed the fish?"

"You promised the safety of my crew if I helped you," Teriana said, her fingers cold.

"The crew listed on the document *you* signed," Marcus replied. "This one's name wasn't on that list, and I'm not about to start guaranteeing the safety of every idiot you *claim* is part of your crew."

Bait grew quiet, the whites of his eyes bright against his dark skin as he finally realized how much trouble he was in. Teriana licked her lips, trying to think of a way to get Bait back into the water. Even without Magnius, he was more than capable of swimming to shore. Getting past Marcus and his men would be impossible—they were armed and far more capable fighters. The only chance she had was convincing them to toss him overboard without injury.

She let her shoulders slump as though in defeat. "Be merciful then. Throw him overboard so that the sea can take him."

Bait's jaw dropped. "Teriana?"

"Be merciful," she repeated, lowering her head.

The only sound in the cabin was the creak of the ship and Bait's anxious, heavy breathing. Cautiously, she peered through the braids that had fallen across her face. Marcus had risen to his feet, and he was staring at her, brow furrowed. When their gazes met, he looked away first. "Put him in with the rest of her crew," he told his men. "Make sure he gets there in one piece," he added when the men jerked Bait to his feet none too gently.

He waited until the three had left the cabin before going to the door and latching it. He then went to the window and stared at the moonlit wake. Teriana stayed fixed in place, her feet refusing to move. "Why'd you let him live?" The words croaked out of her dry throat.

"You asked for mercy."

Marcus didn't turn around to answer her, only rested his elbows against the ledge, shoulder muscles flexing from the motion. He was stripped down to the linen undershorts that the legionnaires wore beneath their tunics, and her eyes latched on numbers tattooed harsh and black against the golden skin of his back. *1519.* She felt the sudden urge to touch them—to see if the mark of the legions felt different from the rest of him. But before she could move, he turned to face her.

"Why do they mark you like that?" she blurted out.

He glanced at the 37 inked on the right side of his muscled chest. "It's a mark of honor," he said, and she thought she caught a faint hint of anger in his tone. "I wouldn't expect you to understand."

"But I do!" The words were out before she could think. "I do understand that one. Just not the other . . ."

One of the muscles in his jaw twitched. "For expedience. It's useful in identifying deserters. And in identifying the dead."

Pulling the window shut, he started toward the bedroll laid out on the floor. "Go to sleep, Teriana. And in the morning, urge your new crew member to exercise a bit of caution. I'll dole out the punishment if one of my men kills him, but that won't make your friend any less dead."

She nodded, but Marcus didn't look at her as he pulled the covers up and rolled to face the wall.

Dimming the lamp, she replaced it on its hook and got under her own blankets, her mind reeling. Why had he spared Bait's life? He'd had no obligation to do so, and her idiot friend had certainly done a good job ensuring his own demise. She had no doubt Marcus had let him live for a reason, but what could it be? Was it so he could use Bait against her in the future? She ground her teeth in frustration. Why could she never predict how the Cel legatus would behave?

Rolling over, she buried her face in the pillow and forced all the questions from her mind. Bait had said their guardian was here, and it was long past time they spoke. Cautiously, she stretched out her mind. *Magnius?*

I am here.

A wave of relief passed through her, and Teriana realized how afraid she'd been that Magnius had turned his back on her. *Things have happened.*

I assumed there was a reason my ship was full of Cel. There was no missing the anger in his voice. *The souls of many of our people have passed on.* He listed the names of the *Quincense* crew members who'd died and then the names of the Maarin of the other ships who'd been killed. The pillow beneath her face was damp by the time he finished.

I didn't know what to do. And rather than explain what had happened, she remembered it, knowing Magnius would see and feel it as she had. She didn't justify or explain her actions; she didn't need to. He would make his own judgments.

He was silent for a long time after she finished her remembrance, and if not for the weight of his mind in hers, she would have thought he'd left.

You are not forsaken, he finally said. *Madoria has a different path in mind for you.*

Teriana exhaled with relief, but it was only momentary. *What do you mean, a different path?*

The dominion of the Six is in grave danger. Visions of a great battlefield played through her mind, the piles of the dead and dying filling her with horror. She recognized banners of the Twelve Houses of Mudamora soaking into the blood and the muck, crushed beneath the feet of an army. An army with the burning circle of the Seventh emblazoned on the flags they carried. The vision blurred and flickered, and abruptly she was staring at the rear of a fleet of ships, the golden Cel dragon flying high in the rigging, open seas ahead of them, darkness behind. *Enemies approach from both sides.*

And here she was, trying to open the door so one of those threats could come waltzing through. Her jaw ached from clenching her teeth, as she wondered if Magnius was about to tell her that the ocean paths were closed, that despite everything she'd done, her crew was doomed to die.

Will you open the path for me? she asked reluctantly.

If it is what you want.

Teriana dug her fingers into the blankets. She didn't know what she wanted. Whether she was in this position because her goddess had chosen her or by chance, it was in her power to stop Marcus, if she was strong enough. She could refuse to open the path and suffer the consequences.

What would Marcus do? she wondered. Would he kill her quickly or would he put her to torture again in an attempt to change her mind? A slow-building icy fear crept through her. She hadn't been strong enough to stomach having her fingernails pulled off. Why did she think she'd be able to resist blurting out anything and everything to get them to stop if it came to it again? Even if she did and they killed her, it still didn't mean the Cel would be stopped. Marcus was many things, but stupid wasn't one of them. He'd work his way through her crew, maiming and torturing every last one of them until someone agreed to open the path. Her dying wouldn't stop the Cel; it would only delay them. She'd just be passing the burden to her crew. Visions of Yedda and all the rest falling under legionnaire blades filled her mind, and her stomach twisted.

There was no way she could stop the Cel and save her captured people. And in her heart, she knew which one she would choose. Which meant she'd failed already.

I've told you before, Teriana: there is more than one way to cross the world.

The pain in her jaw eased, and she considered his words. *You think that even if we deny them passage, they'll find another way?*

Madoria believes it inevitable. Others do not.

So we give up? The very idea of it tasted sour. *Let the Cel conquer the West and drive the gods from Reath?*

An echo of laughter that held no amusement filled her head. *Do not deny them passage, Teriana. Let them through, then defeat them.*

"I don't know how." She bit her lip, realizing she'd whispered the words aloud, and lay still for a long moment, waiting for any sound of Marcus stirring.

Don't be so sure, Magnius's voice filled her head. *And remember, Teriana, he who desires passage must be the one to request it.*

Teriana blinked as the guardian retreated from her mind. Was it possible that Madoria *wanted* her to bring the legions through the path?

The faint light of the lamp was enough for her to see Marcus's bare shoulder. Without a doubt, Marcus was the *he* Magnius had referred to. Which meant she had a very interesting conversation in her future. It had been one thing to convince Lydia of the existence of a demigod. It would be quite another to convince a Cel legatus to beg a boon from a sea serpent. Quite another thing indeed.

21

MARCUS

While the morning sun was bright, the hold of the ship was dark, forcing Marcus to walk blind for several strides before his eyes adjusted. The space normally dedicated to cargo was filled with his men, and those who were awake quietly rose and saluted him as he passed, mindful of their dozing comrades. The air stank with the smell of too many men in too small a space, though it was much improved with the absence of vomit.

These were the best of his men. They were the strongest, the fastest, and the smartest of the Thirty-Seventh, but they were also the worst when they got bored. They tended to pick fights—not with one another but with whoever else was about. And in this case, that meant Teriana's crew. Which was the last thing he needed.

Although Servius had already been through, Marcus made his rounds, checking their kits, ensuring armor was gleaming and blades were sharp. His presence kept them on their toes, but he knew he was doing it to keep his mind busy.

"Good morning, Legatus," Servius said with a grin as he approached. Gibzen silently saluted, but Marcus didn't miss the feral gleam in the primus's eyes. He was first of the Thirty-Seventh's centurions because he always got the job done, but he had a mean streak. Gibzen had been born in the tiny province of Timia, and when he'd arrived at Campus Lescendor he hadn't spoken a word of Cel. He had quickly received the reputation of being one of the worst bullies of their year, and he had been Marcus's most persistent tormenter until he'd negotiated a truce in exchange for teaching Gibzen to speak Cel. After that, he had become one of Marcus's staunchest defenders.

"I slept like a babe last night," Servius said, stretching his arms wide. "How about you?" The grin on his face could only be described as shit-eating.

Marcus scratched his arm, absently looking around. "What I don't understand is where he could have hidden."

The other two grunted and nodded. "Lad's only got half a foot," Servius said. "I'd have noticed that if nothing else. Plus he's the only boy of that age in her crew." The big legionnaire frowned. "What was he doing sneaking in there anyway? Do you think they're . . . ?" His frown turned into a full scowl.

"I didn't ask, and I don't really care," Marcus replied. "What I do care about is how he managed to stow away undetected for an entire day."

Servius and Gibzen exchanged uneasy glances and shook their heads. "Should have strung him up by his guts from the mainsail," Gibzen said. "I heard what he said to you—Thirty-Seventh doesn't tolerate that kind of disrespect. Makes us look weak."

Marcus didn't entirely disagree with the primus's sentiments. "We need them," he replied. "To get there and, if needs be, to get back."

"We need *her*," Gibzen argued. "And enough of them to sail the ship. No more."

All the men in the hold were silent, watching and listening. Marcus struggled to keep his face smooth. It wasn't that Gibzen had never questioned his decisions before, but he knew not to do it in front of the men. That he was doing so now was troubling. One of the desirable aspects of this mission was that it got the Thirty-Seventh out from under the Senate's thumb, which meant Marcus could do things *his* way. But it also meant that he no longer had the power of the Empire to enforce his orders and maintain his ranks—it was all on him now.

"I believe it's advantageous to maintain what goodwill we have with Captain Teriana," Marcus said, knowing he needed to come up with justification for his decision to spare the Maarin boy. "She'll take care of disciplining her crew."

"She'll." Gibzen spit a glob of phlegm onto the deck. "That's the problem, isn't it?—that we're dealing with a girl."

"The *problem*," Marcus said, "is apparently your shortsightedness, Primus." He spoke loud enough that everyone could hear. "The captain and her crew know everything there is to know about where we are going, whereas we know next to nothing. If we keep them happy, we have an asset we can use. But turn them further against us? Then we go in blind or worse." He let the corner of his mouth twist up. "We'd still win, but any fool knows it would come with a greater cost." He stepped forward so that he and Gibzen were nose to nose. "I don't know about you, Primus, but my pride's tough enough to take a few insults for the sake of saving the lives of my men."

Gibzen stared him down for a heartbeat, then nodded and dropped his gaze. "Another reminder as to why you're the one in command, sir." He shifted his attention to the watching men. "What are you lot staring at? Next rotation on deck now, or you'll be scrubbing out shit buckets for the rest of this miserable journey."

Marcus gave Servius a warning look to keep an eye on the primus, then made his way back on deck.

His explanation had sounded good. A logical reason for not punishing the Maarin boy for his insolence. Unfortunately, it hadn't crossed his mind until Gibzen had questioned him.

Marcus dug his fingers into the wood railing, remembering the calculated way Teriana had tried to save her friend from what she presumed was Marcus's bloodthirsty nature. He hadn't spared the boy because it was a good idea but rather because he wanted to show her he wasn't just a killer. "Idiot," he muttered, then turned around so that he could see what was happening on deck.

The *Quincense* was quite unlike any ship he'd sailed aboard, and he'd been on plenty. She was beautifully made and well cared for, her sleek lines and gleaming surface making it seem as though she were alive rather than a structure made of wood and nails. Despite having only half their blue sails up, she flew across the sea with speed that was curtailed only by the need to keep the other ships in sight.

The crew, too, were different. They sailed with the ease with which most people breathed, reacting instinctively to changes in the wind or sea with only the occasional order from whoever manned the helm. They worked hard but not always. Even now, a group sat conversing in a circle on the deck. More than crewmates. More than friends. They were family. And the ship wasn't just their livelihood; she was their home.

A home you stole from them.

Marcus shoved the thought away, focusing instead on his men, who were all staring up into the rigging. Casting his gaze upward, Marcus watched as a nimble Maarin sailor named Jax climbed, his muscled legs bare from knees to ankles, revealing mahogany skin. He wasn't the only crew member who appeared to have a parent or ancestor outside the seafaring race, though all possessed the color-shifting eyes that rippled like waves. Ancestors, he suspected, given the Maarin reticence to discuss the topic, who hailed from one of the innumerable kingdoms of the Dark Shores. Servius had made several attempts to pry the information out of Jax and Yedda, and even the cook, Polin, but in all matters pertaining to the West, the Maarin only shrugged and told Servius to direct his questions to their captain.

Marcus's gaze moved to where Teriana sat cross-legged on the quarterdeck. She appeared freshly scrubbed, her ebony skin gleaming in the sun. The older woman, Yedda, knelt behind her and was finishing a series of elaborate narrow braids that pulled Teriana's hair back from her face. It was a different style than she'd worn before, showing off her cheekbones and large eyes, which were currently a shade of deep blue, probably because she wasn't looking at him. Yedda, who he had discovered was Teriana's deceased father's elder sister, saw him watching and whistled in a way that made his cheeks burn. Teriana looked up, but he turned away before she could catch him out.

He'd spent the better half of the morning picking her brain for details on the continent where they were headed, and he wasn't sure he could take any more of her sarcastic comments.

Teriana got under his skin to the point where he wasn't certain whether he liked her or hated her, or whether it mattered at all. She was brash, insufferable, and had a tongue fouler than most of his men. But she was also tough, seeming to take everything that had happened to her in stride. The only time he'd seen her truly crack was when her mother had turned her back on her. Marcus knew what that felt like—to be not good enough. To be abandoned. It was why he'd lied to Teriana and said she'd used up her chance to visit her mother. He'd spoken to Tesya in the wee hours before Valerius had come to retrieve her, and she'd refused to acknowledge that she had a daughter. It had seemed better for Teriana to hate him for being cruel than for her to suffer *that*.

A whistle from the lookout overhead caught his attention and, shading his eyes, Marcus made out a pair of rocky islets in the distance. Crossing the deck, he climbed the stairs two at a time and made his way to where Teriana stood at the helm, deep in conversation with Yedda.

"Last chance to turn around and go home, handsome," the old woman said, giving Marcus a wink.

Teriana made a noise of exasperation. "We're at the edge of the doldrums. Those rocks there mark the current that will take us through. But once we're in, there's no turning back, am I clear? The only way out is the xenthier stem."

Marcus lifted his head to eye the full sails. "Winds look strong to me."

"Aye. They'll be strong right up to the point they abandon us entirely." She crossed her arms. "And you didn't answer my question."

She'd explained the Maarin route through the Sea of the Dead to him before, describing the thin river of current that meandered through the pockets of deadly calm that had captured more than their fair share of Empire ships, dooming the crews to starvation or worse. The navy captains of his fleet had argued intensely against entering the doldrums of this deadly region of the Endless Seas, calling it suicidal, and it had only been the Senate's deep pockets full of gold and Cassius's deep pockets full of secrets that had caused them to agree to the plan. And the only reason Marcus had agreed to risking his men was because he knew the lengths that Teriana would go to protect her crew. She wouldn't sail them in if there were no way out.

"You know my feelings on retreat."

She rolled her eyes. "All right, then."

Turning the wheel, she rested her chin on it, eyes fixed on the nearing islets. "The captains of your fleet must keep to the center of the current. They must not attempt to alter course or to turn around, or they'll be caught in the doldrums. If one of them falls off course, no one else may stop to assist them, or they'll be lost as well. You could lose the whole fleet to a singular error, you understand?"

"Yes." He understood the lives of his legion hung on the nerve of the captains of those ships, which was why his men would be watching like hawks for any deviation from Teriana's orders.

The *Quincense* drove toward the pair of islets like an arrow, the only sounds the creak of the rigging and the splash of the surf against the hull.

"Last chance," she murmured.

Marcus didn't bother answering, his eyes fixed on Teriana's hands, her knuckles blanched from how tightly she gripped the wheel.

"Lower the sails!" She turned her head to look at him, expression unreadable as she added, "Drop the anchor."

The anchor rattled down, the ship losing momentum as they entered the gap between the two islets, coming to a halt at the midpoint.

"Mark the path."

No one spoke as one of the Maarin sailors tossed a bucket of what appeared to be crimson dust onto the sea, where it floated on the surface. At first it appeared nothing was happening; then the dust began to move, catching in an invisible current and marking a narrow pathway west.

"Hoist the anchor," Teriana ordered once the dust had traveled a hundred yards or so from the ship. "And give our fleet something to follow."

The *Quincense* began to move, gaining speed, the ship no longer rocking on swells but running forward as though they traveled down a river, not across the sea. Marcus's skin prickled with the unnaturalness of it. At the impossibility of it. "How?"

Teriana's eyes left the sea to meet his. "You Cel believe everything has an explanation, but that's not the case. Some things just *are*. Xenthier. This current. And what you've seen is only the beginning, Marcus. It's time for you to let go of the lies Mother Empire has whispered in your ear and start seeing the world for what it really is."

"And what is that?"

"Inexplicable. Limitless." Her gaze went back to the ocean. "Divine."

They exited the gap between the two islets, following the trail of red, and Teriana murmured, "Welcome to the Sea of the Dead."

22

MARCUS

About two miles after they'd passed the islets, the winds died.

Not a slow death but a demise as abrupt as having one's head severed from one's shoulders. The air was still, close; and though Marcus could see for miles around, the sensation was claustrophobic, as though he were trapped in a box.

Or in a tomb.

The reason for the sea's moniker became clear soon after the winds died. Half a dozen ships with limp sails dotted the horizon—ghost ships, Yedda called them—and countless more graced the seafloor to either side of the crimson path, the waters so clear and still that the wrecks seemed close enough to touch. Ships that had blown off course in storm winds or lost their bearings in the night, only to find themselves caught in the doldrums with little chance of escape. Such windless phenomena occurred closer to the Empire's coastline, but they lasted a matter of days. Maybe a week. To be trapped in the Sea of the Dead's doldrums meant eternity.

"It's a bad way to go."

He turned his head to regard Yedda, who had appeared at the rail by his elbow. "Dehydration? Once the initial stages of thirst pass, it's actually a fairly peaceful way to go."

She chuckled. "Oh, they don't often go from thirst, Legatus. Once they realize they're caught, the Windless Madness takes hold. Most often they jump into the sea and drown themselves, but there are worse tales. Men slaughtering their own crewmates as they sleep. Cannibalism. Vampirism. Men who eat their friends down to the bone, surviving for months, even years, before they begin to consume themselves."

He lifted an eyebrow. "If no one ever escapes, how do these stories make their way out into the world?"

"Oh, someone always escapes," she replied. "Though whether they escape with their minds intact is another question."

"Why don't they just lower the longboats and row?" Servius asked, having come up to the quarterdeck. "Seems to me they all die of laziness."

"How do they decide who gets a spot in the longboat?" Teriana spoke for the first time since they'd left the islets. "Maybe half the crew would fit into the boats of the average merchant vessel, fewer if you factor in the supplies they'd need to bring. Men fighting their friends, slaughtering each other for the chance to survive. It's a madness, a chaos, that has no place anywhere other than the underworld."

"It could be done in an orderly fashion," Servius argued. "By drawing lots. Or volunteers."

"No, it can't."

"How do you know?"

"Because I've seen it happen." She kept her attention fixated on the crimson path ahead of them. "If they catch sight of a Maarin vessel, they abandon ship to try to reach us, even though it's impossible. The current is too swift, and we don't dare try to stop."

Impossible or not, those deaths haunted her. Marcus could tell by the tension that sang through her body, the muscles of her bare forearms flexed tight enough that they stood out against her flawless skin.

"Sometimes the longboats get caught in the current, but by the time they reach the mouth of the xenthier stem they're empty of everything but bloodstains. Same with any ships." She shook her head. "There's madness in the stillness of these waters. It makes men and women not themselves."

Unease crawled down Marcus's spine like a thousand stinging ants. "Check the status of the fleet," he ordered.

"No point," Teriana said. "If they're not with us, they're lost."

Marcus had them check anyway.

Time seemed to stand still as the fleet meandered its way through the Sea of the Dead, the only marker of change the sun overhead and the ghost ships they passed. Servius and Gibzen were working the men hard to keep them distracted, but a thousand push-ups wouldn't be enough to drive away the eerie sense of wrongness that had stolen over the ship. Marcus watched how his men's eyes went to the stranded vessels, heard the distinct lack of banter among them, and felt their uneasiness like it was his own.

It *was* his own. Because he had brought them into this. They trusted him, would follow him anywhere, and while it had been easy to agree to this mad plan back in Celendrial, now he wondered if it had been a different sort of madness that had driven him here.

As they ventured deeper into the Sea of the Dead, there were more and more ghost ships dotting the horizon, clusters of them sitting to either side of the path. The current pulled them close to an ancient vessel, the sails in tatters and the bottom nearly rotten through. Walking to the rail, Marcus leaned over, eyes searching the deck as they passed, but it was empty. No bleached skeletons. No abandoned bottles or cups. No sign the vessel had ever had a crew at all. The rigging swayed with the motion of the ship, a piece of metal striking the mast with each swell.

Clank.

Clank.

Clank.

The sound echoed in his skull, seeming to grow louder and louder, and he shook his head to clear it, then made his way to the quarterdeck. The stowaway, Bait, was standing next to Teriana, the two deep in conversation, though Teriana's eyes never left the path.

Pausing at the top of the stairs, Marcus eyed the younger man. Taller than him but gangly as a colt, the Maarin boy had curly hair that stuck out from his head like a black halo, the shifting waves of his eyes currently a deep indigo, shifting quickly to a turbid green as they landed on Marcus. "What do *you* want?"

"Answers. Why are there more ships the farther we go into the doldrums? How do they get here if this path"—he gestured outwards—"is the only current?"

"It's not the only current, you idiot," Bait responded, causing Marcus to grind his teeth. "There's a deeper current created by the xenthier that draws the sea toward it, pushes it out the other side."

In their discussions prior to their departure, Teriana had told them the Maarin sailed their ships directly into the genesis stem and were deposited by the terminus off the coast of the southern continent of the Dark Shores, reversing the trip through a genesis in the deep north that returned the ship in a terminus off the coast of Sibern. The ledgers Cassius had taken from the various ships confirmed this circular pattern of trade, but the word *deeper* struck a chord of unease in Marcus's chest. "Exactly *how* deep is it?"

"About a mile." The boy smiled, his teeth gleaming white against his dark skin, even as Teriana let out an aggrieved sigh.

"I *told* you I'd talk to him about this, Bait."

A rutting mile? He'd expected a few feet. Maybe something only reachable at low tides. Something . . . Something . . . "How—"

He was interrupted by a piercing shriek.

"We've got a live one off the starboard side!" one of the lookouts shouted.

"We'll talk about this later," Marcus said, pointing a finger at Teriana before returning to the main deck to join Servius, who was standing at the rail, a spyglass in his hand. His skin, normally a deep brown, was blanched pale.

"Shit," Servius muttered. "Shit."

"What is it?"

"Look for yourself."

Taking the glass, Marcus peered through, swearing under

his breath at what he saw. The vessel wasn't weathered like most of the others—was probably sailable. Or would be, if the corpses of the crew weren't all hanging from the rigging. Another shriek filled the air, and Marcus jumped despite himself as the corpses began to dance, their limbs tied to lines like rotting marionette dolls.

He panned the deck, searching for whoever was making that rutting-awful shrieking sound, his gut twisting as he caught sight of a naked man tugging on the lines with wild fervor. The sailor's skin was burned red and covered with lesions, and when he turned, the contents of Marcus's stomach threated to rise.

The man's face was covered with deep scratches, and his eyes were nothing more than bloody sockets.

"The Six protect us," Marcus heard one of the Maarin crew members mutter as they drew closer, everyone on deck taking a collective step back as the survivor leapt onto the railing and scuttled down the length like a deranged monkey, shrieking as he went.

Marcus's pulse roared in his ears, heart galloping in his chest even as his breath came in too-fast pants. "Someone get me a crossbow," he ordered.

The sailor must have heard his voice, because he paused in his progress around the ghost ship, sightless eyes turning in their direction. "Dance!" he screamed. "Dance, little puppets. Dance! Dance!"

Gibzen appeared at his arm with a crossbow, and Marcus jerked it out of his grip. Loading the weapon, he aimed it at the sailor.

"Long shot. Wait until we're closer," Gibzen muttered.

"No." Marcus let the bolt fly, swearing when it passed to the shrieking man's left.

"Dance! Dance! Dance!"

Sweat trickled down Marcus's back as he loaded another bolt, took a deep breath to steady himself, then let it loose.

It punched into the sailor's chest, knocking him back and onto the deck. A mortal wound, but he kept up his chant, somehow managing to catch hold of one of the lines, sending the corpses into a frenzy of motion. "Dance, little puppets! Dance!"

"Set it on fire," Marcus ordered. They were nearly alongside the other vessel now, only twenty yards between them, and his eyes skipped over the gore on the deck. Strange messages painted in blood and the damned sailor who just wouldn't shut up and die. "Burn it!"

Rattled or not, his men were trained, and in moments bolt tips wrapped with burning tar–soaked cloth were flying into the dry deck of the other ship. Into the mast. Into the sails, lighting them up like paper.

The *Quincense* passed the vessel by, but Marcus leaned over the rail to watch the other ship slowly turn into an inferno, sparing the rest of his fleet the sight. They had enough haunting their dreams.

As did he.

Darkness fell, and though it hid the ghost ships and the endless stretches of calm ocean from sight, that somehow made everything worse.

The red dust the Maarin used to mark the path glowed faintly, the effect otherworldly and strange, his men frequently stopping in their exercises to stare blankly at the crimson current, Gibzen and Servius hoarse from ordering them back to work. The brightly lit fleet trailed behind them, signal horns regularly sounding to ensure everyone was accounted for.

Through it all, the Maarin sang. Marcus could only pick out a few words, but the melody was haunting, the voices of the men and women echoing across the decks and out over the water.

Whether it was the light or the sound Marcus wasn't certain, but their presence seemed to wake the ghost ships floating in the darkness. Wails of agony and despair floated over the waters, cries for help and for mercy, but it was impossible to know exactly where they were coming from, and even if it were possible, there was nothing Marcus could do to help. The worst was the weeping of what sounded like a female voice, great ragged sobs that seemed to come from all directions and none, inescapable, making Marcus want to shove cotton into his ears. Knives into his ears. Anything to drown it out.

Sometime in the darkest hours before dawn, Teriana abandoned the helm to Yedda's care and approached him. "We'll be there by midafternoon," she said. "So I suppose we ought to discuss the specifics."

Sweat rolled down Marcus's back, his skin icy, and when a shriek echoed across the seas he jumped. "One does not," he said between his teeth, "*just* sail into a stem located a mile beneath the ocean surface."

"No," she replied. "One doesn't."

"You lied to me." He had no right to level accusations at her about truthfulness, but that bloody incessant weeping was fraying on his nerves. Turning to the sea, he muttered, "Would you shut up and die already!"

When he refocused on Teriana, she was staring at him with unease. "Keep it together, Marcus," she said. "The survival of my people depends on you being alive, so I really don't need you jumping overboard to silence the voices of ghosts."

The weeping was growing louder, hurting his ears. "How do we reach the xenthier?"

Wiping her hands against her trousers as if to clear them of sweat, she said, "Madoria needs to open up the seas for us to reach it."

His head was throbbing, each wail and shriek sending sharp jabs of pain into his skull. "You're going to ask a *god* to open the seas?"

"No." Teriana exhaled a long breath. "You are."

23

MARCUS

All sound had ceased.

As had all motion.

The fleet floated on still waters, nothing around them but the blue of ocean and sky, the sun sinking down toward the western horizon.

They were trapped.

Marcus sat on the steps to the quarterdeck, elbows resting on his knees and fragments of Teriana's explanation of how to reach the xenthier stem skittering through his mind. He couldn't seem to piece together what she'd said—it was though he were trying to remember something told to him years ago or something he'd heard in a barely understood language. Or something that made no sense at all.

He was meant to be paying attention, to be giving orders, but the words *demigod* and *blood ritual* kept repeating themselves over and over in his head as he stared out over the vast expanse of ocean.

He'd been wrong about Teriana. He'd believed she wouldn't do anything that would put her crew's lives at risk. But instead, in one fell swoop, she'd managed to defeat nearly ten thousand of the Empire's soldiers without lifting a single weapon. Because they were all dead men. Destined to succumb to madness, to tear one another apart in desperate attempts to survive a few days longer.

And when his men realized what had happened, they'd kill her first. Then probably him next.

"You all right?"

Marcus looked up to find Servius standing in front of him, and the sudden motion was just enough to tip his tenuous control. Shoving his friend out of the way, he staggered to the railing and proceeded to heave his guts into the sea.

"What's wrong with him?" Teriana's voice sounded distant.

"Seasick."

He could hear the two talking. Hear Servius giving the orders to batten down the hatches. More orders to send everyone not needed below. More tricks. She was planning something. An attack. Perhaps the Maarin had a way out and their plan was to kill the men aboard the *Quincense* and then leave the rest of the fleet here trapped.

Twisting around, he struggled to keep his balance. "Stop!" The legionnaire holding the signal flags gaped at him, and Marcus snatched one of the flags out of his hand and threw it to the deck. "This is a trap."

"What are you going on about?" Teriana demanded. "I'm doing what you asked and now you tell me to stop? Did you lose your mind along with the contents of your guts over the side of the ship?"

He tried to grab hold of her, but Servius's hand clamped down on his arm. "Marcus, what's going on?" he asked under his breath.

"She duped us." He tried to pull away, but Servius's grip was implacable. "There's no path—or if there is, she's got no intention of revealing it."

Servius turned to Teriana. "Is that true? Did you lie to us?"

Her eyes were a stormy grey. "I told him how to open the path—he just didn't like my answer."

"Lies!" Marcus jerked out of Servius's grasp and lunged at Teriana, but she scampered away. "She brought us here to trap us. To kill us." He stalked her across the deck, but he felt wild and unsteady with fury and misery. Why had it come to this? Why did everything have to end in death?

She tried to run to the railing, perhaps to leap overboard, but his men hemmed her in. He caught hold of her, knocking her to the deck and pinning her.

"I'm not lying!" she screamed, struggling against him. "I can prove it—give me the chance to prove it."

"Do you have any idea how badly they'll react when they find out you've doomed them?" he asked, letting his head drop so that he was whispering in her ear. "They're going to kill both of us. And it won't be an easy death. Not with these men."

"Marcus, don't do this," she pleaded. "I know you don't believe—I know you think what I'm telling you is pagan madness, but you must trust me. You'll see that I've told you the truth!"

Her words were dull noise in his ears. Everything had been for naught. He'd thought he could get away from Cassius, thought he could save his family, thought he could save himself. He'd put all his coins on one roll of the dice and lost. It was time to pay up.

"I'll do it now," he said, half to himself. "I'll make it quick, and by the time they know why, it will be too late to hurt you any more." The words were familiar, and her face blurred into that of a pale-skinned girl with inky dark hair.

Marcus started to reach for a blade, but the thought of cutting her made him sick, so he reached for her neck instead. "I'm sorry," he muttered. "I'm so sorry."

Then droplets of seawater were raining down on him. His skin prickled, and without loosening his grip on Teriana he turned his head.

And found himself face-to-face with a mouthful of teeth.

An enormous serpentine creature had risen out of the water and was looming over the deck, its eyes filled with wrath.

"Kill it!" Servius shouted, but before the men could respond, Marcus countered the order.

"Hold!"

"Magnius," Teriana whispered, and when Marcus looked down, her eyes were glassy and alien. "He wishes to speak with the one who would request passage."

Marcus yanked his hands away from her and the creature snapped his teeth once before sinking back into the water.

Scrambling to the railing, Marcus watched the sea serpent circle the ship, his gut filling with a primal fear.

"I'm never going in the water again," Servius said, blade in hand and face pale.

Teriana shouldered her way next to him, her face streaked with tears though her eyes were dry.

"Proof enough for you, Legatus?" she snapped. "This is Magnius, guardian to the *Quincense,* and scion of the goddess Madoria." She watched the water, head tilted as though listening to an unheard voice. "If you wish passage, it is he whom you must ask. Will you speak with him?"

"Yes." The word came out as barely more than a croak, and though it was madness, he repeated, "Yes. I'll speak to him."

He let her take the knife from his belt, knowing that she'd be within her right to stick it in his back. She pulled his left arm over the water and, without warning, sliced the blade across it. Blood and pain welled up from the gash, droplets raining down into the open mouth of the creature below.

Marcus felt the first droplet hit. Felt his mind snap open, invaded and expanded at the same time.

Who requests passage through the deeps?

Marcus swallowed hard. The voice was clear as day inside his head, but he could tell from the reactions around him that no one else had heard. Except for Teriana. Her expression was cold, her grip tight on the knife handle. "Well?"

"I do," he said quickly. Then louder: "I request passage."

His men looked at him in surprise, then exchanged worried glances with one another.

Silence.

"He wants your name." Teriana's voice was toneless.

He nodded once, watching the serpent swimming below. He could feel the creature in his head, and he suspected that he didn't need to speak aloud for Magnius to hear him. But the idea of such a conversation ran counter to everything he knew. "I am Marcus, legatus of Celendor's Thirty-Seventh Legion, and

I request passage from the . . ." His voice faltered. "From the goddess Madoria."

He could feel the eyes of his men upon him—feel their astonishment at his words. He could only hope their judgment would be tempered by the creature in the water before them.

I care not for titles and false names.

The blood rushed from his face, and Marcus clenched the rail. *How could it possibly know?* was the first question that came to mind, but he immediately dismissed it. This thing called Magnius was in his head—he knew what Marcus knew. The second thought was whether the creature would give away his secret. He glanced at Teriana—her brow was furrowed and he could see the question in her eyes.

"It is the only name I know. The other I gave up when I was given to the legions."

Lies. You keep part of it with you. The voice was loud enough to hurt. *Give me your name.*

He shook his head sharply. "No."

That is the price of passage.

Marcus ground his teeth, his mind racing. How was it that a name was capable of causing him so much grief? Gaius Domitius was the name he'd been born to—the name he'd been called for the first eight years of his life. But for the past twelve, everyone had called him Marcus. It was what his friends called him. It was the name his men chanted at every victory. It was who he was. Everyone who knew him as otherwise had forsaken him. But he had not forgotten.

Marcus straightened his shoulders. "I am Marcus Domitius, legatus of Celendor's Thirty-Seventh Legion, and I ask the goddess Madoria for passage." Some trick of the wind caught his voice, making it echo loud across the ship and sending it flying across the sea.

It will be done.

The serpent sank under the water, disappearing from sight. Marcus rounded on Teriana. "What happens now?"

Her face was pale and grim. "We do our part. Send everyone belowdecks."

"You heard her!" he shouted. "Everyone belowdecks!"

They obeyed, but he could see that they were looking at him with a new light. Would losing his anonymity change things? Would they treat him differently knowing that he was from one of the wealthiest and most influential families in all the Empire? He didn't know.

"You too," he said to Servius, who hadn't moved from his position at the rail.

Servius shook his head. "If you're losing your mind, I need to be here. But if what I think is happening is actually happening, then you need me here even more."

"Fine."

Teriana was shouting orders at her crew, who were all battening down the hatches. Polin rolled a massive drum onto the deck and fastened it down. He then proceeded to tie himself to the mainmast before calling Teriana's name.

She nodded once.

The cook began pounding on the drums, the beat rhythmic and urgent. And the Maarin began to chant. Marcus didn't know what they were saying, but there was no mistaking what their dark eyes and tight grips on ropes meant. It was going to be a rough ride.

Wind lashed across the deck, in a gust made more violent by its long absence, every one of the Maarin crew stopping what they were doing to exchange worried looks even as the sun disappeared behind clouds that were gathering and blackening with unnatural speed. Lightning flickered across the sky, followed seconds later with a roar of thunder that drowned out the chanting sailors. Marcus stared skyward, fixated on the circling clouds. What was happening? How was any of this possible?

"Bugger me cross-eyed," Servius whispered. "Look at that."

Marcus tracked the direction the big legionnaire was pointing.

The ocean was no longer still.

Like the swift current of a deep river, the sea was moving, and it was pulling the ship with it. It gathered speed, tugging the *Quincense* along until the wind of their passage rivaled that of the storm. Marcus's eyes stung as he tried to make out the other vessels against a sky that had grown black as night. From what he could tell, they were as caught up in the current as the Maarin ship. Turning his attention back to the ocean, he saw the water dip downwards, and he understood in an instant how the xenthier was reached.

A whirlpool.

The pace of the drumbeats increased.

Wrenching his gaze from the widening mouth in the sea, Marcus searched the deck for Teriana. She was crouched to the side of the helm, her eyes wide and hands gripping the railing. He shouted her name, but the wind drowned him out. Dodging chanting sailors, he sprinted across the deck and up the stairs, shaking her shoulder to get her attention.

"Something about this isn't right!" he shouted into her ear. "I can see it on your face!"

Teriana nodded. "The storm! Madoria has no influence over the weather. That is Gespurn's domain." She cast her face upward. "He doesn't want us to pass!"

Gespurn. The unfamiliar name rolled across Marcus's mind, and he knew she was referring to another god. Less than a quarter hour ago, his mind would have balked, but that seemed ignorant now. There were forces at work that he didn't understand—and if the Maarin wanted to give them names, so be it. "Can we stop it?"

She shook her head. "This is between the gods. We are at their mercy."

Lightning lanced across the sky, bolt after bolt illuminating the darkness as they struck the sea. The *Quincense* was closest to the mouth of the whirlpool, lower already than the rest of the ships. A charge filled the air, making his skin crawl. Lightning streaked toward the ship, but before it could strike, a column of water shot into the sky to meet it. The two collided with a thundering boom, and steam jetted in all directions. It happened over and over—the sky attacking the ships and the sea rising each time in their defense.

But one bolt struck home. Flames exploded from the rigging of one of the ships, and Marcus's stomach plummeted when he recognized it as Felix's. It was filled with Marcus's men—men he had brought here. Men who were caught in this whirlpool of storm and terror because of him. "Please, no," he said, the howling wind tearing away his words before anyone could hear them.

Or perhaps not.

A sheet of water rose next to the burning ship and slowly collapsed against her, extinguishing the flames. Thunder roared across the sky in a bellow of fury, and the clouds swirled and coalesced until an enormous face formed. The head turned, black eyes searching the seas until they latched on to the *Quincense*. A vortex of air formed a massive hand, and it reached for them, jostling the ship like a toy as it brushed the rigging.

A familiar shout filled the air. Servius was dangling from the rail, feet hanging over the deadly water. Marcus moved to help his friend, but the god's hand jarred the ship again, and he slipped and fell. "Servius!" he shouted. "Hold on!"

Then Jax was at the rail, hauling Servius back on the deck, the Maarin sailor holding the big legionnaire steady until he found a rope to hang onto, then turning to spit curses as the hand reached through the sails once again.

The *Quincense* circled faster, the whirlpool dragging them deeper into the sea. There was no way to escape the pull of the water. They were trapped by one god and about to be crushed by the fist of another.

Motion caught Marcus's attention. Teriana was standing, her face tilted to the sky, wind blowing her braids wildly. She shouted at the cloud god, but whatever she said was answered with a blast of thunder that rattled the rigging. The hand reached down and closed around her waist, lifting her off the deck.

"No!" Marcus lunged, catching one of Teriana's hands. But his weight made no difference to the god. Marcus's arm strained as he was lifted off the deck, and he barely managed to catch hold of the rail with his other hand. His body screamed as he was stretched between Teriana and the ship.

"You can't have her!" he shouted, but the wind only tore at his face, snatching away his breath. He tried to suck in another, but he might as well have tried to breathe in sand. His heart hammered, his fingers slipping. Then water crashed against them, and both he and Teriana fell hard against the deck.

Marcus didn't waste time recovering. Clambering onto hands and knees, he pulled Teriana upright. "Are you all right?"

She shook her head and pointed.

A figure formed of water had risen out of the sea and was engaged in battle with the cloud god. It . . . *she* swung a sword made of ice and carried a shield of the same. Lightning flew from the fist of the cloud god, and it smashed against her defenses, sending frozen chunks hurtling into the water.

Steam erupted from each blow, and a fragment of ice flew toward them. Marcus flung himself on top of Teriana. The ice slammed against the metal armor covering his shoulders and he collapsed against her. Her breath was hot and ragged against his cheek as he eased onto one forearm.

"How much longer?" he shouted into her ear.

She shoved him off and dragged him toward the side of the ship. It was hard to move, the circular force of their progress tugging them backward. Crawling, with fingers clawing against the boards of the deck, they finally made it. Marcus peered over the edge and into the twisting funnel of water below.

He could see it. The glittering crystal of a xenthier stem so many times larger than any he had seen that it seemed wrong to call it by the same name. It sucked the water resolutely downwards, and it would only be minutes until the ship reached it.

As he looked up, his guts twisted. They were farther below the surface of the ocean than he'd ever believed possible, the other ships arrayed like children's toys above them. In the midst of it all fought the two gods, air and water doing battle against each other.

The water goddess seemed to be holding her own when a funnel-shaped cloud descended, tearing her translucent shape apart. The cloud god surged past her, eyes black as the darkest night and hand growing in size as it reached toward the *Quincense*.

"Hold on!" Teriana screamed, and the xenthier reared in front of them. Marcus caught hold of her and dragged her down onto the deck; then all sight was washed away by brilliant and blinding white light.

24

TERIANA

Though she had passed through the ocean paths countless times, panic still took hold. Teriana felt nothing, not the planks beneath her knees, not Marcus's hands where she knew they gripped her shoulders. There was no sight, no sound, no smell. It was as though her body had ceased to exist and all that was left was her mind.

The ship shot out into the air, crashing down onto the surface of the sea with a spray of surf. Teriana's skin stung and burned with pins and needles. She blinked against the brilliance of the early-morning sun and shoved Marcus away from her. He appeared dazed, but only for a moment. Then he was on his feet.

"Sails up!" she shouted. "Get lines and boats ready. If any of the ships don't make it intact, we'll need to pick the survivors out of the water."

Her crew threw themselves into action, allowing Teriana to guide the ship out of the current the moment the sails caught the wind. The *Quincense* turned just as another ship came through the passage. She landed hard but intact, the crew frozen in shock, not moving from their handholds as the water jetting out of the xenthier carried them swiftly south. Another ship came through in much the same manner, then another and another.

"Do you know what's happening on the other side?" Marcus's voice was strained.

She shook her head.

"Does it . . . does Magnius know?"

She glanced at him out of the corner of her eye, trying to keep her attention on guiding the ship to where she would do most good. He was pale. She wondered if it was because he feared for the lives of his men or if it was because he feared his conquest was in jeopardy. "He hasn't crossed through. The path will close when he does."

Marcus nodded once. "Four left."

One of which was the vessel that had caught fire—the ship Elephant Ears was aboard.

"Everything will come through, no matter what state it's in," she said. "Get your men ready to fish survivors out of the water. Find the one with the flags and have him signal the others. Get them ready to do the same. The current will push everything in their direction."

What she didn't tell him was that if any of the ships had broken up, all they'd be fishing out of the sea were corpses. The impact of the water coming out of the xenthier combined with the weight of their armor was sure to drown all but the luckiest.

Two more ships arrived, both damaged by fire and listing badly. One wouldn't make it to shore. "Marcus!" she shouted. "That one needs to be off-loaded."

He bellowed orders at the sweating soldier frantically waving flags at the distant ships. Another man had a horn, and he was red faced and blowing more signals.

A loud crash signaled the arrival of another vessel, and Teriana swore when she saw the state the ship was in. It was Elephant Ears' monstrosity, the rigging destroyed by fire and the hull punctured by four large holes. Teriana suspected there was a fifth hole on the far side—one for the thumb of a giant fist.

The ship was already sinking when the last vessel flew out. She bounced once against the water; then the current caught her, sending her hurtling along at twice the speed of the sinking ship. None of the sailors were moving from the handholds they clung to, and nobody stood at the helm.

"Get their attention!" she screamed. "They need to steer around!"

Horns blared, but it was too late. The last ship collided with the bow of the sinking vessel with a deafening crash. Teriana watched in horror as the ship keeled over, spilling dozens of men into the churning waters.

Magnius, shut the path! She sent the thought out as a scream, praying he would hear. Then she hauled on the wheel and sent the *Quincense* into the fray. "Ready the longboats. Prepare to come alongside." She didn't dare lower the small craft until the path was closed. The sea was too rough—they'd be swamped. Coming alongside would be no small feat, either. She was as like to send the two ships colliding into each other, but there was no other option. The ship was sinking, and if she went down, four hundred lives would be lost. The deck of the other ship was full to capacity with men, and those still in the hold would be waist deep in water by now. As it was, not even half of them would fit on the *Quincense*. Another vessel, at least, would be needed, and as much as Teriana doubted her own ability to come alongside in the rough seas, she *knew* none of the Cel ships could do it.

Teriana sailed cautiously, knuckles white on the wheel as they approached. Elephant Ears was standing next to the captain, waving his hands and shouting orders. Soldiers were throwing barrels and planks of wood—anything that floated— to those struggling in the waves. The ship's longboats were lowering into the water where they'd be filled in seconds.

"Servius!" He was standing closest to the flag-wielding legionnaire. "Tell them not yet! It's too rough." Frustration filled his face, his eyes going to the men in the water. But he barked an order at the soldier, who immediately beat his flags through the air. Seconds later, the boats stopped their descent.

Close the path! Aloud she called, "Drop the sails!" It was all on her now. Sweat trickling down her back, she judged the rise and fall of the massive swells, turning the ship to slow her speed. Her crew dropped bumpers into place on the starboard side to lessen the impact and stood ready with hooks and lines. The other had sunk enough that her rail was only a few feet higher than that of the *Quincense*.

"Get ready!" Her ship rose on a swell, then slid down with irreversible speed, slamming against the doomed vessel. Wood splintered and cracked, and the impact knocked almost everyone off their feet. "Lines!" The ships pulled apart and then slammed together again. Her crew were on their feet in an instant, tossing hooks up to the larger ship and attempting to lash the vessels together as best they could.

Marcus shouted orders, and seconds later soldiers surged onto her ship in a surprisingly orderly tide. Their faces were pale and their jaws tense, yet their conditioning to obey held even now. But would it be enough to hold those who had to stay aboard and wait for another ship to arrive? If they swarmed the *Quincense,* she'd be swamped and they'd all drown. Even now, she could feel the ship slipping lower in the water from the growing weight of the legionnaires filling her already-full hold and crowding her decks.

"Marcus!" she called. "We need another ship. You get them all aboard and we'll go down."

He nodded grimly. Pushing through his men, he climbed on her rail and leapt onto the sinking ship.

"The Six help us," Teriana prayed, shutting her eyes for a heartbeat. "Madoria, keep us safe." Opening them again, she shouted Bait's name, searching for his face. He was up in the rigging. He pointed, and she saw the fleet had finally recovered from the shock of the whirlpool and was moving. One of the smaller ones was sailing in their direction, clearly looking to come along the port side. "Get in the water and help those you can!" He nodded and dived into the rough seas.

The tide of soldiers flowing onto her deck abruptly ceased and the lines holding the two ships together went slack. Instinct had her calling for her crew to raise sails, then turning the wheel so that the *Quincense* rotated away from the sinking vessel, but her attention was all for Marcus, who stood in the midst of the countless men still on the deck.

"You have to go back!"

Elephant Ears was pushing up the stairs toward her.

"He's still aboard!"

Teriana looked from the frantic tribunus to the very calm-looking legatus standing at the helm of the sinking ship. Marcus met her gaze and shook his head.

"Lower the longboats," she ordered, trying to force the tremble out of her voice with excessive volume. They'd drifted far enough away from the jetting xenthier tip that the waters were starting to calm, and Bait needed somewhere to put those he rescued.

"Are you listening to me?" Elephant Ears shouted, though he was right next to her now.

"He doesn't want us to go back," she snapped, moving the *Quincense* so she was out of the way but close enough to . . . Frankly, Teriana didn't know how being close would help at all. "Look, the other ship will be there in minutes."

Apparently that wasn't good enough. He shoved her hard, then grabbed the wheel.

Fury filled her. The idiot was going to get them all killed. Balling her fist, Teriana slugged him in the side of the face. It was his turn to fall back, but in an instant he came at her swinging. She leapt out of the way, the wheel jerking and rotating with no hands to steady it. "He knows what he's doing," she hissed. "We'd be going against his orders if we go back."

Felix hesitated. "What orders?"

"He needs us to get these men safely to shore. He ordered me to do it." The lie slipped easily from her lips. She gestured at the crowded deck. "Get as many below as you can so my crew has room to move."

His eyes narrowed to slits. "I don't trust you."

"I need him alive!" she shouted, her frustration chasing away her fear. "He's the one my agreement is with. He's the only one who can give me back my mum. Last thing I want is for anything to happen to him." Her words echoed over the ship, and the men crammed amidst all the gear on deck looked up. The pathway had closed, the sudden silence more noticeable than the roar of the jetting seawater had been. The waves instantly calmed, but not in time to soften the impact between the incoming ship and the sinking one.

A dull groan and the sharp sound of snapping timber washed over them as the massive ship keeled over, the four holes on the starboard side plunging under the swells. Most of the men managed to find a handhold, but several slipped into the water before the ship righted itself, several feet lower and sinking fast.

"The Seventh take you, you incompetent Cel idiots!" Teriana shouted, her heart hammering in her chest. They only had minutes before the ship went down, and it looked to her as though Marcus intended to be the last man off.

They were moving fast, clambering onto the rails and leaping to grasp the arms of their friends, but there were so many of them. She didn't see how they would all make it in time.

Bait had rescued those who had fallen into the water, but the longboats were full to the brim, men forced to cling to the edges. They wouldn't be much help if the ship went down with soldiers still on board.

They were lifting one another up now, standing on shoulders in order to reach hanging ropes and reaching hands. Marcus was in the thick of it, helping his men and shaking his head whenever one of them tried to get him to go. *Has he lost his mind?* Teriana abandoned the wheel to Yedda's capable hands, elbowing Elephant Ears so he would make room at the rail.

"Damn it, Marcus, you blasted brave fool," she heard the tribunus whisper. They stood together in silence, unable to do anything but watch and wait.

It happened quickly. One minute, the deck was above water; the next, the stern was beneath the surface, tipping the bow upward at an increasingly sharp angle. Teriana clenched her fists, unable to look away from the few remaining men hauling themselves up the deck until they were high enough to reach the rail of the other ship.

Then Marcus was the only one left aboard. The ship bobbed

once, then sank like a stone. He jumped, catching the hand of a legionnaire leaning far over the railing.

Not just any legionnaire: it was Titus, Cassius's son.

Marcus dangled in the air for an instant, and then he was falling. His feet hit the disappearing bow; then man and ship were sucked beneath the waves.

Teriana reacted without thinking. Leaping onto the rail, she took a deep breath and dived off the edge.

The suction of the sinking vessel pulled her into the depths. She couldn't see anything through the bubbles rising from the ship, but then they cleared, revealing Marcus trying to free his foot from where it had tangled in some rigging. She kicked hard, but the ship was heavier, her momentum lost. She was going to lose him to the sea, and with him, any chance of freeing her captive people.

A dark shape brushed against her. Magnius. She caught hold of his dorsal spike and they plunged, her ears popping. *Faster,* she thought. *Faster.* Then they were upon the ship.

Marcus's struggles had the frantic edge of one almost out of air, and when Teriana caught his wrist he tried to pull away. Then their eyes locked, and with one mighty thrash of his tail Magnius pulled Marcus free and dragged them toward the surface.

Teriana's chest burned, and if she needed air this badly, Marcus needed it more. The sun grew brighter and brighter, but his grip was weakening.

Hold on!

Then they shot into the air, Magnius rising out of the water in a massive breach. Both she and Marcus lost their grips, but Teriana sucked in a mouthful of air before she hit the water.

Marcus sank, and she caught hold of him, kicking hard and dragging them both up until their heads broke the surface. He coughed and choked, and it was everything she could do to keep him afloat until Magnius swam under, lifting them onto his broad back. She held Marcus in place while he gasped in air, the guardian swimming in lazy circles around the ship.

"You going to live?" she asked once he finished coughing.

"Yes." His voice was hoarse. He rolled onto one elbow, and she gave him a dark little smile when he realized exactly what he was lying on and froze.

"Don't fall off."

His eyes widened. "Would he . . . ?"

"Been known to happen, though you're a bit skinny for his tastes."

One of Marcus's eyebrows rose. "I prefer the term *lean*."

"You shouldn't have told me that."

Against all odds, he laughed. He had a good laugh, she concluded, watching his shoulders shake. It made him look less like the ruthless killer she knew him to be. It didn't last.

"You saved my life," he said, ignoring the ropes his men tossed down from the *Quincense*.

Teriana stared at the water, unable to meet his gaze. "I need you alive," she muttered. "Let's just say, I'm not all that confident that Titus will pick up your end of the bargain should you meet an untimely end."

"It might've been an accident."

She spit into the water. "If you're that big an idiot, then you deserve to be sitting at the bottom of the sea."

"I didn't say I didn't think it was on purpose," Marcus replied, absently picking a splinter out of his ankle. "Only that I can't prove it. Which means I can't *do* anything about it."

"Suppose that means I'll have to watch your back if I ever want to see my mum again."

The corner of his mouth turned up. "I suppose it does." They circled the stern of the ship and he reached for one of the dangling ropes, but she caught his hand and tugged it away.

Kneeling on Magnius's back, she pointed off in the distance to the haze darkening the horizon. Marcus held up a hand to shade his vision, and his lips parted with a soft sound of astonishment. "Is that it?"

She nodded, hoping, praying, that she knew what she was getting into. "Welcome to the Dark Shores."

25

TERIANA

If Legatus Marcus of the Thirty-Seventh was troubled by his near brush with death or the manifestation of gods, he did not show it as he calmly delivered orders from the quarterdeck of her ship. Blood dripped down the side of his ankle and from the knife wound on his arm, but he'd refused offers to have the injuries bandaged in favor of taking reports, pausing from time to time to examine the nearing coastline with a spyglass.

He has a plan in mind, Teriana thought to herself. Then again, so did she.

It was a balancing act. A fine line she needed to walk between helping them enough to fulfill her half of the bargain and sabotaging their conquest. Between saving her people and sacrificing the West to the Cel scourge.

The xenthier stem was off the eastern coast of the midpoint of the Southern Continent, which was both vast and diversely populated. Her crew had been of a mind that she trick Marcus into landing the fleet in Gamdesh. There they would most certainly be crushed by the Sultan's armies, which were large, well trained, and commanded by the Sultan's god-marked daughter, who was known to be one of the finest generals of the West. Yet as tempting as such a proposition was, it was unlikely to incite Marcus to write the letter Teriana needed saying she'd upheld her end of the bargain.

Such a letter was a more certain thing if she took them to the far south of the continent to the peaceful plains of Katamarca, which was full of farmers, not warriors. Most of the god-marked living there were blessed by Yara, who would do them little good against two Cel legions. Landing them there would ensure the West would never be rid of them.

There were other options she could've guided Marcus toward, each with their pros and cons, but it still required a choice on her part. Which nation would she throw to the sharks? In the end, it had been Arinoquia.

"Jungle," Marcus muttered, lowering the spyglass. The water soaking his tunic had long since dried in the hot sun, and the stiffened straps of his armor creaked when he moved.

"That's what I told you," she said, praying her voice betrayed none of her concerns. "If we go north, it's mangroves, and the plains are four days' sail to the south."

"Assuming all that you've told me is true, this is precisely where I wish to be."

Marcus had barely spoken to her after she'd told him about how to reach the xenthier, but prior to that he'd questioned her about the thousand miles of coastline, no detail seeming too small to escape his notice. Size of villages and cities, the nature of their fortifications, and their military strengths. Descriptions of the landscape and vegetation. Understanding of trade and commerce and politics.

But mostly he was interested in strife. Conflict. War.

And she supposed that made a certain sort of sense. What better place to strike than one he believed already weakened by years of infighting? One that could be wiped out easily and a stronghold established.

"I'd be a fool to lie," she said, then shouted an order to lower a sail. The *Quincense* sat low in the water, and the last thing she needed was to bottom out her ship. Her crew members were still rattled by the manifestation of Madoria and Gespurn—the gods did their work through those they gifted with god marks, and it had been longer than living memory since one had stepped onto the mortal plane in such a grand display. It was not lost on Teriana that it had been *her* choices that had motivated those manifestations, but she kept forcibly shoving the thought from her head, because to do otherwise would render her a weeping mess on the deck. "Me lying would give you a reason to renege on our bargain. I'm not that stupid."

And she hadn't lied. At least, not overtly. A generation ago, the coast of Arinoquia had been conquered by invaders from an island off the southern tip of the continent, the majority of those native to Arinoquia retreating inland to the Uncharted Lands, where they presumably remained, though no one ever saw them.

With the loss of the unifying force of war, the conquerors had broken back into their familial clans—and fallen back into old rivalries. Eventually, one of the clans ruled by a man named Urcon had taken control of the region and claimed himself the ruler of all of Arinoquia, establishing his base of power in the ancient city of Aracam.

When she'd described Arinoquia to Marcus, Teriana had told the truth: that the region was engaged in continual back-and-forth raids between rebellious clans and Urcon's vicious militia. What she hadn't told him was that the clan members, men and women, were as competent with weapons as they were with fishing poles, and that rather than being weakened by the years of strife, the region had grown more militant. She'd not warned him this would be no easy conquest, but then again, he hadn't asked her opinion.

"That's the town?" He gestured with the spyglass toward the cove north of that in which she intended to anchor.

"Village," she muttered. "It's small—fewer than a hundred people—just as you asked."

All the cities on the coast of Arinoquia were walled fortresses, but Marcus had requested a rural landing point, despite the impracticalities of off-loading an entire fleet without a proper harbor. Mining her memory of the coast, Teriana had come up with this place, remembering the *Quincense* having stopped at this particular village to trade when she was younger.

The wooden buildings and singular dock were only barely visible, but she was certain she could see motion on the beaches.

Run! she wanted to scream at them. They'd have seen the fleet by now, and it wouldn't take them long to pack what they needed and melt into the jungle. Warning would spread up and down the coast, and by the time the Cel had unloaded their ships and gotten themselves settled they'd find themselves pitted against not a singular village, but the united force of an entire clan's warriors. Better yet, if the legions ventured into the jungles, they'd find themselves pitted against something far worse than staff or steel, for the Uncharted Lands were the god Lern's domain and there was a reason Urcon and the rest of the invading clans had never pressed very far inland.

The cove drew closer, the turquoise water and white beach idyllic and lovely. Well suited for a bonfire and rum and stories passed around until the sun lit the East. Not this. Teriana bit her lip, then ordered the last sail dropped as she listened to her crew call the depths. The ship drifted in, and a rocky outcropping obscured her view of the village. But it didn't matter; they'd still see the rest of the ships and know what it meant.

"Drop the anchor," she shouted, and a second later Marcus lifted his hand and his men surged into action. The centurion Gibzen barked commands at a group of soldiers who were armed to the teeth. And, with no regard for the fact that this was *her* ship, ordered the longboats dropped. Within seconds of them hitting the water, the men were clambering down ladders and rowing hard for shore.

Row as fast as you like, she thought. *They'll be long gone by the time you get there.*

"Securing the beach?" she asked, leaning against the helm.

"Taking the village."

His voice was calm and confident, and it took a great deal of willpower to keep a smile off her face. Then the ship pulled against the anchor and turned. Shock hit her like a bucket of water to the face at the sight of the empty sea behind them. Snatching her own spyglass, Teriana scanned the horizon, and the fleet leapt into view, much too distant for the naked eye to make out from shore.

"What are they . . . ," she started to say, then broke off, watching her crew tie down the sails. Blue sails marking the *Quincense* as a Maarin ship.

The longboats had reached the beach, the legionnaires leaping into the water and running toward the jungle and the unsuspecting village. The Maarin brought trade, not violence, and the men of the Thirty-Seventh would catch them completely unaware. And there was nothing she could do to stop the soldiers. The villagers would be slaughtered, and it would be all her fault.

"They're waiting for my signal," Marcus said, starting toward the stairs. He hesitated upon reaching them and glanced over his shoulder at her. "This is what we do, Teriana." For a moment, it appeared as though he might say more, but then he strode down the steps and into the organized chaos of men off-loading her ship.

"Well, that didn't go nearly as badly as I expected." Yedda came up the steps two at a time, her agility belying her age.

"They've gone to take the village."

The old sailor shrugged. "What did you expect them to do? Lie down in ranks on the beach and sun themselves?" She smiled. "Though wouldn't that be a sight to behold."

"Quit making jokes!" Teriana rounded on her, hands balling into fists. "None of this would've happened if I hadn't told our secrets to Lydia. I've brought war to these shores. People are going to die because of what I've done." She flung a hand in the direction of the neighboring cove. "Won't be long until we hear their screams, and I might as well be the one slitting their throats."

Yedda's smile fell away. "'I, I, I,'" she snapped, reaching out with one hand and flicking a finger between Teriana's eyebrows. "What conceit to think you single-handedly managed this feat. The crew sailed the ship because the alternative was joining our kin on the gallows. That one"—she pointed a finger at Marcus—"requested passage through the deeps, which Magnius granted. And Madoria defended the fleet when by all rights Gespurn would've seen the lot of us at the bottom of the sea. Nearly all you've done is whine and complain and antagonize the boy leading this mad venture."

"He's not a boy," Teriana grumbled, not knowing why she felt the need to clarify her opinion on *that* matter. "And I don't recall any of you jumping in to save his heavy Cel self."

"But instead of capitalizing on the goodwill you earned, you're weeping in a corner like a child deprived of a toy all because everything is happening like you *should've* expected it to."

Teriana glared at her, knowing Yedda was right but hating to admit it. "What do you suggest?"

"You're supposed to be finding out what they're planning."

"You think I haven't tried?"

Yedda rolled her eyes and shook her head. "Ever stop to think you might be going about it the wrong way?"

Teriana exhaled slowly, trying to keep the anger bubbling in her guts from boiling over. She knew what the woman meant, but the idea of . . . *ingratiating* herself with her captors was disgusting. Only not trying to do what she could to stop them was worse.

Turning on her heel, she started for the stairs, but Yedda's voice stopped her. "Teriana, you're a pretty girl. And"—she gestured at the sea of legionnaires below them—"you don't have much in the way of female competition. Mind the way you go about doing things."

Teriana opened her mouth to snarl at the advice but then snapped her teeth shut, realizing it wasn't a suggestion. It was a warning.

Down on the deck, she dodged men and supplies, making her way to where Servius directed the process. Not that much direction seemed to be required.

"That was something," he said, slapping her across the shoulders hard enough that she staggered. "Wouldn't have believed it if I hadn't seen it with my own two eyes. I've used the paths a time or two, but it was nothing like that. Felt spun around like a top. Who were they?"

"Gods," Teriana replied, peering around him at Marcus, who stood watching the proceedings while his servant polished his armor and fastened a crimson and gold cloak to his shoulders. As though sensing her gaze, he glanced in her direction, and their eyes met for an instant before a group of soldiers carrying barrels walked between them.

"Gods." Servius rubbed his chin. "The Senate hang me for paganism, but seems as good a term as any. Gods . . ."

"So what's the plan?"

"Will take the rest of the day to off-load the ships and set up camp. There will be injured who need tending, and we'll need to do a roll call to see who was lost."

"Right." She scratched at her healing fingers. "And after?"

Servius regarded her with silent scrutiny. "These are questions better directed to the legatus."

"Oh, aye. I know. But he's busy getting prettied up." She bit her tongue, remembering Yedda's words and wishing she could take back the sarcasm.

He laughed. "Sometimes it's important to look the part. Speaking of Marcus . . ." He lowered his voice and Teriana leaned in to hear him over the noise. "Bastard's too proud to thank you for saving his arse, so I'll do it for him: we owe you. This legion would follow him to the ends of Reath and back, and by nightfall there won't be a one of them who doesn't know you saved his life. And the lives of all the men on that ship."

Not a bastard, she thought, remembering the admission Magnius had requested in exchange for passage. Marcus Domitius, a son of one of the most powerful families in the Empire. She'd no doubt that *that* information would spread just as quickly, and she wondered if it would make a difference to the men. She considered asking Servius whether he'd known, but then thought better of it. "If he was killed, Titus would take command?"

Servius's face darkened, confirming that he'd witnessed what the other man had done. "He'd try."

"That's what I thought," she said, nodding as though she'd time for such complex thinking before diving into the water. "Seems to me that Marcus is the lesser evil."

"I'll take that as a compliment."

Spinning round, Teriana found the man in question behind her, armor gleaming in the sunlight. Before she could respond, a horn sounded, filling the air with its mournful wail. It came from the direction of the fishing village, and her heart sank.

"Call in the other ships," he ordered, then gestured to the rope ladder hanging from the rail. "After you."

"Where we going?" she asked, noting that the longboat was already full of grim-faced soldiers.

"The village."

A foul taste rose in the back of her throat. "What do you need me for?"

"Our agreement was that you would advise me. That means you go where I go. So quit dallying and get in the boat."

It was only fair. She'd sacrificed the village, so she deserved to see the consequences. Grasping hold of ropes, she swung over the edge and clambered down with practiced ease, landing with barely a thud among the men. Marcus followed, the wind catching at his cloak and making the sinuous creature picked out in gold seem almost alive. He set the boat to rocking as he landed, then went to the fore and sat. "Row."

Relying more on strength than skill, the two men at the oars drove them through the waves. The boat rose and fell, slapping against the water, but Teriana refused to look up, staring instead at the knees of the soldier facing her. At the fine hairs on his tanned legs. At the strips of metal-plated leather hanging like a strange skirt from his waist, and the heavy sandals strapped to feet callused from a lifetime of walking.

She knew they'd rounded the point when the rowers' breathing eased and the boat launched forward with every wave, but still she did not look up. A waft of woodsmoke tickled her nostrils, and sweat broke out on her skin. *Would this be another Chersome?*

Teriana had seen men and women dead from battle before—had killed a few herself. But they'd all been fighters who knew what they were getting into, not innocent fishermen. Not children.

Silently, she prayed for the oars to break. For a wave to swamp the boat. For the tide to miraculously turn and pull them out to sea. Anything that would delay the inevitable horror that awaited on the beach.

None of the gods answered her prayers. The boat slid onto the sand, and the men leapt out, dragging it farther ashore.

"Teriana." Marcus's voice was inflectionless, but there was no mistaking it for anything other than an order. *Get out of the boat.*

The smell of smoke was stronger now. She did not want to see. She did not want to know. But she had no choice.

Clenching her teeth, Teriana looked up.

26

MARCUS

The lesser evil . . . Teriana's words sat heavy in Marcus's mind as his men rowed around the point and into the impossibly blue cove containing their initial target.

Evil. Evil. There was something about the word and its meaning. Not just doing foul deeds, but delighting in their doing. And the way she'd said it. Not as an insult, but as a statement of fact.

And yet she'd risked her life to save his. Staring at the clear waters, he remembered the drag of the ship pulling him down and down, the futility of his struggle. The pressure growing in his chest, the desperate need to breathe that had haunted him his entire life. And then the feel of her hand closing around his wrist, pulling him toward salvation.

What did it say about her that she would save evil's life?

Marcus forced the thoughts from his mind. Turning, he examined the motionless village. The wooden homes were unlike anything he'd seen before. Elaborate two-story structures built up off the ground with stone pilings, they had bridges made of carved wood running between them, both design choices indicating they frequently experienced storm surge or flooding. The windows of the homes were made of colored glass with shutters to protect them from the elements, the roofs meticulously shingled with rectangles of what looked like tree bark, the overhang wide and clearly intended to protect the narrow balconies that encircled the homes at bridge level.

Small, well-made fishing boats littered the beach, with a few larger tied up to a floating dock that could be pulled ashore during storms. Behind the village, the jungle reared green and dark, teeming with life.

Acid burned in his belly as a wave swept them onto the

beach. This strategy was tried and true, but it had failed him before. With disastrous consequences.

Chersome is a world away, he reminded himself. *This place will be different.*

The boat hit the beach, and Marcus jumped out, feeling the need to have solid ground beneath his feet. His sandals sank into the cold, wet sand, and for a second he stood still. A whole continent to explore, and they were the first Cel to step foot upon its shores. If he'd had his choice, Marcus would've dropped his weapons and started walking. Up one coast and down the other; walking until he'd seen all there was to see and finally found a place where he wanted to sit still. But that wasn't the reason the Senate had sent him, and his men were relying upon him to keep them alive in this new world.

"Sir?" One of his men spoke softly from behind, and Marcus turned to find Teriana still sitting in the boat, head lowered and hands resting on her knees. He waited and when she did not move said her name once.

She looked up, and he nearly recoiled at the dark pools that were her eyes. He'd seen them this color before, but they'd always been stormy, turbulent seas of anger, not the still reflections they were now. His skin prickled cold despite the intense heat as he watched her pan the sand, the tightening of her jaw unwarranted by the empty beach.

"Let's get this over with," he said, turning back to the village.

The jungle had gone eerily silent on their approach, the tree branches motionless as though whatever lurked within was watching. They worked their way between the pilings holding up the homes, the network of bridges and balconies a good ten feet off the ground, accessible only via ladders that could easily be pulled up if the village came under attack. Reaching out with one hand, Marcus ran his fingers down one such ladder, holding up his hand to examine the waxy coating, which smelled faintly like sap.

"Comes from a tree," Teriana muttered. "Doesn't burn. The buildings are all coated in it."

Clever, Marcus thought, wiping his hand on his tunic, his eyes drinking in every detail. The laundry hanging from a line. A ball sitting in a puddle as though those who'd been playing with it had stopped midgame. The scent of fish from the latest catch. There was something haunting in the familiarity of it, as though, despite the difference in the landscape and architecture, he could've been walking through a coastal village back in Celendor.

They passed signs of struggle in the mud. A spilled basket of fruit. From above, his nose caught the scent of burning bread, and he gestured to one of his men to deal with it before they had a fire on their hands. But nowhere were there signs indicating that anything had gone other than according to plan.

The mournful wail of an infant pierced the air, and Marcus heard Teriana's sharp intake of breath. *She's afraid.* Then they rounded a corner and stepped into an open space encircled by seven different shrines.

The men he'd dispatched formed a perimeter, weapons out but lowered; in their midst sat around fifty villagers with tanned skin and fair hair, eyes of every color staring back at him. Most of the men and women wore loose trousers that were cuffed just below the knee, with shirts tucked into wide belts made of what looked like snakeskin. The fabrics were loose weaves dyed mostly dark brown and green, and most wore sandals made of leather and rope. A pile of their weapons sat out of reach, blades and bows and spears, the metal gleaming and sharp. *Not just villagers,* he amended. *Warriors.*

"They did not resist, sir," Gibzen said, then lifted a shoulder. "As usual, your gambit worked."

One of the villagers, a tall blonde woman whose eye was swelling shut, rose to her feet. Her knuckles were split and bleeding, and Marcus wondered which of his men she'd gotten a piece of. She shouted something, and he didn't need Teriana to translate to know what it was.

But that didn't stop Teriana from rounding on him. "Where are their gods-damned children, Marcus?"

All across the Empire, Marcus had witnessed the way small coastal towns and villages responded to the arrival of a Maarin ship. The way the children would run down to the beach, dancing in anticipation of the crew's arrival, the Maarin not only bringing goods from far-off places, but also notoriously kind and generous to children. And the parents always let them go, because they knew their children would be safe. That the Maarin could be trusted. They were on the far side of the world, but it seemed in this regard, things were the same.

"On the beach in the neighboring cove," he answered. "Under the care of the Maarin and my men. They won't be harmed." And having them there meant they wouldn't be underfoot if his gambit went sideways.

Servius had been under orders to take Yedda and Polin to shore to manage the village children, Marcus banking on the Maarin sailors' ability to communicate with the children and keep them calm. Just as he'd banked on this village of warriors surrendering without a fight when his men arrived shouting the words, "Stand down! Your children won't be harmed" in Trader's Tongue, a language the Maarin had done a fair job spreading across all of Reath.

Children changed things.

The same people who'd die a thousand painful deaths to defend them would shy away from anything that risked them. It was one of the innumerable reasons that the Empire's legionnaires weren't permitted any relationships outside of the legion. Children and family were a weakness he and his men weren't allowed to have.

"How could you?" Teriana hissed. "Is there anything you won't do?"

There were plenty of things he wouldn't do, including harming children, which meant Marcus had always needed to find creative methods to accomplish the same ends his peers did with violence. Smarter methods. Half of his campaign strategies were built around understanding the ways the minds of people worked and how to manipulate them. And he'd learned long ago that the imagination bred fiercer fears than reality ever could. "Tell them their children are unharmed, Teriana, or we are going to have a fight on our hands."

She said some words, and the fear diminished from the group's eyes, replaced with anger as they realized he'd tricked them. Before that anger had a chance to grow, Marcus said, "Teriana, find out who their leader is."

Her speech was stilted, but she managed to get her point across, and the villagers moved to clear a path for a grey-haired man with a long scar bisecting one eyeless socket, the other a shade of amber Marcus had never seen before. The man said something to Teriana, to which she gave a discomforted shrug before turning to Marcus. "The Arinoquians are broken into seven clans, which are lead by—" She broke off, frowning as she searched for the Cel translation of a word. *"Imperators."*

It was an old Cel title no longer in use, primarily because an individual who held it would appear to contest the power of the Senate, but Marcus understood what it meant. A leader who was a commander, as though each clan were an army. That Teriana had chosen to translate the Arinoquian title as such told him a great deal.

"These people's imperator lives in a town north of here, but this man, Flacre, will speak on behalf of her."

Marcus repeated the name in his head, committing it to memory. "What did he ask you?"

"When Maarin ships started taking passengers."

It was unfortunate that the ruse would only work this once. Which meant Marcus needed to make it count. "I want you to translate what I say precisely, no embellishment."

"Go slowly," she muttered. "I'm out of practice."

"I am Legatus Marcus, supreme commander of the Thirty-Seventh and Forty-First Legions of the Celendor Empire. We have been sent across the seas by our leaders for the purposes of exploration and the establishment of trade."

Teriana's chin twitched with the obvious effort it took not

to interject her own views into the conversation. This was why he hated using translators—that she was an opinionated sailor with her own agenda only made matters worse. Scowling, she rattled off a string of words and then crossed her arms.

The man's eyebrows rose even as he gestured toward the sea in disbelief before responding.

Teriana gave an exasperated sigh. "He doesn't believe it. They think there is nothing but ocean."

"They, as in this village, or they, as in everyone living in the West?"

Her jaw tightened. "Everyone."

Interesting. It made a certain sense that the Maarin had kept the existence of the Dark Shores a secret from the Empire, but their motivations for being equally unforthcoming with those of the West were less clear. It implied that the Maarin kept to themselves across all of Reath, and it suggested to him that that their relationship with the governing bodies of the various realms was likely as limited as it was with the Senate. And if the rest of the people of the Dark Shores were as disbelieving of the existence of the Empire as this fellow, it would only be to Marcus's advantage: what doesn't exist isn't a threat.

"Tell him we were equally unaware of the existence of these shores until recently, but having learned about them from the Maarin, we desire to foster trade relations between our people."

She translated his words, the length of time she took to do so suggesting she was adding a bit more color than Marcus would like.

Flacre's brow furrowed, and he eyed Marcus for a long moment before responding.

"He says you don't look like merchants—that you look like an army set on taking what you want."

"Does he think that because you suggested as much?"

She rolled her eyes and shook her head. "It's because he's neither blind nor an idiot."

"Invader," Flacre said in accented Trader's Tongue.

"He called you—"

"I know what he called me," Marcus interrupted. "Do they speak Trader's Tongue fluently?"

"The language is called Mudamorian, and most of them would only speak a bit of it. You got lucky on that one with your little bit of trickery."

Marcus bit the insides of his cheeks, thinking. "Tell him we've no intention of bringing violence to this village unless they invite it upon themselves. That our army has been sent because to send unarmed merchants into foreign lands would put their lives unnecessarily at risk."

Waiting for Teriana to translate, he then added, "We've been told that this region is made dangerous by the imperator Urcon, who uses force to extort wealth from the clans of this region, setting himself up as a false king. We've been told that many clans, including yours, are actively resisting his rule."

He didn't need Teriana to translate the old man's response to know that her description of the situation in the region had been squarely on target. Flacre spit into the dirt when Teriana finished speaking, then spouted a string of what Marcus suspected were curses.

"Urcon is worse than an unchecked plague upon the people. He . . ." Teriana trailed off, her frown deepening as she posed a question to Flacre and listened to his response, her gaze flicking briefly to one of the shrines, which was made from black stone. "He takes the children of those who can't pay."

Cordelia's words echoed through Marcus's head: *Cassius plans to take the fourth sons of families who can't afford to pay.* "For what purpose?"

"No one knows. They're never seen again."

Marcus nodded grimly, suspecting the children were probably sold in some capacity. Or worse. His having used their children against them, given the circumstances, was a dark mark that would take time to fade. But what was done was done. "Such a ruler is not conducive to peaceful trade between nations.

We would like to propose an alliance with your clan to put an end to his practices. And to him."

"The last thing you want is an alliance," Teriana hissed under her breath.

"Do not presume to know what I do and do not want," Marcus replied. "Now translate."

The villagers stared silently at him after Teriana repeated his words, and then a flurry of whispers filled the air. Flacre spoke.

"What would be the terms of such an alliance?"

"We are newcomers to this land, and we need the advice of those who know it well," he said. "We need supplies and guides and liaisons, and we have the means to compensate you and your people, if you are willing to provide those things to us. Part of that compensation will be that we provide the army needed to remove Urcon."

Someone in the group shouted something, the rest nodding in agreement. "We don't need an alliance with a foreign army to fight our battles."

A statement that was probably true, but for this strategy to work, Marcus needed to convince them otherwise. He needed to convince the Arinoquians that they needed the legions, when in truth, it was quite the opposite.

Lifting his arms in a shrug, Marcus said, "I believe you are capable, but how long will it take? How many of your people will die fighting against Urcon's mercenary army? How many of your children will grow up without parents? How many of your children will grow up only to pick up the swords of their fallen family members to keep fighting the same fight?"

Servius arrived at that moment in the company of Yedda, Polin, and perhaps two dozen children, who immediately rushed to their parents' sides as Teriana translated.

"You can fight this war alone for years," he continued, once they had settled. "Or you can ally with us and end it in a matter of weeks."

Whispers once again stole through the group, heated debates breaking out between individuals as they considered the offer.

Considered their options. Considered the consequences of saying no. And as they did, Marcus considered his own knowledge of rebellion.

He'd been trained to quell it, but that training had driven him to seek a deeper understanding of what it took to drive people to fight back against a power greater than their own. What it took to force people to risk *everything* they cared for at chance for something better. And often he'd wondered what it would take the Senate doing to push those living under the Empire's rule to fling themselves against legions like his. What it would be like for Celendorian civilians to take up arms against armies of men who'd been trained to fight all their lives, armies of men who had nothing they loved to protect. Armies of men who had nothing but their own lives left to lose, which they would if they didn't fight.

Finally, Flacre responded, but his tone was one of someone who is unconvinced.

"He says that even if they agree to such an alliance, what you propose to do is impossible with only one, umm—" She coughed. "—commandeered Maarin ship full of men."

"Of course not," Marcus said, silently wondering if he *could*. "But fortunately, we don't have to."

Nodding at the soldier holding the signal horn, he waited for the series of notes the man blew to signal flagmen on the *Quincense* and then turned to the ocean.

In the distance, but clearly visible to the naked eye, was his fleet flying toward the coast. And with the uncanny timing of a well-orchestrated plan, massive crimson banners unfurled from each of the ships nearly as one. He looked back at Flacre and the Arinoquians behind him. "We can tear this tyrant from power," he said. "And we will."

27

TERIANA

Teriana's feet felt like blocks of lead as she trudged back to camp, the soldiers loosely arrayed around her not looking half as tired despite the fact that they'd done twice as much work. Which was saying something, because she couldn't remember the last time she'd been hustled so hard.

The Cel were merciless in their efficiency. The pair of engineers had immediately enlisted her to translate their conversation with Flacre, muttering between themselves and scribbling drawings and calculations on scraps of paper before setting off to the beach to begin construction of a pier capable of servicing the fleet. Next was an officer of some sort who requested she translate as he and Flacre determined certain laws both the legion and the village would be held to, along with the punishments for transgressions. She'd hoped the Cel demands would be egregious, but instead they'd been disappointingly reasonable and Flacre had only nodded in agreement. Then she'd spent several hours negotiating the purchase of supplies, primarily fish, for which another Cel officer had paid in unmarked silver without argument. Then it was back with the engineers, where she was set to explaining to the villagers they'd enlisted how they were to assist with the construction and how much they'd be paid for their efforts. Which was all to say that she'd had no time to strategize and certainly no opportunity to plant seeds in the villagers' minds that the Cel were not as they seemed.

It would have all been much easier if Yedda and Polin had remained with her in the village, but Marcus had taken them back to the *Quincense,* allowing Polin only the length of time it took to check Teriana's healing fingers.

"Be mindful you keep these clean," the cook muttered, his big hands gentle on hers as he eyed her healing fingernail beds, which itched like the fires of the underworld. "And be mindful what you tell the Arinoquians. Especially when *he's* in earshot." Rubbing salve onto her fingers, he added, "That boy's got the knack for language, so you won't be slipping things past him for long. And if he catches you saying something you shouldn't . . ." Polin shook his head. "Don't get caught."

"I won't."

"It should be one of us older folk taking on this burden. Isn't right that it be you."

"I'm the captain," Teriana replied. "It's my duty to protect the crew." And even if it wasn't, she'd been the one to ink the bargain. She'd see it through.

"Captain or not, it was hard enough thinking we'd lost you once. None of us care to go through that again."

"Quit fussing over me, Polin," Teriana replied, feeling Marcus's eyes on them and knowing she needed to put on a show. "I'm not a child."

"You'll always be my little tadpole, girl."

An unexpected burn rose in her eyes. Her own father had died when Teriana had still been a babe in her mother's belly. A small injury that had turned foul while they'd been trading in the East, and the *Quincense* hadn't made it back west to find a marked healer in time to save him. Polin hadn't exactly taken on the role, but he'd been as much an uncle as Yedda was her aunt. He'd watched over her, taken care of her. But now it was her duty to protect him. To protect all of her crew.

And that thought had weighed heavily on her mind hours after Polin and Yedda had departed the village under Marcus's watchful eye.

Swearing under her breath, Teriana kicked at a rock, but her toe caught a root in the darkness and she stumbled. One of the engineers steadied her without comment, but when she looked up she stopped in her tracks. They'd reached the beach, but where once lay swaths of untamed jungle now sat what could only be described as a fortress.

Walls of raw tree trunks rose from the earth, too high to be scaled without rope and manned at regular intervals by legionnaires whose attention never seemed to shift from the growing darkness around them. It was massive and menacing, but the men surrounding her picked up their pace, expressions those of one returning to a familiar home, not a structure that had been torn from the jungle in the space of half a day.

Crossbows glittered in the torchlight, leveled at the approaching party until passwords were exchanged, then the gate swung open to reveal a sea of white tents lined up in perfectly neat rows.

"Legatus wants to see you," one of the men at the gate said, nodding toward the large tent sitting in the center of the camp. "Immediately."

Her gut instinct was to balk at what was obviously an order, but Yedda's advice echoed through her head, and Teriana kept her mouth shut. Obeying would give her a chance to study the inner workings of a Cel camp, and her continued compliance would earn their trust.

Eventually earn their trust, she amended, pretending not to notice the two men who broke off from the group to follow her.

If perfect organization counted for anything, the Cel camp would be nothing short of impenetrable. The spaces between tents appeared to have been set with a measuring stick, the campfires were at exact intervals, and everything was organized identically, giving her a sense of déjà vu as she walked through row after row. There were a few soldiers sitting around the fires playing dice or cards, many more sound asleep on bedrolls, and countless others standing guard on the walls or patrolling within the well-lit camp. Not only would it be almost impossible to break in or out, even sneaking around inside would be challenging.

The Cel dragon flapped on the sea breeze as she approached

the tent, the gold serpent appearing to lunge and snap in the firelight. One of the men flanking the entrance ducked his head inside, then pulled back the flap and nodded as she passed within.

Lamps were scattered around the tent, revealing an interior that was as austere and practical as she'd come to expect. It was stifling hot and smelled of steel, leather, sweat, and the vestiges of the fish they'd eaten for dinner. Standing at the entrance, Teriana waited for one of the ten young men standing around the folding table to acknowledge her, but they were all intent on a large map covered with markers and figurines.

"We'll target here and here," Marcus was saying, but Teriana couldn't see what he was pointing at around Servius's bulk. The others made noises of agreement and straightened. "Bring me the numbers when you come back," Marcus said, then stepped away from the table. The others saluted and left, most smiling at her as they passed, with the exception of Felix, who ignored her entirely.

Only Titus paused. Teriana's hackles rose with her knowing that *this* was Cassius's son. But a broad smile broke across his face. "That was some amazing sailing you did today. There's a lot of men who owe you their lives."

She opened her mouth to make a snide retort, but Marcus gave a slight shake of his head. So instead she shrugged. "I've a reputation to live up to."

"Still, if it hadn't been for you . . ." Cassius's son glanced over his shoulder at Marcus, then back to her. "Thank you. We owe you one. *I* owe you one."

One knife in the back, she thought, but remained silent as he strode out into the camp, red cloak fluttering behind him. "You sure it's wise to let him in on your plans?"

"I think it's wise to keep him close," Marcus replied, watching his servant gather empty tin plates and cups. "I'll need you ready at dawn. We'll be sending out more scouting parties, and I want to enlist some of Flacre's people as guides."

"I suppose they might be interested if you keep paying," she said, casting her eyes over the map in the hopes of gleaning what his strategy might be.

He gestured to the padlocked chests sitting under the table. "We'll pay. I don't intend to make enemies of the Arinoquians."

"What do you intend?" she asked, the question sneaking out before she could think. *How clever, Teriana,* she silently chastised herself. *What a talented spy you make.*

"I intend to do exactly what I told Flacre and the rest," he said. "I intend to ally with the clans rebelling against Urcon's false rule, and together, we will pull him and his underlings from power, likely using force. Then the clans can return to governing themselves individually, as they did previously."

"Why? What's in it for you?"

"A strong alliance would mean the long-term support of the Arinoquians."

Teriana's stomach plummeted, the sudden understanding of his strategy like a slap to the face.

"Rebellions are bloody uphill battles," he said. "Urcon has more power and more resources than the clans rebelling against him, plus he has a paid mercenary army at his disposal. Flacre and his people, it seems they are skilled fighters, but they aren't career soldiers. Their days are spent making lives for themselves and their families, and every time they have to fight, it takes them away from those responsibilities. It risks their lives. It risks the lives of everyone they care about, because of a certainty, Urcon retaliates. That they are willing to fight anyway is testament to how intolerable they consider his rule."

She stared at him, tongue frozen.

"My men, on the other hand, *are* career soldiers," he continued. "This is what we do. It is *all* we do, because the Senate ensures we are provided with every resource we need. The nature of the legions ensures that we have no one outside of our own brotherhood to protect, and even if some of my men have lingering sentiments for the families they left behind, the Empire is on the far side of the seas and untouchable by Urcon or anyone else seeking to retaliate."

She couldn't breathe.

"And I should think the reasons for why I want a strong alliance with the Arinoquians would be obvious. They will continue to aid us, and in exchange for coin, they will continue to supply us with food and resources. We will be able to establish a strong foothold here, which will allow us to explore farther afield in search of xenthier genesis stems while we wait for one of the Senate's path-hunters to find us. Once we are successful, I'll write up the necessary documents for you to present to the Senate as proof you fulfilled your end of our deal. You and yours will be free to go about your business, unmolested by the Empire."

How well Teriana saw it would go. Village after town after city capitulating without a fight because of the allure of such an alliance. By the time they toppled Urcon, which she supposed was inevitable, everyone in Arinoquia would see the Cel as gods-damned saviors, not the subversive conquerors they were.

Marcus had known exactly what sort of place this would be from the information she'd given him, and he'd known exactly how to manipulate the strife in the region to his benefit. Rather than setting them up for failure, she had given him the exact circumstances the Cel needed to entrench themselves in the West. Worse still, knowing that she couldn't be trusted, he'd put her in the position of knowing that if she undercut him, she'd be stealing away these people's opportunity to rid themselves of their current oppressor.

"You're a slimy, wretched bastard," she snarled. "Hiding behind the face of a benevolent hero until these people have lost all capacity to resist, then sending the Empire's tax man to knock at their doors. Replacing one tyrant with another."

Marcus didn't so much as blink. "Thanks to your friend Magnius, we all know my parentage isn't in question. And the Empire won't tax them beyond their capacity to pay—it wants them to thrive, because that's how the Senate makes money."

"Oh, really?" she said, keeping her voice low enough that his men outside couldn't hear. "Does Chersome thrive? Or is it still a smoldering pile of smoking corpses? Although I suppose the Senate could forgive you killing all those potential taxpayers, because you made it so they could buy a child's indenture for less than a loaf of bread. As always, the Empire wins."

"Yes," he replied, rubbing at his temple with one hand. "It does. But be glad it's currently winning with gold and diplomacy, or you'd be standing in a field of corpses right now."

There was nothing Teriana could say to that. She needed to get back to the *Quincense*. To talk to Yedda and Polin about how they might use this information. "Anything else?"

He shook his head.

Teriana turned on her heel. "Then I'll be—"

"Staying right here." Before she could do more than open her mouth to argue, he added, "This tent is constantly under guard." He nudged a bolted chest with one foot. "Gold. Maps. Plans. It's the safest place in camp."

Swallowing the rest of whatever was in his cup, he set it on the table and went to the rear of the tent, pushing aside a flap of canvas and disappearing. Teriana reluctantly followed, taking in the dimly lit space divided down the middle by a sheet. There was a bedroll on the ground, a small stack of her clothing and belongings sitting on top of it. On the other side of the sheet lay another bedroll, which Marcus stood next to. "This is *your* tent," she said.

"It's the command tent," he replied. "Since I'm in command, I sleep here. Amarin sleeps out front," he added, seemingly as an afterthought.

"I can sleep in a regular tent," she stammered.

"Too risky to have you unguarded. We know Cassius would rather kill you and risk stranding us than ever deliver on that contract, so you can bet Titus will aim to make that happen. I don't intend to give him that opportunity." Marcus crossed his arms. "And I'm not pulling men from other duties to watch you sleep when those guarding this tent can do the task just fine."

Sleeping in the same room as him on her ship had been one thing. But this tent . . . There'd be only a foot of space between the two of them. She'd rather try her luck naked in the jungle. "I'll be safe on my ship."

"That's not an option."

"Why? It isn't as though we can sneak away in the night. Her decks are still swarming with *your* men."

"If your word is good, then I shouldn't have to worry about you sneaking off," he said. "But that isn't what I meant—you staying on your ship is impossible."

"Why?" Her head shot up from her inspection of the tent. But the lamp cast shadows across Marcus's skin, rendering his expression unreadable.

"Because," he said, fiddling with the buckle on his wrist guard, "the *Quincense* is gone."

"What do you mean, gone?"

"I dispatched the *Quincense* under the command of your aunt Yedda to an island we passed on our way in, where the ship will be anchored. They have some of our injured, along with enough of my men to ensure there is no trouble. They'll remain there until your contract is fulfilled and it's time to send you back to Celendor."

Teriana stared at him, barely able to process what he was saying. She *needed* them in order for there to be any chance of smuggling the information she learned out of the legion camp.

"I know you can communicate with Magnius," Marcus said, seeming to hear her thoughts. "But by my reckoning, that requires a certain proximity, which I don't intend to allow, because I don't *trust* you."

The crew was her family, the *Quincense* her home. The longest she'd been parted from them was when she'd been captive in Celendrial. It could take weeks for her to figure out a way to sabotage the legion's mission, likely months. Maybe even years. And she'd have to spend them surrounded by her enemy, completely cut off from everyone who mattered to her. She clutched a handful of her hair, trying not to burst into tears as the tiny ornaments woven through it dug into her hands, because all she could think about was with Yedda gone, who would braid her hair?

"You, you . . ."

"I'm not bringing them back, Teriana. Not until we find land-based xenthier paths to and from the Empire and we're through with each other."

Or unless things go very badly for them. The thought must have been written across her face, because his darkened. "I've spent every day since I was a small child with this legion. With these men. Just how well do you think it would go for you if I believed you caused harm to befall any of them?"

She huffed out an angry breath, because the alternative was a sob. "Yet you expect me to stand here and take whatever you dole out without comment?"

"Oh, I expect plenty of comments from you, Teriana," he snapped. "But right now, I want you to go outside and find a campfire to sit next to, because I've plans to make. And you'll excuse me for not wanting you close enough to hear them."

28

MARCUS

Marcus squinted at the map, turning up the lamp in the hope that the blurred lines would focus. But the light was no cure for exhaustion.

After he'd dispatched Teriana into Gibzen's care, Felix and Servius had returned, the two of them digging through reports from the scouts, engineers, and cartographers, trying to get the lay of the land while Marcus reviewed more unfortunate material. The legion's casualties from the xenthier crossing had been prepared. Twelve drowned. Forty-six injured, but only eight hurt badly enough not to march, all of those sent to the island with the *Quincense.* All the injured and dead were from the Thirty-Seventh. It could've been much worse. All four hundred on that ship might have been lost if not for Teriana's swift action, Felix included.

The official list was a bound book of numbers, each representing a man of the Thirty-Seventh, which the Senate required they keep updated. Deaths. Discharges. Desertions, of which there had only ever been one. Servius kept a secondary list that was the same, only it also included the men's names. It was this list Marcus was staring at, the names of the dead stamping themselves on his memory.

"We aren't going to want to wait long on this." Felix broke the silence, tapping his finger against a dot marking the small fortress city of Galinha, which was a day's march north of their current position. "From what we're gathering, all the militia forces harassing the towns and villages in this area are based here. Better to take them out at the source rather than picking them off up and down the coast."

Marcus made a noise of agreement, but he wasn't really paying attention to what Felix was saying, his mind replaying his conversation with Teriana. The way her eyes had turned the color of storm-tossed seas, the venom in her voice. How she'd thrown Chersome in his face.

"You even listening to me?" Felix demanded.

"Yes." *No.* "If we move too soon, we risk the population turning hostile. We want them to want us."

"And risk Urcon moving men from his stronghold in Aracam to bolster the city's defenses?" Felix jabbed a finger at a dot farther north. "Right now, we'd take Galinha easily. We delay, that might change."

"It might." Marcus rubbed one temple. "But we'll stay the course until the scouts get back with more information on numbers. And we'll see what information Teriana can dig out of the Arinoquians."

Felix's hand stayed frozen where it was pressed against the map. "You trust the information she provides?"

"With a grain of salt." Marcus straightened, his back cracking. "She's dependent on our success."

"Or plotting our failure," Felix said. "She doesn't want us here."

Replacing one tyrant with another. Teriana's voice echoed through his skull.

"Do you remember home?" Marcus asked, the question rising to his lips before he'd taken the opportunity to think through the consequences of asking.

Both his friends lifted their heads. "The Empire?" Servius asked. "Or Campus Lescendor?"

"No. Before that."

Felix and Servius exchanged looks, the latter eventually shrugging. "Sometimes I'll see something that makes me think of it. When I see sisters together, it makes me think of mine."

"Baking bread," Felix said. "The smell of it reminds me of sitting in my family's bakery before the legions took me."

"Do you remember the tax man?" Marcus asked, watching their reactions. It was possible they'd been too young to have noticed, but even as the thought crossed his mind both of them nodded slowly.

"A man came once a month," Felix said, expression distant. "During bad months, I remember him always offering an *arrangement* to my parents that would allow them not to pay. Only they always did, even if it meant weeks without meat."

Marcus picked at the edge of the table, peeling off a splinter of wood. "The Empire makes a great deal of money off usury. They were smart not to take the deal."

"My family paid in grain," Servius said, his brow furrowed. "Or livestock. They'd come around with wagons under legion guard. We used to sit in the trees and watch them march, and I'd brag that I'd be in their midst one day." He laughed, but there was something uneasy about it. "Seems twisted to think about that now."

"You?" Felix asked, and Marcus gave his friend a long look, knowing that he was using the question to dig for information on something else.

"Tax men do not knock on senators' doors."

"I suppose not." Felix rubbed a bit of grime off his wrist guard. "That patrician you beat bloody . . . He was your brother, wasn't he? And your father is Senator Domitius?"

There was no way he could deny it now, but Marcus fervently wished he hadn't opened up this line of questioning. "Yes."

"Why the secret?" Felix asked, ignoring the warning look Servius gave him. "It wasn't as though everyone didn't know you were from the Hill: it was in your speech, the fact that you could read and do sums, and that you knew twice as much as the rest of us. Shit, Marcus, I remember your hands being soft as a girl's."

Do not let anyone learn your identity. His father's words echoed through his mind. *If they do, our family will be ruined. Do you want your sisters forced to whore themselves on the streets? Your brother and me hanging from a noose?* He swallowed, remembering how afraid he'd been of being discovered. "I didn't want anyone to know."

"Why? There were dozens of patrician boys in our ranks. No one cared then, and they sure as shit don't care now."

"Then why are you asking?"

"Because! I want to know why you were willing to tell some pagan sea creature what you refused to tell your best friends for twelve years."

"Let it alone," Servius said, trying to step between them, but Felix shoved him back.

"Ever since we got back to Celendrial, you've been acting strange. Doubly strange since Teriana was thrown into the mix, but at least the reasons for *that* are obvious. I'm sick of you keeping secrets from us, especially since we are now stranded in this place."

Would it be so bad to tell them the truth?

It would be, and Marcus knew it. It was one thing to keep things from them, but if his friends found out he'd been lying to them all these years? That he was not who he claimed to be and was part of a scheme that broke one of the most sacrosanct laws of the Empire? There'd be no coming back from that.

"You want to know why I didn't tell you? Fine." Picking up a cup of water, he drained the contents. "My family was ashamed of my illness. They sent me to the legions expecting— and hoping—I'd die. They wanted to forget I ever existed, so I did them the same courtesy." Chewing on the insides of his cheeks, he added, "Cassius knows who I am. He remembered that I was sick as a child, and he threatened to reveal the information if I didn't help him. And I think it's safe to say that Titus knows as well."

"So the reason they recalled us, the reason they chose us for this mission, was because Cassius had you marked for blackmail." Felix's ears were a brilliant shade of red. "That rat bastard. And Titus? Do we need another reason to kill him?"

"I'm not murdering a man because of what he *might* know, Felix."

"What about the fact that he tried to murder you? A knife in his back would end this. You wouldn't have to worry."

"No," Marcus snapped, as much angry at himself for finding the idea appealing as he was at Felix for suggesting it. "Drop it."

"Fine."

Before any of them could say more on the matter, Gibzen and Teriana staggered in, arms slung around each other's shoulders, the spicy scent of rum wafting with them.

"She's fleeced us, sir," Gibzen hollered, dropping a sack of coins on a stack of maps, then depositing Teriana on one of the stools.

She was grinning like a mad fool, her eyes an alarming shade of cerulean. "Your men gamble poorly, Marcus."

"You've been drinking," he said, and Teriana slowly clapped her hands together.

"Not just a pretty face, are you, *Legatus*?"

They stared each other down, her irises shifting and darkening. "I need to sleep," she muttered, getting up and walking toward the rear of the tent. "G'night, Gibzen. Tell your boys I'll let them try to win back their coin tomorrow night."

"Night, lovely!" Gibzen stretched, folding his arms behind his head, then finally seemed to notice Marcus glaring at him. "What? You told me to keep her out of the way until you were finished. Mission accomplished."

"Get out." Exhaling softly, he waited until the primus was gone, then said to his friends, "We'll pick up again tomorrow."

Gathering Teriana's winnings, he went into the back, tossing the sack on her bedroll.

"Didn't think you'd let me keep it," she said.

"If they're stupid enough to gamble with a Maarin sailor, then they deserve to lose."

Lifting her head, she said, "*I'm* not stupid, you know. For one, drunks don't win at cards. Two, I'm not foolish enough to sacrifice my wits in a camp full of soldiers."

"Only *pretending* to enjoy their company, then?" He shifted sideways so that Amarin could pass, the man setting a basin of water on the ground next to Teriana.

"Thank you." She smiled at the servant before shifting her gaze back to Marcus. "Who said I was pretending? They're fine company, and I was happy enough to spend an evening with them."

It was just him she hated.

Stepping to the other side of the curtain, he held out an arm, and Amarin unbuckled the straps, carefully setting the pieces aside for cleaning. Teriana had turned up the lamp, and when she stood he could see her outline clearly through the sheet. She lifted her arms over her head, pulling off her shirt, then hopped on one foot and then the other as she tugged off her trousers. As the splash of water filled his ears, he realized he was staring and jerked his gaze away from the curtain.

Amarin had an amused smile on his face. "Don't even think of saying it," Marcus growled, jerking off his own tunic and throwing it in a pile on the floor.

"Saying what?" Teriana demanded.

"You might turn down the lamp, miss." Amarin's smile widened further as Marcus waved his hands, trying to get to him to stop speaking. "Lamp oil is precious."

The light dimmed.

Amarin handed him a washcloth and Marcus threw it back at him. "I don't think so."

The other man wrinkled his nose and set the cloth next to a basin of water. "You might want to reconsider, sir." Then he gathered up the pieces of armor and departed.

All Marcus wanted to do was collapse on his bedroll and sleep, but instead he found himself scrubbing away the sweat accumulated during the day before putting his weapons in easy reach and lying down. Moments after he did, the lamplight winked out, leaving him in the dark with only the ambient sounds of the camp, the drone of insects, and the soft sound of Teriana crying.

Guilt was an old friend, but it raged against him with a vengeance. *This is your fault,* it whispered. *She's crying because of you. You brought her here. You tore her away from her family.*

She's alive because of me, he reminded the guilt. *As are they.*

But the reminders did nothing to silence the emotion. Or to silence Teriana's tears.

"Sending them to that island was the best option I had for protecting them for you," he said.

Teriana didn't respond, but her snuffles quieted. She was listening.

"If they'd remained, they would have done so as prisoners within this camp, and there would've been little I could do to make those conditions ideal. They'd have been used as a resource, for translating and whatever else, which would mean they'd be constantly in danger—from my men and from Urcon's. On that island, they are apart from all of this. Your crew is as safe as it can be."

Wind rustled the canvas of the tent, and some of his men laughed uproariously in the distance.

"You could've let me say good-bye."

He could've. He probably should've. "I made the decision before anyone had the chance to question whether the *Quincense* and her crew might have a better purpose than sitting on a white sand beach in the middle of nowhere."

Silence.

"It's only for a short time," he said.

"While you use me to get everything you want."

If she only knew.

"You've already given me everything I wanted," he said, knowing he was treading a fine line.

"But—"

"The rest of what you have to do to free your people? That is for Cassius. Not for me. But for the sake of your people, I'll help you get it done." Rolling over, he glared at the darkness, hating how even on the far side of the world Cassius had him under his thumb. "Get some rest, Teriana. Dawn will come early."

Soon after, her breathing quieted into the slow rhythm of sleep, likely more as a result of the rum Gibzen had given her than any comfort from Marcus's words. And as the minutes passed and sleep didn't come, it made him consider sending Amarin to find him a bottle. Only that was a slippery slope that he didn't care to set himself upon. He didn't like being drunk, didn't like the way booze loosened his tongue and sense of self-control. He had too much to lose, and what relief he might gain for losing himself in the bottle for a night wasn't worth the potential price.

Sighing, Marcus rose to his feet, pulling a tunic over his head. Carrying his weapons and sandals out into the command tent, he silently donned them and stepped out into the night.

The guards encircling the tent quietly saluted him as he passed, and he strode through the neat lines of tents. The camp was split between the two legions, and though the halves were identical, he could have closed his eyes and spun around like a top and still been able to point to the half containing the Thirty-Seventh. If nothing else, the smell of alcohol would've given them away.

Reaching the gate, he said, "I'm going to the village."

"A moment, sir, and we'll organize an escort," the soldier in command of the watch said, but Marcus shook his head.

"Don't need one. I won't be long."

The young man—one of the Forty-First—opened his mouth to argue, but a long look from Marcus kept any argument from passing his lips. The gate was cracked to allow him to pass, Marcus snaking one of the burning torches as he strode through. Of a surety, one of them would already be running to rat him out to Felix, but he'd still have some time alone. Time to breathe.

A path to the village had been cleared, and Marcus walked swiftly through the darkness, listening to the drone of insects, the calls of birds and monkeys in the trees, and the crash of the ocean against the distant beach. The air smelled of moisture and dirt and trees, clean in comparison to the camp. He'd been to places with the same sounds. Same smells. Yet there was something different here. A charge of energy, and a sense of . . . watchfulness that made his skin prickle.

He reached the outskirts of the village, nodding to the guards who had been posted, four of Flacre's and four from the legion. The legionnaires were Thirty-Seventh, so not an eyebrow rose at the sight of him. As much as they didn't like his midnight wanderings, his men were used to them.

The village itself was quiet, the people in their homes, though Marcus doubted they were enough at ease with his army's presence to sleep. He meandered between the pilings holding up the buildings until he reached the open space in the center, the perimeter dominated by seven stone shrines. Each of them was unique, bearing detailed carvings of male and female likenesses, the eyes seeming to shift and move as he circled the clearing. The shrine made of black stone he approached last, a strange desire to touch the slick rock coming over him even as he studied the carving, which was little more than a suggestion of a face, the eyes dark pits.

Reaching out, Marcus hesitated, his fingers suddenly chilled to the bone. The sensation grew, the cold beginning to burn as though his hand had pressed against a block of ice too long.

It hurt, but he couldn't draw back.

A dull glow filled the carving's eyes, and they shifted, *seeing him.*

Then a hand closed on his wrist, pulling him back.

Reaching for the blade at his waist, Marcus froze at the sight of Flacre, a fussing baby in the man's arms. The old Arinoquian pointed at the black shrine and gave a warning shake of his head.

Pulse still roaring in his ears, Marcus said, "Why do you have it then? Why not destroy it?" He pantomimed breaking the rock, but the man only shook his head. Rocking the child, he gestured to each of the shrines, then pressed his hand to his chest. Then over the child's chest. Then, reaching out, the man pressed his hand over Marcus's thundering heart.

"Get your hands off of him!"

Felix's voice split the night, and the baby, who had fallen asleep, began to howl.

"It's fine, Felix," Marcus said, wincing at a particularly loud shriek. To Flacre, he said, "Sorry. He's . . ." Trailing off, he cursed not having had the opportunity to learn at least some of the Arinoquian language before he arrived, and his limited Trader's Tongue failing him.

Expression more amused than anything, the old man hugged the baby tight and said one word. "*Protective.*" Marcus smiled and nodded, repeating the word. Committing it to memory.

Flacre inclined his head, then walked away, murmuring soothing sounds to the child as he disappeared into the darkness.

Felix stood with his arms crossed between two of the shrines. "We've talked about this," he said.

"I know. I know." Casting an upward glance at the night sky, Marcus watched the way the stars sparkled. "I couldn't sleep."

"She snore?"

Laughing, Marcus shook his head. "No worse than you."

"I only snore when I sleep on my back."

"You always sleep on your back."

Felix shrugged. "Want to walk?"

They strode through the village and down to the beach, where Marcus's men had begun construction of a pier capable of servicing their fleet. Sandals clacking against the cut stone, he and Felix walked to the end of it and sat, legs dangling off the edge and elbows together as they stared out to sea. "How are they doing?"

Felix always had a better sense of the morale of the men than Marcus did, because he was one of them in a way Marcus had never been able to manage. Even before he'd been put in command, he'd always felt apart. Like he didn't quite fit in with the camaraderie of all the other boys. It had been a relief in more ways than one when the commanders at Lescendor had marked him as a future officer and he'd been able to spend more time in the library studying the history of the Empire's wars. Learning strategy. Mastering tactics. Hunting victory.

"Some better than others. The idle time in Celendrial took its toll, and that voyage . . ." Felix shook his head. "Not sure if it was better or worse for those in the hold who couldn't see what was happening. As it is, the sailors did their fair share of talking before we got everyone off-loaded. Servius needs to get his hands on more drink or we're going to have trouble in the ranks."

"We'll have trouble if we're attacked and a third of our men are drunk."

"We'll have just as much trouble if that third is losing their minds from exhaustion." Felix exhaled a long breath. "Most can't sleep, and when they do, they have dreams. The drink is the only thing that helps them."

Dreams. Of the things they'd seen. Of the things they'd done. Of the things they feared being done to them.

"It's not your fault," Felix said.

Marcus didn't answer. Didn't have to. They'd been assigned as bunkmates when they'd first arrived at Lescendor, but they'd been best friends since the first time Felix had dragged Marcus off the ground where he'd collapsed during the first day of training. He still remembered seven-year-old Felix's voice in his ear: *Get up. You have to get up. There is no quitting here, only dying.* Or the first time Marcus had had one of his attacks and Felix had hidden him rather than asking for help from the medics, instinctively knowing it was Marcus's only chance at survival. That if his weakness were discovered, he'd be purged.

"It's your job to keep the Thirty-Seventh alive," Felix said softly. "And against every odd, you've done it. And it's my job to keep *you* alive. But to do that, I need you to quit taking these risks, understand? We need you."

Marcus felt his friend's elbow bump his, and he knew that he should turn. To acknowledge what Felix had said. To reassure him. But the words wouldn't come. "We should get back," he said. "With the dawn, we need to start showing this Urcon that we are here to stay."

Felix grinned. "And the Thirty-Seventh doesn't fall back."

They would never go back.

29

TERIANA

Teriana awoke to the rhythmic inhale and exhale of someone breathing hard. She blinked at the white canvas over her head, only barely illuminated by the coming dawn, and groaned, her head throbbing with a hangover. Mornings were not her favored time on the best of days, and another few hours—or six—of sleep would not have hurt. But clearly that was not on Marcus's agenda.

Marcus.

Despite the rum she'd consumed last night, Teriana had tossed and turned for a long time after their conversation through the sheet, turning his words over in her head. In Celendrial, while he'd bandaged her hands, he'd spun pretty words about his interests being aligned with hers when it came to protecting her people from Cassius, but she'd brushed them off as him trying to manipulate his way into her good graces. Same with him allowing her to deliver the bodies of her fallen people to the sea. How could she think otherwise when the contract she'd signed with him had demanded so much—a whole half of the world on a silver platter? That he'd been willing to give the Maarin their freedom was like tossing her bread crumbs. A paltry cost for what he'd gain.

But what he'd said . . . *You've already given me everything I wanted. The rest of what you have to do to free your people? That is for Cassius. Not for me. But for the sake of your people, I'll help you get it done.*

A soft thud caught her attention, and Marcus's breathing again took on a slightly strained rhythm.

"By the Six!" she snarled. "What are you doing?"

Rolling on her side, Teriana jerked up the sheet hanging

between them and found herself face-to-face with a pair of grey eyes. Or were they blue? *Doesn't matter. They're his.*

Marcus was frozen in the lower half of a push-up, his face turned in her direction. "Exercises."

He resumed pushing up and down, muscles moving back and forth beneath his stupid Cel skin. Rolling onto his back, he started doing sit-ups, and she watched because she knew it would annoy him, then said, "You look like an idiot," and dropped the sheet back in place.

"Fitness is important."

She rolled her eyes, annoyed that she was already hot when the sun wasn't yet up in the sky. "Well, when you're done flailing about, maybe you could take a walk. I need some privacy."

"Latrine pits are at the rear of camp."

Because the Six forbid she have a damned moment alone. Cheeks burning, she pulled on her boots and made her way through the empty command tent, passing Amarin as she went. "Good morning," he said. "Would you like your breakfast here or will you queue with the men?"

"I'll figure it out," she muttered; then her eyes latched on a stack of blank paper before dancing to the pencils littered across the table.

"I think Marcus wants you for something," she said, and when the man started toward the rear of the tent she snatched up some paper and a pencil, shoving them into her pocket before pushing outside and taking a deep breath of fresh air.

Two men fell in behind her as she made her way toward the rear of the camp, and remembering Yedda's advice, she asked, "What did you two do wrong to get the job of following me to the shitter?"

They both laughed. "Nearly came to blows us fighting over the job," one said. "And as for the other, I think Servius has something rigged so you don't have all the little boys in the Forty-First deciding they need to take a piss at the same time as you."

"He's a good one, that Servius," she said, relieved that she wouldn't have to do her business in view of a few thousand men every day and storing the slight against the other legion's maturity in her back pocket for later consideration. If there was conflict between them that went beyond what was between Marcus and Titus, maybe she could use it to her advantage. "And since we're going to be thick as thieves, what do you call yourselves?"

"Quintus," he replied. "That's Miki." The other legionnaire grinned, the corner of one of his eyes twisted up by a fresh set of stitches. Even without his name it was obvious Miki wasn't Cel by birth. What hair he had was concealed by a helmet, but his eyebrows were a shocking shade of red and his pale skin was more freckle than not. Likely from Sibern, the great barren wastelands to the north of Celendor proper.

Quintus, on the other hand, was as Cel as Marcus or Felix, with the ubiquitous golden skin, fair hair, and light eyes. Yet there was something familiar about him. "I've met you before," she said. "You're the sewing-circle soldier."

Miki burst into laughter, the spear he held in one hand shaking. "Oh, that's good. You're never going to live that one down."

Quintus sighed. "Thanks for that, Teriana. The whole rutting legion is going to be dropping off their mending in front of my tent."

"Will finally give that needle of yours a purpose," Miki said, and they devolved into a banter that grew more off-color as it progressed.

They reached the latrines, which true to their word had a roofless structure off to one side with her name carved into the door, along with the warning that trespassers would find themselves digging ditches for the next year.

Lydia will die laughing when she hears about this—

The blood rushed from Teriana's face on the heels of the thought, fury at herself rising in its place. Fury at allowing herself to forget even for a minute that the other girl was the reason Teriana was standing here at all. Stepping inside, she closed the door and pushed the rudimentary latch into place. It took her a matter of moments to do what she'd come for, but despite the stench clinging to the air around the pits, she lingered in the tiny closed-off area, extracting the pieces of paper and the pencil she'd stolen from the command tent. Writing swiftly, first in Gamdeshian and then in Katamarcan, she detailed the situation as best she could, describing what she knew about Marcus's intentions, as well as the greater threat of the Empire. She pleaded for assistance—for herself, for her people, and for the people of Arinoquia, requesting that resources be sent to drive back the Cel threat. Finishing, she wrote her titles and signed her name with as much flourish as was possible with a dull pencil.

Peering through a gap in the wall, she eyed her two guards, who were chatting companionably with another legionnaire, whose back was to her. The letters in her hand all of a sudden made her skin crawl, because they were requests that the rulers of the West come kill these men. Quintus and Miki hadn't chosen to come to this place. They hadn't even chosen to become soldiers. Every aspect of their lives was mandated by the Senate, and by *Legatus Marcus*. She made a face and turned, resting her shoulders against the door, shoving the letters deep into her pocket.

They aren't innocent, you idiot, she told herself. They were trained killers and none of them would hesitate to slit her throat if given the order, so why should she?

"Teriana?"

She froze at the sound of Marcus's voice, then peered through the crack. *He* was the third soldier, but he wasn't wearing any of his usual officer's regalia, which was why she hadn't recognized him.

"Do you need to talk to one of the medics?"

Why would she . . . ? Every inch of her burned hot, and she shoved open the door, stumbling over her own boots as she exited. "I'm fine," she said, glaring at Quintus and Miki, annoyed they hadn't the decency to warn her.

Sorry, Quintus mouthed.

"The diet can be difficult." Marcus crossed his arms, and she noticed his muscles were all hard lines from his stupid exercises. "If you need something, talk to a medic. Don't let it become a problem."

Diving into the pits behind her would've been preferable to this conversation. "I'm fine. I was just . . . thinking."

It was impossible to tell beneath the helmet, but she was certain one of his eyebrows rose. "Think on your own time. We've work to do."

Grinding her teeth, Teriana fell into step next to him, the other two trailing behind. "We?"

"Yes, we. The surrounding towns and villages need to be met with, so you're needed to translate."

"Obviously. But what are *you* needed for?" The comment came out with more sarcasm than she intended, and she heard a stifled snort from behind her.

"A cold coming on, Quintus?" Marcus asked without turning around. "If you're feeling unwell, I could find you a less strenuous task. Mending, perhaps?"

"I'm fine, sir. And sorry, sir."

"Didn't think you had a sense of humor," Teriana muttered.

"I don't know what you're talking about."

Marcus's voice was inflectionless, but she turned her head just in time to see a ghost of a smile cross his face.

In the company of fifty men, they left the camp and made their way down a trail that followed the coast. It was too wide to be called a goat track, too narrow to be called a road, but after an hour Teriana was convinced it was the path to the underworld.

It wasn't because she was out of shape, because she wasn't. It was only that she so very rarely *walked* anywhere. Her legs ached, and it felt like her boots were sanding the skin off her heels. The sun was cooking hot, and it seemed as though she were drinking as much as breathing, the air was so humid. To make matters worse, Marcus insisted on bombarding her with questions, no detail too small to escape his scrutiny, not even those that should be beyond his tiny Cel mind.

"Those shrines in the village—they are for your gods?"

Her stomach tightened as she remembered her history of the Empire. How similar-type monuments were destroyed.

"I'll take that as a yes," he said. "I've heard you mention the Six, but there were seven shrines."

"The Seventh is the Corrupter," she muttered. "He demands a place in the god circle, but only those with evil in their hearts invoke his name."

"But they all have powers like those we saw in the crossing?"

"Gespurn commands the elements." She eyed the sun, wishing she could blame the heat on the god but knowing it was typical of Arinoquia. "Madoria's domain is the sea. The others have different powers."

"Such as?"

"Why? You looking to take up prayer?"

He let out an exasperated sigh. "If they are a threat, I need to know about them."

It was the individuals the gods marked who'd be the threat, but Teriana had no intention of telling Marcus that. "Lern rules the beasts. Yara has dominion over the earth. Hegeria over the body and spirit, and Tremon over war." Stories told that there had once been more gods, deities beyond counting, but now only these seven remained.

"The things men and women care about," he mused. "And they are worshipped all across the Dark Shores?"

It was her turn to sigh. "*Yes*, Marcus. North and south and everywhere in between. They are called different things in different languages, but they are the *same* gods, and everyone pays tribute to them in the same ways."

"With the circle of little temples?"

Teriana made a face at the word *little*. Such a typically Cel thing to believe size was what mattered. "The temples of the god circle in Gamdesh's capital of Revat tower so high, they touch the clouds. We consider them the greatest feat of architecture on Reath." Casting a sideways glance at him, she added, "Though you'll no doubt dismantle them and drag it all back to Celendrial."

"We'll see," he responded, and Teriana stomped on a beetle crossing the path rather than voicing what she thought about *that*.

"Urcon," he asked after a merciful few minutes of silence, "have you ever seen him?"

"No." Her clothes were drenched with sweat, and she'd already consumed the entirety of the contents of the waterskin Amarin had given her. "Aracam is an ancient city, built before the clans conquered Arinoquia and drove those native to these shores inland. It's on our blacklist and has been for nearly a decade. Urcon's port tax is excessive, and he's known for taking cargos without paying. And for burning ships. The Maarin only trade with the smaller settlements, but it's not particularly profitable."

"They have a currency?"

"The island the clans originally came from functions primarily on a barter system, but here they prefer Gamdeshian coinage. Gold. Silver. Copper." Casting a sideways glance at him, she said, "Speaking of, why are you using unmarked coins? I'd have thought you'd be keen to spread the Celendorian dragon everywhere you went."

"I requested unmarked coins. Gold has a way of garnering attention, and if enough Cel dragons find their way into Gamdesh, I might find the Sultan and his armies casting their eyes my direction sooner than I'd like."

Teriana scowled at the path, because arranging for some of that coinage to move north to Gamdesh had been one of her plans to convince the Sultan of the severity of the Cel threat.

Marcus pushed his helmet up and wiped the sweat away. "How deep into the interior does Urcon control? Do the people living there ever fight back against him?"

Each step she took was an act of will, her feet hurt so much. "Marcus," she snapped. "This is the longest I've ever been off the ocean. How in the name of the Six am I supposed to know what's going on miles inland?"

He eyed her up and down. "I suppose that explains your snail's pace."

"Would you prefer we run?"

"Your feet hurt?"

"I'm fine." Her boots were probably filling with blood, but she'd let them rub down to the bone before she'd complain to him.

"No, you are not. Stop walking."

Everyone stopped, but Teriana belligerently kept down the trail.

"Teriana."

She ignored him.

"Why must you make everything so rutting difficult?"

She opened her mouth to retort, but something snagged her ankle and suddenly she was lying on her back. Marcus caught one of her ankles and before she could kick him away jerked off her boot.

"You bloody idiot," he snarled, then shouted, "Medic!"

There was a flurry of motion, and then a soldier pushed through the ranks toward them. He was indistinguishable from the others but for the satchel he carried, and he let out a sigh at the sight of her foot, which Marcus still had in his grasp.

"What a mess," the medic muttered. "Surprised you could even walk."

"I'm not." Marcus jerked off her other boot so the medic could assess her raw heel. "Bloody stubborn, pigheaded mule of a girl. If you cut off her feet, she'd walk on the stumps."

"It might come to that."

Teriana left off trying to kick her way out of Marcus's grip. "That bad?"

"It's not good." The medic poured water over her heels, then rubbed a salve that burned like fire across the bloody mess, but as he wrapped bandages around her feet he smiled. "But not that bad." Pushing up the leg of her trouser, he secured the bandage with practiced hands.

"Can she walk?" Marcus's arms were crossed, his tone frigid.

The medic shook his head. "No, sir. Not for a few days."

"I can," she protested, but the medic shook his head.

"She'll need to be carried."

Teriana blanched. "No. Absolutely not!"

Her arguments fell on deaf ears.

Marcus leaned down, his armor digging into her stomach as he flipped her over his shoulder, grunting more with annoyance than with strain as he lifted her.

"Marcus, put me down. Or get someone else—"

"Oh, don't worry," he snapped. "I'm sure we'll all get a turn."

For all he'd called her a stubborn mule, Marcus proved he was the same and worse, insisting on carrying her all the damn way to the small walled town, through the open gates, and past countless raised homes until they reached the center. There he dumped her unceremoniously on her feet in the middle of the god circle where the imperator, who it turned out was an imperatrix, waited.

She was tall and wiry, her dark blonde hair streaked with grey. Her vibrant green eyes were marked with crow's feet, and her cheeks carved with deep lines suggesting she smiled often, though she was not now. In the ranks of warriors behind her were individuals from Flacre's village.

"Seems they know about you already," Teriana muttered.

"Yes, I asked Flacre to arrange an invitation to speak with them about our proposed alliance. Their acceptance came this morning while you were loitering in the latrine."

Teriana's cheeks burned even as she ground her teeth in frustration. Polin, it appeared, had been more than correct in his assessment of Marcus's gift for language.

The imperatrix nodded to Teriana in greeting. "My name is Ereni."

"Teriana."

"These are the men who came on the ships?" Ereni asked.

"Aye," Teriana said. "They come from the Celendor Empire across the Endless Seas. They mean to establish trade."

The woman eyed Marcus as he approached. "These are no merchants, and"—her gaze flicked back to Teriana—"we've heard you don't serve them voluntarily."

"Heard from whom?"

"A Maarin boy with only half a foot has been paying visits to my clan. He paints a dark picture of these golden young men."

Bait. It was all Teriana could do not to smile. Marcus thought he'd been so clever, imprisoning her ship on that island, but Bait didn't need a boat. Especially not with Magnius to speed him along. "Then you know the gods hold no sway in the East and the Cel would see that it is so wherever they go."

Angry mutters circulated among the Arinoquians, and Marcus sighed. "Stick with the script, Teriana."

"Yeah, yeah," she muttered, then started in on the speech Marcus had prepared for her, knowing better than to deviate with him paying such close attention. The legions were here to establish peace, the Senate unwilling to risk Cel merchants to areas ravaged by war. They understood that Urcon was the source of the strife in Arinoquia, and they desired an alliance with the clans who wished to see him removed from power. That they'd defend those who helped them, and would pay for what food and supplies the clans could spare.

Imperatrix Ereni rubbed her chin as Teriana finished. "And if we say no?"

"What happens if they say no?"

Marcus rocked on the soles of his feet, seeming unconcerned by the question. "Nothing, as long they do not bring violence against my men, or support those who would. We will take our trade elsewhere, and the consequences of that are as they have always been."

The woman frowned as she listened to the translated message. "A poor choice," she said. "Feed the invaders in exchange for coin or have no coin to feed our own."

Teriana shrugged, feeling Marcus's eyes digging into her back.

"What they say about Urcon," Ereni asked, "about allying with us to pull him from power, do you believe they will do this? They won't choose to ally with him instead in order to use his army when they move north and south?"

A sourness burned in Teriana's belly as she realized that despite Bait having told them the truth about the Cel, Ereni was still considering an alliance.

"What did she ask?"

Teriana couldn't answer Marcus's question, not without revealing that someone had told the villagers the legion's true intentions. And given the *Quincense* was anchored miles offshore, she'd be the obvious suspect. "I didn't understand. Let me ask her to rephrase." To Ereni, she said, "They aren't known for sharing power?" inflecting her words to make it sound like a question.

She'd expected a negative reaction to *that,* but the woman only rubbed her chin. "Are they *capable* of defeating Urcon? He has more warriors, and the city of Aracam's walls are thick."

"She wants to know if you're capable of beating Urcon, as he has more soldiers than you."

Marcus didn't so much a blink. "Yes."

"He's undefeated," Teriana said to the woman. "Not only that, he's rumored to be *undefeatable.* The Empire boasts an army of over two hundred thousand men just like the ones you see, and he's said to be the most brilliant of them. Been commanding armies since he was twelve years old, and he's never so much as retreated."

"*Yes* is one word, Teriana."

"He's been instrumental in the defeat of four nations, so I don't see why Urcon will pose a problem for him."

"Teriana!"

The woman and all the other Arinoquians present were eyeing Marcus in a whole new light. "What?" Teriana said, resting a hand on her hip. "I was talking you up. Bragging about your victories back east so that they don't doubt you're capable of doing what you say."

"Don't." His tone was unconcerned, but his eyes were livid.

"Why?" she asked. "Aren't you proud of your accomplishments?"

"Seal. The. Deal."

Shrugging, Teriana turned back to the imperatrix. "What say you?"

"He wants Urcon gone." The woman gave Teriana a slow nod. "I say the enemy of my enemy is my friend."

The words brought Cassius to mind, as well as the look of pure hatred on Marcus's face when they'd sailed past him out of the Celendrial harbor. "If you allow them to entrench, all the West will pay the price."

"What is the alternative?"

To fight. But, knowing she'd stretched Marcus's patience to the limit, Teriana only shrugged. "So what do you say, friend? Do we have an accord?" A second later, a heavy drop of rain smacked against her forehead.

30

MARCUS

The air turned to water.

There was no other way to describe the rain that descended upon them with such density and force that it was a struggle to breathe. Returning to camp in these conditions would border on impossible, so Marcus ordered signals sent that his return would be delayed, the horn's notes relayed by the soldiers stationed between.

"Ereni invited us inside to wait it out," Teriana said, gesturing to a large structure, which like the rest was held off the ground on pilings. Children were in the process of running through the town, closing the shutters over the colored glass in the windows, protecting them from the storm. "They say the coastal road is prone to flash floods and mudslides, so it's best to avoid it until tomorrow."

Scowling at the delay, he asked, "Is this your storm god interfering again?"

"Afraid not, *sir*," she responded. "This is just Arinoquia at its finest."

Marcus watched her climb a ladder leading to the network of buildings and bridges, her soaking-wet trousers stretched tight across her curved ass, which he only realized he was staring at when Miki muttered, "Eyes up, sir," as he passed. *Why* he was staring at her ass was lost on him, because the entire day she'd been nothing but a pain in *his*.

"Perimeter on the building," he growled at those awaiting orders. "Ten on patrol in the town and ten in the trees outside the wall. Mind you don't drown yourselves in this rain." Then he climbed the ladder and stepped out of the deluge.

The storm had turned the afternoon light dim, but the

interior of the building was filled with a warm glow courtesy of a dozen blown-glass sconces mounted on walls painted with elaborate murals depicting what he suspected were representations of the gods. It was exceptional work, and Marcus found his eyes lingering on each scene, trying to glean details about the natures of these deities of which he was woefully ignorant.

Shifting his attention to the rest of the room revealed several long tables made of polished planks of wood, the legs carved with twisting vines and blooming flowers, the benches flanking them equally ornate. Each of them bore vases containing elaborate arrangements that wouldn't have been out of place in a senator's home.

But as he looked closer, Marcus saw the dings in the paint on the wall. The gouges and marks in the furniture. Chips in the vases, and stains in the woven rugs that no amount of washing would remove. The signs of age and wear that indicated these people were lacking in either time or means, possibly both. Signs that life had, at one point, been different for these people. Had probably been better.

But mostly what he noted was that the building was completely dry, which, given the deluge, was bloody remarkable. Eyeing the rafters, Marcus made a note to have Servius look into some of the men learning their building techniques and what materials they used, along with some consideration to how they elevated their homes, as he was certain his camp was resembling muddy soup at this point.

Teriana sat on one of the benches, deep in conversation with Quintus and Miki. Throwing back her head, she laughed at something the former had said, pulling off his helmet and running a hand across his shorn hair until he playfully batted her arm away. She was entirely at ease with both of them despite the fact that they were two of the more deadly members of the Thirty-Seventh, Quintus in particular. He was trained as an assassin, used for selective strikes against key members of the enemy or for kills the Senate wanted attributed to someone other than the legions. He was very good at his job.

Or had been.

Quintus had cracked toward the end of the Chersome campaign. He hadn't been alone in that, but he *had* been the only one to do so in the middle of the command tent in front of Marcus and half his officers, screaming that he couldn't do it anymore, that he couldn't be a murderer anymore.

Gibzen had pushed Marcus to have Quintus discharged, arguing that he was too dangerous and unpredictable to be allowed to remain. Marcus had been inclined to agree, had been about to sign the paperwork, when Miki had forced his way into the command tent. The redheaded Sibernese soldier was typically devoid of temper, but he'd gotten right up in Marcus's face. *Quit using him as your own personal butcher!* he'd shouted. *Quit using him to do your dirty work, and he'll be fine. Just don't send him away. I'll keep him together. I'll hold him together. Just don't send him away.*

Then he'd wept.

And Marcus had ripped up the paperwork.

"I assume you have coin on you so I can negotiate with them for something for us to eat?" Teriana's voice pulled Marcus from his thoughts, and he focused on the Maarin girl, whose arms were now crossed, all laughter gone from her face.

Ereni and several of her people had filtered in as well. Marcus stood between them and his men, the tension in the room thick enough to cut. Anxiety from the Arinoquians at having strange men bearing arms in their midst, and his men, knowing they inspired such emotions, looking like they'd rather be out in the deluge. He cast his eyes over the Arinoquians, noting how lean they were despite being next to abundant seas, the proof of which he'd seen in the size of the catch they'd hauled in from their boats. With what they could hunt and forage for in the jungle, they should've been able to trade for what they needed, but Marcus knew hunger when he saw it. "Negotiate, please," he said to Teriana, then turned to one of his men and murmured, "Collect a day's worth of grain ration from the men. And all the booze they have on them."

The man blinked. "No one has—"

Marcus fixed him with a stare, the soldier coloring before he saluted sharply and left the building.

Teriana had her bargaining face on, her voice taking on the rhythmic lilt it did when she was negotiating. Already he was recognizing Arinoquian words: things like *fish* and *fruit*. *Silver*. *Friend*. Language had always come easy to him, and he spoke every major language of the Empire fluently. So he easily recognized it when Teriana said, "We have a deal, then?" She turned to Marcus after Ereni nodded. "They'll provide three meals of fish, fruit, and tubers."

"Whatever you negotiated in silver," he said. "Or this." The soldier had already returned with a large sack, along with several small bottles of spirits. Taking the sack, Marcus set it on the table and gestured at Ereni to look. The ration was mixed grains straight from the fertile fields of Celendor proper, and Marcus had a great deal of it sitting back at camp. *Silver or grain.* He waited to see what they would choose, because it would tell him much about just how hungry these people were.

The imperatrix pointed at the grain, her hands marked with scars that had gone silver with age. *Hungry.*

Marcus nodded, then extracted a heavy gold coin from his belt pouch. Pushing it across the table, he said in Arinoquian, "My men are terrible cooks."

The imperatrix smiled the first genuine smile he'd seen from her and nodded.

They feasted on grilled fish and roasted tubers, the Arinoquians bringing in trays of sliced fruits at the end, his men stuffing their faces with a greediness that bordered on embarrassing, though the townsfolk seemed pleased with it. Marcus handed over the rum he'd pilfered from his men, and in exchange they'd received some sort of spirit the Arinoquians distilled themselves that was strong enough to make Marcus's eyes water.

With Teriana at his elbow translating, he bombarded the

Arinoquians with questions about what sort of fish they caught, the weather, what sort of creatures lived in the jungle, whether any were poisonous, all the while watching as spirits lifted, more people entering the common room to satisfy their curiosity. Soon there were children running between legs, laughter filling the air, and judging from giggles coming from outside, at least one of the women in the town had taken a shine to one of his men.

The only individual frowning was Teriana.

"You're manipulating them. Do you think I don't see that?" she muttered. "Pretending to be their friends so that they'll lower their guard and you can strike."

"You're acting like I'm going to wake up tomorrow and stab them in the back," he growled, drinking some of the potent spirit despite having ignored his cup all night.

"I didn't say it would be tomorrow."

Draining his cup, he set it down. It was late, all the children having been dispatched to bed, even the pair who'd been running about wearing Quintus's and Miki's helmets, whacking each other in the head with sticks. Resting his elbows on the table, he caught the attention of Ereni. "I think it is time we discussed Urcon."

Teriana tonelessly translated, everyone crammed into the room growing silent. "Tell me his story."

Ereni's words were stilted at first, but gradually her tongue loosened as she described the rise of Urcon. The Arinoquians had come to these shores almost a generation ago, leaving behind their inhospitable homeland, which Teriana said was an island nation south of the continent. "Ice and rock and not much else," she muttered. "I wouldn't want to live there, either."

After driving those native to these lands inland, they'd established themselves and then broken back into their clans. Urcon was the leader of one of those clans—a charismatic man and gifted warrior who, having had a taste of the power of the clans united into one, desired more of the same. With an army of his men, he set to forcing the other clans to accept him as ruler, to bend their knees and tithe to him as though he were a king.

At first, they resisted, but Ereni said, "We'd come to these shores for a chance to stop fighting, to live in a place where our people could thrive. So we gave him what he wanted, believing he'd let us live in peace."

But that wasn't how it went. Instead, Urcon demanded more from them, stripping away wealth, burning and destroying the homes of those who attempted to resist, killing those who fought back. And with the money he took, he was able to build himself a mercenary army that no one could stand against. It was then he began taking the youths of those towns and villages who couldn't afford to pay. Youths who were never seen again. So once again, the clans picked up their swords and began to fight back.

"And no one knows what happens to those taken?" Marcus asked, persisting with the question despite having been told by Flacre that it was a mystery.

"No," Teriana said; then she hesitated, listening to Ereni. "They don't know."

She wasn't translating the whole of the story. Marcus knew she was constantly filtering the information he received, but in this moment he wasn't willing to let it slide. "They know something. Tell me."

Teriana sucked her cheeks in, and he watched her gaze darken as she debated whether or not to concede. "There are . . . rumors. Rumors that Urcon worships the Seventh god. Rumors that the children are . . . sacrifices."

Marcus's brow furrowed, his skin turning cold as he remembered the shrine in Flacre's village. How the featureless face had seemed to look at him, its eyes burning. "What would he stand to gain from such behavior?"

Giving a discomforted shrug, Teriana said, "I don't know."

"Speculate."

Her face darkened. "I don't know, Marcus, all right? I haven't made a habit of spending time with those who bend the knee to the Seventh."

Turning back to Ereni, he asked, "Why don't the other gods intervene?"

One of the young Arinoquians in the room spit and said something that was undoubtedly a curse. Ereni barked a reprimand at him, and he left the room with a scowl on his face.

"It's not the gods' way to intervene," Teriana said. "Only to hold men and women accountable for how they lived their lives when they come to the end of them."

She was lying. There was more to it; Marcus knew it. He'd seen Gespurn and Madoria rise from air and water and go to battle over his fleet. There was no chance that they and the rest would idly watch events like these pass them by without acting. But he wasn't going to pick a fight with Teriana about her deception in front of these people and burn away all the goodwill he'd earned.

Ereni said something more. Teriana made a face and then said, "She wants to know why someone like you who knows no gods shows so much curiosity about them."

Answering the question with his men listening was dangerous ground, but Marcus found himself doing it anyway. "It's true that I was raised to believe that the idea of gods was lies and myth, but since coming to the West I've seen things that make continued disbelief seem . . . recklessly ignorant."

Picking up his cup, which someone had refilled, he swirled the contents before setting it back down. "In truth, I find certain appeal to the idea that in this world where so much injustice reigns that in our final hours there is someone—or something—that holds us to account."

For once, Teriana said nothing, and when Marcus turned his head, for the first time since they'd met, the ocean waves of the eyes gazing into his own were a tranquil blue.

Ereni allowed them to remain in the common room for the night, Marcus and Teriana taking the small adjoining chamber while his men rotated between taking watch shifts and sleeping in the main hall.

Teriana had said nothing to him since his conversation with Ereni had ended, and even once they were alone she'd done nothing but pull a thin blanket up over her shoulders and turn away from him.

Exhausted from carrying her, and the potent alcohol burning in his blood, Marcus turned down the lamp. Sleep came quickly.

As did the dream.

It was always the same. Him, walking alone across the Chersome plains, his breath misting in the cold air. Ahead, a village situated next to a copse of pines, buildings and trees smoldering, the smoke rising into the grey sky. A gust of wind hit him in the face, carrying with it a stench that he swore would linger in his nose for as long as he lived. A sickening combination of burnt pork and charred hair, the iron tang of seared blood, and something . . . something that his basest instincts recognized as human.

He did not want to go into the village, but his feet dragged him closer. The wind blew again, and he shivered, reaching for a weapon only to discover it wasn't there. And it didn't matter. What good was steel against the dead?

Then he was in the village, the small homes blackened where they were not glowing red. And all around him lay bodies. Men and women. Children. Babies who hadn't seen a year of life. All of them dead. All of them burned, though the fire did not erase the other violence that had been leveled upon them.

As one, they stood. Like marionette dolls, the strings attached to their spines lifting them straight. They turned on him, arms pointing in accusation.

"I'm sorry," he pleaded. "I didn't mean for this to happen. It wasn't the plan."

They didn't hear. They didn't care.

The corpses converged on him, and their number swelled to thousands upon thousands. They hemmed him in, burnt hands clutching and pulling at him, eyes nothing but empty holes and mouths open in silent screams.

"I'm sorry!" he shouted, trying to fight them back. "I'm sorry, I'm sorry—"

"Marcus, wake up!"

He froze, feeling his attacker pinned beneath him in the darkness.

"It's me. Teriana. You were having a dream, so I woke you up."

His skin was icy. "A dream." *The dream.*

"Aye."

He inhaled and exhaled, calming himself easily only because he'd had a great deal of practice. It was then he noticed that she was near to naked beneath him, having stripped down sometime in the night. Only a linen camisole was stretched tight over her full breasts, whatever undergarments she wore leaving her legs bare where they were twined with his. He had her wrists pinned to the blanket, and he could feel her pulse rapid against his palms. And the entirely inappropriate thought that he should kiss her crossed his mind.

Instead, he asked, "Did I hurt you?"

"No."

She shifted, her leg moving and their hips pressing together in a way that made him ache. Before his body could betray him entirely, he sat up, pulling her with him. Her braids swung, brushing against his chest, the tiny ornaments cold against his skin. He held her steady, her shoulders warm and sleek beneath his hands, waiting for her to push him away. To tell him to get off of her.

"I'm sorry." His voice was hoarse, and he swallowed, wishing for a glass of water. "Sometimes I have dreams."

"What about?"

He could only just see her outline in the darkness, but her breath was hot against his cheek, her lips only inches away. "Chersome." The truth came out without thought.

Teriana was quiet for a long moment; then she placed both

hands against his chest, pushing him back and climbing to her feet. He watched as she crossed the room to her pallet, hesitating next to it.

"Good to know your victims plague your dreams," she said, and the hate was back in her voice. "Next time, I won't wake you."

31

TERIANA

Teriana awoke with a start, staring at the unfamiliar ceiling for several moments before remembering where she was. And whom she was with. Opening her mouth to deliver a few sarcastic remarks at Marcus's expense, she rolled over.

He was gone.

Disappointment filled her, and she shoved the feeling aside, replacing it with annoyance. *He's your enemy,* she reminded herself. *He's a manipulative bastard, a liar, and a killer.* Yet the reminder did little to chase away the memory of his bare skin against hers, the heat that had throbbed low in her belly as his hips had pressed down, holding her against the floor. How for that brief moment her traitorous body had wanted to wrap her legs around him, to peel away those few scraps of clothing between them and let what would happen, happen.

It's lust, nothing more, she told herself. *He's good to look at and you aren't blind, that's all.* It still troubled her that, of all the men she'd known, it would be he who'd inspire those feelings. What did it say about her that she'd wanted the hands of a murderer on her skin, to taste the lips of a man who'd taken thousands of children from their homes, broken up thousands of families? Her stomach soured, but she relished the sensation, because it was appropriate.

The door opened, and Quintus leaned in. "Wakey, wakey," he said with a grin. "It's a beautiful morning."

"It's not," she said, pulling her clothes on. "It's horrible. And my feet hurt."

Her whole damned body hurt.

"I brought you something to eat," he said. "Maybe that will help change your outlook."

"If it's gruel, I'm going to throw it right back at you."

His grin only grew. "You'd make a bad soldier."

"My heart is broken."

"Fortunately for you, Miki's been making friends and he secured us a few of these." He pulled his arm out from behind his back and handed her a banana.

"I can see why you love him," she said, peeling back the yellow skin and taking a bite.

"It's the hair, actually," he replied with a smirk. "Always had a weakness for redheads. And for freckles."

"Fair enough," she said. "Though the Six knows what he sees in an ugly golden bastard like you."

Quintus laughed. "I take it back. You'd make an excellent soldier with a mouth like yours."

Bowing deeply, she finished her banana and asked, "Where's our darling supreme commander?"

"Outside with everyone else. We're waiting on you."

Lovely.

Every muscle in her body screaming, Teriana walked slowly after the soldier, feeling the scabs on her feet tug and pull with each step, despite the salve she'd smeared on them the night before.

Marcus's back was to her, for which she was profoundly grateful, because her cheeks warmed at the sight of him.

"Dawn, Teriana," he said, turning around. "We rise at dawn. Get used to it, because I grow weary of waiting around for you."

"Kiss my ass," she muttered in Mudamorian.

"I tried that route, and it didn't work," he said, and when she gaped at him added, "Your crewmember Jax taught me that particular phrase. Now let's go."

He moved to lift her, but Teriana caught sight of a symbol carved into the door of one of the buildings—a symbol she'd been desperate to see—and she pushed him back. "I need to see their . . . ," she searched for a suitable Cel term, "herbarius before we go."

"Talk to one of the medics."

Planting her hands on her hips, Teriana stared him down. "Your medics have much experience treating female conditions?"

Color rose in his cheeks, and he looked away. "Be quick about it."

Moving gingerly on her aching feet, Teriana climbed into the elevated town, wove across several bridges, and then knocked on the door.

"Come in."

Pushing inside, she waited for her eyes to adjust to the dim light, eventually catching sight of an older man grinding herbs in a stone bowl, Hegeria's mark tattooed onto his forehead. His eyes immediately went to the bandages on her feet, a sympathetic noise passing his lips as he rose. "Come here, child, and let me see to those injuries."

Teriana stepped back before he could touch her, knowing that was all it would take. "No. You can't. If these men learn what your mark allows you to do, they'll use you until you're in your grave."

If her words shocked him, it didn't show. "Are you here to warn me, then?"

Shaking her head, Teriana said, "I need a favor."

"I'm listening."

She pulled two folded letters from deep in one of her pockets and passed them to him. "I need you to get these to the temples in Katamarca and Gamdesh, and for the Grand Masters to pass them on to the Queen and Sultan, respectively."

His hands stilled. "What do they say?"

"They're a warning," she said, then swallowed hard. "And a request for aid on behalf of the Maarin people. My name's Teriana. My mother is Tesya, captain of the *Quincense* and Triumvir of the Maarin Trade Consortium. The Cel aren't here for peace. They're here to conquer. It says all that in there"—she pointed at the letters—"but I have no way to get them delivered. But you do."

Picking up his mortar and pestle, the old man went to the

window and twitched aside the curtain, grinding the herbs as he looked out. "Is it a lie, then, that they plan to dispose of Urcon and allow us to govern ourselves?"

"Yes! No." Teriana pressed a hand to her forehead. "It's what they mean to do in the short term. But once they've found xenthier paths between here and the Empire, all this kindness? It will disappear. Cassius is just as bad as Urcon. Worse."

His hands paused. "I believe you, Teriana. But I fear your warnings will fall on deaf ears among my people, especially if this *Legatus Marcus* continues as he has. My people know no other fear greater than Urcon, and many have lost faith in the Six, blaming them for abandoning us in our time of great need. They might welcome this regime from across the seas, not seeing the danger that lurks beneath the surface until it is too late."

"You need to help me make them see it," she said. "They need to fight back. They must!"

"I think you need to consider what will happen if they don't."

Teriana's stomach had hollowed as he'd spoken, but now that space was filled with fear. She'd banked everything on the belief that the nations of the West would be able to fight back the Cel, to send them into retreat. But if what the healer said was true, then the Arinoquians might not just capitulate; they might welcome the Cel with open arms. And only once it was too late would they realize their mistake.

"Teriana!" Marcus's voice echoed through the walls of the building. "Are you finished?"

The healer poured the contents of his pestle into a linen sack and handed it over. "To add credence to whatever excuse you gave to see me."

Teriana lifted it to her nose and sniffed, instantly recognizing the scent. "I don't want this," she said, trying to return it.

"But you might need it," he replied, pushing it back. "My name is Caradoc should you need help these men can't give you."

A knock sounded at the door, and a moment later it opened to reveal the face of the medic, who smiled and inclined his head respectfully. "Teriana," he said, "the legatus said this man specializes in plants and herbs? A physician of sorts?"

Her chest tightened. "Why?"

"We're well supplied, obviously," he replied, eyes drifting over the shelves filled with jars. "But on the assumption we'll eventually start to run short, I'd like to start working on understanding which local plants I might use as alternatives. Would you ask if he's willing to talk?"

Relief flooded through her. "Please don't tell me that Marcus is willing to sacrifice his fine-tuned schedule to discuss *plants*."

"He is." Marcus answered for himself, stepping inside the home and leaning against the wall. "If this man is willing to share his knowledge."

Scowling, she asked Caradoc, who only shrugged and nodded, proceeding to answer the medic's seemingly endless questions. Teriana translated, but her attention kept drifting to Marcus, it being impossible to focus with his eyes on her.

"Don't you have something better to do?" she said to him. "Maybe go try to buy me some sandals or something so that I can walk. My ribs can't take any more of your bony shoulders."

He cracked his back. "It's already taken care of."

Taken care of turned out to be the purchase of a donkey that was nearly as round as he was tall. By the time they'd finished in the other towns and villages and were heading back to camp, Teriana's ass hurt nearly as much as her feet.

"Every gods-damned minute with you is more miserable than the last," she muttered, eyeing the setting sun. "I hate this. I hate being on land. I hate how hot it is. I hate all these mosquitos. I hate walking everywhere. I hate everything."

"I hope you didn't mean to include all of us in your little rant, Teriana," Miki said from where he strode next to her right knee, the donkey so short the legionnaire was eye level with her. "Quintus's feelings are easily hurt, and you and I are going to have words if you make him cry."

To her left, Quintus pretended to weep into her donkey's sweaty neck.

"Not you two lovebirds," she said, shoving Quintus away with one bandaged foot. "Mostly," she said, her voice growing louder with each word, despite Marcus walking next to the donkey's head, "I hate the asses in our company who seem to be working together to rub the skin off my backside."

A sharp series of whistles filled the air and the legionnaires were all moving in an instant.

Quintus pulled Teriana off the donkey and dragged her to the side of the path, pressing her against the ground. Over the rush of her fear, she heard Marcus snarling orders, but all she could see was Miki's sandaled foot next to her face, the metal of Quintus's breastplate digging into her back.

"What's happening?" she whispered.

"Possible ambush," Quintus replied. "We stay down until it's safe."

The ground was moist beneath her head. A twig or a root, she wasn't sure which, dug into her ear. A spider scuttled toward her, but Quintus flicked it away before it could climb into her hair. Her breath came in fast little rasps that she was certain anyone who was hunting would be able to hear, because Quintus and Miki were silent. A tear squeezed its way out, dribbling down her face.

"It's going to be all right," Quintus said, easing off of her. "Legatus is coming this way now."

"Help her up."

"I can get up myself," Teriana muttered, climbing to her feet. Only then did she realize that it hadn't just been Quintus and Miki with her but ten other soldiers arrayed about her.

Marcus's face was pale beneath his helmet, expression grim. "What happened?" she demanded, her gaze skipping to the other legionnaires who were with him. All the humor that had been on their faces moments ago was long gone.

"Can you tell me what this says?" he asked. Pulling a knife from his belt, he scratched out a series of words into the ground.

The Arinoquian language used different letters than Cel and some he'd formed badly, but the message was clear enough. "'Those who ally with the dragon will pay the price.'"

Lifting her head, she asked, "This message was left on the path? As a warning to the Arinoquians?"

Pulling off his helmet, Marcus wiped sweat off his face. "A warning to us." Turning to one of his men, he said, "Is there a way around?"

"No, sir," the soldier responded. "Not unless we backtrack and cut deep inland. They chose that spot for that reason, which is why when we saw"—his gaze cut to Teriana, then away—"when we saw the message, we suspected an ambush."

"No helping it, then." Marcus jammed his helmet back on. "Your donkey bolted down the trail, Teriana. We'll catch him for you on the other side."

"Other side of what?"

"Can you walk for ten minutes?" he asked, ignoring her question.

"Yes, but—"

"Let's go."

The group started walking, the path cutting closer to the sea until it was skirting the edge of a cliff, sharp hills rising on the other side. She remembered the spot from when they'd passed through the prior morning—they weren't that far from camp.

Marcus caught hold of her arm. "Close your eyes."

"Why?" she demanded. "What's there that you don't want me to see?"

The muscles of his jaw flexed. "Close your eyes, Teriana, or I'll blindfold you."

She took a step back. "Whatever it is, I should see it."

"No."

"I will stand here and fight you on this all day," she said, but her voice shook, because right then the wind gusted in their direction and she caught the tangy copper scent of blood.

"I'm not letting you see." He moved, pinning her arms to her sides, his other hand clamping down over her eyes.

"Let me go!" she shouted, struggling against him, but he was stronger.

"Walk, or I will drag you."

Her feet moved, but she kept fighting. Kept fighting even as her bandaged feet stepped in something warm. Something stickier than mud. It splattered against her legs, squished between her toes. "Let me see!" she shrieked. "Let me go!"

"No." His voice was strained. "Hate me all you want, Teriana, I'm not letting you see this. Because if you do, you will never be able to unsee it. It will be burned into your mind, and you will see it every time you close your eyes."

"I don't care."

"I do," he said into her ear. "I care."

"Not your choice." His hand had slipped slightly in her struggles and, not caring about the consequences, she bit him. Hard.

Swearing, Marcus jerked his hand away from her face.

There were things in the world that shouldn't happen. That shouldn't be. This was one of them.

Blood. Blood, everywhere. And pieces . . . Logically she knew they formed bodies, but her mind couldn't seem to fit them together. Couldn't seem to turn them back into the people they'd been. As she watched, one of the men knelt, closing the eyelids of a young woman's face, his hands shaking.

Twisting away, Teriana stumbled backward and away from the slaughter, but her foot slipped in the mud and she fell on her ass, jarring her spine. The pain barely registered as her eyes fixed on her feet. The once white bandages were brilliant crimson, entirely soaked through with blood.

Arinoquians. That's who the dead were. Some of the townsfolk they'd spent the night with. It was the blood of the West that was coating her feet. And it was her fault. She'd brought the Cel here. She'd negotiated peace between the Arinoquians and the Cel. This was her fault. Her choice. Her doing.

"Get them off." Her voice shook, sobs tearing from her lips even as she tore at the bandages, but they were sticky and tangled and there was blood on her hands. "Get them off! Get them off!"

Marcus dropped to his knees in front of her, unraveling the bandages and tossing them aside. But her feet were still covered in it. Her hands were covered in it.

Her whole body shook, her breath coming in fast little gasps. Her ears filled with a loud roar and the world seemed to shift around her, swimming. Darkening.

And then she was in the sea.

Waves washed over her, Marcus's arms around her waist to keep her from drowning.

The sea surged up the white sand of the beach, and then down, taking the blood staining her skin with it. Calming her. Bringing her back to herself.

"Are you all right?" Marcus's voice was low, only audible because his face was near her ear, one arm wrapped around her, one braced in the wet sand.

She nodded, and he let her go, standing next to her in the water. He pulled off his helmet, and though he was motionless, Teriana could feel a seething energy to him, like a geyser waiting to blow.

Teriana focused on the sting of her raw heels rather than the pain in her heart. "This is my fault."

"This is not your fault, Teriana." He swallowed hard. "It's mine."

"I brought you here."

He didn't respond, only stared out over the water as though his eyes could stretch all the way back to the Empire.

"Fuck!" he abruptly screamed, and in a violent motion threw the helmet at the waves, the metal bouncing once before sinking. He swore again and kicked the water before doubling over like he'd been punched in the gut.

Teriana watched him in silence. Watched as he slowly sank down to sit next to her, elbows resting on his knees, face in his hands. For a long time, he didn't speak. Didn't move. And though the weight of what she'd seen sat heavily on Teriana's shoulders, she found herself transfixed by this uncharacteristic crack in composure.

Marcus finally straightened, droplets of water running down his face. *But not all of it,* Teriana thought, *is from the sea.*

"Thousands of hours of training," he finally said. "Every book the Empire possesses on strategy and tactics and politics and negotiation crammed into my head. Campaign after campaign, and yet this is *always* where I fail."

"You've never lost." The words came out of her mouth as a whisper, barely audible over the waves.

But he heard.

"I've lost a hundred times," he said, turning to her. His eyes were red. "A thousand times. Every time someone died because I failed to predict just how low men and women will stoop when pushed. Just how evil they can be if pressed."

He looked away. "Cross the world, and it's the same." And then, so low Teriana barely heard it, he said, "It's happening again."

"What do you mean?" she asked, curious and fascinated and horrified, because that massacre on the pathway—that was part and parcel of his *life.*

But Marcus didn't answer, only rested his face in his hands again, staring at the water between his knees. All the power of ten thousand soldiers behind him, an Empire behind him, and in that moment he looked like nothing more than a boy.

Go home, she silently whispered. *Go back to the place that bred you. That made you. Don't make me destroy you.*

Abruptly he twisted onto his knees in front of her, gripping her forearms. "You know whose fault this is, Teriana? It's the fault of the men who wielded the blades. And the fault of the man who ordered them to do it."

"Urcon wouldn't have given that order if I hadn't brought you here," she said. "They'd still be alive."

"Would they?" His eyes bored into hers with an intensity unique to him, and she found herself deeply aware of where his skin touched hers. Where his knee pressed against the inside of her thigh. "Because from what we've been told, Urcon has killed plenty of Arinoquians with no more motivation than the desire to build his own power."

Letting go of her with one hand, he pointed a finger up the slope in the direction of the gory scene. "Those people died because they traded with us for food. Because they hosted us for a night. Because they agreed to help *feed us* and *guide us* and perhaps one day to fight alongside us. And for that, Urcon had them cut into pieces and left as a gods-damned message on the trail.

"He did it to try to intimidate us," he continued. "And as a way to intimidate his *own people*. To make them fear the consequences of rising against him. But mostly Urcon did this because he is afraid."

Marcus's hands slid down her arms to grip hers, and Teriana stared at their interlaced fingers, unsure of why she didn't recoil. Of why she gripped them back to try to stop his hands from shaking.

"Do you think Urcon should be allowed to remain in power?" he demanded, leaning forward. "Do you think he should be allowed to continue as he has?"

"Of course I don't." Her voice was hoarse.

"Then help me tear him down." His face was inches from hers, his breath rapid and warm against her cheek. "Help me give him a taste of justice."

It was more complicated than that. Deep down, she wasn't sure it was Marcus's right—or even her own—to bring Urcon to justice, but her battered mind couldn't form the argument that she knew was there. Not with his eyes burning into hers, his fervor lighting her own blood on fire.

"The Arinoquians didn't choose Urcon. They don't want him, and he punishes them for it." Marcus rose to his feet, pulling Teriana with him. "And it's time his rule came to an end."

32

TERIANA

If Urcon believed that his message would put fear into the hearts of Ereni's clan or send Marcus and his legions running back to Celendor, he was mistaken. For the Arinoquians were no cowards, and the Thirty-Seventh had never fallen back for a reason.

Teriana didn't know exactly what had happened, for Marcus had sent her back to camp under the watchful eye of Quintus and Miki, but Marcus had returned to see Ereni with Gibzen and several other hard-eyed legionnaires in tow. They didn't return until late the next day, and Marcus would say nothing other than that justice had been delivered.

And his alliance with Ereni was sealed in blood.

Justice did nothing to ease Teriana's guilt over her complicity in the slaughter on the road, her belief that those Arinoquians would be alive today if not for her choices, and the only thing that kept her anguish from drowning her in the bottom of a rum barrel was that the legion worked her harder than she'd ever worked in her life.

Teriana was constantly on the move, negotiating with towns and villages within Ereni's sphere of influence to provide the legions with fish and supplies, for which she struck hard enough bargains that even her mother would've been proud. For two days, she was forced to ride that gods-damned donkey led by either Quintus or Miki until her feet had healed, but once they had, she marched along with the men, teaching them the rudiments of the language even as she joked and laughed with them, burying all her other emotions for a time when she could put them to better use.

It had been her strategy to make the men like her. To make

them trust her. She hadn't expected them to win her over. But they had.

Before, she'd always seen them as a thousand replicas of the same creation, trained and groomed by the Empire that owned them. Now, she saw them as individuals with unique personalities and quirks, some of whom she liked, some of whom she didn't. Their names piled up in her mind as she ate, diced, and drank through her evenings in their company.

It didn't help that they weren't the blackhearted menaces she'd believed them to be. As a rule, they were considerate to the Arinoquians, communicating with the words they'd learned, hand gestures, and smiles, requesting that Teriana teach some of the youths how to speak Cel to better bridge the gap.

Ereni's clan now came to them with offers of assistance beyond what goods and supplies they sold. Warriors, with their imperatrix's blessing, offered their services as guides and spies, but Marcus took it a step further, integrating the men and women into legion patrols, his men under strict instruction to learn from them and heed their advice.

The young Arinoquians flirted with the legionnaires, and she did not fail to notice when they'd tug a young man out of sight, or their flushed cheeks when they returned. Teriana had held her breath the first few times, worried that the soldiers would cross the line and someone would get hurt, but Marcus held militantly to the laws he'd negotiated with Ereni, and his men did not cross him. "You hear even a whisper of unprovoked violence toward man or woman, you bring it to me directly," he told her. "These people are our allies, and they are to be treated as such."

And as much as it ground on her nerves to hear the people of the West referred to as allies, what could she say when it ensured their protection?

Urcon's bands of men made several more attempts to attack villages and towns peopled by Ereni's clan, but Marcus's men and Ereni's warriors met them at every turn, slaughtering them with no mercy. Teriana had thought seeing the bloodthirsty side of the Cel might put the Arinoquians off, but it only seemed to win them further favor. To win Marcus further favor.

Once, she'd heard Titus question Marcus as to why they didn't take Galinha, the city north of them. It was controlled by Urcon, peopled by his clan, and was where a large portion of his raiders were garrisoned. "Why don't we just take them out at the source?" Titus had complained. "Why are we marching our men up and down the coast and spreading ourselves so thin?"

"Because," Marcus had answered, "if we take Galinha out now, it will be our victory. The Empire's victory. But if we turn the Arinoquians into our allies, it will be their victory, too."

"We have Ereni's clan already."

"One isn't enough."

"How many do we need?"

"All of them," Marcus had said. "Then it will be the victory of a nation."

Too late, Teriana was coming to understand why they called him the Prodigy of Campus Lescendor. Why he'd won all those battles and wars. What made him so damned good at what he did. Marcus understood people. Understood their fears, their desires, their motivations. How to get them to do what he wanted. How to give them what they wanted.

And the worst of it was, he *actually* seemed to care about whether the Arinoquians were happy or not. Rising religiously at dawn, he worked continuously through the day, consulting the clan imperators who'd joined the alliance, Ereni and Flacre permanent fixtures in the command tent. He directed every aspect of the campaign down to the smallest detail, a single lamp burning in the command tent long after Teriana had collapsed onto her bedroll. It was taking a toll on him; that much was clear from the shadows beneath his eyes, his already-lean frame now only skin stretched taut over muscles kept solid by his stupid exercises. When he did sleep it was fitful and plagued by dreams, his violent tossing and turning and muttered pleas for forgiveness tearing her from sleep night after night, consuming her with guilt each time she stuck by her word and refused to wake him.

He deserves it, she silently told herself, forcing her mind to recycle the stories she'd heard about him. His violent and bloody history.

How many have died because of him? How many forced into servitude?

He is the enemy. He is your enemy.

Yet every day, it felt harder to reconcile the commander she'd heard so many stories about with the young man she now *knew*. The young man she knew well, because she'd been at his side every day since they'd landed, translating, negotiating, and, to her growing dismay, actually advising him. It was nearly impossible not to—not when Marcus fixed her with that intense gaze of his, digging knowledge out of her that she hadn't even realized she possessed.

Being around him wasn't comfortable in the way it was with the other men. With the others, she could sit around the fire and relax, gamble and tell stories, and it was easy. Thoughtless. But with Marcus, Teriana felt hyperaware of everything she said. Everything she did. Every breath she took. It was like being in the rigging during a storm, conscious of every step. Of every handhold. Because to relax even for a heartbeat might mean catastrophe. Except with Marcus she was no longer certain what *catastrophe* meant. And there was a part of her, buried so deep she could barely admit it to herself, that wanted to find out what would happen if she let go.

"The Arinoquians have stopped listening to me," she said quietly, resting her elbows on her knees as she regarded Bait swimming below. They'd met like this before, Teriana pleading the need for a proper bath, the distance Miki and Quintus gave her for privacy enough to disguise the sounds of her and Bait's conversation. And even if they suspected, it was nothing for Bait to sink under the waves.

"I've told them every story I know about how the Empire conquered the East," she continued. "The worst. The goriest.

The bloodiest. About how rigid the Cel laws are, how everyone is forced to conform. About the taxes and the child tithes to the legions. About how they don't follow the Six. About how the Six aren't even present across the seas. They either don't believe me or don't care. I'd be better off spitting into the wind."

"They can't see past their full bellies and even fuller purses," Bait replied. "He's making Arinoquia better than it's been in decades."

"All he's doing is paving a smooth path for the arrival of something worse."

Bracing a hand against the base of the pier, Bait sighed. "Maybe we did it to ourselves by keeping knowledge of the East from them. It's all stories and myth to them, whereas Urcon is a tangible threat they've been dealing with for over twenty years. And . . ."

"And what?" she demanded.

"I was able to make contact with another Maarin ship," he said. "They had news from the north. Derin breached the wall and has invaded Mudamora under the banner of the Seventh god."

"What?" Teriana whispered even as she remembered the vision Magnius had shown her of the field of corpses, the banners of the Twelve Houses sinking into the mud even as soldiers with flags bearing the burning circle of the Seventh god marched past.

"They're led by a priestess who is said to be one of the corrupted."

Her blood chilled. Those marked by the Seventh god were able to kill with a touch, draining the lives of their victims to bolster their own, leaving only desiccated corpses in their wake. She'd only seen one once, in Mudamora, and the woman had killed dozens of trained soldiers before she was finally taken down. Even though Teriana had watched it all through a spyglass from where the *Quincense* had been anchored in the harbor, part of her had still been terrified the woman would leap across the waves and kill her next. But the information triggered another thought in her head.

"The Arinoquians think they're being abandoned by the Six." She gave a slight shake of her head. "And in truth, there is something to their fears. There is only one healer in Ereni's clan. One, where there should be dozens. And I've not so much as heard a whisper of anyone marked by the other gods."

Neither of them spoke, but Bait reached up to rest a comforting hand on her knee.

"Bait, sometimes it feels like Arinoquia was set up for invasion," she whispered. "It's been too easy."

"Or maybe he's just as good as they say."

"Maybe."

"Regardless, the eyes of every kingdom are on the outcome of Mudamora's war with Derin," he said. "What's happening here with the Cel . . . No one cares. Arinoquia is on its own."

"And the Arinoquians don't seem too troubled by that fact."

Bait's jaw worked back and forth. "Urcon is rallying his armies. Maybe he'll defeat them."

Neither of them spoke, but a question that had been lurking in her chest found its way out. "What do you think will happen to the allied clans if Urcon does defeat the Cel?"

Before Bait could answer, Quintus shouted, "Teriana, we need to go!"

Pulling on her boots, she said, "You need to go home to Taltuga, Bait. Convince the other triumvirs to start meeting with the rulers of the West to make them see the magnitude of the Cel threat."

"Too many of them are holding to the mandate, Teriana. East must not meet West. They're afraid there will be consequences if they talk about the Empire here. That they'll be punished."

"Considering there are close to ten thousand Cel legionnaires currently camped in the West, I'd say that ship has sailed," she snarled. "Convince them. I can't leave, and the *Quincense* can't sail. It has to be you to go, Bait."

"Are you talking to someone?" Quintus called, and she flinched as his sandals clacked against the pier.

"Just to myself," she called back, then to Bait, "And if you can't convince the triumvirs, you need to go to Revat to speak to the Sultan of Gamdesh. Use my name to get yourself in—he'll listen. Steal some of the Cel coinage from your guards and take it with you as proof."

A hand rested on her shoulder right as Bait sank beneath the waves. "Come on, Teriana. Tonight's not the night to test your limits."

"Why?" she asked. "What's going on?"

Quintus opened his mouth, but Miki beat him to it. "If the legatus had wanted you to know, he'd have told you. Either way, he's the one who wants you back within the camp walls ten minutes ago."

Teriana's stomach clenched, sweat pooling beneath her breasts despite the breeze coming in off the sea. It took them only a matter of minutes to return to the camp, and the moment she stepped through the gates she knew.

It was empty.

Not entirely empty, the walls still manned, but mostly empty, which damned well never happened. Her chest tightened, her feet drawing her toward the command tent at a pace that bordered on a run.

"What's going on?" she demanded.

Marcus didn't look up from the page he was reading, but Titus turned to her. "We're attacking Galinha shortly."

Though she'd known the attack was imminent, her skin still prickled with nerves. Two days ago, Marcus had ordered the camp moved to a location farther north, within spitting distance of the city—the legions efficiently packing, moving, and replicating the camp in the space of the day. Since then, the allied imperators and their warriors had been gathering in camps nearby. That they'd move against Galinha, and soon, had been obvious. It was equally obvious that she was the only one who hadn't known it would be tonight.

"It's almost dusk," she said, not knowing why she bothered. "Who starts a battle in the middle of the night?"

"I do." Marcus straightened, nodding at the men filling the tent. "Proceed. Tell Imperatrix Ereni that I'll be along shortly."

Gods-damn it! Even Ereni knew and kept it from me.

Marcus waited until they'd left, then sat on one of the stools, examining the map of the city in question. Then he said, "Most of the civilians will be in their homes and out of the way, which will help reduce incidental casualties."

"Incidental?" Her tone was biting and one she reserved solely for him. "How can you claim any death unplanned when you're *attacking* their city?"

He rubbed his temple with one hand. "Fine. It will reduce the number of deaths of people who don't deserve it. Is that better?"

"Would be better if you didn't attack them at all."

"Would it really? You've heard as much testimony as I have as to how the people in Galinha are treated, and they are *part* of Urcon's clan. By now, they will all be aware that there's an alternative to Urcon's rule—a chance at a better life. They're primed to turn on his men, which means they'll not get in our way when we attack, and they won't cause us trouble once we've taken the city. If we wait longer, we'll risk them growing embittered over the loss of their southern supply chain, and they'll rise against us or try to overthrow Urcon's men themselves. Either circumstance will result in more civilian casualties, which, despite what you seem bent on believing, is not what I want."

She did know that wasn't what he wanted, had overheard countless discussions he'd had with the rest of his officers and the imperators. It was the reasoning behind it that wouldn't allow her to see his actions as benevolent. "Oh, I know civilian deaths aren't part of the plan," she said. "The Six forbid that you have to send corpses back to the Empire rather than living, breathing slaves."

Silence. Then Marcus slowly got to his feet, cup clenched in his fist, his face full of enough anger that she wondered if she'd finally pushed him too far.

"It always comes down to Chersome, doesn't it?" he snarled, then to her shock threw the cup in his hand across the tent, where it splattered water against the canvas. "No matter what I do, it will always come back to that damned island."

He was agitated and angry, and Teriana knew she shouldn't push this. But she couldn't let it go. "That will happen when you murder thousands of innocents. It's not something people forget."

"Murder." He slowly turned to face her, his golden skin blanched of color. "Is that what you think?"

"It's what I know."

"No." He stalked toward her, and it took every ounce of bravery she possessed not to take a step back. "It's what the Senate wants you—wants everyone—to believe. Better for you to think us heartless killers, to fear the Empire's wrath, than to know the truth."

"What truth?" she asked, annoyed with her curiosity. For wondering if there was something he could say that would make the decimation of a country and the enslavement of its entire people palatable. For hoping that there was.

His eyes searched hers, and then it seemed that all the heat rushed out of him in an instant. Sitting on one of the folding stools, he rested his elbows on the table, staring blankly at the map laid out before him. "The truth is that nothing about that mission went as I'd wanted it to."

He was silent, the only sound a flock of birds screeching overhead. Teriana held her tongue, waiting.

"It was supposed to go peacefully," he said quietly. "We'd land and infiltrate them. Pay for what we took, give them a taste of what it meant to be part of the Empire. Convince them to voluntarily cede control to the Senate and accept the taxes, while avoiding armed conflict where at all possible. It had worked before. Has worked since. But . . ."

He licked his lips, his breathing raspy, and she knew he was remembering.

"But it didn't go that way," he continued. "We landed. As we marched, all we discovered were burned-out villages, the inhabitants dead by flame or blade. Men, women, and children. Little babies dead in their mothers' arms." His throat convulsed as he swallowed. "I've seen things that make what Urcon's men did to those villagers on the path look like child's play."

Those were his dreams, or at least some of them. The ones that made him thrash about in his blankets until he woke in a cold sweat. "Who killed them?" she asked.

"Their own people. Chersome had a warrior caste that lived apart from the rest. They were systematically moving across the island and slaughtering everyone."

"Why?" Teriana asked, unable to comprehend how or why they'd do such a thing. Those villages would have been full of their families. Their friends.

"Because they believed it was better for them to be dead than to be under the control of the Empire. Better for the entire island to go up in flames than the Senate to profit from its lands."

She bit her lip, wondering if there was something to the idea. Was it better to be dead than to live a life stripped of everything you valued?

"We captured some and tried to make them see reason," he said. "Only they wouldn't listen. Would burn themselves alive, fall on a sword, or hang themselves with whatever they could find. So . . ." He drew in a shaky breath. "So we fought them. I broke the legion up and sent it across the island in a coordinated strike with orders to kill every warrior they came across, no exceptions. Only then the men in the villages started behaving the same way: killing their families and themselves. So I rounded up the women and children and sent them back to Celendor."

She remembered when it had happened. How the markets had collapsed under the supply, indentured children going for little more than the cost of a loaf of bread. It had been disgusting, and her mother had taken the *Quincense* west for a time so they didn't have to bear witness to it. "They say one hundred sixty thousand Chersomians were processed within the space of three months." And everyone, everyone, had known *he* was the man responsible.

Marcus nodded. "But they were alive."

"So?" she demanded, the memory of those indenture markets, filthy and stinking and jammed full of children with dead men's eyes something she'd never forget. "You tore apart families. Ruined lives. Maybe it was better for them to die than to suffer what they did!"

"Maybe it was!" His anger was back, and he was on his feet, beads of sweat forming on his brow. "Only they had the right to make the decision of whether to live or die themselves—not to have it forced upon them."

"You forced it upon them," she spit, storming across the tent until she was in his face. "If you hadn't gone there and forced the Empire down their throats, maybe all those people would be alive."

"You think that was my choice?" His shoulders were shaking, face white as a sheet. "Those were my orders. The Senate did not ask my opinion on whether Chersome should be conquered. They only told me to see it done in the most expedient way possible. To have taxes flowing before the year was out."

"You didn't have to do it." Even as she said the words, she knew it wasn't so simple.

He stared at her unblinking for a dozen heartbeats, then said, "You're right. I could've said no. And they'd have strung me up on the gallows and selected someone else from the ranks who understood that to be in the legions means obedience. And if by some strange stroke of fate, my legion chose to follow me, chose to fight back, the Empire would have sent six more to crush us. And when they were finished, they'd have moved on to Chersome."

Every word seemed torn from his chest. "We are not free,

Teriana. We were never asked whether this was the life we wanted to live. We were merely given the choice: obey or die, and more often than not, obeying *means* dying.

"This legion is my life, the men my brothers. The Senate believes that they gave me this legion as a tool to enact the Empire's will, but I say *I've* been given to the legion as a tool to protect the lives of the men within it. And I will *always* make the decision that protects them."

And Teriana understood. How could she not, when she'd fed up an entire half a world to the Empire in order to protect her crew? Her people? She was no better. No better at all.

"I agreed to this mission because it was a way to escape, for me and for my men," he said. "Back east, we must go where the Senate tells us to go. Do what the Senate tells us to do. But here, *I* am in control." His breathing was rapid, ragged. "It could take a year to find xenthier paths. Five. Ten. And in that time, I decide what we'll do here, and as much as you might think otherwise, conquest isn't what I want."

"Then don't look for the paths," she whispered. "Don't give the Senate back its power."

"I'd do it gladly if not for the fact that you would pay the price." His face was deathly pale. "My freedom at the expense of yours. My men's freedom at the expense of your captured people."

And her people's freedom at the expense of the West. "Go back," she pleaded. "Load your men onto your ships and I'll take you back."

"To go back, I have to be defeated," he said, "And that means sending my men to be slaughtered." Dragging in a breath, he said, "I'm never going back. I can't."

He was ill with something, but she couldn't think about that. Not when he'd put her in this impossible position of having to choose. "Why did you do this to me?" she demanded, it taking all her control not to scream the words at him. "Why didn't you just let Cassius kill me?"

Horns blasted in the distance, long and mournful, and

Marcus turned his head in their direction, closing his eyes for a heartbeat before looking back to her. "Do you know why I stopped the questioner from torturing you?" He laughed, but it turned into a cough. "Do you know why I interfered?"

He swayed on his feet, and Teriana eyed him with alarm. His breathing was coming in tiny little gasps, and he looked ready to collapse. "Marcus—"

"Because I couldn't handle your screams," he choked out, panic rising in his eyes. "I didn't even know you, and I couldn't watch them hurt you. But instead of saving you, I damned you."

Then he collapsed.

Teriana caught him around the waist, but his weight pulled them to the tent floor. "Marcus, what's wrong?"

The only answer was the desperate wheeze of air.

"I'll get help." She settled his head against the ground, but before she could get up, his hand closed around her wrist.

"They. Can't. Know." There was panic in his eyes. "Get. Amarin."

"Okay." She pulled free, then stumbled out the entrance. There were legionnaires in a perimeter around the command tent, close enough to stand guard without overhearing their commander's conversations. Quintus and Miki were mercifully absent. "Marcus doesn't want to be disturbed," she told them. "But he wants Amarin for something."

"Went that way," one of them replied, leaning on the butt of his spear.

Teriana scuttled in the direction he'd pointed, walking as swiftly as possible without running. Whatever was wrong with Marcus, he didn't want anyone to know, and rushing around would only draw attention. Relief flooded her as she caught sight of the tall servant, and she shouted his name. Hurrying up to him, she whispered, "There's something wrong with Marcus. He can't breathe properly. Told me to find you."

Amarin blanched, and he glanced at the fading sunset. Teriana did as well and knew the battle was almost ready to begin.

"Find Servius or Felix," he said, gripping her arms hard enough to leave bruises. "None but them."

"I understand," she said, but he didn't let go.

"None but them," he repeated. "Or I'll cut your heart out myself, you hear?"

She ran.

33

TERIANA

Despite the heat and humidity, Teriana's hands felt like ice as she made her way through the ranks of legionnaires, moving toward the knot of young commanders watching the proceedings, Ereni with them, along with two of her warriors. It occurred to her that some of those she passed would die today. That they were going to fight a battle and anything could happen.

Yet that seemed a distant concern compared to Marcus. It was like some invisible hand had been choking him, slowly cutting off the air to his lungs. *Please don't let him die,* she silently prayed. Whereas before all she'd cared about was her bargain with him, now something else was digging little icy splinters into her heart: the fear of losing *him.*

"Straighten up those ranks," Servius bellowed, and Teriana smiled at the soldiers standing guard over the officers before ducking between them. Servius was still shouting orders, so she reluctantly approached Felix, who eyed her sourly.

Stepping close, she murmured, "Amarin sent me. There's something wrong with Marcus."

Felix sucked in a breath, and she knew that whatever it was afflicting the legatus, this wasn't the first time it had happened. And that it was every bit as bad as she feared.

"Servius," he said, his tone betraying nothing. "Legatus wants a quick word."

The big legionnaire nodded, and Teriana turned, nearly colliding with Titus.

"What's this about?" he asked.

She shrugged and tried to go around him. "He didn't say."

Titus stepped into her path. "If there's been a change of

strategy, I should be part of the discussion. As should the im-peratrix."

A sly move on his part, as while he couldn't argue with Mar-cus's officers, Ereni most certainly could.

Ereni's eyes flicked their direction, drawn by the word she knew to be the Cel translation of her title. "You know how par-ticular he is," Teriana said to her. "He probably just wants to ensure all the banners are blowing the right way in the wind."

The imperatrix frowned, then shrugged. She'd wanted to be on the field with her warriors, and it had taken some con-vincing on Marcus's part to convince her to stay behind the lines. Nothing short of the truth would take her back to the command tent.

"No changes, sir," Felix interjected, shoving Teriana be-tween the shoulder blades to get her past the other commander. "He likely has a last few questions that need answering."

"I should be there."

"Men are moving into position," Servius said. "Command is yours and the imperatrix's until we return, sir."

There wasn't much Titus could say to that, and they knew it. Neither Servius nor Felix said anything until they were out of earshot; then the latter demanded, "What did you do?"

"Nothing," she said, wishing he would shut up. That they'd walk faster. Hoping that one of them would know what to do when they got back to the tent. Praying that Marcus was still alive when they did. Her heart hitched as she remembered his words to her: *I couldn't watch them hurt you.*

"His attacks don't just happen," Felix snapped. "What did you say? What did you do?"

Teriana tried to swallow, but her throat tightened. "I asked about Chersome."

Felix's glare dripped with hate. "If he dies, I'm personally going to—"

"Shut up, Felix," Servius said. "Threatening her isn't going to do him any good." He nodded as the guards surrounding the tent saluted, then pushed his way inside.

Amarin had dragged Marcus to the rear of the tent behind the table, so she heard Marcus before she saw him. A gasping, wheezing sound that made her own chest tighten. She hung back while the two soldiers flanked the table. "How bad?" Servius asked.

"Worse than in Celendrial," Amarin said. "We're going to have to put in the tube."

"Shit. Shit!" Felix swore. "Titus will have the men marching. Marcus needs to be out there now."

Amarin said something Teriana couldn't make out, and she edged her way around until she could see. And instantly wished she hadn't.

Marcus's eyes were open but unseeing, his skin a faintly bluish hue. His legs were moving, heels digging into the ground, muscles straining as he unconsciously fought against Servius, who had his shoulders pinned to the ground. Felix was prying open his jaw, but he looked up at her approach, gaze full of accusation. *This is your fault.*

The room swam, and Teriana gripped the edge of the table for support. It didn't seem like him. Not the brilliant, unshakable, resolute Marcus who never showed a moment of weakness. *Except when you pushed him!* she snarled at herself. *Made him relive his nightmares, and screamed in his face, blaming him for the deaths of thousands. The enslavement of thousands. And he never had a choice.*

Amarin had a narrow tube in his hand, and he muttered at the two officers to hold their commander steady.

"What are you doing to him?"

"Piss off, Teriana!" Felix snarled, but Servius shook his head. "We can't stay with him. We need her."

"If we don't get this in now, he's done," Amarin snapped, interrupting the pair.

"Okay, okay," Servius muttered, and his massive arms strained. Felix's wrists trembled as he held Marcus's head steady, a piece of wood stuck between his teeth. Amarin slipped the tube into the legatus's throat, and Teriana turned her head, unable to watch but unable to block out the sounds of him gagging and choking, of the men swearing as they tried to save his life.

While she stood there and did nothing.

"It's in," Amarin said, and Teriana exhaled the breath of air she hadn't known she was holding. Nails digging into the table's surface, she turned to watch Amarin holding the slender tube in place while Servius and Felix unfastened Marcus's cloak, pulling it out from under him.

Felix knelt holding the cloth, face pale. "I can't."

"You have to," Servius said. "You two are the same size, and with his helmet on, no one is going to notice in the dark."

Horns blared, and in the distance Teriana picked up the sound of marching feet.

"We're out of time," Servius said, shaking his friend's shoulders. "Already Titus and Ereni will be wondering about the delay. Marcus needs to be on the field, and since he can't be, you have to do it for him."

Felix shook his head. "I don't want to leave him. Not like this. Not with her."

His spite was like a slap to the face, but Teriana kept her mouth shut. She and Felix would have it out one of these days, but today was not that day.

"If you don't, he's a dead man!" Servius snarled, shoving the smaller man back so that he slammed into a stool. "If you don't, the legion will find out. Titus will find out. You *know* what that means."

As answer, Felix unfastened his own cloak, replacing it with Marcus's elaborate one, the golden dragon glittering in the lamplight. Watching them. Then he jammed Marcus's helmet down on his head, the nose and cheek guards covering enough of his face that he could easily pass for the other man.

The horns sounded again, and Teriana flinched as Servius took her by the shoulders, expression intent. "You know what will happen if this gets out?"

"I do." She lifted her chin. "I won't let it." To Felix, she said,

"I'll keep him safe." He only ignored her, making his way to the entrance of the tent, Servius swiftly following.

"Servius," she called, and he turned his head. "Try not to lose too badly."

He grinned, and then they were gone.

The whistle of Marcus's breathing through the tube demanded her attention, and Teriana closed the distance between them, dropping to her knees. Amarin held his head steady, one hand gripping the narrow tube protruding from his lips. His color was not as bad as it had been, but he remained unconscious, and when she took his hand it was icy to the touch.

"How long will it last?" she asked Amarin, wrapping her other hand around Marcus's as though keeping his fingers warm might somehow make a difference.

The servant's face was grim, and he shook his head. "It should've begun to ease by now. It's been years since a fit has taken him this thoroughly."

Her chest tightened, her pulse deafeningly loud in her ears. "But it *will* ease?"

"For all our sakes, I hope so." He unbuckled the rest of Marcus's armor, carefully easing it off, along with his weapons. "He isn't getting enough air, and if it lasts much longer . . ."

She knew what he meant—had seen sailors brought back from drowning without a marked healer's intervention and their minds were never the same. A tear dripped off her nose and landed on his cheek, and she wiped it away, furious at herself. For the part she'd played in him lying here helpless, and for caring that he was.

Amarin rested one ear against Marcus's chest, listened, then pulled away, exhaling softly as he shook his head.

"No," Teriana snapped, unwilling to concede without a fight. "I'm going to get help."

She tried to scramble to her feet, but Amarin caught her arm. "There is nothing anyone can do, and he won't thank you if you let his secret out."

"Let me go!" She heaved, but the slender man was stronger

than he looked. "The Seventh take you!" Balling her fist, she swung, catching him in the face. His grip loosened, and she tore away, snatching up one of Marcus's knives and running to the entrance before slowing her pace so as not to alarm the guards watching over the tent and its precious contents.

The camp was quiet and empty, no one questioning when she strode in the direction of the latrines. She waited until she was out of sight of the men guarding the command tent, then ran silently between the rows of tents until she reached the wall. She clambered up, her fingers and toes unconsciously finding holds as she searched the darkness for the guards, knowing the variations in their patrols like the back of her hand.

A shadow moved, and she dropped to the base of the wall, waiting, waiting, and then she ran, not caring if they heard. It was too dark for any of them to hit her with a crossbow, and they'd only pursue her so far into the jungle.

Shouts of alarm filled the air behind her, but they only made her run faster, branches lashing against her arms and face as she tore through, running in the general direction of the town. She tripped and fell, was back on her feet in an instant, ignoring the pain in her body. *I will not let him die. I will not let him die.*

Ducking behind a tree, she crouched, listening to the sounds of her pursuers. Something crawled across her hand, but she forced herself to stay still, praying that whatever it was wouldn't bite.

One of the legionnaires passed her hiding spot, blade in hand. His steps were silent, the darkness not seeming to hamper him. He paused, and she held her breath, convinced he'd hear her heart beating. *Go back, go back,* she silently chanted, her shoulders slumping when he shook his head and retreated toward camp.

She waited until he was out of earshot, then crept onward, praying to Lern not to let her run afoul of a snake or worse. The air was filled with the drone of insects, and above her things moved in the canopy. The moon and stars were obscured by the dense foliage, and she relied on her sense of the sea, the distant roar of the waves, to keep from losing her direction. Still, it was no small amount of relief when she stumbled onto the narrow path leading into the town, the warriors standing at the gate admitting her without question, her face well known to them.

Breaking into a run, she wove between the pilings holding up the buildings, making her way in the direction of the healer's home. Shoving in the door, she found Caradoc readying supplies for the injured warriors who'd be brought to him. "I need your help," she blurted out, then clenched her teeth together.

Because what sort of help could she expect him to give? She'd warned him not to let the Cel see what his mark allowed him to do, and if she brought him back to camp to help Marcus there would be no hiding it. Marcus would know, and there was no chance—none at all—of him not using marked healers to help his men. The healers were an advantage the West had over the Cel. Did she dare give it up to save one life?

It was a life she needed. Her deal was with Marcus, and her mum, her crew, and her people depended on her seeing this through. Except Teriana knew that wasn't the reason she was here.

Whose side are you on?

The Cel were the enemy. And as much as her opinions of him might have changed, Marcus was their leader. He was the enemy. Her enemy.

"Teriana?" Caradoc asked.

"The Six forgive me," she whispered, then more loudly, "I need you to come with me."

"I can't," he said. "The battle is underway, and I must prepare to deal with the injuries that will come from it."

"This is urgent. You can come back after."

"Is it one of *them*?"

She considered lying to him, then said, "Aye. He's sick. He'll die without your help."

"You yourself told me that these men are godless. That if they learned about Hegeria's mark, they'd use me until I am dead."

"I know what I said." She bit the insides of her cheeks. "But I need him to live."

The healer's eyes were too shrewd. Too knowing. "It's their leader, isn't it?"

Teriana didn't answer.

"I do not wish death upon this young man," he said slowly. "But my clan relies upon me, and I will not jeopardize them for the sake of one."

"Please reconsider."

The healer eyed her; then he shook his head. "No."

I will not let Marcus die. The knife made a cruel little sound as she pulled it out of her boot, the Cel steel wicked sharp. "Start walking."

"You can't make me heal this man."

"You let him die, and I'll tell the rest of them that you could've helped and chose not to," she whispered in Caradoc's ear as she led him through the town. "What do you think they'll do to you then? What do you think they'll do to your people?"

It was a cruel threat, and she wasn't certain if she meant it. But she needed his help, and she did not think he'd give it willingly.

"They are godless," he replied, but the reassuring smile he gave those standing guard told her the threat had worked. "What if Hegeria chooses not to help him?"

It was a real risk. She'd seen firsthand that the gods were taking sides in this, and she did not know where the goddess stood. Except this was Marcus's only chance, so she had to try. "I suggest you pray it doesn't come to that."

The journey back to camp didn't take nearly as long as her dash through the jungle, and she walked purposefully toward the gates, praying the guards didn't stop her. Didn't question her. Didn't insist on following her to the command tent.

"Stay silent," she muttered, and not for the first time she was grateful to be the only one who spoke fluent Cel. "You raise a fuss, they'll cut you down without hesitation."

"Halt!" one of the guards shouted, and she recognized the voice as that of Avitius, one of her regular gambling companions. "Identify yourselves."

"It's Teriana."

A burning crossbow bolt flew through the air, digging into the ground in front of her, and she carefully pulled it out of the ground and held it up so her face was illuminated.

"Shit," Avitius said. "When did you leave again? And where the hell are Quintus and Miki? The battle's begun—the legatus isn't going to be happy to hear about this."

"He knows," she shouted back, hoping volume would hide the quiver in her voice. "This man is an herbarius in Ereni's town. Marcus had questions for him about medical supplies, or something like that. I'm supposed to keep him here until the battle's won."

This was the test. She'd done all she could to earn the trust of the Cel legion, and now it was time to discover whether it would pay off.

Yawning, she rocked on her heels as though the entire procedure bored her, doing her best to ignore the fact that her sweaty shirt was glued to her back. They could refuse to let the healer in. Or worse, they could insist on escorting her back to the tent, and there'd be no way to stop them from discovering Marcus. But what choice did she have? Without the help of a marked healer, he'd die.

Maybe he already has.

"This is the first we've heard about this," Avitius called down, and her fear turned to panic.

"That's because I was supposed to be back before they marched," she said, struggling to hide her agitation. She didn't have time for this. "You can ask Marcus when he gets back, if you doubt me so much."

They conferred among themselves; then the gate swung open

wide enough to admit the two of them. "Stay silent," she repeated, then pulled Caradoc inside.

"We're breaking the rules for you," Avitius said. "The legatus doesn't confirm your claim, both you and I are going to be sitting pretty for the next few weeks."

"Good thing I gamble just as well standing," she replied, watching as they searched the healer for weapons. "And I promise, I won't let him out of my sight."

"He needs an escort," the legionnaire replied.

"I'm pretty sure I can mind one man for the length of time it takes Marcus to return." Teriana made a face as she walked backward into the camp, tugging Caradoc with her. "I thought this was supposed to be an easy fight? After all the bragging I've heard, I'm surprised they aren't back already."

The legionnaires laughed, and she held her breath.

"Keep an eye on him," Avitius said. "This one's on you, Teriana."

She grinned and saluted, then headed straight for the command tent, lifting a hand in greeting to those standing guard outside. "This man is Ereni's herbarius. Marcus wants to talk to him. I'm supposed to keep him entertained. Amarin's in there, too."

One of the legionnaires shrugged and waved her inside, Ereni having spent enough time here that having one of her people inside was no cause for comment. Not with the maps and gold kept under lock and key.

The first thing Teriana noticed when she pushed through the flaps was the silence. And a knife carving her from stem to stern wouldn't have gutted her so completely. *No.*

Amarin had stood when she'd entered, and she had to tear the question from her throat. "Is he . . . ?"

He shook his head, and a faint prickle of hope filled her. "Not yet."

"But very nearly," Caradoc said, pushing past her. Amarin's face darkened at the sight of him, but his lack of reaction only confirmed how far gone Marcus was.

"Nothing can be done, Teriana," he said. "If none of the greatest physicians in the Empire were able to cure him, there is no chance a herbarius from some backwater fishing village will do better."

She bristled, but there was no time for arguments. "Well?" she demanded of the healer.

He dropped to his knees, and she knew from past experience that he was weighing and measuring the life left in the legionnaire, his god mark allowing him to see where and what damage had been done. "He's close to death."

"I can see that."

"This will cost me."

"So will doing nothing. You know the stakes, so make your choice."

If her soul wasn't already forsaken, it was now. Teriana had been raised to believe that a healer's touch was a gift, not something one demanded. And certainly not something one forced on pain of death.

The healer bowed his head. "Hegeria willing, the damage can be repaired. However, the affliction is part of him, and there is nothing I can do to keep it from happening again."

"I understand." Her fingers felt like ice, and her knees trembled as she crouched next to Marcus's head. "If you help him, I'll . . . I'll be in your debt."

"No, you won't," Caradoc replied, and he reached and removed the narrow tube that was all that kept Marcus alive.

"No!" Amarin gasped, but Teriana shoved him back.

"This is his only chance."

And it wasn't going to work. Marcus twitched, his pasty skin turning blue. Whether Caradoc had done it on purpose or Hegeria had refused his call, the healer was letting him die, and it was her fault. Her fault, but she'd make him pay.

Jerking the knife out of her boot once more, she leveled the blade at Caradoc, and only then did she see that he'd aged. And though she'd witnessed it a dozen times before, the impossibility of watching the years drain from the healer to save another still struck her to the core. His grey hair turned white, skin wrinkling and mottling, his shoulders drooping as though they'd carried a great burden for half a century or more.

And Marcus's color was returning, his breathing steadying and losing the horrible gasping wheeze.

The healer collapsed.

Neither she nor Amarin moved, both of them staring, transfixed. Then the servant reached down, his fingers hesitating over Caradoc's throat before pressing where a pulse should be. He shook his head. "He's dead."

A dull roar filled Teriana's ears; then she crawled on her hands and knees to the corner and retched. Her body spasmed and jerked as though it were trying to rid itself of the horrible press of guilt, but the feeling kept growing and expanding and . . . the Six help her, she'd killed a man—a marked healer, an innocent—to save her enemy. To save the man set on conquering the entire world. What had she done? What had she become?

"Teriana?" Marcus's voice. His hands on her shoulders. "What has happened? Who is this dead man?"

She shrugged his hands off, refusing to respond, because what answer could she possibly give that wouldn't make things worse?

Traitor.

Traitor.

Traitor.

34

TERIANA

The late-afternoon sun was blindingly bright, the air full of the smell of sweat from the crowd of thousands standing before the platform. Teriana's eyes drifted over their heads to fix on the Cel banner flapping from the pole Marcus had ordered erected in the city's center, having officially claimed Galinha as liberated from Urcon's unlawful rule. *How long,* she wondered, *until liberated turned into conquered?*

Marcus coughed softly, jerking her attention from the flag to his face, a shot of panic lancing through her. But he only cocked one eyebrow at the page she clutched with sweating hands. *Translate.*

Clearing her tired throat, she belted out the crimes of the line of men and women standing under guard on the platform, then their sentence. They were thieves, all, and for their crimes they'd each lose an index finger and spend a month in prison. Ereni and the other imperators had agreed to the laws to which their clans—and their enemies—would abide, but Teriana wondered whether they realized that those laws were a version of the Empire's laws, carefully curated by Marcus to ensure they'd agree to them. As were the punishments.

The cheers of the crowd were *almost* loud enough to drown the screams as the fingers were removed, methodically and efficiently, a pair of medics calmly cauterizing and bandaging the injuries before more soldiers dragged the criminals off to the bulging prison that the engineers were working to expand and fortify.

Averting her eyes from the spray of blood, Teriana wiped the sweat from her brow and took a long swallow from the waterskin hanging at her belt. They'd been at this for hours, and she wanted to be done. Needed to be done with this seemingly endless day of listening and translating the testimonies of the citizens of this city. For years, they'd lived in fear under Urcon's rule—his soldiers and cronies milking every last copper from the people, even as they'd thieved, raped, murdered, and terrorized. Now all that was over.

Until it is replaced by a new regime.

"We're almost through," Marcus murmured, and his elbow bumped hers as he reached for the last sheet of paper listing names and crimes.

His touch made her skin tingle, and though she should've moved to give him more room, Teriana stood her ground, greedily anticipating the next time his hand would brush hers. For longer than she cared to admit, she'd been acutely aware of his presence, everyone else fading into the background when he was near. She'd justified it with a thousand different reasons and maybe they hadn't been lies, but neither had they been the truth.

As she took another mouthful of water, her mind drifted to the early hours of the morning when they'd returned the healer's body to the town. After prying an explanation out of her and Amarin, Marcus had given life to her lie, appearing visibly irritated that the herbarius had the audacity to die before he'd had the chance to speak with him about supplying the legion, and openly chastising those who'd allowed Teriana to bring him into camp after dark for breaking protocol, because to do otherwise would've drawn more attention. He hadn't even given Felix and Servius the truth, telling them after they'd orchestrated the switch that Teriana had procured a tonic from the Arinoquian that had relieved his attack, though the contents of the concoction remained a mystery.

With Caradoc shrouded on a litter carried between two of Marcus's men, he'd accompanied her to the town, ostensibly to undo any damage that had been done.

The expressions on the Arinoquians' faces when they'd arrived would remain burned on Teriana's soul for the rest of her life, several of them falling to their knees in tears as they realized their healer was dead. Caradoc had been born in that town—was likely related to many of them in some fashion—but his loss was greater than that. Having a child marked by Hegeria was considered one of the greatest gifts the gods could give, because it allowed the clan to survive illness, conflict, and disasters. They would feel the healer's death long after their grief faded to dust.

"Is there anything I can do?" Marcus asked once he'd ordered his men back to camp. "Gold or some other form of recompense? Anything?"

She shook her head. "Would be an insult. They believe his death was the will of the gods, not something to be profited from." Besides, if anyone deserved to pay, it was her. It didn't matter that she hadn't expected Caradoc to die from healing Marcus—he had. And it was because she'd given him no choice. A healer's touch was a gift, and she'd stolen it to save the life of the man leading the Cel tide.

The Arinoquians said nothing as she explained that their healer had passed saving the life of a man near death, knowing they would mistake her tears as grief rather than guilt. Hating that she was too much of a coward to correct them.

As they set to building a pyre, Marcus moved to leave, but Teriana caught his wrist and he didn't argue. The Arinoquians placed the healer's body on the stacks of wood and fuel, his white hair dangling down one side. Except all she could see was the face of a man with years of life in him, with so much left to offer.

A copper coin was placed on his forehead. "To pay his passage," she explained. "They're hoping Madoria takes him so he can be with his family in the afterlife."

"Copper?"

Swallowing felt like it was tearing her throat apart. "It's all they can afford."

Marcus fumbled at his belt, then tripped as he stepped forward, holding out a gleaming gold coin to Ereni. The imperatrix stared at it for a long moment, then nodded, and Marcus carefully replaced the copper coin with the golden one. When he turned, Ereni was holding out a flickering torch, and without hesitation Marcus took it, circling the pyre until the whole of it was engulfed. Then he returned to Teriana's side.

"You didn't have to do that." *Why didn't I?*

"It's only gold."

And she knew it wasn't that he had chests full of it back at camp but rather that he valued life over wealth. Over glory. Over the ambition of the Empire. While his end goal ensured his place as the enemy, the many-layered truth that had been uncovered made it impossible to hate him for what he'd done. For what he would do. It was all shades of grey: moral justification for immoral ends. A good man pushed into the role of a villain—not just for the sake of his own survival, but for that of his men. And her control crumbled, tears pouring down her cheeks, because Teriana knew, if given the choice, that she'd do the exact same thing again. Would do whatever it took to protect his life.

Traitor.

The beat of drums pulled her from the uneasy memory, and her eyes fixed on the prisoners the legionnaires were dragging onto the platform. The crowd went mad, rotten fruit and worse sailing through the air to smash against the criminals. The Cel were caught in the crossfire, but they were too well trained to react. And besides, this was the reaction they wanted.

There were ten of them. Murderers and rapists, and Teriana had heard firsthand of the things they'd done to terrorize their own people. To keep them quelled. She'd translated the stories while Marcus and Titus had listened, even Cassius's wretch of a son losing his color at the things he heard.

"Make them short nooses," Titus had said before he'd walked out. "Let the bastards choke to death."

Marcus had said nothing, but to Teriana the ropes appeared of the typical length, as mandated by the Empire, the drop enough to break necks. He waited until his men nodded, then he held up one hand, and to Teriana's amazement, the crowd fell silent. Then he balled up the sheet of parchment and let it fall to his feet, and she did not need to see the surprised expressions on Servius's and Felix's faces to know this was out of character.

He stared at the criminals for another long moment, then gave Teriana a nod before turning to face the crowd.

"For two decades," he shouted, "you've lived under the rule of the tyrant Urcon. For two decades, he has stolen from you. Beaten you down. Burned your homes and stolen your children. Anyone who dares stand against him has found their lives cut short. For two decades, you've lived in fear while these murderers"—he jabbed a finger in the direction of the prisoners—"lived like kings off your labors."

He paused, and Teriana instinctively translated, belting out the words so that everyone in the crowd could hear.

"That fear ends today!"

The crowd screamed their approval.

But not all. Ereni stood stock still among her cheering peers, her jaw tight and her expression fixed on the hanging men. Then it shifted to Teriana. And she knew. Knew that for the first time, Ereni was truly seeing the danger of the Cel invasion. Was seeing that she and her fellow imperators were no longer the ones in control.

"Urcon believes himself untouchable," Marcus shouted. "He believes himself safe in his fortress surrounded by his mercenary army, but today, Galinha is free. Tomorrow, we begin our march on Aracam. And when we arrive at the gates, it will be Urcon's turn to know fear!"

When she translated his words, the crowd roared and surged against the line of legionnaires in front of the platform, arms reaching toward Marcus like he was some sort of god, and it was all Teriana could do not to step back in the face of their intensity. But he wasn't through with them yet.

"We have come from lands across the Endless Seas," he continued. "From a place known as the Celendor Empire, where rulers are chosen by the vote of the people. Where all men and women, regardless of their station, are subject to the same laws. And the same punishments."

More cheers erupted from the crowd, but they were soon replaced with a sort of manic anticipation as Marcus strode toward the gallows. "These men have been charged with murder, rape, extortion, and theft. And after the testimony of dozens of your friends and family who were victims, they have been found guilty of their crimes. I, Legatus Marcus, supreme commander of the Thirty-Seventh and Forty-First Legions, under the laws of the Empire, do sentence you—" He listed their names from memory. "—to death by hanging."

Teriana watched the criminals as she translated their sentence. Most of them were weeping, and some had lost control of their bladders. Yet she felt no pity. Her only regret was that they wouldn't suffer as much as their victims.

You belong up there with them.

The drum rolled, the beat accelerating, and Teriana's heart followed suit. Faster and faster, sweat dribbling down the back of her neck, the parchment in her hand trembling in her grip. Then the drumroll stopped. One long beat, and Marcus nodded.

As one the soldiers manning the gallows shoved the levers, and the trapdoors fell open with a thunderous clatter. The men dropped. Over the silence of the crowd echoed the snapping of ten necks.

And the people who believed themselves liberated screamed their approval.

Teriana stood still as Marcus walked back across the platform.

"You all right?"

Her body was still shaking from the adrenaline coursing through her veins, but she managed a nod.

"It was justice," he said, his eyes searching hers. "Men like that don't deserve to live."

"I know." But what power to be the one who made the decision. To determine who was guilty. Who lived and died.

Marcus hesitated as though he wasn't sure if he believed her, then let out a long breath. "Take some guards with you and arrange for the purchase of meat and libations for the men. Tonight, we celebrate."

"And here I didn't think you knew how to have fun," she said, the noise of the crowd fading into the background.

He smiled and leaned down, his breath warm against her ear. "When will you stop thinking you know everything about me?"

"How old is this place?" Quintus asked as they walked through the narrow streets of Galinha, running his hand along the scarred and pitted stone of the buildings, which had gone green from the ceaseless humidity of Arinoquia.

"Ancient," Teriana answered. "Six or seven hundred years old."

And she could feel every year of it, the city so deeply steeped in history and blood, life and death, that it seemed almost sentient. As though even if it were devoid of people, it would still be alive. Would still be watching.

"Don't know why, but it reminds me of the redwood forests in Bardeen," Miki said, casting his gaze up as he crouched to walk through a tunnel low enough that even Quintus and Teriana needed to duck their heads. "I swore those trees had eyes."

Quintus grunted in agreement, his hands shifting reflexively to the hilt of his gladius as he stepped out of the tunnel. Teriana gestured to go left, following the directions she'd been given to a distillery known for its passable rum. The streets were relatively quiet. Most of the citizens were still in the square containing the gallows, celebrating the execution of their tormenters. But some people were going about their business, ducking in and out what seemed almost comically small entrances. Galinha had been built by a people of shorter stature than those who currently resided in it.

They didn't fit.

But it wasn't just their size that made Teriana think that. This wasn't the sort of place the Arinoquians would build: theirs were towns made of wood and glass, open and airy and somehow impermanent. Galinha was thick stone, tunnels and narrow buildings that made Teriana feel claustrophobic. The Arinoquians belonged here no more than she or the Cel soldiers did, all of them invaders in some capacity.

"A word, Teriana."

Teriana jumped, almost as startled by the swiftness with which Quintus and Miki unsheathed their weapons as she was by Ereni's sudden appearance.

"Of course, Imperatrix," she replied, trying to ignore the rapid patter of her heart. She hadn't spoken to the woman alone since the death of the clan healer, and a cowardly part of her didn't want to. Still, she nodded at the legionnaires to give them some space.

Ereni eyed the two, then said in passable Mudamorian, "You need to explain yourself."

Teriana frowned at the choice of language, because it meant that whatever Ereni intended to say, she didn't want the legionnaires to understand. Miki, in particular, had been a quick study of the Arinoquian language. "Explain what?"

"Explain why *you* were the one who took our healer into their camp."

Biting the insides of her cheeks, Teriana didn't answer.

"You were the one who told us that his god mark needed to be kept secret from these men at all cost," Ereni hissed. "You were the one who said they'd use it for their gain. And yet you do this?"

"Everything all right, Teriana?" Quintus asked.

It wasn't. Not even a little bit. "It's fine."

"It was their leader, wasn't it?" Ereni asked, deliberately not using Marcus's name. "I know it wasn't him who commanded the battle—it was his second. These golden men are so used to following that they do not stop to question. But *I* do not follow."

"You do now." The words slipped past Teriana's lips before she could think them through. "Because that's what this is about, isn't it, Ereni? Not that your clan's healer died to save *his* life, but that *he* is the one in control, not you."

Closing the space between them, Teriana stared the old warrior down. "I warned you. My crew member Bait warned you. But you decided the risk was worth ridding your people of Urcon, because how great a threat could these *golden men* be if they had no easy way to cross the Endless Seas? Well now you've seen. Now you know."

"Yet for all your talk, Teriana, still you saved their leader's life."

"And I'd do it again, because in order to protect *my* people, I need him alive."

Ereni's green eyes burned into hers, then she shook her head. "The gods will judge us both."

As if Teriana didn't know that. As if she didn't expect all the gods to turn their backs on her now. As if she didn't know she deserved it.

"Ereni! Teriana! Why the tense words on this joyous day?"

Servius had appeared from around the corner, and he slung a casual arm around Teriana's shoulder, tugging her back. "You both should be celebrating."

"Perhaps later," Ereni replied in broken Cel. "I must visit the families of my warriors who lost their lives in battle. Good day to you."

Ereni strode away, a pair of her warriors appearing from the shadows to flank her. Servius exhaled a long breath. "Care to explain why my boys here were about ready to poke holes in our ally?"

Turning, Teriana grimaced. Both Quintus and Miki had their blades in hand, gazes predatory.

"It's nothing," she muttered. "Though you might want to mention to Marcus that the imperators are used to delivering their own justice and they aren't best pleased about him doing the honors."

"Why she complaining to you about that and not him?"

Teriana shrugged. "Guess she thinks he's more likely to listen to me."

"Smart woman," the big legionnaire said. "Now let's get to walking. If I lift my nose to the wind, I can smell the rum from here."

Servius accompanied her to procure supplies for the celebration, handing over golden coins without argument after telling her that the amount of rum she'd negotiated for wasn't enough.

"Fighting is thirsty business," he said. "And when we drink, *we drink*."

"I can respect that," she said, her head already buzzing from sampling the wares in an attempt to drown her guilty thoughts. "Though it seems a bit reckless to let your army get sloshed when Urcon is only two days' march from here and probably priming for a fight."

"A third."

"Pardon?" She motioned for the merchant to load the casks, then looked up at her friend.

"Only a third get the night to celebrate and the morning to sleep it off. The rest will be at camp or here keeping the order and working on repairing what was damaged in the fight. It's a rotation."

Of course it is. "You part of the celebrating third?"

"Always." He grinned and drained the rest of the cup of rum in his hand. "Though in all seriousness, I was supposed to be on duty, but Felix volunteered to take it."

"Why?"

A slight frown crossed his face, but then he shrugged. "Wants to see this one through, I suppose."

Given he'd commanded the battle, albeit disguised as Marcus, she could understand the motivation. Except part of her believed it was something else, and that the something else was her. She knew the tribunus resented the amount of time she and Marcus spent alone together and it had nothing to do with her dubious loyalties. It was jealousy. She'd had her suspicions before, but seeing Felix's reaction during Marcus's attack had been confirmation that he was in love with his commander. And it was an affection to which Marcus appeared oblivious.

She followed Servius onto the street, where carts laden with casks and sides of meat were already gathering. A slight flutter of nerves passed through her stomach as she asked, "What about Marcus? He part of the third?"

Servius shouted at the men to get the carts moving, then turned back to her. "He doesn't drink much."

That wasn't a huge surprise. The legatus liked to be in control, and he hated making mistakes. Shrugging, Teriana followed the carts, but the massive legionnaire caught hold of her arm and hauled her back.

"What?" she demanded, the unhappy set of his mouth both surprising and discomforting. "You got something you need to say?"

Servius's jaw worked back and forth; then he said, "Don't do anything stupid, Teriana."

"Noted." She jerked out of his grip, annoyed and embarrassed, although she wasn't entirely sure why.

They walked in silence toward the broken city gates, but as they rounded the bend a pair of brightly dressed and very pretty prostitutes leaned out of a doorway, smiling at the passing soldiers.

Servius's arm moved and Teriana caught the gleam of a golden coin flying through the air, which one of the girls caught and tucked away in a pocket. The legionnaire grinned at her, then inclined his head, and the girls both nodded and retreated inside.

"Speaking of stupid," Teriana said, "you know those girls are going to show up at camp tonight."

"Good," he replied. "Let's hope they bring their friends."

35

TERIANA

It was long after dark by the time Teriana squeezed into a spot next to the fire between Gibzen and another centurion whose name she couldn't remember.

"Cards?" the primus asked.

She shrugged. "Eager to lose more of your coin?"

"It was an unlucky streak," he protested, digging into his belt pouch and extracting a deck. Most of the men had discarded their armor back at their tents, but a clutter of weapons lay around the fire in easy reach. The smell of rum and ale filled the air, but she strongly suspected that even three sheets to the wind, they'd be deadly.

"Winning at cards isn't luck. It's skill," she said, winking. "I've played in every port across Reath, against rich men and poor men, sailors, fishermen, and nobles. You want luck on your side, maybe we should stick to dice."

Gibzen handed her the deck. "You deal."

Teriana absently shuffled, but her eyes were circling the group as she wondered where Marcus was. There were dozens of similar circles scattered throughout the camp—men gambling, telling stories, and singing rude songs—but this fire, where the golden dragon standard glittered, was where he would be.

Accepting a cup of rum, she dealt in several other players, eyed her cards and their tells, and folded.

Gibzen snorted, but she ignored him, discreetly searching the darkness with one eye half on the play. Another hour passed and she amassed a sizeable pile of coins, but Marcus had still not shown his face. Where was he?

"This is cruel," she declared to Gibzen. "I can't in good conscience take any more of your money. I'm out."

The men groaned and pleaded with her to let them win it back, but she shoved the coins into her pockets and moved to where Servius sat telling stories with the others. He silently filled her cup from the jug he was drinking from directly and continued to regale the group with the story behind the six-inch scar running up his thigh.

She sipped her drink, and when he was finished she said, "Servius, you're full of shit. Everyone knows you got that scar trying to shave your legs."

The group erupted into laughter, none louder than Servius, and then the conversation turned to everyone sharing the stories about their varying scars, the volume increasing as the rum disappeared down throats.

"What about you, Teriana?" Servius asked. "Beautiful as you are, a pirate has to have a few scars with stories."

She flipped her braids over one shoulder and batted her eyelashes at him, then hauled off one of her boots to reveal a jagged scar running down the top of her foot. Everyone made sounds of appreciation, and she paused dramatically and took a big mouthful before beginning.

If there was anything she and all Maarin were good at, it was spinning a yarn, and within moments she had them captivated with a tale of the crew of the *Quincense* battling a giant octopus in the Twisted Seas off the coast of Derin.

Across the fire, a shadow approached, the firelight glinting off polished armor. She recognized his stride and faltered mid-sentence as Marcus stopped just outside the circle, a half smile on his face. "Don't let me interrupt."

"Not much else to say," she said. "It had me by the ankle and was dragging me across the deck toward its gaping maw. My foot broke through a shattered plank, slicing me open. But it was just the leverage I needed to reach the blade that had been knocked from my hand. It was a desperate throw, but the gods must've been guiding my hand, because it caught the beast straight in the eye. The noise the cursed creature made rendered the whole crew deaf for a week, but it let go of my leg and slipped back into the sea. Whether it lived or died I could not say, but of it we saw nothing more."

The men all clapped and whistled, and she inclined her head, barely noticing the rest of them with Marcus's gaze fixed on her.

"Entertaining story," he said, sitting in the space his men made for him on the opposite side of the fire. "Except that's not how you got that scar."

Her skin warmed, and it had nothing to do with the log Gibzen had tossed on the blaze. "Oh?"

Accepting a cup, he shook his head.

She slowly clapped her hands together. "Congratulations on your choice of commander, my friends. Apparently he's not *just* a pretty face."

The noise was deafening with the shouts of "Truth! Truth! Give us the truth!"

Grinning, she pulled her boot back on. "We were drinking and dicing in a port city in Gamdesh, and my crew picked a fight. We had to skedaddle quick, but on our way back to the ship I put a foot through a lobster trap and had to be carried the rest of the way."

"That sounds more like it," Marcus said. "Drunk?"

"Obviously." She grinned. "What about you, Legatus? Surely you have a few scars with stories."

"Nothing worth telling."

Several of the men snorted into their cups, and Servius's cough sounded distinctly like "Bullshit," as he scratched dramatically at one cheek.

Marcus crossed his arms, and though it was hard to tell by the light of the fire, it appeared to Teriana that his cheeks had reddened.

"Since our dear legatus appears to be lost for words, allow me," Servius said, rising to his feet. "We were deep in the forests of Bardeen, part of a coordinated strike intended to finally bring the country under the Empire's control. We were primed for battle when the infamous Thirty-Seventh was dealt a blow that was nearly our doom." He paused, and the men groaned as if on cue. "Who can say whether it was the undercooked chicken, the vegetables of dubious quality, or the stream water rife with beaver shit, but over one thousand men were confined to the latrine pits while they exploded from both ends. And none were afflicted worse than our dear commander."

Teriana clapped a hand over her mouth, trying not to laugh as Marcus buried his face in his hands. "I hate you, Servius," he said, but the massive legionnaire only grinned.

"Our camp was deep in enemy territory, our walls—as high as they were—little protection with trees soaring hundreds of feet into the sky." He reached up high, then crouched low so the fire made shadows on his face. "Our fearsome commander was doing his best to fill the latrine holes we'd thought we'd dug so deep when out of the darkness came a flurry of arrows. One. Two. Three." Servius danced around the fire ducking and dodging.

"Alas, one of the enemy aimed well and"—he sliced a finger across his cheek—"Marcus the infallible, the untouchable, the invincible, was forever marked."

Laugher tore from Teriana's lips, and when she could finally control it enough to speak she asked, "This true?"

The embarrassment written in red across Marcus's face was answer enough. "What do you think?"

"Oh, it's true," Gibzen said. "He came stumbling back into the main camp covered in blood, shit, and worse, bellowing orders to catch the man who'd shot him."

"Did you?"

"No," Marcus answered, shaking his head and grinning. "Rat bastard got away." He leveled a finger at Servius. "There's going to be retribution for this."

His friend rubbed his hands together in anticipation, but before more could be said a trio of shadows approached the fire, hips moving with a distinctly female sway. Teriana's good humor fell away as the prostitutes stepped into the light, four more appearing soon after. They were all pretty and polished and clean, and Teriana was aware that she hadn't had a proper bath in far too long, her clothes were worse for wear, and her braids were fuzzy from neglect.

The soldiers' attention snapped from her to the other girls, who separated from their little groups and spread among the men, smiling and laughing, the fact that they didn't speak the same language mattering not in the slightest. One of them, a tall girl with long copper-colored hair, pushed between her and Servius, stepping hard on Teriana's foot. She barely noticed, because two others had flanked Marcus. But he only smiled and gestured at the broader group.

"Teriana. Teriana." Servius was poking her in the arm. "Tell her she's the most beautiful girl I've ever seen. That I've been across all of Reath and that none compare to her."

Teriana rolled her eyes and took a mouthful from her cup. But the rum no longer tasted sweet, so she set it on the dirt, where the girl's sandaled foot promptly knocked it over. "He thinks you're pretty," she told the prostitute, but the girl only raised one eyebrow, so Teriana added, "He can pay. They can all pay, and if they don't, they'll get in trouble."

The girl smiled and then cooed at Servius, kissing him on the lips. He winked at Teriana, flipped the prostitute over his shoulder, and with her giggling wildly departed into camp.

All around, coins were glinting as they exchanged hands, the soldiers departing with young men and women dressed in brilliant clothing designed to catch the eye. The trade itself didn't bother her. Everyone had to make a living. And it wasn't as though she could expect anything more or less from a legion full of young men who had no choice but to go and fight where they were told.

Teriana's stomach tightened, and she stared at her spilled drink wishing she could syphon out the dirt. *Would he go with one of them? Who would he choose?*

Why do I care?

A hand reached down in front of her and righted her cup,

an amber liquid of a finer quality than what she'd been drinking filling it up. A cloak brushed her arm, red and golden, and a not-unpleasant shiver ran through her.

"The gifts have begun arriving." Marcus tapped the side of her cup with the rum bottle, then took a long swallow before returning to the far side of the fire. Quintus and Miki had disappeared, and with the exception of the golden dragon glaring down at them, she and Marcus were alone.

Teriana took a small mouthful, for once at a loss for words. "Where were you?" she finally managed to ask.

"Handling some problems," he replied, leaning back on one hand. "There is an alarming amount of administration that comes with taking over a city, especially when one's translator is busy getting drunk with one's men."

"I'm not drunk," she said, though if she kept at it she would be. *Don't do anything stupid.*

He watched her as though weighing the truth of her words, and she looked away, taking in the lovely young people strolling through camp to ply their trade. "Feel free to find yourself some entertainment," she said. "Seems like everyone else is."

His gaze shifted to the fire. "I'm not leaving you to wander alone in a camp full of drunk men."

"Then set some guards on me," she said. "I'm tired anyway. All I'm likely to do now is go to sleep. You can go with one of them, if you want—"

"I know I can go," he interrupted, eyes fixed on a fire that had died down to embers. "But I don't want to."

Neither of them spoke, the only sounds the snap and pop of the burning wood and the distant laughter of soldiers. Teriana toyed with the handle of her cup, her eyes tracing over his features, which were so perfectly Cel. High cheekbones, straight nose, and a square jaw, his shorn hair a golden brown. The scar across his cheek that had inspired so much comedy, when it shouldn't have, because that arrow had almost killed him. And if it had, she wouldn't have met him.

How different would the world be if he had died in that moment?

"If you're tired, I'll walk you back to the tent," he said.

Nodding, Teriana waited until he'd kicked dirt over the coals, then fell in next to him as they walked the short distance to the command tent. His hand brushed hers, and a warm ache grew deep in her belly, her heart racing with anticipation.

Don't do anything stupid.

36

TERIANA

Marcus held aside the tent flaps, then followed her in, setting the rum bottle on top of a pile of maps with uncharacteristic carelessness. Teriana moved it where it couldn't do any damage. "Going back out to the celebration?"

"No." He glanced at her, then strode toward their sleeping quarters, unfastening his cloak as he walked and tossing it over a stool. "Tomorrow will be busy."

"Where's Amarin?" The man seemed to have an innate sense for when Marcus had need of him, but he was nowhere to be seen.

"Gave him the night off. He's in the city making friends his own age. He can take care of himself."

"Oh." She watched him turn up the lamp, then begin unbuckling his wrist guard.

Shoving aside all thoughts of right and wrong and consequence, she closed the distance between them. Pushing aside his hand, she unfastened the buckles, letting the piece of leather and metal drop to the ground before turning to his other wrist.

"I do know how to take it off," he said, but he didn't push her away.

"I know." His skin was hot beneath her fingers, and she fumbled at the buckle before finally dropping it at their feet. She unfastened one shin guard, then the other, following the pattern she'd witnessed every night since they'd landed. Only watching and doing were entirely different things.

Neither of them spoke, the only sound her breathing. And his.

Straightening, she moved on, the heavier pieces of armor

making soft thuds where she dropped them. Marcus stared straight ahead, but the rapid flutter of his pulse belied the steady expression on his face.

Teriana tugged hard on his belt, and he swayed toward her, saying nothing as she carelessly discarded his weapons behind her. Then there was nothing left but clothing, the fabric of his tunic worn where the armor had rubbed it. Her heart thundered in her chest as she lifted the hem, wondering if he'd stop her, whether she'd pushed him too far, whether he wanted this as much as she did. But he only lifted his arms and lowered his head, allowing her to tug the garment off and discard it with the rest.

She'd seen him stripped down to his undergarments before, but this time, she greedily drank in the sight. Hard muscles that cut and defined his torso, shoulders, arms, his stomach rippling with the hard edges of abdominals that she ached to run her fingers over. Training and walking and rations ensured there wasn't a spare ounce of flesh on him, his body every bit as much a weapon as the steel on the ground behind her.

And that face.

She lifted her own to look upon it, surprised to find his eyes closed, lashes longer than she'd noticed before. Resting one hand against his shoulder, she traced a fingertip over the number inked on to his chest. His inhalation was sudden and ragged, the sound of it answered by an almost unbearable ache in her core.

"I thought it would feel different," she whispered.

"Why?" His voice was hoarse, but his eyes were open now and fixed on her.

Because it defines you, was the first thought that crossed her mind, but she discarded it, because it was the opposite. He defined it. The number was the legion, and as much as the Senate had created it, he had shaped it into what it was today. He was its heart. "Because it means so much."

He gave an almost imperceptible shake of his head that wasn't a denial, and before she could lose her nerve Teriana slid an arm around his neck, his skin smooth beneath her hand. Then she rose onto her toes and kissed him.

It was little more than a brush of the lips, but it sent a charge through her that made her tremble. *This* was how it was supposed to feel. Like standing on a cliff high above a turquoise sea, terrified to jump but desperate for the thrill of the fall.

Their foreheads rested together, and his hands were on her hips, her skin burning beneath his touch.

"Why are you doing this?" he asked, and his breath smelled like the spice of expensive rum.

Warnings echoed through the back of her mind, but she ignored them all. "Because I want to."

One hand left her hips, rising to cup her cheek, tilting her face back so they were looking each other in the eye. The calluses on his hands were rough against her skin, and she leaned into them, a sound that verged on a moan coming from her throat as his thumb traced the edge of her bottom lip.

"You deserve better than this. Better than me."

There was desire in his voice, but also grief. An old hurt. And Teriana wondered if she'd ever know all that he had seen, had done. All that had been done *to* him. "That's my choice to make," she said.

He stood unmoving for the length of a breath; then his lips were against hers. The kiss was hard and fierce and deep, his arms dragging her closer, the length of her body pressed against his. She clung to his neck, not trusting the strength of her own knees as his teeth scraped her jaw, her throat, her collarbone. Then his hands were tearing at the laces of her vest, throwing it aside as she dragged her shirt over her head.

He groaned softly, and she let her head tip back, let her spine arch, trusting he wouldn't let her fall, relishing the feel of his hand against the curve of her breast. He tugged her trousers over her bottom, where they tangled around her boots until she kicked them free. Then there was nothing left between them, and he lifted her as though she weighed nothing before lowering her onto the blankets.

Marcus pulled back then, resisting her attempts to drag him against her. Resting on one elbow, he brushed aside the braids that had fallen across her face. Kissing her carefully, he said, "Teriana, are you sure?"

Before she could answer, he pressed a finger against her lips, holding them closed as though he could force her to think in a moment when it seemed thought was impossible.

But she was sure.

So very, very sure.

Taking his hand from her lips, she interlocked their fingers and lifted her head to kiss him, to taste him, to fall for him. "Yes."

Teriana awoke to the faint glow of dawn, her eyes gritty from only a handful of hours of sleep and mouth dry from the rum but feeling strangely content. She was pressed against Marcus, their legs tangled together, and his arm curved around her stomach. Both of them were slick with sweat from the torrid heat, but she would've been happy to lie there for hours more if not for the painful press of her bladder.

Carefully, she untangled her legs from his and eased out from under his arm, surprised that the motion didn't wake him given how lightly he slept. But Marcus didn't stir, his breathing slow and steady. She watched him while tugging clothes over skin sticky enough that she was going to have to go for a swim, marveling at how much younger he appeared when he was asleep. It was hard to believe, sometimes, that he was only nineteen. Two years older than her and the commander of an army.

And hers.

As soon as the thought passed through her mind, she made a face at the foolishness of it. He wasn't hers. And even if he wanted to be, which she had no business being certain of, he couldn't. The Empire owned its soldiers, and it had rules for them. They were allowed nothing outside of the legion until their commission ended, and Marcus was nothing if not a stickler for rules.

So what exactly did she expect from last night? Their time together had always had an end date. Either they succeeded in finding land-based xenthier stems that would allow travel to and fro, or they'd be defeated and she'd drag the sorry lot of them back through the ocean paths. Never mind that *she* was supposed to be working to ensure their defeat.

How in good conscience could she be the lover of the man she was trying to sabotage?

Why would I want to be?

Feeling abruptly ill, Teriana crept through the command tent and out into the open air. The men standing guard around the tent smiled and nodded at her, and she hoped none of them had been listening too closely in the dark hours. Quintus and Miki were with them.

"Have a good time last night?" Miki asked, and she prayed to the Six that her complexion hid the fiery burn spreading across her cheeks.

"Oh, sure," she replied. "I keep gambling with your commanders and I'm going to be rich as a senator. But at the moment, I'd give it all up for a proper bath."

They laughed, falling in behind her as she headed toward the main gates. She needed to pee, and a swim in the ocean would go a long way to clearing her thoughts. An irrational wish that Lydia were here hit Teriana hard in the guts. This was exactly the sort of thing she could *only* talk about with Lydia. Except that wasn't possible now. And never would be again.

"Teriana!"

She grimaced, but as much as she might want to, ignoring Titus wasn't an option. "Morning."

"Good morning." He fell into stride next to her. "I need to talk to you." His eyes flicked to Quintus and Miki. "In private."

Neither of them moved.

Exhaling an irritated breath, Teriana gave them a nod. "Meet me at the gate?"

She could see the hesitation in their eyes, but both reluctantly continued toward the front of the camp. Turning on Titus, she said, "Make it quick. I need to piss."

"Marcus has tasked me with keeping an inventory of, umm, structures related to pagan practices. I know about the circle with the seven buildings in the center of Galinha, but are there others?"

A chill dripped down her spine, spreading out into her arms and legs, turning them to ice. "Why?"

"Marcus intends to leave well enough alone until we're established," he continued. "But then . . . Well, you know how it goes."

The Empire would tear them down.

"Why are you telling me this?" she snapped. "And do you think I've any intention of helping you?"

"Marcus said—"

"Sure he did." She rolled her eyes and kept walking.

"Excuse me?" Titus caught her arm, dragging her to a stop. "If you don't believe that he gave me those orders, feel free to ask him," he said. "In case you hadn't noticed, this is *his* campaign, and nothing happens without him sanctioning it first."

She did know that. Just as she knew that Titus wouldn't risk being caught in a lie.

Her eyes dropped to the straps of his sandals. "He's only following the Senate's orders."

"Is that what you think?" The pity in his voice made her cringe. "Do you know what it takes for a runty, patrician child like he was to make it to the top?" Titus tapped the side of his head. "Genius. And ruthlessness. He's a bloody legend at Campus Lescendor, and here's more proof of why; you should hate him, but instead he's got you mooning after him like he's the hero out of a poem instead of a killer set on conquest."

Her cheeks burned, but for once, she was lost for an appropriate retort.

Titus stared out over the camp. "I know we got off to a rough start, but I like you, Teriana. And he doesn't need to do this. Doesn't need to hurt you more than you've already been hurt."

"Why would the son of Cassius care what happens to me?"

Silence.

"My father's a slimy bastard who doesn't give a squirt of piss about me beyond what advantage my victories bring him." Titus spit into the dirt. "And besides, it wasn't me who handed him the consulship. You can thank Marcus for that."

The sun burned, and all she saw was white light. "You're lying."

"Ask anyone." He leaned in, voice little more than a whisper. "The Thirty-Seventh marched into Celendrial and, to a man, voted for my father."

"You're full of shit, Titus." And before he could say anything more, she hurried toward the camp gates.

He's got an agenda, she told herself. *He's not telling you these things for your sake—he's got something to gain.* But that didn't mean what he'd told her was a lie.

Reaching the gate, she stumbled to a halt. Quintus and Miki were talking to Avitius, so she mindlessly exchanged pleasantries with the men standing guard, waiting for them to finish. All of them were from the Thirty-Seventh. The question came out without thought: "Did you vote in the elections?"

They exchanged looks with one another; then one of them shrugged. "We all did."

"For who?" Her tongue felt numb.

"Cassius."

"Why?"

There was a flash of discomfort in the soldier's eyes; then he said, "*He* didn't give us much choice."

He. Marcus.

"Right." Her feet carried her through the gates, the sun all of a sudden seeming much too bright. Then Titus appeared again at her arm.

"Satisfied?"

Teriana tasted blood, the insides of her cheeks stinging. She'd killed a man to save Marcus's life. And not just any man—a marked healer.

"He's duped you," Titus said, leaning in as Quintus and Miki approached. "For the sake of your sanity, do what you need to do to get through this, and then sail as far away from Marcus as you can get."

37

MARCUS

"I leave you to your own devices for one night and this is how you treat your equipment?"

Marcus jerked awake, eyes going to Amarin, who was eyeing the pile of armor and weapons lying haphazardly across the floor of the tent. "Where's Teriana?"

One of Amarin's eyebrows rose. "Not where you expected her to be?"

Marcus ignored the comment. Rolling out of the tangle of his bedding, he availed himself of the bowl of water the man had brought, then dragged a clean tunic over his head. Leaving Amarin to fuss with his armor, he buckled on his belt as he walked through the command tent and out into the open.

The sun was fully up and wicked bright, forcing him to squint. "Which way did she go?"

One of his men pointed toward the main gates, and Marcus strode in that direction, paying little attention to the salutes of those he passed.

He hadn't meant for last night to happen.

Not because he hadn't wanted it to, but because it could only lead to trouble.

He'd told her the truth about Chersome because he'd wanted her to think better of him. But there were countless other truths he hadn't told her that would do the exact opposite. How much would she hate him if she knew?

How much worse would it be now that they'd been together?

He was a piece of shit for letting it happen, for allowing his own desires to take precedence over being a decent human being. But despite knowing that, Marcus couldn't help but wonder if there was a way to make it work, because his feelings for her weren't limited to lust.

Far from it.

Rattling off a string of curses under his breath, all directed at himself, he scanned the tents, looking for the dark gleam of her hair. He needed to make sure she was all right, to try—although he didn't know how—to undo the damage he'd done. To make her understand that in another world, another life, maybe things could be different. If he were not who he was . . .

And for the first time in years, Marcus allowed himself to feel bitterness at the hand he'd been dealt. To hate his father for sacrificing him to a life where he could have nothing of his own. Where any relationship beyond the brotherhood of the legion was forbidden and by the time he was released, he'd be too old and bitter and broken to care. It was not fair.

Because he wanted this, and he wanted *her,* but it could not be. And even if it could, she deserved far better than him. Someone who wasn't lying to her. Someone who could give her more than a canvas tent and a soldier's rations. Someone who wasn't destined to hurt her.

You are her enemy. You are her captor.

"Marcus!"

He jumped at the sound of his name, turning to see Felix striding toward him. "You losing your hearing?" his friend muttered. "I called you three times."

"Sorry." His gaze drifted over Felix's shoulder, searching, searching.

"I need to talk to you about something we found in Galinha last night," Felix said. "We found a house, one of the fancier ones, and it was full of—"

Where is she?

"Are you even listening to me?"

His attention jerked back to Felix, whose face was dark with irritation. "I am."

"Clearly not, given I just told you that we found the bodies of some of the missing children and you didn't even blink."

That caught his attention. "How many?"

"A hundred or so."

So many . . .

"We're still sorting through them," Felix said. "Some are little more than bones, but others . . . There's something strange about them."

"How so?"

"They're child sized, but they look—" Felix shook his head. "You need to see it for yourself."

It is the last thing I want to see. "Send word to Ereni. And to Flacre," he said. "Have them come and see if any can be identified."

"What about you?"

"I'll come; I just . . ." *Where is she?* "There's something I need to do first."

He started walking to the gates, hearing Felix call his name, but not turning around. "Have you seen her?" he asked the men standing guard.

Because there is only one her.

"Wanted a swim," one of them answered. "Quintus and Miki are watching her back."

Swallowing hard, Marcus left the camp, making his way down through the trees to the sound of crashing waves. "You can go," he said to the two men standing at the edge of the sand, his eyes all for the girl standing knee deep, her clothes dripping and the sun glinting off the gold and gems decorating black braids that hung to her narrow waist. She was beautiful.

But as much as he might wish otherwise, she was not his. And never would be.

Taking a deep breath, he walked out onto the beach.

38

TERIANA

The *thud, thud* of heavy sandals against the sand pulled Teriana from her dismal reverie, the rehashing of Titus's words that no amount of scrubbing with soap and sand could erase from her mind.

It was him. She knew it was him, and she wanted nothing more than to throw herself into the waves and swim until the sea sucked her down into its depths. Anything to avoid this conversation.

"When I woke, you weren't there."

She didn't turn around. "Needed to get clean."

It was true. She'd been sticky with sweat and grime from the heat and exertion. From living in a tent. Except that wasn't what she meant, and from his silence, he knew it.

"Teriana, I . . . I wanted you to know—"

She stepped out of the water, facing him and cutting him off. "Nothing to be said, Marcus. It isn't a big deal. It isn't as though it meant anything."

There'd been a glint of emotion on his face, but it was gone in an instant, replaced by an unblinking stare. "I see," he said.

The words were inflectionless, which usually meant he was annoyed. *Good,* she thought. *Let him believe his plan to manipulate me hasn't worked.* Never mind that it was a lie. Never mind that he'd rattled her worse than she'd believed possible.

Picking up her boots, she tugged one on. "It's a matter of convenience. You've made it clear all your men are off-limits, and you seem set and determined to keep me near you every moment, so . . ." She shrugged, then tugged on her other boot. "It worked for both of us. For a night."

He didn't respond, only stood staring at her. Silent. Probably thinking of ways to alter his strategy now that he knew she wasn't some stupid little girl to be so affected by a night between the sheets.

"If it helps"—she pulled on the vest that had been lying next to her boots—"think of me like those girls in the camp last night."

"Like a prostitute." He blinked once. "Well, in that case, you know where we keep the gold. Take whatever you thought it was worth."

Without another word, he rotated on one heel and strolled back to camp.

It was worse than if he'd spit in her face. But what had she expected? He had the advantage in this game they were playing, because he didn't care. She had cared.

And I still do.

Though if he thought she'd sit here in the sand and weep, he had another thing coming. Taking several quick steps, she fell in next to him. "No need for that," she said. "With the way your men gamble, it will all end up in my pocket anyway."

The muscles in his jaw flexed. "There isn't going to be time for cards in the coming days," he said. "Not for you. You're going to be marching up and down the coast ensuring the supply chains we've set up are functioning as intended. We'll be marching on Urcon's stronghold in Aracam shortly, and the last thing I need to be worrying about is feeding my men."

He was sending her away.

She should've let him die.

Had he always been planning this, or was this his reaction to her not playing into his ploy? When he'd believed she was a lovestruck fool, it had been safe enough to keep her around. Only now that he knew otherwise, what better way to keep her from sabotaging his plans than to send her away just before the fighting intensified?

"You need me here. Who else will translate for you?"

"I don't need you," he said in Arinoquian. "For translation or otherwise."

She flinched and hated herself for it.

They'd reached the gates, and he stopped while they were still far enough that the men couldn't hear them. "Pack what you need and be ready to go in an hour. And Teriana . . ."

"What?" The word was supposed to sound sour, but instead it was strangled.

"Your usefulness is waning. Best you come up with a way to pick up the slack, or I might find cause to reconsider our contract."

39

TERIANA

Teriana stared at the pitted and scarred wood of the table, idly tracing shapes with the condensation pooling at the base of her glass.

"You in or out?" Miki asked, shuffling the deck.

She gave a slight shake of her head and took a mouthful of ale, wondering how much she'd regret it if she drank to the bottom of a keg tonight. Probably no more than she had the first night, or the second, or the third since they'd been in Galinha, the tavern and inn above bought and paid for with Cel gold for the men who remained here to keep order.

"You in, Quintus?"

"Nope." Her bodyguard shifted, elbow bumping hers. "Teriana has all my money."

The group laughed, but she barely heard it, attention drifting around the room. Seeing an Arinoquian tavern filled with Cel was strange but not, she supposed, for much longer. *How long will it take?* she wondered. *How long until Arinoquia is as nestled into the Empire's fold as Atlia, Bardeen, Sibal, and Chersome?*

Teriana would've given anything to talk to Bait, but Magnius hadn't answered her calls any of the times she'd tried to summon him under the guise of taking a swim. Which, she hoped, meant that Bait had heeded her order and gone with their guardian home to Taltuga, the Maarin islands off the coast of Mudamora. She prayed that he'd have more luck gaining the assistance of the two other triumvirs than she had in stopping the Cel. Not that luck had been on her side in anything lately other than cards.

The server walked by, and Teriana motioned for him to bring another round, paying for it with her winnings.

Sensing eyes on her, she turned her head and met Quintus's gaze. "Something on your mind?" he asked.

The Arinoquians' deaths on the road. Caradoc's death. The fact she'd fallen on her back for the Thirty-Seventh's commander. All her mistakes.

She pursed her lips and shook her head. "Just thinking about what's left on that list for me to accomplish." Before Marcus had booted her out of camp, he'd penned a dozen items on a piece of paper in his obnoxiously elegant script and told her not to return until she'd crossed out all of them.

"It's make-work, you know," Quintus said, accepting a foaming cup. "Point and pay. Anyone could've done it. Didn't have to be you."

"I drive a harder bargain than anyone else."

"You do," he agreed, pushing the bowl of fried bits of batter in her direction. "But given about the only thing that rat bastard Cassius did right was supply us with enough gold, that's not the reason the legatus sent you away. Am I wrong?"

"I need some air." Pushing back her stool, Teriana wove between the tables, trying to keep her annoyance in check as Quintus followed. *The Six forbid I have a moment of privacy.*

"You're not going wandering without a full escort," he said, pulling her to a stop. "So get your fresh air right here."

"Piss off," Teriana muttered, but didn't argue when he leaned against the wall next to her.

"What's had you in such a twist these past days?"

"That's a stupid question, Quintus. I'm a prisoner being forced to help those intent on conquering the world and wiping out my religion. And if I don't help, they'll kill my mum, then slaughter my people."

Her bodyguard blew out a breath between his teeth, nodding as he did. "Point made." Then he turned to look at her. "Except something's made things worse. Am I right?"

"Aye." But a big part of what had made it worse was nothing she had any intention of admitting. "I didn't think Marcus was involved with the decision to capture Maarin ships. I thought that was Cassius."

"It was."

She spit into the dirt. "Bullshit. Without Marcus, Cassius wouldn't have been able to give those orders. Titus told me about the vote."

"Titus doesn't know shit."

"He knows enough! Cassius murdered dozens of my people, tortured my mum—tortured me. Made me choose between the lives of my people and the lives of the thousands of people you lot will likely conquer or kill. And Marcus was the one who put him in power."

Quintus shook his head slowly. "If you're going to blame him for that, then you might as well blame the lot of us, because we all voted. And his token didn't count for any more than mine."

"But you had no choice. Marcus ordered you to vote for Cassius."

"No," Quintus said. "He didn't."

Her mouth was open to retort, but instead her teeth clicked shut.

"We were recalled from Chersome, no reason given, and left to languish outside Celendrial. Cassius called Marcus to a private meeting and tried to blackmail him into ordering us to vote for him. Told him that if he didn't win the consulship the Thirty-Seventh would be sent to some shit hole full of pestilence where our ranks would be slowly whittled down to nothing by disease. But if we voted for him, we'd be rewarded."

Blackmail. "You all voted for him. Titus told me so."

He nodded. "We did. Most of us, at any rate. Except Marcus didn't order us to do anything: he told us the truth and let us vote how we wished." Leaning against the building, Quintus tilted his face toward the sky, studying the moon. "Maybe it was the wrong thing for us to do, to vote for Cassius, because the people of the Empire won't thrive under his leadership. Except what have they ever done for us? Why should we suffer any more than we already have for their sakes?"

It was tempting to be all high-and-mighty, to say they should've voted to support the greater good. Only Teriana wasn't that big a fool. When given the opportunity, people voted in their best interests, and for the Thirty-Seventh that had been Cassius.

"You said Titus told you this? He's not the greatest source."

"Aye." She hadn't thought Titus brave enough to lie about something she could so easily confirm, but neither had she thought him clever enough to hide his deceit in a layer of truth.

"A consul isn't a king," Quintus said. "Cassius still needs a majority vote to do much of anything, and that includes deciding which legion to send on a particular mission. There wasn't a chance of the Senate agreeing to an inexperienced legatus like Titus commanding a mission of this importance. But to send him as second to the best commander the Empire has in service? That was an easy sell. Made easier still by the fact that they were glad to send the Thirty-Seventh, and our black reputation, to the far side of the world. Out of sight, out of mind, right?"

She nodded.

"Except that same distance means that the Senate can't stop Titus from taking command if something were to happen to Marcus, so don't think for a second that he isn't doing everything he can to make that happen."

"How is making me hate Marcus supposed to accomplish that?"

Quintus shrugged. "Got me. But I do know he wouldn't have done it without cause."

There was movement in the shadows up the street, and Quintus's blade was in his hand in an instant, his free hand pushing her toward the door. However, the men who materialized from the darkness were Cel, and he instantly relaxed.

"Got a message from camp," one of them said. "Legatus plans

to give Urcon an ultimatum. Surrender, or we attack Aracam. He wants Teriana back as soon as possible."

"Guess that means we're leaving at dawn," Quintus said. "Enjoy your last night sleeping in a proper bed, Teriana."

The sun was high in the sky and her feet ached, but they still hadn't made it to the new camp. *Have things changed?* she wondered. *Will my belongings still be in Marcus's tent, or will he have moved me somewhere else? Somewhere out of the way?*

Lost in thought, she walked into Quintus's back, her knuckles clanging painfully against his armor. "The Seventh take you, Quintus! What—"

"Would you be rutting quiet," he hissed, and it was only then that she noticed the jungle had gone silent. No birds chirped. No monkeys screeched. Even the insects seemed to have ceased their endless drone.

The legionnaires eyed the trees. Watchful. Uneasy. Blades slipped into hands, and Quintus muttered, "This is an ambush. We need to move. Now!"

Teriana's ears caught the muffled twang of a bowstring, and a second later an arrow was jutting just below Quintus's collarbone. Another took him in the arm. Another in the leg. Then he dropped even as she heard Miki scream his name.

Teriana caught Quintus, his weight dragging her to the ground as dozens of warriors exploded from the jungle, the air full of their battle cries. The legionnaires stood their ground, fighting with ruthless efficiency, cutting down warrior after warrior. But they kept coming.

"We need to retreat!" Miki shouted, gutting one of their attackers even as he stepped back, reaching for Teriana to haul her up. "Teriana, let him go."

She could see the words cost him. Could see the tears on his cheeks.

"We need to run!"

She started to rise right when their attackers parted like a wave and a man strode through them, dark eyes fixing on them.

Teriana took one look and screamed. "He's corrupted! Kill him!"

Miki threw a knife, and it embedded in the man's chest with a meaty *thunk,* but the corrupted only laughed, plucking it out and tossing it aside.

"Run!" Teriana howled. *"Run!"*

But instead Miki sprinted toward the corrupted, blade in hand. The corrupted lifted a sword and they fought, the air filling with the crash of steel, but then the creature had her friend by the neck, Miki's face ageing before her eyes.

"No!" Her voice was shrill and frantic. Grabbing a fallen knife, she threw it, the blade embedding in the corrupted's arm. It hissed and flung Miki aside, his body hitting a tree with a sickening crunch.

Sobbing with grief, Teriana flung herself at the creature, carving her way through the men standing between them with Quintus's gladius.

"Don't hurt her! We need her alive," someone bellowed, but the words only made her fight harder, not with the lethal efficiency of a legionnaire but with the nastiness of a pirate. Knowing they wouldn't stab her in the back, she fought to maim, the razor-sharp gladius removing limbs and opening guts.

They fell back from her in an ever-widening circle, and she hazarded a glance over her shoulder to check on her guard.

All there was were still bodies. Parts. Blood. They were dead. All of them were dead.

"You bastards!" Teriana screamed, and she threw herself at the corrupted even as she felt the dart pierce the skin of her neck.

40

MARCUS

"How much longer?"

Felix cleared his throat. "Three hours."

Three hours left for Urcon to surrender Aracam, or the legions and the allied clans would attack the city and take it by force. Marcus had given Urcon the opportunity knowing that the man wouldn't take it. Men like him never did.

One of the Forty-First stepped inside. "Powder casks are unloaded from the ship, sir."

"Good," Felix said. "We'll set the charges after the sun sets. Remind the men to keep the casks away from open flame. Don't want to blow ourselves up."

The soldier saluted and departed. "We'll blast a few holes in that ring wall," Felix said. "Urcon won't know what hit him."

"If it works," Marcus muttered. But it wasn't the effectiveness of the new weapon that was plaguing his thoughts.

Teriana and her bodyguards should've been back from Galinha this morning, but it was already late afternoon and there was no sign of her. Agitation prickled at his skin, and every time he heard the flaps to the tent open, his heart skipped, his eyes flicking to the entrance to see if it was her.

But it was always someone else.

Footsteps stole his attention from Felix, and he turned in time to see Servius and Gibzen walk in, followed by Titus and his second and third. He listened to their updates, noting, not for the first time, that the other legatus had turned out to be quite different than he'd expected. He was smart and attentive, never argumentative, although he did not hesitate to raise his concerns. He kept his emotions in check, which, lately, had made him more of an asset than Felix.

"Sir?"

The guard he'd dispatched to find out if Teriana was lurking somewhere else in the camp had finally returned. "Well?" he demanded.

"I asked at the gate, sir. Teriana and her bodyguards haven't returned."

Marcus's skin prickled, and the nerves that had been troubling his stomach amplified to the point he felt sick.

"They should've been back hours ago," Servius said.

"Who cares," Felix replied. "Teriana probably slept late and slowed them down."

Except that wasn't her way. She might bitch and complain until she was blue in the face, but she was a hard worker. If she said she would do something, she did. If she said she would be somewhere, she was.

"Could've been an accident on the road." Gibzen's face reflected the grimness of his tone. "Twisted ankle or the like. Want me to send a few men out to find them?"

"Yes," Marcus answered, even as Felix said, "Come on! Our army is already half in position, and the rest will be marching soon enough. We can't spare the resources, and even if we could, what's the point? They'll get here when they get here."

Marcus dug his fingernails into his palms as he struggled to keep his anger in check. Instead of answering his second, he nodded at Gibzen. "Do it. Tell them to hurry."

Never had Marcus wished harder for time to stop, but never had it flown faster, the sun passing overhead as though it were being chased by one of this land's gods. Maybe it was.

"Time's up," Felix said from where he stood with his arms crossed in the corner. "Shall we?"

Urcon hadn't capitulated.

Teriana hadn't arrived at camp.

But Marcus could not stand here waiting for news of her when his army was about to march into battle. *Focus.* He took a deep breath and nodded once.

"They were ambushed!"

There was a flurry of motion at the front of the tent, and a legionnaire staggered in, breath coming in great heavy gasps. Marcus felt hollow, the dim tent abruptly too bright. "What?"

"They're all dead but Quintus and Miki, and they're both in bad shape. Miki might not make it. They're with the medics now."

All of them. All of them. A loud whining ring filled his ears, and Marcus stared at the man, seeing his lips moving but not hearing the words.

"What about Teriana?" Titus demanded, and the sound of her name snapped Marcus back into the moment.

"Not with them. The others are still looking."

Felix barked out a bitter laugh. "And the bitch finally shows her true colors."

Marcus snapped. Twisting around, he struck, catching Felix in the face and knocking him back. Only it wasn't enough. Not nearly enough.

He flung himself at his so-called friend, and the table collapsed beneath their weight, maps, markers, and tin cups flying. "You think she did this?" he screamed. "This was done *to* her. We were supposed to keep her safe, and now she's dead."

Hands latched on him, dragging him off Felix, slamming him on his back. Servius and Gibzen held his arms and Titus sprawled across his legs. He fought against them as Felix staggered to his feet, nose bleeding.

Then the anger rushed out of Marcus in a flood, leaving a void behind. Teriana was dead, and it was his fault. He'd sent her away from the safety of the camp, and not because she'd deserved it, but because of his lack of willpower. Because his rutting *feelings* had been hurt. And now she was gone.

Servius's face was inches from his. "We'll find her, but right now, you've got to get your shit together, because you've a battle to win."

Titus eased off his legs. "The men Gibzen sent are good trackers, Marcus, plus they have four of Ereni's warriors with them.

Together they'll find her, and if . . ." He trailed off, then clenched his teeth. "We'll make them pay."

"Those were my men with her," Gibzen added. "We'll find the bastards who did this and show them ways to die that they never dreamed of."

Marcus heard everything they said, but it meant little. Revenge wouldn't bring her back. And burning this whole continent to the ground wouldn't make her death any less his fault. Servius dragged Marcus to his feet, keeping between him and Felix.

"Marcus, you know I—" Felix started to say, but Marcus cut him off.

"Save your breath."

"Sir?"

One of the guards stood at the front of the tent, his eyes drifting back and forth between the mess of furniture and maps and his angry commander.

"What?"

"We've got a man, a local, outside. He wants to talk to you."

"Now isn't the time," Servius snapped at him. "We're about to march—"

"He was shouting Teriana's name."

Hope shot through Marcus's veins. Maybe she'd escaped to one of the villages. Maybe she was alive. "Bring him in."

The man they escorted in didn't deserve the word. He was a boy, little more than twelve or thirteen, and Marcus recognized him as one of the children from Ereni's clan who Teriana had been teaching to speak Cel. Both of his eyes were blackened, and blood dripped from his nose. "You do this to him?" Marcus demanded, but the soldier shook his head.

"We found him like that, sir."

"Teriana," the boy blurted out.

"Where is she?" Everyone pressed close, but Marcus motioned them back.

"Urcon's men. They . . . took her." His words were accented and shaky but clear enough.

"Where did they take her?"

The boy shook his head and lifted his shoulders in mute appeal.

"What do they want?" Marcus barely heard the question, despite it coming from his own lips. Because he knew.

"He say, you—"

The boy broke off, fear making him forget the Cel he'd been taught. Marcus knew how the child felt, because every bit of Arinoquian he'd learned seemed to have vanished from his head. Taking a deep breath, Marcus focused his thoughts and dragged the words he needed forth: "What did this man tell you to tell me?"

"He said you need to take your army and leave. To get back on your ships and go home."

"Or?" Marcus's pulse roared in his ears.

The boy's throat convulsed as he swallowed. "Or Teriana dies."

41

TERIANA

Teriana woke to the sound of beating drums, only to realize that the sound was a throbbing pulse inside her skull. Groaning, she lifted a hand to her head, and the events on the road came crashing back. Her friends lying still among the bodies of the enemy. Hearing the order not to kill her. The dart that had taken her in the neck.

Fear chased away the pain, her lashes sticking and pulling as she pried her lids open.

And saw nothing but blackness.

Breath coming in frantic little pants, she stretched out her legs, but her feet thudded against something solid. They'd put her in a box. Panic crept through her veins, and she reached out, feeling little relief as her fingers bumped against wooden bars. Not a box, but a cage.

Keep it together, she ordered herself, shifting as best she could to test the limits of the enclosure, eyes growing accustomed enough to the darkness that she was able to make out what lay beyond the bars. It was a building of some sort, windowless, but light faintly outlined a door.

Which suddenly opened.

She squinted at the man who'd come inside.

"You're awake," he said. "How delightful."

"You've made a mistake." Her voice was hoarse. "When they track you down, which they will, you're all dead men."

"Oh, I doubt that." The man knelt next to her cage. He wore a sword belted at his waist, and there were knives strapped to his forearms and calves, along with several knife-shaped bulges under his shirt. But all that steel meant nothing. Nothing,

nothing, nothing, as the eyes of the man who'd stolen Miki's life met hers.

Corrupted.

She recoiled against her cage, which shook with the impact of her shoulders. All it would take was one touch. One touch from someone marked by the Seventh god and all the remaining years of her life would be gone.

"We were careful to lay a dozen false trails," he continued. "Besides, we won't be here long."

"Where are you taking me?" she whispered.

"Depends." He smiled, and his teeth gleamed white against the brown of his skin, the dozen rings in his left ear glittering. He was Gamdeshian. Or at least, *had* been.

"Depends on what?" She needed to keep him talking, to discover as much of their plans as she could, figure out how much time she had, and then think of a way to escape.

"On how much your friends value your life."

"Then I suppose you should kill me now," she said, "because they aren't my friends. I'm their prisoner."

He laughed. "You don't act like much of a prisoner, Teriana. You see, we've been watching you. And *him*."

There was only one *him*. Marcus. "What do you want?"

"As we speak, a message is being delivered to the commander of your boy army." He drew a finger down her cheek to mimic Marcus's scar, and when she recoiled he grabbed a handful of her braids and jerked her forward. "Either he withdraws his army, or we send you back to him in pieces. I was of a mind to send you back aged into an old woman, but we did not want to risk them not recognizing you."

After how she'd left things with Marcus, the chances of him withdrawing the legions on her behalf were next to nothing. Yet she had to ask: "And if he agrees?"

A feral gleam filled the man's gaze. "Oh, we'll still send you back in pieces, when the moment is right. No doubt they'll attack Aracam in retaliation, but by then our reinforcements will have arrived, and we'll see how this army of boys fights a two-sided battle against grown men."

Not only did Teriana not relish an early end to her life, her people's freedom depended on her making it out of this situation alive, because that gods-damned treaty with the Senate was with her. If she died, what would happen to her crew? To her mother? To those of her people captive back in Celendor? She needed to do anything, risk everything, to escape before Marcus laughed in their messenger's face and she was cut to bits.

How much time did she have? An hour? Two? And how in the name of all the gods was she going to get past a minion of the Seventh? The answer to that was obvious: she wasn't.

Which meant it was time to start negotiating.

"You're wasting your time," she said. "He couldn't care less if you kill me. But for you, I'm much more valuable alive than dead. I know their plans and strategies. How they fight. I'll tell you everything if you give your word to let me go after you defeat them."

"Here's the thing." He tapped her on the nose, and she flinched. "I think he *does* care for you, and I think he'll do whatever it takes to get you back."

If only that were true. Teriana bit the insides of her cheeks, the pain steadying her nerves. "You're mistaken. Killing me gains you nothing."

The corrupted shook his head. "You are a liar, Teriana. We know he keeps you with him at all times, shares his tent with you—and his bed. Our informant told us as much when he provided the time and place for our ambush, and even if he had not . . . We have our own spies."

Teriana exhaled slowly, trying not to react. *Our informant . . .* Who could it be? "You'd trust a man who'd betray his own?"

The corrupted shrugged. "The fool was so caught up with his desire to be rid of you that he failed to see the weapon he was handing over. Was paying us to take." He laughed and extracted a handful of gold coins. They were stamped with the Cel dragon, which meant they hadn't come from the chests in the command tent. But none of the legionnaires she'd gambled with had that amount of wealth in their pockets, only silver and bronze.

"He went on and on about how you'd been nothing but trouble. How his commander was making a fool of himself chasing after you. How everything would go back to normal once you were dead." His mouth twisted in a smirk. "It was quite obvious he idolizes him. Love makes men into fools."

Felix. Who else could he be talking about? Felix disliked her more than anyone else, and if he'd found out that she and Marcus had been together . . . Well, it wasn't like she hadn't suspected how deep Felix's feelings ran for his commander. Everything the corrupted had said pointed to the second-in-command, and as an officer, it was possible he had access to that amount of gold. . . .

"Trying to figure out who the traitor is?" the corrupted asked. "I'd describe him, but they all look the same to me."

She had to escape. Had to warn them. Had to stop Marcus from making a mistake that might cost both of them everything. Had to tell him she hadn't meant a damned word of what she'd said on the beach.

Think. If they intended to kill her regardless of what Marcus did, why hadn't they already done so? There had to be a reason why they were keeping her alive, and maybe she could capitalize upon that.

"But what about you, little Maarin girl?" the corrupted asked. "We know this boy commander is enamored of his prisoner, but is the prisoner such a fool as to have fallen in love with her captor?"

She met his dead stare for a long moment, voiced a silent prayer to the Six, then spit in his face.

Very slowly, he lifted his sleeve to wipe his cheek, and for a heartbeat Teriana thought she'd misjudged him. Then, quick as a viper, he reached through the bars and caught the front of her shirt. He jerked her forward and she tried to brace her hands against the bars, but he was infinitely stronger. Over and over, he slammed her face and shoulders against the cage and she shrieked and cried, because it hurt. When her hands slipped through the bars, fumbling against him as though in an effort to brace herself, he did not notice that she palmed one of his knives, slipping it up her sleeve with practiced ease.

He tossed her against the rear of her cage, and it was no act when she curled up in a shuddering ball, her eyes swelling, nose dripping blood.

The door opened. "Ashok," another man said. "The messenger has gone into the Cel camp to deliver your demands."

"Splendid." Ashok rose to his feet. "Now let's see what this boy values more: your life or his pride. Not that it will make much difference to you, in the end." Laughing, he walked out of the building.

42

MARCUS

No one in the tent spoke.

Withdraw, or Teriana dies. Marcus felt numb, and he only dimly heard the others continue questioning the boy as he turned away. Righting the table, he gathered the maps, laying out the ones he needed and replacing the scattered markers in their correct locations. *Withdraw, or Teriana dies.*

"Marcus?"

Was this always the way it was to be? Those he cared about being put in jeopardy in order to manipulate him? First his family and now Teriana. His affection was a curse, and maybe it was better for all if he wiped the emotion from his heart. If he truly became the cold, logical creature the Empire had trained him to be.

But it wouldn't save Teriana.

"Marcus." Titus was across from him, his face flushed. "What do you want to do?"

Whatever it takes to save her.

"This is Teriana we're talking about," Titus said. "You've got to do something. You can't just let them cut her up."

Marcus flinched. *Was that what they'd do?*

"We'll delay the attack," Titus said, leaning over the table, bits of spit flying with the intensity of his words. "It's the only way to save her. Then we'll find her and make them pay."

"Shut up, Titus." Felix shoved the younger soldier aside. "Marcus, listen. I know you're angry with me, but you have to see reason. If we withdraw, do you think they're just going to hand Teriana over to us unharmed? There'd be nothing to stop us from attacking them, and they'd have lost the only leverage they have against us. No matter what we do, we're not going to get her back alive."

His chest ached. "What are you suggesting?"

Felix licked his split lip, then looked away. "I know you're fond of her, but . . . but this is the Thirty-Seventh. We do not negotiate. And we do not fall back."

"How shocking that *his* advice is to let her die!" Titus snarled. "Don't listen to him, Marcus. We can find her; all we need to do is buy some time. The men will understand why."

"What they'll understand is that their commander is making decisions based on his feelings for a girl," Felix retorted. "Never mind what the clan imperators will think about this. They're in position, too."

"I'm not listening to this." Titus kicked a stool. "I'm going to find out whether the trackers have had any luck." Motioning for his men to follow, he stormed out of the tent, leaving Marcus alone with Servius and Felix.

"How much time do we have?"

Servius cleared his throat. "The boy didn't know much, but from what I gathered before I sent him off with a medic, we have less than an hour to comply or they—"

"Cut her up," Marcus finished, his mind filling with that horror. Of having to see her perfect body reduced to parts, her beautiful eyes still and unseeing. Her voice silenced. And it would be his fault.

"Yeah." Servius's voice was thick with emotion. "That's the threat."

"Sir—"

Marcus cut him off. "I know, Felix. I know everything that you're going to say, and you're right. We should attack, because we are the Thirty-Seventh and we do not fall back."

Felix straightened in surprise.

"I know what my orders should be." Marcus swallowed hard, knowing that nothing would be the same after this. "Only I don't think I can live with myself if I give them."

Silence.

"Just how much do you care about this girl?"

Marcus didn't answer, only met his friend's gaze. *Too much.*

Felix looked away first. "Right. Well, the decision is yours, sir." He saluted sharply. "If you'll excuse me, I need some air."

Tick, tock. The second hand of the clock made a slow progression around the face.

"You need to make a decision," Servius finally said. "Whatever your orders are, you need to give them."

Marcus shook his head once, never taking his eyes from the clock. He felt paralyzed, unable to make a decision. "I don't know what to do, Servius."

"Recall them or march the rest into position, but you have to do something. We have men in the field and we can't leave them hanging."

Tick, tock.

He knew what he had to do.

"Marcus, we're running out of time."

It was only a matter of finding the courage to do it.

"Give the rutting order!"

The second hand hit the hour, and he swallowed the stickiness in his throat. "I—"

"Wait!" Gibzen flew into the tent, nearly knocking into the table as he slammed his palm down against the surface. Lifting his hand, he revealed a tiny golden hair ornament that Marcus would've recognized anywhere.

Gibzen's grin was vicious. "We've found their trail."

43

TERIANA

You have to escape. You have to escape. You have to escape. Teriana kept the chant going in her head as the sunlight filtering through the open door faded into dusk. Except the three guards in the building never left her alone and try as she might, she couldn't think of a way to subdue all three without making a racket. She was a good fighter, and she'd picked up her fair share during her time with the legions. But she wasn't that good.

And time was running out.

A laughing Ashok had told her that the legions and the allied clans were withdrawing from their positions, which she could scarcely believe. Yet the proof was that she remained alive, not quartered pieces in a sack on its way to be delivered to a man she'd convinced herself didn't care whether she lived or died.

It made her furious that Titus had seen the truth when she had not, and played her like a fiddle. And now look at the mess she was in. If only she hadn't let Titus bait her. If only she hadn't jumped to conclusions. If only she hadn't said those things, the legions and the allied clans would be on the verge of defeating Urcon and pulling him from power.

Because it was past time she stopped denying that was what she wanted. There would be long-reaching consequences to such a victory, but if it meant the Arinoquians being free of Urcon, they were worth it. At least she hoped they'd be worth it. Prayed they would be . . .

But if she didn't get free to warn Marcus, it wouldn't matter what she prayed for. He and his men would be dead, and Urcon would seek revenge against all the Arinoquians who'd fought against him. And if Cassius and his ilk learned she was dead, her people would be the next to suffer and die. She couldn't let that happen.

Fiddling with the handle of the blade tucked beneath her bottom, Teriana eyed her guards. They weren't corrupted, so if she could get one of them close enough for her to put a knife to his throat, maybe she could negotiate her way out with him as a hostage. Or maybe bribery would work.

"You know," she said, "the Cel have chests of gold in their camp. More than you've ever seen in your entire life. They'd pay to get me back alive."

All three lifted their heads.

"We sell you back, what's to stop them from resuming their attack on Aracam?" the big one asked.

"Nothing." She lifted one shoulder. "But you'll be rich as princes, so what would you care? You could go anywhere you liked."

The men eyed one another, wheels turning in their minds as they considered her proposal.

"We'll get all that gold when we defeat them," the big one eventually said. "No need to turn traitor to get it."

"Urcon will get it," she corrected. "You'll be lucky to see a handful of copper."

All three glared at her.

"You've got to know that," she said. "That's what he does, isn't it? Takes and takes and takes . . ." Trailing off, she gave them a weighted look. "Doesn't have to be that way. You could be the ones doing the taking. You want proof, look in my pockets. Unless you've taken what was in there already."

The big one shrugged at his comrades. "Might as well. She's not going to need it."

Teriana schooled her breath, her fingers tightening and loosening around the blade handle. Why did it have to be him? Why couldn't it have been any of the others? Only she didn't have time for another ploy. It had to be this one, and she had to make it count.

When he reaches in, get the knife on his throat, she told herself. *If he fights back, slit it. Break the bars. They're flimsy. It won't be hard. Take his sword and fight your way out. Then run.*

It was an awful plan, but it was all she had. Already it was full dark, and who knew how long it would take for her to find her way back? She had to warn Marcus. Had to tell him that in trying to save her he'd put everything at risk.

"Which pocket?"

"Left trouser," she said, easing the blade out from under her bottom. He crouched down, and was reaching through the bars when the ground shuddered. A second later, she heard a distant boom. Then another and another.

The big man turned away from her cage, and she swore, pulling out the blade and swiping at his retreating back.

She missed.

But it didn't matter, because a second later the night filled with screams.

The men pulled their blades, but it did them little good as a knife whistled through the air, catching the short one in the chest. He stumbled back and fell unmoving, and then a legionnaire stormed through the entrance, gladius flashing.

He engaged the young one, their blades clashing once, then twice, before the boy fell screaming, one hand clutching at the guts spilling from his stomach.

There was a flash of motion outside, and as the legionnaire turned to fight, the moonlight reflected off his face.

Marcus.

He cut down two more men in quick succession, but that was when the big man decided to make his move.

"Marcus!" Teriana screamed, slamming her heels against the bars of her cage, the wood snapping. "Behind you!"

He twisted, raising his weapon.

It was too late.

44

MARCUS

Marcus whirled at the sound of his name, lifting his blade to meet that of the giant man who'd been lurking next to Teriana's cage. The angle was awkward, and the force of the impact knocked the weapon from his hand.

Swearing, he pulled a knife and lunged before the beast of a man could regain his balance. It slid between a pair of ribs and into a lung, and the serrated edge ensured the wound was mortal as Marcus jerked it out.

He might as well have stuck the man with a pin.

Roaring with fury, the man lunged, and all the air rushed from Marcus's lungs as his back slammed against the ground. Gasping for breath, he stabbed the man in the kidney but lost his grip as his opponent reared, pulling Marcus with him by the front of his armor.

And threw him against the ground.

The impact rattled Marcus's teeth, but he caught hold of the knife strapped to his leg. As the man slammed him down again, he embedded the weapon between another pair of ribs.

And it was as if he'd done nothing.

The man choked and frothed blood, but his strength didn't diminish as he beat Marcus against the ground like a rag doll, not even seeming to feel his injuries.

"Die, you stupid bastard," Marcus croaked, smashing the bridge of his helmet against the man's nose, breaking it. Blood rained down in a torrent onto his face, but the only effect was the berserk bull of a man let go of Marcus's armor and took hold of his throat.

He could not breathe.

Marcus struggled, employing every dirty trick he knew, his

grip on the man's fingers the only thing keeping his throat from being crushed. They were both dying. It was just a matter of who'd get there first.

His vision darkened. He could feel his strength fading. Then a hot flood of liquid spurted into his face, and the beast's grip slackened as he toppled sideways, landing with a thud.

Gasping for breath, Marcus wiped a hand across his face, trying to clear the blood from his eyes as he pushed onto one elbow, reaching blindly for his weapons.

"Never thought I'd need to show you how to kill a man." Teriana's voice was shaky, but her grip on the knife she'd used to slit the man's throat was steady.

"Don't get used to it." His voice was hoarse. "Are you all right?" She wasn't; he could see that. Her face was swollen and bruised, her lip split, and the cut on her hairline needed stitching. But she was standing, and talking, and not dead.

"Better than you." She dropped to her knees, wiping blood from his face with her sleeve. Her hand was icy cold, and he caught it with his, needing that small reassurance that she was alive. That he hadn't been too late.

A shudder ran through her, twin tears cutting through the blood and dirt on her face. "You came for me. I didn't think . . . I wasn't sure . . ."

The disbelief in her voice hurt more than the beating he'd just taken. That he'd given her cause to think he'd abandon her without a fight. There were so many things he wanted to say, to make her understand how he felt. Only he'd spent so much of his life burying his emotions behind a wall that he had no idea how to put them into words.

"I'm sorry," he said. "For causing you to doubt that I would."

A strangled sob tore from her throat, and then her arms were around his neck. He held her close, her braids tangling in his fingers, and he knew he should be watching the door, be on his feet with weapon in hand. He didn't care. Because he wanted this. Wanted her. And he needed her to know it. "Teriana—"

A cough interrupted him, and he twisted on his knees, fumbling for the blade that still lay on the ground.

It was only Gibzen.

"How nice to see you are still alive, sir," the primus said, cocking one eyebrow on his blood-splattered face. "Surprising too, given that you running in here like a madman wasn't part of the plan you so clearly articulated to us."

It hadn't been, but when he'd seen the enemy moving toward the shed where they were keeping her all he'd been able to think of was Teriana. How he refused to come so close to saving her only to lose her for the sake of caution toward his own life.

"We have prisoners," Gibzen said. "When you're through with your little moment, you can decide what to do with them."

Those prisoners were the ones who'd taken Teriana. Who'd beaten her and put her in a cage. "Kill them."

Gibzen shrugged, but Teriana shouted, "No!"

Pulling out of his grip, she shoved past Gibzen and out of the shed.

"Teriana," Marcus called after her, but he might as well have been shouting into the wind.

"I get it," Gibzen said, reaching down to haul Marcus to his feet. "I like Teriana, and if I were in your position, I'd do the same. But if you lose your edge because of her, it won't go well."

"I know." And this was always what would come between them. Because he was here to lead the army that would conquer this half of Reath in the name of the Empire, and no matter what there was between them, no matter what she felt, he knew she intended to stop him.

Which made the sight of Teriana shaking and shouting at one of the prisoners all the more surprising. "Where are they?" she screamed. "What direction are they coming from? How many men?"

The prisoner spit at her, and she slapped him hard before lifting the knife with obvious intent.

"Teriana, no." Marcus grabbed her arms, hauling her back.

"I need to make him talk."

"You don't need to do anything. We'll deal with them."

"There's another army," she blurted out. "That was the point of capturing me. To delay your attack against the city so that you'd be caught between the two of them."

Marcus had known something like this would happen. Not the specifics, only that there'd been a better reason to take Teriana than a misguided belief that the Cel would abandon their campaign entirely just to save one girl. He'd hoped that the few hours of false retreat wouldn't make a difference, that he'd get away with it.

He'd been wrong.

And now how many of his men, how many of his allies, would die because of a decision that he'd made? A mistake he'd made?

Teriana is alive, and that is not a mistake, he told himself. It was cold comfort. If everything went to shit and he lost control, he'd no doubt his men would cut her down as soon as they were finished with him.

"How much time do we have?" he asked.

She grimaced. "What do you think I was trying to find out?"

Over her shoulder, he met Gibzen's eyes and nodded. Then to the three prisoners who were all that remained alive in a sea of dead, he said, "The first one to answer her questions lives."

One pissed himself, but none of them spoke.

"Are you so afraid of Urcon that you'd rather die by my hand than survive to face him?"

"Not him," Teriana whispered. "Ashok."

Fear rippled through them like a tide. "Who's he?"

Teriana licked her lips, wincing as her tongue passed over the split in her lower one. "He's a . . . He's in the employ of Urcon, but he's more powerful. More dangerous."

Marcus eyed her, gauging her reaction and feeling his temper flare as he drew conclusions. "He's the one who beat you."

She gave a short nod, and there were angry mutters among Gibzen's men. "Aye. But it wasn't the worst he could've done.

Even if he'd beat me to death, it wouldn't have been the worst he could've done."

There was something she wasn't saying, but Marcus let it go.

"He will take all the years of our lives and all of those of our families, if we betray him."

Marcus only caught a portion, but it was enough to understand the threat. "When we take Aracam, we will find this Ashok and hang him for what he has done."

Teriana translated, and before she finished, the man laughed. "You will not catch Ashok. Not him. And one who counts his life in centuries can take his time with revenge."

"You won't catch him," Teriana said. "He's a slippery sort, but one more than willing to bide his time for revenge."

It was the first time Marcus had ever caught her mistranslating, but he didn't think she'd do it without reason.

He stared at the three for a moment, debating whether it was worth it to dig the information out of them. If there was an army coming, his men would be ready, no matter how many or which direction they came from. And regardless, now that he knew to look, his scouts would find that information soon enough. What mattered now was making it back to his legion.

"Kill them."

Taking Teriana's shoulders, he turned her so that she wouldn't watch as their throats were slit.

"I just killed a man in front of you. You don't think I have the stomach for this?"

"This is different," he said. "This you don't need to see."

He pressed his hands against her ears as the prisoners struggled and begged, the distinct choking gurgle of slit throats filling the air. And then a shout, "North!"

Turning his head, Marcus nodded at his man to lower the knife pressed against the lone survivor's throat. "How many?"

"Ashok did not say," the prisoner wept. "Only that there were enough, and that they'd be here by dawn. I swear on the Six, I know nothing more."

Marcus nodded. "Bind his wrists and ankles," he ordered.

Dropping his hands from Teriana's ears, he extracted what little gold he had on him and shoved it in the man's pockets. "Once you get free, I suggest you run fast and far. And wherever you go, I would have you tell them that you were shown mercy. That your comrades who died today did so for their crimes, and that their punishment dies with them. Their families will not suffer by my hand for that which they have done. Tell them to consider wisely who they would choose to fight for, and who against."

He left Gibzen to deal with the rest, drawing Teriana away. "We're going to have to move fast. The retreat was only a ruse, the siege already underway. If we make it back before dawn, I can get the men in position and . . ."

"I'll keep up," she said. "Marcus, there's something else. Ashok got his information about . . . us, and where and when to ambush me, from one of your men."

A traitor. "He could've been lying." The idea of one of his men turning on him . . . turning on the *legion,* seemed impossible. They'd been together since they were children, had fought and bled together. Certainly there were personal grievances between men—between him and certain men—but this traitor had caused the deaths of the soldiers who'd been protecting Teriana and put all the rest at risk. And that was something else entirely.

"He wasn't lying." Her brow furrowed and she looked at Marcus's feet. "There's things he said that . . . implicated a particular individual."

"Who?"

She shook her head. "This will be hard."

"Who?" He barked out the word, because they did not have time for this and because he *knew* the name she was holding back and there could be no greater betrayal. "Spit it out, Teriana."

"Felix."

His name drove the air out of Marcus's lungs as surely as a punch to the guts, and her voice sounded distant as she repeated the things this Ashok had told her.

"It's not proof," she said once she was through with what seemed like fairly damning evidence to the contrary. "I could be wrong. Maybe it was Titus."

"Titus?" Gibzen and his men, who had finished tying up the prisoner and were waiting at the edge of the camp, shifted uneasily. They wanted to be gone. "Titus argued that we do what was needed to save you. It was Felix who wanted to let you die."

"And you're here saving me, while Titus leads the legions and the allied clans to their most significant victory on the Dark Shores. Think about it."

He was thinking about it. About how Felix had disliked Teriana from the beginning, how blasted irrational he'd been lately, and, most of all, how quick he'd been to throw Teriana to the wolves. Yes, Titus had motive. But so, apparently, did Felix.

"Don't do anything you'll regret," Teriana said, the press of her hands against his forearms doing more than her words to pull him from his thoughts. "Wait until we have proof."

He didn't answer.

"If you act and you're wrong, you'll regret it for the rest of your life."

I can add it to my list of regrets. "We need to go."

45

TERIANA

They had no choice but to use torches, despite the target it painted on their backs. The jungle canopy blocked the moonlight, and the last thing they needed was someone twisting an ankle or worse in the dark. And moving slowly wasn't an option.

They'd been running for hours when Teriana's sides cramped, nausea rising from her belly. She tried to ignore it, but then the torchlights began to pulse, and the next thing she knew, she was on her knees retching in the dirt.

Marcus was next to her, holding her hair back and pressing a waterskin to her hand. "When did you last eat?"

She couldn't remember. Everything hurt.

"Did they feed you?"

She shook her head, knowing they didn't have time for this. "Go. I can get back myself."

A snort was the only response he gave; then he was lifting her, pulling her arm over his shoulder. "On your feet," he said. "It's not much farther."

The world seemed to fade in and out, and all she wanted to do was lie down. Yet her feet kept moving, her weight half-suspended between Marcus and Gibzen until they reached the road and she reached her limit.

"I've got her." Marcus's voice, his breath warm against her ear as he lifted her up.

"Want me to send men ahead? Warn them?"

Whatever Marcus said she didn't hear, the night slipping away. When she regained consciousness, it was to the sounds of voices and light. Blinking, she focused on the breastplate pressed against her cheek, and lifting her face, she was able to make out Marcus's chin, the straight line of his jaw. He was carrying her, his breath ragged and strained. And beyond, the distant beat of drums and echo of horns. The battle.

"Put her here, sir."

He lowered her, the soft press of the cot beneath her little comfort compared to his arms. All around, lanterns were burning bright, the tent canvas white above them. A familiar face leaned over her—a medic in the Thirty-Seventh. They were back.

"Exhausted, dehydrated, and she took a beating." Marcus was standing over her, speaking to the medic. "Stitch her up, and then keep her here."

"Yes, sir."

Teriana struggled to sit. "I'm fine."

"Give us a moment." Marcus waited until the medic had moved off, then pressed her back against the cot with one hand, pulling his helmet off with the other. His face was covered with the blood of the man she'd killed, and his throat was already purple with bruises in the distinct shape of fingers.

"They'll take care of you," he said. "And then you'll stay here where it's safe."

"I'm fine," she argued, not wanting to let him out of her sight. He was angry, and she was desperately afraid that anger would cause him to make a mistake.

"Then you can help," he said. Tilting his head, he listened to the horns before adding, "They'll be bringing the injured here soon enough. I have to go."

Even if she'd had the energy for it, there was no arguing with him. Catching his hand, Teriana squeezed it tight. "Promise me you won't do anything until we have proof."

His jaw clenched, the muscles standing out in the lamplight. "Fine."

A small amount of relief filled her, because he would not break his word without cause. Though she knew he needed to go, needed to be on the field giving commands, she held tight. "Thank you."

And she didn't mean for the promise.

He stood still, his eyes searching hers. And Teriana wasn't certain what she expected him to say or do, only that she felt like they were standing at a fork in a road. That he would acknowledge that there was something between them. Something more than lust. Something significant enough to move traitors and enemies to act, and to make both of them risk everything. Or he would not, and this would be where it ended.

Marcus squeezed her hand once, then carefully lowered it to the cot. "Be safe, Teriana." Then he turned and walked away.

46

MARCUS

Leaving her there, battered and bruised and ill, had felt wrong, and if there'd been a way Marcus could have remained, he would've done so. Except already he'd lost the chance to see Titus's and Felix's reactions to the news of the incoming army from the north by choosing to send Gibzen ahead rather than going himself. Which meant he'd be resuming command with no confirmation of who the traitor was.

And it wasn't what he should be thinking about anyway. *His* army was in danger, as were the hundreds of Arinoquian warriors led by the allied imperators, and he needed to put them in the best position to triumph no matter what came at them. Yet as he left the medical tent, heading toward the path leading to the hill he'd selected for its unencumbered view of the city, his mind refused to quit its obsession with the idea that one of his men was a traitor.

The legions knew that it was Titus in command, that Marcus had gone after Teriana instead of directing the largest battle since they'd arrived on the Dark Shores. And that would have consequences. If it went badly, he'd be blamed for abandoning them to an inexperienced commander, and if it went well, the credit for the win would go to Titus.

The conversation she'd repeated for Marcus twisted and turned through his thoughts. *Titus or Felix. Titus or Felix.* Though there were more consequences to it being Titus, he almost wished it was Cassius's son, because the betrayal wouldn't cut so deep. He'd known from the moment that Titus had dropped him onto that sinking ship that the man sought to replace him as commander, and given the blood running through his veins, it wouldn't surprise him if Titus chose a circuitous plot to stab him in the back rather than to wield the knife himself.

But . . .

Felix had been unreliable for weeks now: bitter, angry, and not himself. Although perhaps that was wrong. Maybe he was more himself, certain truths Marcus had chosen to ignore pushed to the forefront by Teriana's presence.

A series of horn blasts rippled through the air, and he listened to the signal. The walls had been breached some time ago, but now the enemy had begun to surrender. Not that that meant much. It would take time to root out the soldiers and pockets of resistance, especially given his orders to avoid civilian casualties. It would've been faster and easier to sack the whole city, but his orders had been explicit. He hoped it wouldn't cost him everything.

"Stop where you are! State your rank, name, number, and purpose."

He'd reached the end of the tree line, the hilltop overlooking the city bare and rocky. Its perimeter was guarded by one hundred men of the Forty-First, their spears practically shaking with excitement, and it ground his nerves that it wasn't his men.

"Legatus Marcus, supreme commander of the Thirty-Seventh and Forty-First Legions, number one five one nine. And you bloody well know my purpose."

The soldier gaped, then saluted. "Sir, I didn't recognize you without . . . We didn't think . . ."

"Move," Marcus barked, shoving the soldier out of the way and striding to the hill's summit.

It was a scene of organized chaos, messengers coming and going with information and orders, officers taking and sorting through the mess of it, three men with signal horns blasting messages over the valley, and Titus standing in command of it all.

Marcus forced down the swell of anger that made him want to jerk the command unceremoniously out from under the younger man's feet. Until he knew for certain who had betrayed him, he needed to handle the situation carefully.

"Report." They all turned, Titus stumbling as he did.

"You missed the party," Servius replied, slapping Marcus on the back. He winced, his shoulders tender from the beating. "Though Gibzen told us you had one of your own."

"Is Teriana all right?" It was Titus who asked with what appeared like genuine concern. "Gibzen said you were taking her to Medical."

"Bruises. She'll live."

"Good." He started to say more, but Felix interrupted.

"All has gone as you anticipated. Our ships blockaded the harbor, allowing the allied clans to take it from the water and the beaches while we took the city itself. The black powder was as effective against the walls as we were told it would be— absolutely a worthwhile addition to the arsenal. Fighting was tense at the points of breach, but the last holdout fell moments ago. They're surrendering. We should have the city by dawn, which puts us in a good position to deal with this force Gibzen says is coming in our direction."

"I think—" Titus said, but Felix wasn't done.

"Neither our scouts nor Ereni's have reported any sign of an army, but I've sent more out, north and west, instructing them to roam farther afield. On a chance this was a ruse, I've only redeployed our fourth, six, and eleventh centuries to hold the ridgeline, and our ninth, twenty-third, and thirty-sixth are holding their positions midground—"

"It's not a ruse," Marcus interrupted.

Felix lifted his face from the map he was holding and focused on Marcus's face for the first time, the map falling from his hand as he closed the distance between them. "Are you hurt?"

Marcus stepped out of reach of his second's hand. "I'm fine. It's not my blood." Turning to Titus, he said, "Well done. A night assault is no easy thing to command."

Titus nodded, eyes unreadable.

"Sir! Look."

Their heads all turned north in time to watch a scout's signal flare burn out in the sky.

"Not a ruse," Marcus repeated, estimating from the flare that they had an hour or two, tops. "Get the rest of those men up there. I want the high ground. Titus, continue as you were. Felix, stay with him. Servius, with me."

"Where are you going?" Titus asked.

"On the field. Someone get me a horse."

Amarin appeared out of nowhere, the rest of Marcus's gear in hand. Without comment, he fastened the cloak to Marcus's shoulders, exchanging the plain helmet he'd been wearing for that of a commander. "Your mount is the white one, sir," he said, pointing to the gleaming horse picketed below. "I selected him myself."

"I appreciate the foresight." Walking down the slope, Marcus checked the girth out of habit, then motioned Servius over.

"There is a man named Ashok who may be in the city," he said, providing the description Teriana had given. "He's dangerous, but I want him alive."

"I'll spread the word, though rooting out a specific man might take time." Servius held the horse's bridle while Marcus mounted. "What's so special about him that you dragged me down here to talk about it?"

He had no reason not to trust Servius, but caution told him to keep the information close. "He's the one who roughed up Teriana."

"Right." Servius glanced up the slope to where Felix and Titus stood, their backs to them.

"Something you want to say?" Marcus demanded, the horse sidling sideways beneath him.

"Nope."

"Have Titus and Felix keep the imperators and their warriors in the harbor. This fight is ours."

"Yes, sir."

Marcus dug his heels into the horse's sides, riding down the trail to the fields below, where he broke into a swift canter toward the men he'd redeployed. It was rare that he took the field, but if there was ever a time it was now. The wind caught and tore at his cloak, sending it trailing out over the horse's hindquarters. Men's heads turned as he passed, his name rising on their lips as he fell into stride next to Gibzen. "I've another job for you."

"Name it."

Leaning out of the saddle, he gave the man his orders. "Show them no mercy."

"Understood."

His orders rippled through the ranks, but Marcus was already on the move, riding among his army, redeploying men by the hundreds, and when he heard the horns declaring the city was taken, by the thousands. His strategy formed in his mind as scouts and messengers brought him information on the incoming force. He would win, and it would be decisive, and they would remember why *he* was commander.

Dawn rose in the east.

Marcus sat on his horse, watching the cleared fields and the distant jungle beyond, his only company a signalman, who held the tool of his trade loosely in one hand, and the Thirty-Seventh's standard, the golden dragon brilliant in the rising sun. On the ridgeline stood three hundred of his men. A pittance against what his scouts estimated as close to ten thousand enemy.

A scout sprinted across the field toward him. "They're coming!" he gasped, stopping next to Marcus's horse.

"Any hesitation?"

"None."

There wouldn't be. Not when he'd let their scouts get close. To see his men with their backs turned and the allied clans busy in the harbor, all woefully unprepared for an attack from the rear.

Marcus nodded, and the signalman blew a long note on the horn. Marcus did not look back, knowing his men, trained in a way a mercenary army could never be, were now moving into position. Not the easy, unprepared target the enemy scouts thought them to be.

In the distance, he heard a faint roar. The sound of thousands of men running and screaming. He nodded again at the signalman, who blew two notes.

The roar grew louder. "Steady!" Marcus shouted.

Across the fields there was movement.

A second later, the enemy broke from the trees.

The front-runners were mounted, and the horses broke into a gallop the moment they hit the open space, perhaps five hundred total. Behind them came a horde of men, weapons gleaming in the light.

Marcus knew this sort of foe, and he knew it well. Mercenaries. Men, and sometimes women, who were often skilled warriors in their own right. Except they fought as individuals, an uncoordinated mass that barely deserved to be called an army.

Urcon's mercenaries raged across the field, their eyes fixed on his three hundred men, and Marcus's stomach tightened, because this was where he'd have his casualties. "Hold!" he shouted.

Wait.

Wait.

The horsemen were close enough now that he could see their faces, wild with bloodlust and the certainty of victory. Behind them, the footmen were deep into the field, the safety of the jungle lost to them.

Closer.

Closer.

"Now," he said, and the signalman blew his battle cry.

His three hundred stepped back, revealing a line of sharpened stakes even as another thousand of his men stepped over the ridgeline, forming a wall of shields and bristling spears eight men deep.

The front-runners tried to pull up, but it was too late, their momentum too great. They smashed into the stakes, horses and men screaming and dying and then falling up against the wall of shields and spears his men had formed. The rest of the cavalry pulled up, the horses refusing to charge into the fray, eyes wild with terror as their riders tried to heel them into the melee.

There was hesitation in the flood of enemy on foot; and, eyeing the distance, Marcus nodded once. "Loose."

The horn blew a trio of notes, and a second later the air whistled and turned dark with bolts flying overhead. They fell in a deadly rain, swaths of men dropping injured and dying even as he ordered volley after volley, one eye on his men who were decimating the enemy cavalry not twenty paces from him.

The enemy was going to break. He could see the hesitation in the ranks, the desire not to be the first, but certainly not to be the last, to turn tail and run.

"Flank them."

His signalman's horn was met by the call of two others, but for a time there was nothing to see.

Then the enemy broke.

Urcon's mercenaries fled across the field, but as the frontrunners neared the trees two thousand legionnaires stepped out to meet them. Some of the mercenaries pressed forward, throwing themselves against the wall of legionnaires and steel; others retreated to the middle of the field where they milled about in desperate confusion.

Eyeing the carnage before him, Marcus lifted one arm, and the rest of the Thirty-Seventh marched over the lip of the ridge, stepping over the corpses of the enemy cavalry. An unforgiving line of death that moved forward, crushing the enemy between two forces, much as Urcon had intended to do to Marcus's men.

He watched until it was over, the enemy nothing more than the dead and the dying. Then, pulling the standard from the ground, he hooked the end in his stirrup and trotted to one of the centurions. "We've no need of prisoners," he said, and when the man nodded and saluted he added, "Burn the dead."

Marcus walked his horse back through the ranks of his men, and they began to chant. Not for the Empire. Not for the legion. Not even for victory. They chanted for him.

But he hardly heard them as he rode back to camp. And to her.

47

TERIANA

And there it was. Whatever had been between her and Marcus was over, silenced before it could cause more trouble than it already had. Though she barely felt the ministrations of the medic, she was content to let him believe the slow leak of tears down her cheeks was from the pain of the needle or the prodding of her ribs, which were declared bruised but not broken. She was given water and broth and told to rest. Rolling on her unbruised side, Teriana stared at the rows of cots and the young men setting up what they would need, those of the Thirty-Seventh working with calm efficiency, those of the Forty-First with tense anticipation.

Marcus was right. Whatever there was between them had no future. But knowing it was so did little to ease the ache in her chest.

It wasn't fair.

She knew Yedda, and the rest of her crew, would slap her upside the head for even uttering those words, but that was the sum of it. To want something so badly knowing that it was a mistake.

Because no matter what they felt for each other, in the end they were enemies.

The Celendor Empire had already hurt her and hers in its pursuit of conquest, and it was set on dominating all of Reath. The Cel called the West the Dark Shores, but they were the black tide intent on washing the gods from this world. And Marcus and his men were the weapon they'd use to do it.

She wanted the Empire to fail, to fall. Yet she did not want *these* men to lose, because losing meant dying.

Screams cut the night, and Teriana jerked upright in time

to see a pair of gore-splattered legionnaires come into the tent bearing another man who was twisting and screaming on the stretcher. She took in his injuries, her mind refusing to process the notion that so much could be done to a man and that he'd still live.

The medics fell upon them, transferring the injured man to a cot and dispatching the deliverers. White bandages turned red, clamps and needles and vials put to purpose with practiced hands. But it was all for naught, because moments later the injured soldier went still.

Teriana pressed a hand against a tent pole, not even certain when she'd stood. Her heart thundered in her chest like a drum, but she could not look away as one of the men turned the body and recorded the number on his back.

More came. And more and more. A tide of injuries, some minor, some unlike anything she'd seen before. Some of the men screamed, wordlessly or for a friend or for mercy, while others stared blankly, the shock numbing the pain. It was mostly those who caused the medics to shake their heads and direct the bearers to put them at the far end of the tent. Lost causes.

Blood, blood, and more blood. It was everywhere, but it was as though she watched from a great distance. Or as though it wasn't her watching at all.

"Teriana?" Something caught at her wrist, and she snapped into the moment, the noise loud, the air thick with the stench of sweat, blood, and opened guts. The hand grasping hers belonged to a man passing on a stretcher, the face one she recognized.

"Avitius?" Then she saw the ruins that were his legs, took in the direction the stretcher-bearers were taking him, and she knew.

"They found you." A faint smile crossed her gambling companion's face. "Is it true the legatus went himself?"

"Aye." She stumbled along next to the stretcher, unwilling to break the hold he had on her wrist. "But he's back. Already resumed command."

"That's good." He sighed, and his eyes rolled back before

regaining focus. "Titus has no business commanding the Thirty-Seventh." Then his fingers went limp, and he was gone. Dead, just like that.

"Take him outside," said the grim-faced medic who'd patched her up. But before he could walk away, Teriana stepped into his path.

"I want to help," she blurted out. "Tell me what to do."

"You aren't . . . ," he started to say, then paused. Reaching into the pouch at his waist, he extracted an opaque vial and dropper. "One drop per hour for pain," he said. "Two drops to put them under. Five, if they want to be done. You understand?"

She swallowed down the thickness that formed in her throat. "Isn't there something that can be done for them?"

He shook his head. "No. And even if there was, these aren't injuries they'll want to survive."

Because if they couldn't fight, couldn't be of use to the legion, they wouldn't want to live. It made her want to spit in the face of the Empire. It took away everything from them but the legion, their brothers, and the fight. "I understand."

"No man wants to die alone." He squeezed her arm as he passed. "I'm glad he got you back."

So she spent the rest of the night moving from bedside to bedside, providing what comfort she could, all the while thinking that Lydia, traitor that she was, would've been better at the task, with her calm and pragmatic presence. Some of the men Teriana knew; some she didn't. But all knew her, and she listened or spoke or was silent as they needed. Some joked, some cried, but all were afraid. None asked for more than two drops, and that was a mercy to her, because she wasn't sure if she could've done it.

They were braver than she was.

Word that the city had been taken came in the night, but it was the horns calling the men to their new positions that made her hands turn to ice. Marcus redeploying his men to engage the army marching in from the north, another battle to be fought on the heels of the first.

Please let them win, she prayed, knowing that it bordered on blasphemy to ask for such a thing from the Six.

Then a series of horn blows echoed through the air, and everyone in the tent paused what they were doing to listen. "What does it mean?" she asked the man at whose bedside she sat.

"Retreat."

Her heart skipped. "Ours?"

His bloodstained lips drifted into a faint smile. "We do not fall back."

It was the last thing he said.

Not long after, when she was closing the eyelids of yet another man, this one a boy from the Forty-First who barely looked old enough to shave, she felt a sense of attentiveness sweep the tent. Men, even the injured ones, straightened, and from behind she heard the thuds of fists hitting chests.

Her knees creaked as she stood, but Teriana did not move from the dead man's side, watching instead as Marcus moved through the ranks of the injured. He was no longer dressed like a common legionnaire, once again wearing all the accoutrements of his rank. The dragon on his cloak gleamed, seeming to twist and dance as he moved. A symbol of the Empire mocking her, because it had won.

He went from bedside to bedside, helmet tucked under one arm, face still marked with blood and his throat purple with bruises. He spoke to each man and to the medics attending them, his brow furrowing with attentiveness and concern as he listened. Each man seemed to rally under his attention, and it made her think about what it took to earn that sort of respect.

And that he'd jeopardized it for her.

Just as she'd jeopardized the fate of the West for him.

The air abruptly felt too close, the smell too much. She needed to get outside, away from this. Away from him. Handing the glass vial to a passing medic, Teriana strode out of the opposite end of the tent. The sun was bright and hot overhead, and she did her best not to look at the bodies laid out in neat rows under the shade of some trees.

Instead, she headed up a gentle slope, following a path that had been trod down by countless men. Up and up she went until she reached a rocky point overlooking Aracam. The walls were collapsed and smoking in a dozen spots, and fires burned in other parts of the city, although they'd be doused in short order. In the distance, she could see the allied clan camp, which was where their injured warriors had been taken, no doubt to keep the Cel away from any marked healers they had in their midst. It was a secret she doubted they'd be able to keep much longer.

The wind blew in from the sea, the smell of salt clearing the stench of death that clung to her nostrils, and she closed her eyes, breathing deeply.

"Teriana?"

Her heart leapt at the sound of his voice, and slowly, she turned. Marcus stood at the base of the rocks, helmet still held loosely in one hand, the breeze catching at his cloak. He was battered and filthy, but instead of detracting, it made him seem more like the leader that he was.

"You won." And though she was a riot of emotion, her voice came out flat.

"Yes." He scrubbed a hand over his hair, and she noticed it was longer than she'd ever seen it. "It went as planned. Very few casualties, though it might not seem that way to you, given where you spent the night." He hesitated. "The men told me what you did. Thank you."

"It was nothing; I only sat—"

"It wasn't nothing. Not to them. Not to me."

There was something in his voice that twisted at her heart, and she closed her eyes, afraid the color would betray her.

"We captured Urcon, who's apparently so old he can barely walk, and dozens of his men, but *Ashok*"—his voiced soured at the name—"managed to escape. It appears he's just as deadly as you claimed. The other army arrived just after dawn, but I'd already redeployed a dozen centuries and the enemy broke on their first charge. A few escaped, but they're a problem for another day—"

"Marcus," she interrupted. "Why are you here? Because it isn't to give me an update."

"I suppose it isn't." He stared out at the city he'd just conquered, but she didn't think he was really seeing it. Then he lifted one hand, which was clenched in a fist, and opened it palm up, revealing a glint of gold. "I wanted to give this back to you. It was how we found the right trail. Without it . . ." His jaw tightened. "It's yours."

Curious, Teriana climbed off the rocks and approached. The gold was a tiny fish ornament, and her hand went instinctively to her hair, catching at locks she hadn't even realized had come loose from their braid. "My mum gave that to me when I was ten," she said, taking it from him, the brief contact of her fingers against his palm making her skin flash with heat and hurt. "I would've been sad to lose it. Thank you."

He nodded, and then they were both silent. But the air was thick with the tension of much unsaid, and at once, they both blurted out, "I wanted to talk to you about—" and then broke off.

"Go ahead," Marcus said, and she cowardly wished he'd spoken first.

"After that night, when we were . . ." She swallowed, feeling her cheeks warm. "Anyway, when I left the tent, Titus waylaid me, saying that he needed my help identifying temples within the city." She carefully repeated the conversation as best she could remember. "When you came down to the beach, I was so angry, because I thought you hated Cassius. The idea that you'd willingly put the man who'd killed and hurt my people in power, and then slept with me was just so, so—" She broke off.

"Teriana . . ."

She shook her head, forestalling him. "But then Quintus told me the truth. That Cassius had blackmailed you, and the whole damned legion, into voting for him, and I understood why you did it, though I wish you'd told me." She took a deep breath. "And I know Titus was manipulating me into believing you're worse than you are—"

"Forget Titus," Marcus interrupted. "He's his father's son. When I find some proof he's a traitor, then I'll not hesitate to hang him by a short rope, never mind what the Forty-First thinks about it. But . . ." He grimaced and shook his head, before meeting her gaze. "He didn't lie, not really. Yes, Cassius threatened to ship us off to the middle of nowhere, among other things, if he didn't win, but I could've fought that if I'd been willing to face the consequences of doing so. Instead I made sure to present the facts to my men in a way that would ensure they voted the way I needed them to. I knew what he was, that he wasn't fit to be consul, and that the Empire would not prosper under his leadership, but I helped put him in power anyway. Because it benefited me and my men."

Teriana stared at his chest, hearing what he was saying, this ever-shifting truth, but it wasn't sinking in.

He gripped her arms, his hands dampening the fabric of her shirt. "I do hate him, Teriana. More than you can ever know. He has threatened and hurt everyone who has ever mattered to me, and his reach seems to extend across the Endless Seas. He's made me do things that I'll regret until the day I die, but the fact remains that I helped him win." Marcus swallowed and winced as if it pained him, then said, "And I understand if you hate me for it."

"How can I hate you for making the same choices as I've made?" she whispered.

"It's not the same." He carefully cupped her face, fingers barely grazing the bruises. "Please don't try to give me absolution, Teriana, because I don't want it. And I don't deserve it. I have done horrible things in my life. I've killed people with my own hands, hanged dozens for disobeying laws the Empire forced on them, and slaughtered tens of thousands of those who fought against me. Hundreds of thousands have been forced into indentured servitude because of the decisions I've made.

I've burned and pillaged, bent entire countries to the will of a group of pampered men who care not for them but for the taxes they'll pay. And yes, you can say that I had no choice. That I'm motivated to protect the lives of my men, who are like a family to me. But that does not negate the damage that I've done."

"I know."

"And if we are to make *this* work in whatever way it might, you must see me for what I am, not as you might want me to be."

Make this work. "What is *this*, Marcus?"

"I don't know." His voice was hoarse, and his hands trembled where they touched her face. "I have too much power, and you too little, but sometimes it feels like if you asked—" He broke off. "I cannot set you free, at least, not in a way that would allow you to retrieve your mother and protect your people. The Senate will hold both of us to our word, and that means you stay until we have land passage to and from the Empire and the Dark Shores, and we are far from that."

"I know," she said, leaning into his touch, feeling an aching need drive deep into her core. "I signed the same document as you. But you didn't answer my question."

"I'm here to win. And it won't always be against tyrants the world is better off without." One hand slipped around the back of her head, tangling in her braids. "At some point, I'm going to cross a line that you won't be able to accept."

"I know." *And then I'll have to stop you.*

"It will end badly."

She nodded. *One of us will lose.*

"You deserve better than this." He pulled her against him, her chest pressing against the hard steel of his armor. "Better than me. I am the property of the Senate and will be until I'm too old and bitter to care otherwise. I have nothing to give you but soldier's rations, a tent, and a blanket on the ground."

"And you?"

He hesitated. "A part of me, a large part, belongs to this legion. I don't know if what's left of me is worth anything, whether it is enough, but it's yours."

This was something stupid. This was a mistake. This was folly.

She was going to do it anyway. Wrapping her arms around his neck, Teriana rested her cheek against his and said, "It's enough."

GLOSSARY

Certain aspects of the Celendor Empire were inspired by the Roman Empire, and I have used several Latin terms common to that era. I have, however, taken liberties with the definitions of some of those terms, altering them to fit the world that I have created. To that end, those who possess a strong knowledge of Ancient Rome should not hold me to any level of historical accuracy, as *Dark Shores* is a work of fantasy fiction.

Amarin: Marcus's manservant
Aracam: Ancient Arinoquian fortress city; Urcon's stronghold
Arinoquia: Kingdom on the southern continent of the Dark Shores
Ashok: One of the corrupted
Atlia: Province in the Empire
Avitius: Legionnaire in the Thirty-Seventh Legion; one of Teriana's regular gambling companions
Bait: God-marked sailor on the *Quincense*; Teriana's friend
Bardeen: Province in the Empire
Basilius: A senator running for consul
Campus Lescendor: Training school for the Empire's legions
Caradoc: God-marked healer
Cassius, Lucius: A senator running for consul
Castrick: Captain of a Maarin ship sunk by the Cel navy
Cel: Language of Celendor
Celendor: Ruling nation of the Empire
Celendorian dragon: Symbol of the Empire; also the name of Celendor's gold coins
Celendrial: Capital city of Celendor

centurion: A mid-level officer in a legion who is in command of approximately one hundred legionnaires

Chersome: Newly conquered province of the Empire

child tithes: Law within the Empire requiring all second-born sons to be surrendered to legionnaire training at age seven

consul: Highest elected political office in the Celendor Empire

Cordelia: Marcus's older sister

Corrupter, the: see Seventh, the

Curia, the: Meeting house of the Senate

Derin: Kingdom on the Northern Continent of the Dark Shores known to be controlled by the Seventh God

Domitius, Gaius: Marcus's younger brother

Domitius, Senator: Marcus's father

domus: Freestanding home occupied by the upper classes of Celendor

Empire, the: Celendor and its provinces

Endless Seas, the: Seas dividing the Empire (Eastern Hemisphere) from the Dark Shores (Western Hemisphere)

Ereni: Imperatrix of an Arinoquian clan

Falorn, High Lady Dareena: God-marked warrior; High Lady of one of the Twelve Houses of Mudamora

Felix: Tribunus of the Thirty-Seventh Legion; Marcus's best friend

Flacre: An influential Arinoquian

Forum, the: A plaza surrounded by important political buildings at the center of Celendrial

Galinha: Small fortress city in Arinoquia

Gamdesh: Most powerful kingdom on the Southern Continent of the Dark Shores

Gespurn: God of the elements

Gibzen: Primus, centurion born in Timia, taught Cel language by Marcus at Campus Lescendor, one of Marcus's staunchest defenders

gladius: Sword used by the legionnaires

god mark: Powers gifted to individuals by a god; each god bestows different god marks

greater ocean path: Xenthier stems rising from the ocean floor that the Maarin use to cross the Endless Seas

Hegeria: Goddess of body and spirit

herbarius: A Cel term for an individual knowledgeable in the art of plants; the term Teriana assigns to god-marked healers in the Dark Shores to hide their true nature

Hill, the: Large hill in Celendrial where patrician homes are located; the most influential families have homes on the top of the hill, overlooking the sea

Illria: Murdered Maarin sailor

imperator: A Cel term for a commander who is also a leader of a people; Teriana uses this term when translating the Arinoquian word for the leaders of the clans

insulae: Four- or five-story apartment-style buildings in Celendor; occupied by the poorer classes

Jax: Sailor on the *Quincense*

Katamarca: Kingdom on the Southern Continent of the Dark Shores

legatus: Highest-ranking officer in a Cel legion

legionnaire: A soldier in a legion

Lern: God of the beasts

Lydia Valerius: Foster daughter of Senator Valerius; Teriana's best friend

Maarin, the: Seafaring race of people

Madoria: Goddess of the seas

Magnius: the *Quincense*'s sea serpent guardian; demigod and scion of Madoria

Marcus Domitius: Legatus of the Thirty-Seventh Legion

Miki: Legionnaire in the Thirty-Seventh Legion; Teriana's bodyguard

Mudamora: Kingdom on the Northern Continent of the Dark Shores

Mudamorian: Language of Mudamora; also the first language of the Maarin; in the Empire, the language is known as Trader's Tongue

patrician: Highest class within Celendor; each of the patrician families holds a seat on the Empire's Senate

peregrini: Individuals hailing from the Empire's provinces

Phera: Province in the Empire

plebeian: Common Celendorian citizens

Polin: Cook on the *Quincense*; like an uncle to Teriana

praefectus: Third-highest-ranking officer in a legion; individual in charge of equipment and provisions

primus: Most senior of a legion's centurions

province: Nation that has been conquered by Celendor and is now considered part of the Empire

Quincense, **the:** Teriana's ship

Quintus: Legionnaire in the Thirty-Seventh Legion; Teriana's bodyguard

Reath: Name of the planet

Revat: Capital city of Gamdesh

rostrum: Raised platform

Savio, the river: Large river running through Celendrial

Sea of the Dead: Region of the Endless Seas made impassable due to its doldrums

senator: A member of the Empire's Senate; all senators are individuals from patrician families

Servius: Praefectus of the Thirty-Seventh Legion; Marcus's friend

Seventh, the: Dark god known as the Corrupter

Sibal: Province in the Empire

Sibalines: Mountain range in province of Sibal

Sibern: Province in the far north of the Empire

Six, the: The gods worshipped in the Dark Shores: Madoria, Yara, Tremon, Gespurn, Lern, and Hegeria

Taltuga: Maarin islands of the southwest coast of Mudamora

Teriana: Second mate of the *Quincense*; heir to the role of Triumvir of the Maarin Trade Consortium

Tesya: Captain of the *Quincense* and Triumvir of the Maarin Trade Consortium; Teriana's mother

Titus: Legatus of the Forty-First Legion; Lucius Cassius's son.

Treatise of the Seven: Book describing the gods of the west, along with the exploits of those individuals they have marked with powers

Tremon: God of war

tribunus: Second-highest-ranking officer of a legion

Triumvir: One of three individuals who govern the Maarin Trade Consortium

Twelve Houses of Mudamora: The ruling houses of the Kingdom of Mudamora

Uncharted Lands: Mysterious region in the center of the Southern Continent of the Dark Shores

Urcon: Imperator of an Arinoquian clan who has set himself up as a false king

Valerius, Senator: Prior consul; Lydia's foster father

Vibius: Senator Valerius's nephew

xenthier: Crystal veins (paths) running across Reath that instantaneously transport anyone or anything that touches the genesis stem to the terminus stem (one-directional). In the Empire, mapped paths are those where both the genesis and terminus locations are known. There are many unmapped stems scattered across the Empire where the location of the reciprocating genesis or terminus is unknown. Path hunters are the individuals who attempt to discover the terminus of known genesis stems. Path hunting is dangerous, but the Senate provides lucrative rewards to those who successfully map a path. As yet, there have been no land-based paths mapped between the Eastern and Western Hemispheres of Reath. For ocean-based xenthier, see greater ocean paths.

Yara: Goddess of the earth

Yedda: Sailor on the *Quincense;* Teriana's aunt

Acknowledgments

All of my novels have demanded the support of an incredible number of people to take them from a tiny idea floating in my head to a book on the shelves. In the case of *Dark Shores*, it took a whole legion of supporters. I began writing in the *Dark Shores* world back in 2007, and the first novel to emerge from my efforts also happened to be the first novel I'd ever completed. It was terrible, but I was proud enough of it that I set my sights on publication, not realizing, in my naivete, what a long and uphill battle that would be. At that point, I was still working in the corporate world, and my supporters were not fellow writers, but my family, my coworkers, and my friends, many of who enthusiastically read early drafts or excerpts and cheered on my ambition. To that end, I owe a great debt to Christina Carnovale, Donna Healey, Carter Evans, Kevin Henderson, and Stephanie Wong. The *Dark Shores* you're holding now doesn't much resemble that first attempt at a novel, but it would never have reached this point without your early support.

I ended up burying that first novel in my desk drawer, focusing on other projects and honing my craft, though it took many years and several novels until I finally landed that first book deal. But I could never quite let *Dark Shores* go. The characters and the world had a hold on my soul in a way none of my other books ever had, and time and again I'd open up the manuscript file, writing and rewriting iteration after iteration, but never quite meeting the standards of what I needed this novel to be. I was the only one who read those versions, but the individuals who supported my burgeoning writing career over those long years must be mentioned. The hugest of thanks to Bob and Brenda Barrett, Brandi Boothman, Lindsay Bosnak, Steff and

Kris Carlson, Mike Davis, Caroline Diep, Krista Dumonceau, Sandy Duncan, Carter Evans, Courtney Fellows, Shannon Gallagher, Jessica Gallagher, Jason Hale, Kris and Kali Hauser, Donna and Brad Healey, Cheryl Heskett, Kelvin Huppie, Katie Hussynec, Joe and Nancy Jensen, Myron and Joy Kirik, Christine Kups, Kelsey Moskal, Meaghan Müller, Don and Sheila Penry, Doug and Edith Phillips, Isabel Robles, Sunme Scott, Brenda Sears, Stephanie Wong, Carleen and Joel Woodfin, and Gena Wozimirsky.

To my wordsister Elise Kova, thank you for always being an inspiration, especially when it comes to productivity. To Adam Dreece, Suzy Vadori, and Avery Olive, there are no words for the importance of having fellow author friends within easy reach.

Huge thanks to my friend, beta reader, and superfan Melissa Robles for reading countless drafts, being my sounding board on plot tangles, and picking up my slack on social media. I'd be lost without you.

To Kate Couresy, who edited an early (and very long) draft, thank you finding places to tighten the plot—you are awesome! I also owe a debt of gratitude to Renee Harleston for her insight, wisdom, and keen editorial eye. *Dark Shores* is better for your involvement than it ever could've been without—thank you!

Thank you to the team at Tor Teen for giving *Dark Shores* such an amazing home. I have so much gratitude to my fabulous editor Melissa Frain for loving my characters and helping me make them their best selves. Thanks to Whitney Ross for putting my novel in Melissa's hands, to Barbara Wild for finding all my little mistakes, and to Zohra Ashpari for the work you do behind the scenes.

To Tamar Rydzinski, my amazing agent, I could write a hundred pages and never quite come close to expressing how much I value your support and friendship. You didn't blink (at least that I saw!) when I sent that first behemoth of a draft your direction. You kept your faith that we'd find it a good home when I was convinced it would never happen, and I will never stop thanking you for how hard you fought for this novel. As always, I'm grateful to Laura Dail for her support, as well to Samantha Fabien for her help with the manuscript.

To my other half, Spencer, my endless gratitude for your endless encouragement. There aren't many people who would support their partner working for so many years on something that might never pay off, but you never once told me to quit. That matters more than you can ever know. To my little girls, I know having an author for a mom isn't always easy, but you two own my heart and everything I do is for you. To Pat, thanks for being the best mother-in-law a girl could ask for. I'd never make a single deadline if it wasn't for all the help and love you give my family.

To my brother, Nick, and to my parents, Carol and Steve, you three know *Dark Shores* and all the struggles that have come along with it better than anyone. Nick, thanks for supplying me with endless tidbits of military knowledge, even if it nearly resulted in my legions fighting with sporks! Mom, thanks for learning everything you could about publishing so that I'd have someone who understood the craziness that is this business and for pulling me back from the endless breakdowns my chosen career has caused. I hope I'm half as good a mother to my kids as you've been to me. Dad, there are days I feel like this novel is as much yours as it is mine. We've come a long way from the days where you were correcting comma splices, but you've never stopped being an incredible support and resource, my own living encyclopedia. I know I'm often more concerned with making a scene exciting than whether what I'm writing is actually . . . ahh . . . *possible*. Thanks for keeping the worst of my mistakes from the public eye, and for forgiving my occasional need to put plot before physics. This book is for you.

To my readers who have been with me from the beginning and to those who have joined me along the way, thank you so much for your support. I hope you love Marcus and Teriana just as much as I do.